CANDIDATE

FOR

MURDER

A MAC FARADAY MYSTERY

BY

LAUREN CARR

CANDIDATE FOR MURDER

For information call: 304-995-1295
or Email: writerlaurencarr@gmail.com

Designed by Acorn Book Services

Publication Managed by Acorn Book Services
www.acornbookservices.com
acornbookservices@gmail.com
304-995-1295

Cover designed by Todd Aune
Spokane, Washington
www.projetoonline.com

ISBN-13: 978-0692734698
ISBN-10: 0692734694

Published in the United States of America

To My Muse

The Real Gnarly

CANDIDATE

FOR

MURDER

A MAC FARADAY MYSTERY

CAST OF CHARACTERS

(in order of appearance)

Gnarly: Mac Faraday's German shepherd. Before Mac inherited him from Robin Spencer, Gnarly served in the United States Army, who refuses to talk about him.

Lieutenant Frank Watson: Leader of an army unit stationed in the Iraqi desert. He is Gnarly's commanding officer. Those who serve under him call him "Patton."

First Sergeant Scott Scalia: Soldier in Lieutenant Watson and Gnarly's unit.

First Sergeant Belle Perkins: Gnarly's handler and partner when he was in the army.

Private Drew Samuels: Soldier on Gnarly's team. Gnarly stepped up to bat to save him, Private Samuels does the same for him.

Police Chief David O'Callaghan: Spencer's chief of police. Mac Faraday's younger half-brother by their father, Patrick O'Callaghan, Spencer's late police chief.

Police Chief Patrick O'Callaghan: David's late father. Spencer's legendary police chief. The love of Robin Spencer's life and Mac Faraday's birth father.

Dallas Walker: David O'Callaghan's girlfriend. Investigative journalist. Comes from Texas.

Storm: A Belgian shepherd, Storm is Dallas' canine companion and Gnarly's good friend.

Tonya: Spencer Police Department Desk Sergeant. She runs things at the police station.

Nancy Braxton: Candidate for Spencer's first woman mayor. Wife of Nathan Braxton and chair of Braxton Charities. She has been running unsuccessfully for public office for three decades. If she fails in this election, she'll be running for dog catcher.

Nathan Braxton: Nancy's husband. Former professional football player. Super Bowl winning quarterback.

Sandy Burr: Investigative journalist found dead in a bath tub in his hotel room at the Lakeside Inn. Both wrists were slashed with a razor blade. Suicide note found on the bed, but many believe it was murder.

George Ward: State chairman for Nancy Braxton's political party. He'll go to any lengths for her to win.

Erin Devereux: Nancy's executive assistant. She holds the record for longest time in her position.

Officers Fletcher, Brewster, and **Zigler**: Officers with the Spencer Police Department. They serve under Police Chief David O'Callaghan.

Bill Clark: Candidate for Spencer's mayor. Member of the town council. Born and raised locally.

Deputy Chief Arthur Bogart (Bogie): Spencer's Deputy Police Chief. David's godfather. Don't let his gray hair and weathered face fool you.

Fiona Davis: Witness in Sandy Burr case. She had dinner with victim hours before his death.

Bernie and Hap: Two of Spencer's beloved characters. They become Gnarly's campaign managers.

Mac Faraday: Retired homicide detective. On the day his divorce became final, he inherited $270 million and an estate on Deep Creek Lake from his birth mother, Robin Spencer.

Robin Spencer: Mac Faraday's late birth mother and world-famous mystery author. As an unwed teenager, she gave him up for adoption. After becoming America's queen of mystery, she found her son and made him her heir. Her ancestors founded Spencer, Maryland, located on the shore of Deep Creek Lake, a resort area in Western Maryland.

Archie Monday: Former editor and research assistant to world-famous mystery author Robin Spencer. She is now Mac Faraday's wife.

Dr. Dora Washington: Garrett County Medical Examiner.

Jessica Faraday: Mac Faraday's lovely daughter. Attending Georgetown University School of Medicine for doctorate in forensics psychology. Her inheritance from Robin Spencer thrust her into high society, which she left when she married Murphy Thornton.

Murphy Thornton: Jessica's husband. Second Lieutenant in the United States Navy. Naval Academy graduate. He's not your average navy officer.

Tawkeel Said: Murphy's colleague and friend.

Marilyn Newton: She breaks all stereotypes for middle-aged church ladies. She campaigns to win the evanglical vote for Gnarly.

Sheriff Christopher Turow: Garrett County Sheriff. Retired army officer. His wife was killed while serving in Iraq. He's one of the good guys.

Carmine Romano: Owner of Carmine's Pizza. He's endorsing Gnarly.

Cassandra Clark: Bill Clark's third wife. Less than a year after they said "I do," the honeymoon appears to be over.

Hugh Vance: Nancy Braxton's brother. He runs Braxton Charities.

Caleb Montgomery: Reluctant witness in a cold murder case.

Nigel: Jessica Faraday and Murphy Thornton's butler.

Spencer/Candi: Jessica Faraday's blue merle Shetland sheepdog.

Newman: Murphy's bassett hound. He's a couch potato.

Tristan Faraday: Mac Faraday's son. Professional student at George Washington University. He's an intellectual and proud of it.

Sarah Thornton: Naval academy cadet. Murphy's sister. Tristan's girlfriend.

Salma Rameriz: Producer of a local news program. Her type of journalism knows nothing about being fair and unbiased.

CO: Murphy's commanding officer. She leads the Phantoms.

Bruce Hardy: Agent with the Central Intelligence Agency. Worked undercover in the Middle East.

Newt Wallace: Executive Officer to the Director of Operations of the Central Intelligence Agency

Camille Jurvetson: Director of Operations at the Central Intelligence Agency.

Simon Spears: Bill Clark's campaign manager.

Politics have no relation to morals.

Niccolo Machiavelli
Italian Author, born 1469-died 1527

PROLOGUE

Four Years Ago—Iraqi Desert near the Border of Syria

The blazing sun and sweltering heat made it impossible to sleep in past sunrise in the military camp. Members of the army squad moved about quietly as if there was some possibility that their teammates could sleep in.

Courtesy wasn't the sole reason for their silence. The entire camp was grieving over four soldiers who had been killed the afternoon before.

Dressed in desert fatigues, Lieutenant Frank Watson exited his tent into the bright morning sun and stretched. Directly across from his quarters was First Sergeant Belle Perkins' tent, which was eerily quiet. Recalling the events of the day before, the officer sucked in a deep breath.

"Good morning, sir." First Sergeant Scott Scalia trotted up to his commanding officer. "Sleep okay?"

The angst was etched on his face. Rarely, if ever, had the soldier seen the lieutenant smile. "How do you think? Cut yourself shaving, Sergeant?"

Scalia rubbed his fingers along the deep scratch across his jaw. "No, that happened during the ambush yesterday. Still came out much better than many in our team, and it would have been much worse if it hadn't been for your exceptional leadership." The young soldier's face glowed in the morning sun. "Your ability to command in the hottest—"

"Did you get in touch with command?" Lieutenant Watson cut the sergeant off.

"Sending a chopper to pick up their bodies this afternoon," Scalia said. "Unfortunately, sir, it looks like we've got another problem."

"Another?"

"Frost is missing, sir."

Lieutenant Watson's eyes grew wide before immediately narrowing to slits. "Missing? Are you sure, Sergeant?"

"Yes, sir," Scalia said. "Mr. Frost requested that I wake him this morning to give him the ETA for the helicopter transport because he had a pouch going to HQ. I went there just now, and he wasn't in his tent."

"Maybe he's—"

"Not in the mess tent, sir." Scalia was ahead of him. "No one has seen him, sir. Plus his gear appears to be gone, sir."

"Damn it!" Lieutenant Watson said. "We've been escorting that damn contractor all over this hell they call a desert for the last month. We've lost six members of our squad protecting his butt. Two last week and four—"

Scalia shot a glance in the direction of the first sergeant's tent. "The way things went down yesterday—it would have been a whole lot worse if it hadn't been for Perkins and Gnarly. The way they had all of us pinned—"

The howl that came from the tent was heard across the camp. Soldiers spilled out of their tents and ran to First Sergeant Belle Perkins' tent to uncover the cause of her canine partner's distress.

Lieutenant Frank Watson was the first one inside. The interior of the tent was a shambles. The bed had been overturned. They found her German shepherd draped across her dead body. The dog was licking her from one side of her face to the other, and they were unsure of whether he was doing so in the hope of bringing his master back to life or because he wanted to kiss her farewell. When he received no response, he threw back his head and uttered a long, mournful howl.

"Whoever took Frost must have killed Perkins!" When the lieutenant stepped toward them, the German shepherd lunged at him with a hundred pounds of fur and teeth.

Grabbing for his service weapon, the army officer fell back.

"Maybe Gnarly went nuts and turned on her," one of the soldiers said as his canine teammate snarled at them from where he was standing protectively in front of Sergeant Perkins. "I've heard of that happening—PTS."

"Stand down!" Another soldier familiar with dogs pushed through the throng of soldiers, all of whom had their hands on their weapons and were ready to take down the anxious canine. "He got hurt in the ambush yesterday. Dogs instinctively feel the need to protect themselves and their partners—especially when they're injured." Slowly, the soldier inched forward.

"You're going to get yourself killed, Samuels," Scalia said. "We all saw what that dog did to those terrorists yesterday."

"Yeah, I saw." Private Drew Samuels continued inching forward with his hand held out to the German shepherd. "Gnarly stuck his neck out to save our butts. We can stick our necks out to help him—he deserves that at the very least."

Samuels was within striking distance of the dog. Gnarly sniffed his hand.

Aiming his gun at the dog, the lieutenant said, "If he tries anything, I'm taking him out."

"Give me a chance."

Gnarly's grand bronze-colored ears fell back, and he uttered a whine while glancing over his shoulder and back at the woman lying on the floor of the tent behind him.

"I know, boy." Samuels dared to touch the top of Gnarly's head. "We want to help her. Let me look." While stroking the German shepherd, the army medic moved past him to look down at the K-9 handler.

She was dressed in her fatigue pants and a T-shirt. Sprawled out on the floor, she was gazing up at the ceiling with dead eyes.

Everyone in the camp squeezed in through the door. Those unable to get inside stood on their toes and looked past their fellow soldiers to catch a glimpse of the dead K-9 officer and her partner, who was lying next to her with his snout buried in her dark hair.

Looking down at Gnarly, the commanding officer asked, "What happened here?"

CHAPTER ONE

Present Day—Spencer, Maryland

"You didn't tell me you were into blindfolds," Dallas Walker said to David O'Callaghan. "Call me a prude, but I'm gettin' nervous as a fly in a glue pot."

"Whatever that means." David peered closely at her face to make sure that she couldn't see through the bandana he had tied around her head.

While the lanky brunette had never exhibited any trouble moving around in her high heels, the process of walking down the circular staircase in David's luxurious house on the shore of Deep Creek Lake while blindfolded was a different story. Every window in the home, which had been built in the shape of a circle, provided a lake view.

Their long-distance courtship was proving to be a success. Dallas Walker, who was in her midtwenties, owned a thousand-acre ranch in Texas that made some demands on her. As one of the heirs to a billion-dollar fortune, she did have a full staff of ranch hands to keep the operation going, but her love for the quarter horses she bred demanded that she return to Texas periodically.

Yet her investigative-journalism career required frequent and unexpected trips away from both homes to follow leads for particularly juicy cases.

As the chief of police in the small resort town of Spencer, Maryland, David O'Callaghan found that he was enjoying his freedom when Dallas was gone—and enjoying their passionate reunions when she returned.

With his investigative instincts, he had not failed to notice that Dallas was moving into his home one suitcase at a time. The latest piece of luggage was a dog crate that contained a Belgian shepherd named Storm. Slightly smaller than a German shepherd, she had a thick sable coat and a bushy tail that caused her to remind David of a giant fox.

After being apart from Dallas for a full month, David was anxious to pull out all of the romantic stops for her return, including a home-cooked dinner of Chateaubriand for two, candlelight, and champagne. It was his first venture in trying to cook a gourmet meal.

While Dallas had been upstairs getting dressed for their evening in, David had set the perfect table and put on soft lights and music. He then escorted her to the dining area.

As Dallas maneuvered down the stairs in her high heels, David kept a firm hold on her while admiring her long legs, which were displayed in a short skirt. Her thick, wavy locks spilled down to the middle of her back. Once they reached the bottom of the stairs, he ushered her over to the table. "Okay, take off the blindfold."

Anxious to see her expression, David watched her push the bandana up and over her head. Her light-brown eyes met his sparkling-blue ones. Then, as she looked beyond him to the romantically set dinner table, her eyes grew wide with shock. Her mouth dropped open.

Not expecting such a reaction, David turned around just as she let out a shriek followed by loud laughter.

David had set the table for two with a place setting at each end of the table. Painstakingly, he had arranged their main entrée and garnished each plate to make it a work of art. There was a crystal champagne flute next to each plate and a bottle of champagne in an ice bucket in the middle of the table.

Everything was as David had left it when he'd run upstairs to fetch Dallas—except for two additions.

Two additional guests had made themselves at home at the table and were in the process of cleaning the plates of the last remnants of the meal.

David's multimillionaire half-brother, Mac Faraday, had left his dog, Gnarly, a hundred-pound German shepherd, in his care and had taken his wife, Archie Monday, on a river cruise in Europe. While Gnarly had a mind of his own, David usually didn't have any trouble with him—until he met Storm.

The Belgian shepherd's sweet, loving manner concealed her true nature, which David suspected was conniving—especially when she joined forces with Gnarly, the mastermind of the pair. In the very short time that the two dogs had known each other, the hundred-pound German and the female Belgian had become partners in crime.

The only thing worse than one sneaky kleptomaniac canine is two.

At that moment the two culprits were sitting at the table. Gnarly was licking the last drop of sauce from David's plate. Across from him in what should have been Dallas' chair, Storm was standing with her front paws on the table, finishing off her meal by lapping up Dallas' champagne from the crystal flute.

"You—" Unable to think of which nasty word to say first, David sputtered before working up to a scream that sent both dogs flying. The chairs were overturned in the melee that followed. David lunged for Gnarly only to have Storm cut him off, which caused him to narrowly escape falling across the table. By the time David was able to regain his footing, the shepherds were galloping up the stairs.

Both plates had been licked clean. They'd even eaten the parsley garnish.

"I swear!" Dallas was doubled over with laughter. "If they'd run any faster, they would've caught up with yesterday!"

"Do you know how hard I worked to cook that dinner?"

Dallas wrapped her arms around his shoulders. "Really, sugar, it's your own fault."

"My fault?"

"Even in the short time I've known Gnarly, I know he's a thief," she said. "If you were smart, you would have put them outside before leaving our dinner unguarded."

David's eyes narrowed. "I did." Pushing her away, he turned to the French doors leading out onto the back deck where he had put the two food thieves. One of the doors was wide open. With the palm of his hand, he smacked himself on the forehead. "But I forgot to lock it!"

"Lock it?" Her eyes grew wide.

"Gnarly can open doors, even doors with round door-knobs," he said. "But he hasn't figured out how to pick locks yet." He picked up a linen napkin from the floor and tossed it onto the middle of the table. "Give him time. I'm sure if he sets his mind to it…"

Coming up behind him, she hugged him and rested her head on his shoulder. "I'm sure they appreciated it."

"I didn't cook it for them. All I have left in the kitchen is mac and cheese."

"I didn't get a Brazilian wax job for mac and cheese," she whispered before planting a lingering kiss on the back of his neck.

"Storm is a good dog," Dallas said during their drive up to the top of Spencer Mountain to the five-star inn owned by Mac Faraday.

"She ate your dinner and drank your champagne."

"Only because she looks up to Gnarly. I'm willin' to bet he started it."

Chuckling at Dallas' bias toward her beloved dog, David turned the wheel to pull into the inn owner's reserved parking space. Since Mac was out of town, David was sure that no one would be using it. Upon reading the sign announcing that evening's events, David groaned.

"What's wrong, love?" Dallas reached across the seat to squeeze his arm.

He nodded his head at the huge poster announcing the mayoral debate that would take place in the banquet room. "I forgot that the town council is hosting a political debate tonight."

"Maybe we should go see it," Dallas said while watching the crowd of well-dressed patrons cruising past the doormen.

"You've got to be kidding," David said without humor in his tone.

There was puzzlement in her eyes. "Why not? I'm a journalist."

"Spencer is a small town," David said. "The population is fewer than a thousand most of the year."

"And 'bout half of that population was raised on concrete in Washington."

"Didn't use to be," he said. "People only found out about Deep Creek Lake in about the last two decades. Then they started moving in with their mansions and their big ideas about having laws controlling everything from dog leashes to clotheslines."

"Clotheslines?"

"Clotheslines, believe it or not."

Uncertain of whether he was joking, she looked him up and down.

The corner of his mouth curled up.

"Okay, lover, I'll bite. What's the thing 'bout clotheslines?"

"This spring, the town council quietly passed a bill outlawing clotheslines within Spencer's town limits," David said. "No heads-up. No discussion. No debate. No one even knew they were considering it. They were very quiet about it."

Dallas' eyebrows lifted up into her bangs. "*Outlawed* clotheslines?"

David nodded his head. "Can you believe it? I didn't know about it until the law, signed and sealed, appeared on my desk."

"How—"

"Local residents living in this lakefront community are no longer allowed to hang their wet clothes outside to dry. It's a lake community where many families do water sports. Now they have to keep their wet swimsuits inside, where no one can see them. The town council's excuse? Outdoor clotheslines bring down property value."

"If you ask me, the folks on that town council are so low that they'd have to look up to see hell."

"You got it, babe," David said with a sigh. "Within days of the new law's passing—before most of the town's residents were aware that such a law had even been proposed—the city folks bombarded my department with complaints about their lowbrow neighbors drying their clothes outside. The locals have been posting scathing editorials in the newspapers and on social media. I even had to break up a fight between an older woman who liked the smell of her sheets when they were dried by the lake breeze and a Washington lobbyist who didn't want her dinner guests to see her neighbor's bedsheets."

"Are you tellin' me that the clothesline ban was the shot that started a civil war in Spencer?"

"Spencer has been cracking down the middle for the last seven years," David said. "The clothesline prohibition was the straw that broke the camel's back."

A grin came to Dallas' lips. "Sounds like the makin' of a hot debate." With a playful punch to his arm, she giggled. "I can't wait."

"I don't want to go to the debate."

Dallas didn't hear him. She was already out of the cruiser. With a tip of his cap, a doorman held the door open for her and took the time to take in a view of her rear while she trotted inside.

When David caught up with her in the hotel's lobby, where she was looking for the right direction to go in, he repeated his protest. "Wouldn't you rather have a romantic dinner in the restaurant and then go home for dessert than sit in a stuffy banquet room watching two self-absorbed politicians spin one lie after another?"

"Oh, come on, sweetie," she said while brushing her fingertips across his cheek. "From what you just said, this is gonna be livelier than a buffalo stampede."

"I know both candidates," David said. "Bill Clark is the head of the town council. He's an arrogant bully who thinks he's above everyday manners—unless he wants something from you. Nancy Braxton is a compulsive liar."

"In other words, both of them would steal the flowers off of their grandmas' graves." She grinned. "They're politicians. Being crookeder than a dog's hind leg is the first requirement in that job description." Playfully, she grasped the front of his dress shirt and pulled him to her. She locked her brown eyes, which were the color of cognac, onto his blue eyes. After kissing him on the lips, she whispered in his hear. "Just ten minutes. Please. And then we'll go have dinner, and...if you want...we can go back home for dessert, and I'll do that thing that makes you—"

David sucked in a deep breath. Dallas' deep, raspy voice never failed to excite him, even when she wasn't trying to seduce him. After letting out his breath slowly, he whispered, "Ten minutes. Not a second more." He led her by the hand back to the banquet room.

"You know what, darlin'? Back home, we don't consider it to be a proper political debate until fists start flying."

The Next Morning—Spencer Police Department

The jingle of the bell over the front door announced the entrance of the police department's desk sergeant, Tonya. Startled out of the snooze into which he had fallen while resting his jaw against a cold compress, David looked up from her desk.

Tonya slapped a paper bag down onto the desk in front of him. "I thought you could use this." With a shake of her head, the middle-aged desk sergeant took note of the tear in David's suit coat and of his disheveled appearance. Even his blond hair, which was usually neatly combed, was messed with a lock dropping down onto his forehead. His gold police chief's badge was displayed on the utility belt he wore over his dress slacks.

David peered into the bag and discovered that she had brought him a bear claw.

"If anything, you proved your lack of partisanship to the citizens of Spencer," Tonya said. "How many police chiefs would arrest *both* nominees for mayor—*one* of whom is destined to be your boss after the election?"

"How many people running for office would get into a fist fight with their opponent in front of a hundred people?" Taking the pastry out of the bag, he grumbled. "Dad used to say that only a crazy person would throw his or her hat into the ring. So you know that by virtue of the fact that they're running for office, every candidate is mentally incompetent."

"That's why I don't vote." Tonya waved for him to get up from her desk.

David almost choked on his bear claw. "You don't vote! Do you know how many countries in the world have dictatorships where people don't have any say in what the government decides to do? Your vote is your voice. You need to exercise it."

"It's a right," Tonya said. "Not an obligation."

"People like you deserve what you get." David waved the pastry at her. "I don't ever want to hear you complain about our country going to pot again."

The door to the police station opened again. Instantly, Gnarly and Storm charged in, practically dragging Dallas behind them. Once inside, she dropped both of their leashes and closed the door. Since he was in the midst of getting up from Tonya's desk, David was unprepared to defend himself when Gnarly leaped from the floor to snatch the bear claw out of his hand. As soon as he noticed that his breakfast had been taken, David turned to lunge for the German shepherd only to have Storm dart between the two of them to cut him off. Without pausing, both dogs galloped across the squad room and up the stairs to David's office.

"They're like the canine Bonnie and Clyde," Tonya said.

Seemingly unperturbed, Dallas set a lunch container on the reception counter. "That's okay, my love. I brought you a better breakfast." She didn't notice the arched eyebrow Tonya was directing toward her in reference to the danish. "I felt so bad about our date gettin' ruined last night," she said, holding out an egg casserole baked into a single serving dish. "And you had to spend the night here with the candidates in jail—"

"They're still here!" Gasping, Tonya whirled around in her chair. "Do you *want* to get fired after the election?"

"They both assaulted a police officer." David pointed to the welt on his cheekbone. As he took the breakfast goody from Dallas, he gave her a soft kiss on the lips. "After spending all night listening to them blaming each other for getting arrested, an hour ago I called Fletcher and told him to come take over the babysitting."

Dallas followed David to the empty desk where he sat down to eat. "You would think that since they're such high-falutin, important folks, people would have been here like that"—she snapped her fingers—"fixin' to get them released."

"Their party bosses have been calling everyone on the town council and every other political office all night," David said. "These two idiots are the cream of the crop. I can't understand how anyone could've voted for them in the first place. I certainly didn't!"

"I know for a fact that Nancy Braxton didn't legally win her party's nomination," Tonya said with a shake of her head. "My daughter-in-law works for the county clerk. She was there when they tallied the votes. The leaders of Nancy's political party didn't want her opponent to get the nomination. They felt he was too white and had the wrong genitalia to represent their party in this election. It's high time for Spencer to have a woman mayor—even if that woman is an incompetent bitch."

"Are you saying that the party committed voter fraud?" David whirled away from his coffee mug, which he was in the middle of filling, to face her.

"Tiffany told me that the vote was close and that the party leaders just tossed out about a hundred ballots for the other candidate. Nancy won the nomination by only sixty-four votes. If they had counted those other ballots, Braxton's opponent would've been the nominee and would've won by around forty votes."

"Has anybody reported this? Why didn't you contact the board of elections after you heard about it?" David asked over the top of his coffee mug.

"And what would the board of elections have done?" Tonya asked. "They would've asked everyone who was in the room what happened. Everyone would've said that nothing happened, knowing that if they didn't, they'd be blacklisted by those in that party who hold political offices. Worse yet, what if something had come of it? No whistle-blower wants to end up like Sandy Burr."

"Who's Sandy Burr?" David asked.

Tonya's eyes grew wide. She turned to David, who was sitting at an empty desk, and Dallas, who was perched on a corner of it—one long leg draped across the other. They were both looking questioningly at her.

Tonya had known David since his childhood. Over twenty-five years earlier, she had started working at the Spencer Police Department for David's late father, Patrick O'Callaghan, who had been the chief of police.

"Investigative journalist," Tonya said, "who was found in a bathtub at the Lakeside Inn with both wrists slashed. The suicide note found on the bed said that he was sorry. The last person he'd been seen with was Nancy Braxton; they'd been in the hotel's lounge about twelve hours before his body was found by a maid. He'd been doing a story about her charity organization. Your father, who'd only been chief for a few months at that point, and Bogie were the first on the scene. Burr actually told his sister and a couple of friends that if he ended up dead because of the story he was chasing, they shouldn't believe that he'd committed suicide."

"Did Dad ever close the case?" David asked.

Tonya shook her head. "He was forced off of the investigation by the state police because Nathan Braxton, Nancy's husband, complained to the governor. Nancy felt that Pat O'Callaghan wasn't giving her the respect she deserved. Since Nathan was the Redskin's quarterback who took the team to the Super Bowl, the governor couldn't yank the case away from us fast enough. The state police immediately closed it as a suicide—though everyone knows that it was murder and that Nancy did it."

Immersed in the story of the long-cold murder case, they all jumped when the front door opened and a short, exceedingly slender man with black hair and thick, dark eyebrows stepped in. With his slight frame, heart-shaped face, and dapper, tailored suit, he resembled a leprechaun. "I'm looking for Police Chief O'Callaghan," he told, rather than asked, Tonya.

A young woman with short ash-colored hair who was dressed in an ill-fitting pantsuit and flat shoes slipped in directly behind the leprechaun.

David stood up from the desk where he was eating. "That would be me."

Barging forward, he extended his hand to David. "I'm George Ward, the state chairman for Nancy Braxton's party and this is Erin Devereux, Ms. Braxton's executive assistant. I understand there was an incident last night."

David answered him by pointing to the bruise on his jaw.

"The bruise on his cheek came from the other party," Dallas said.

George laughed. "These political debates can get quite passionate."

"'Passionate' isn't the word I would use," David said without humor.

"From what I've been told, Bill Clark started it," George said.

"Those sources are wrong," Dallas said. "Ms. Braxton was the one who threw a water bottle at Mr. Clark after calling him a warmongering fascist. You can see the whole thing from start to finish on the video I uploaded to my blog this morning."

"Did you record the part where Clark called her a fat pig and told her to shut up?" Erin asked.

"She needed to shut up," Dallas said. "It was a debate and his turn to answer the question, and she wouldn't let him get a word in edgeways. I swear, it's like no one ever told her that it's better to keep quiet and let people think you're dumb than to open your mouth and prove 'em right. Every time she opened her mouth, somethin' stupid came flyin' out."

"I guess we know who the police department is supporting in this election," George said. "Can't say I'm surprised."

"Actually, you're wrong," Dallas said. "Mr. Clark isn't any better. From what little I was able to hear from Mr. Clark, it was plain that if he had a brain, it'd die of loneliness. After seein' those two in action, I'd vote for a snake before I'd vote for either of 'em. Snakes are smarter and won't lie to you 'bout plannin' to bite you in the butt the first chance they get."

Tonya let out a loud laugh.

With a roll of his eyes, George dismissed Dallas as unworthy of argument and turned his attention back to David. "With all due respect, Chief, Ms. Braxton was simply defending herself, and you got in the way. She had no intention of striking you. That being the case, I can understand your arresting Clark, but Ms. Braxton?" He tsk-tsked at him.

At the end of the hallway, the door leading downstairs to the holding cells opened, allowing loud curses from the cells below to float upstairs.

"What have you ever really accomplished, Braxton, besides giving feminists a bad name?"

"Shut up, you sexist pig, before I come over there and—"

Fletcher, a young officer with only a few years on the force under his belt, jogged into the squad room. "Chief, how long are we going to hold those two?" he asked while jerking a thumb over his shoulder in the direction of the cells. "They're really getting ugly."

"What do you mean, '*getting* ugly'? They were horrid before the debates even started." Wiping his mouth, David packed up the casserole dish and handed it to Dallas while kissing her on the cheek.

A thin smile crossed George Ward's lips. "With all due respect, Chief, the solution is really quite simple. Keeping Ms. Braxton locked up is going to do your office more harm than good. Word is getting out to the media, and my office will be forced to release a statement about how an overzealous small-town police chief with a political agenda overstepped his authority—"

"Overstepped his authority?" Dallas was on her feet. "Those two polecats would've torn the roof off of the Spencer Inn if David hadn't broken it up."

"Your candidate started it!" Erin said, jabbing a finger in Dallas' direction.

"He's not *my* candidate!"

There was a plea in Fletcher's tone. "Chief, if Clark calls me a loser one more time, I swear that I'm going to shoot him."

David sighed. "Okay."

"So we'll let them go?"

"No," David said with a sly grin. "You have my permission to shoot him."

Fletcher's eyes bugged out. George Ward's and Erin's mouths dropped open.

"Shoot Braxton, too," David said. "We'll tie blocks to their bodies and dump them in the middle of the lake in the middle of the night."

George was the first to find his voice. "That is *completely* inappropriate, Chief!"

"He's joking," Tonya said with a sharp tone. "You are kidding, right?"

"Yeah," David said with a tired sigh. "Bring them up to my office."' When George and Erin turned to follow him up the stairs to his office, he added, "Alone! I want to talk to the children alone."

Her eyes wide, Erin pushed past George so that she could follow David. "You can't interview Ms. Braxton without me."

"Why not?" David's tone dripped with the authority of his position as chief of police. This was his town, and he was the one in control of this matter.

Erin dropped back a step. After regrouping, she gave him a fiery look. "I'm her assistant. It is my job to always be available for her whenever she needs anything. Wherever she goes, I go."

"If she needs anything during our talk, I'll call you."

David's corner office occupied the second floor of a log building that resembled a sports club more than it did a police station. His office windows looked out onto the police dock, which held four speedboats and six Jet Skis. The police fleet also included all-terrain vehicles for patrol or searches in the deep woods up and down the mountain.

When David went into his office, he found Gnarly and Storm occupying the sofa—seemingly licking each other's lips to pick up any remnants of the bear claw. Upon seeing David, the two large dogs stopped and looked at him with questions in their eyes. Their pointy ears stood up tall.

With a shake of his head, David crossed the office to take a seat behind his desk. Within minutes, he heard Councilman Clark and Nancy Braxton loudly protesting their treatment while Officer Fletcher escorted them up the stairs.

Bill Clark shoved his political opponent aside to enter the office ahead of her. His tie was undone. His tailored suit had been torn in the previous night's altercation. "O'Callaghan, I knew you were stupid—"

Upon seeing not only Gnarly but also a second dog only a fraction smaller than the German shepherd glaring at him from the sofa, Bill Clark stopped to regroup.

Past middle age, Nancy Braxton's face, which was as bloated as her figure, was the image of displeasure. To accentuate her equality to men, she was never seen wearing anything but a pantsuit. She glared at David with small, beady eyes. Fearlessly storming past the dogs, she charged his desk. "How dare you lock us up like two common criminals!"

"Seriously?" Showing no fear, David chuckled. "You two assaulted an officer of the law—"

"How were we supposed to know you were a police officer?" Nancy said. "You weren't wearing your uniform."

"You both know me," David said. "You know that I'm the chief of police, and you both threw punches at me."

"I wasn't aiming for you," Nancy said, "I was aiming for him." She pointed at Bill Clark, who had cautiously maneuvered up to the desk while keeping an eye on Gnarly, who was watching him closely.

"Like any good mayoral candidate would have done," David said.

"He started it," she said.

"You started it," Bill said.

"How dare you, Clark, bring up my getting expelled from Princeton Law School for cheating!"

"You were a cheat thirty years ago, and you're still a cheat," the councilman said.

"And you're a blackmailer! I have witnesses who said that you pressured members of the town council into approving your clothesline ban!"

"Enough!" David shouted while holding up his hand. "I've had it up to here with your childish accusations!"

"They're not childish," Nancy said. "Political leaders need to be strong and decisive and of the best character—"

"Which *both* of you *lack*!"

"I've never!"

"On the contrary, Braxton! You do all the time!" David laughed. "I'm not some uninformed, unwitting voter capable of falling under your pathetic-though-well-rehearsed act of sincerity. I know you! I know both of you! You're both the most self-absorbed, corrupt, power-hungry, pitiful excuses for American leaders I've ever seen."

"Watch it, O'Callaghan," Bill said through gritted teeth. "One of us is going to be your boss after this election."

"And since you know us, you know that both Bill and I have *very* long memories," Nancy said.

"So I'd watch my mouth if I were you."

"I'm out there every day talking to the citizens in this town," David said. "You two are so out of touch that you don't realize how angry we are. You don't know the real issues that everyone faces and the divide that has occurred between the locals and the city folks moving in. We see you two and the rest of the town council strutting around—all proud about how we placed our faith in you to make things right—yet none of you have ever lifted a finger to do what we elected you to do."

"That's just your opinion," Nancy said.

"No, it's not," David said. "Yes, you two are the only names on the ballot. How you got there speaks to the condition of the political establishment itself. The fact is that no one in Spencer likes *either one of you.* If we had a real choice, we'd vote for *Gnarly* before we'd vote for you."

Following the wave of David's hand, they turned to where the German shepherd was sitting behind them, scratching his shoulder with his hind leg. His head was down, his ears were falling to either side of his head, and his mouth was hanging open with delight at finally reaching the spot that itched.

Bill Clark laughed. "Yeah, right."

Chapter Two

The Next Morning—Spencer Police Department

The deputy police chief, Art Bogart, who was called "Bogie," had just completed the paper work from the weekend and was enjoying his last cup of coffee for the morning when Dallas Walker stepped through the front door of the police station.

Storm rushed around the reception counter to give a greeting to Tonya, who greeted the dog warmly. "Chief isn't here."

"I know," Dallas said. "He took Gnarly and ran off first thing this morning, saying he had some business to take care of in Mountain Lake Park." Smiling at Bogie, she added, "There's the man I want."

"I'm taken," the sixty-five-year-old career police officer said, chuckling over the top of his coffee mug.

"If I were you, I'd keep my hands off," Tonya said. "His girlfriend is very good with a scalpel."

"Ignore her." Bogie held out his arm to usher Dallas into his office. "She's always cranky on Monday mornings."

With Storm leading the way, they went into the deputy chief's office. Even in her high heels, Dallas noticed that Bogie towered over her. In spite of his silver hair and moustache and weathered face, Bogie had the muscles of a much younger body builder. He shot her a wide grin. "What can I do for you, Dallas?"

"Sandy Burr." Dallas took a seat in front of his desk. "Tonya told David an' me 'bout his murder. Nancy Braxton was your prime suspect. David has no memory of the case."

With a chuckle, Bogie closed his office door. "And being a journalist, you can't resist digging into a murder case in which a political candidate was the prime suspect."

"'Zactly."

"David was just a kid when it happened," Bogie said while pulling out his desktop computer's keyboard. He began typing away. "It was, like, twenty years ago, a couple of years after the Braxtons built their summer place up on the mountain. Nathan Braxton had retired from football, but he was still a big star and was making millions off of endorsements."

"You would think that the wife of a famous Super Bowl quarterback being the prime suspect in a murder would've been big news," Dallas said.

"Nathan Braxton was very popular, especially in this area," Bogie said. "He's a nice guy. Charming. Nobody has a bad thing to say about him. So the media protected him...and her—even though she is a witch."

"If she's such a witch, why is her political party shovin' her down Spencer's throat?"

"Good question." Bogie grinned. "Nancy Braxton runs Braxton Charities, which is a huge charitable organization. Animal rights, the environment, medical research, hunger—it helps tons of different nonprofits. People with lots of money give it to Braxton Charities, which distributes it to the charities under its umbrella." He held up his finger. "One of those charities is Nancy's political party. As long as she's happy, millions of bucks per year keep going to her party. If they don't back her, she has the power to shut off the faucet."

Dallas' light-brown eyes narrowed to slits. "So say I was to start donating several million dollars to Nancy's political party. They would back *me* to run for president of the United States—even if I was a pathological liar with no moral compass who was capable of betraying our country and selling out the men and women defending us on the front lines for cold, hard cash?"

"From what I've seen, pretty much." Bogie shrugged his broad shoulders. "Politics isn't about patriotism anymore, Dallas. It's all about power. Whichever party has the White House holds the power. That's all both parties care about. What's best for America is irrelevant to the parties running the show."

Confusion crossed her face. "I thought it was the people running the show."

"Supposedly."

"My pappy used to tell me and Phil that every single person has the God-given power to change the world," she said. "All they have to do is use it. Momma wrote her books to expose criminals and corruption. Pappy donated money to build hospitals and schools in countries that no one ever heard of and would rather forget existed."

Bogie chuckled at her youthful idealism. "Not everyone is a Walker, Dallas."

"Neither were Rosa Parks and Claudette Colvin."

The deputy chief turned away from his keyboard and computer screen.

"Two women who, separately, back in the sixties refused to go to the back of the bus and started a whole revolution." Dallas grinned at him. "They weren't rich or politically connected. Both of them saw that something was terribly wrong and decided to do something about it. They acted—not in a violent or obnoxious way. They just took stood up, or rather sat down, in the front of the bus and changed the world."

The silver-haired deputy chief and young investigative jouranlist stared at each other in silence.

"Yeah," Bogie finally said, "but how do we use this power your pappy told you about."

"By keeping corrupt killers out of positions of power," Dallas said. "Tell me why Nancy Braxton would have killed Sandy Burr? Were they having an affair?"

"Hardly." Bogie laughed with a shake of his head. "According to his friends and family—he had a sister— Sandy Burr was working on a story about Braxton Charities donating a grant to a research team at the University of Virginia School of Medicine. They were doing research into the effects of repeated head injuries to football players and into how to improve helmets."

"Sounds like research that Nancy Braxton, the wife of a former professional football player, would've been interested in," Dallas said.

"According to Sandy's sister," Bogie said, "a medical student from a team doing the same study in Arizona claimed that the team in Virginia stole their research. Seems that someone in Arizona was dating someone from the Virginia team, and he stole his girlfriend's notes." He waved his hand. "None of that is really relevant. The important thing is that as Sandy started digging into how the Virginia team had gotten the grant, he discovered some of what he called 'irregularities' in how Braxton Charities awarded its research grants."

"What type of irregularities?"

"That, we never got a chance to find out," Bogie said. "Burr got his hands on copies of Braxton's public financial records and talked to a lot of donors to Braxton Charities. He also talked to some people inside the sports-equipment company sponsoring the research into the football helmets. That led him in another direction and then another until he started saying that he was onto something big. He was coming to Deep Creek Lake to meet a confidential informant who was supposed to piece together everything he had dug up."

"Nancy Braxton, the president of the organization herself?" Dallas asked.

"Maybe someone inside the organization, and Nancy got wind of it and decided to confront Sandy to personally put a stop to his investigation. Sandy's sister, Flo, said that he brought all of his notes with him when he came here to Deep Creek Lake. He kept all of his papers in a boot box. This was before the days of laptops and thumb drives." He shook his head. "We didn't find any papers in his hotel room or car."

"But Nancy Braxton was the last one seen talking to Sandy Burr."

Bogie nodded his head. "Sandy Burr checked into the Lakeside Hotel on Friday, April twelfth, at two o'clock. The next day he was seen having breakfast in the hotel restaurant and then spent most of the time in his room alone—or so we think. Around one o'clock, someone saw Sandy having lunch with a man at The Pier." Seeing her writing down the name of their lunch spot, he added, "The Pier is no longer there. It burned down, like, ten years ago." He sat forward. "This is where it gets interesting. At around five thirty that afternoon, Sandy was seen having drinks in the hotel lounge. He had struck up a conversation with a fellow guest, a woman. She was traveling by herself, and they got to talking. He told her that he was a writer. They ended up having dinner together."

Dallas arched an eyebrow at him. "Dinner and what else?"

Bogie smiled. "Nothing else. Her name was Fiona Davis." He watched her write down the name. "She lived in Gettysburg, Pennsylvania. I can give you her address—at least the address we had back then. That was a long time ago."

"What happened then?"

"After they finished eating, they got separate checks. Fiona went back to her room at about seven thirty," he said. "But she told us that she went out later, a little after eight, to go for a walk along the water and saw Sandy in the lounge, at the same table where they had eaten dinner. The description of the woman she saw with Sandy matched that of Nancy Braxton. The bartender knew Nancy Braxton and positively identified her as the woman Burr was having a drink with after dinner. Not only that, but according to the medical examiner who did Burr's autopsy, he was killed less than three hours after he had eaten with Fiona Davis, based on the state of digestion of the food found in his stomach."

"That means that he was dead less than two hours after he was seen with Nancy Braxton," Dallas said. "Did you find any evidence to prove that Braxton killed him?"

Bogie shook his head. "Never got that far. As soon as Nancy Braxton became a suspect, the case was yanked out from under us, and the state police closed it as a suicide."

"Sounds to me like a woman with somethin' to hide," Dallas said. "Besides the guy Burr was seen havin' lunch with, were there any other suspects that you looked at?"

"Let me look at our copy of the case file." Bogie adjusted his reading glasses and studied the information on the screen.

"Was there any physical evidence that indicated anyone else at the scene?" Dallas asked him.

"Fingerprints," Bogie said. "A set of three beautiful prints on the door above the doorknob. We ran them through the system but didn't get any hits. The state police argued that since it was a hotel and so many people stayed in the room, they'd most likely been left by other guests."

"True," she said. "Wouldn't hurt to run them again though."

"Tell that to the state police. It's not our case anymore." Scanning the information on his computer screen, Bogie let out a laugh. "I forgot all about this."

"What?"

"The fat man."

"The fat man?" She laughed.

"The bartender in the lounge said there was a fat man sitting at the bar at the same time that Burr was meeting with Nancy Braxton. He had a feeling this customer was watching Burr, and he noticed that he left right after Burr left the lounge."

"Could've been a coincidence," Dallas said. "Isn't that sometimes the thing with witnesses? They're so anxious to help that they start imaginin' things. The bartender might have just thought he was watchin' Burr because the idea was planted in his mind after he heard heard about the murder."

"That's what makes information from tip lines so diffi-cult," Bogie said. "Thing is, we never identified the fat man. The bartender swore that he never saw the guy before, that the guy paid cash, and that he never saw him again. Plus he left a fresh drink behind when he followed Burr out. That's what made the bartender suspicious."

"Can you see Nancy Braxton gettin' her hands dirty and killin' someone?" Dallas asked.

"No," Bogie said. "That's why we were so interested in the fat man—who we never did locate."

"Maybe I'll have better luck."

Garrett County Board of Elections

"Good morning, Gnarly." A man in farm overalls stopped on his way up to the counter to bend over and pet the German shepherd lying at David's feet.

Gnarly laid his ears back and wagged his tail. The toddler straddling the dog's back giggled with joy.

David glanced down to make sure that Gnarly wasn't playing too rough with the child whose mother was busy completing paper work on the other side of the work counter. Seeing that both child and dog were safe and happy, he checked the registration number on the metal tag in his hand to ensure that he had written it correctly on the form.

"Hey, Gnarly, how's it going?" one of the office clerks said, patting him on the head. After scratching his ears, she continued on through the door and back to her work cubicle without acknowledging Gnarly's human companion.

After pocketing the tags, David signed the application.

"Gnarly! What's up?" a young man said as he hurried by and waved to the dog.

The German shepherd replied with a bark.

"Time to go, Austin!"

"I want to stay with Gnarly," the child said when his mother lifted him by the arm off of the German shepherd.

"Austin," his mother said in a low voice.

With a pout, the toddler threw his arms around the dog. "Thanks for playing with me, Gnarly."

The shepherd sat up and licked the child's face.

"Thank you for watching Austin, Gnarly." The mother gave him a scratch behind the ears. Then, taking her child by the hand, she hurried up to the counter to turn in her paper work.

David led Gnarly up to the counter. Upon seeing the next available clerk, an older woman wearing turquoise reading glasses, his heart sank.

It was Edna.

Bracing for a fight, David clutched Gnarly's leash and stepped up to the counter.

"Chief O'Callaghan, what a pleasure to see you," Edna said with a forced smile.

"Hello, Edna." David slid the paper work in her direction.

Abruptly, Gnarly jumped up to plant his front paws on the counter. The sudden move prompted a shriek from Edna that was heard throughout the office.

Gnarly's mouth hung open in a grin.

"This is—" David said.

"I know Gnarly." She reached over to pat the dog on the top of the head. Her usual sour tone turned agreeable. "What brings you here today?"

"Filing to run as a candidate." David gestured to the paper work in her hand.

Tearing her attention away from the dog across from her, Edna read through the application. Upon reading the name on it, her eyebrows rose up on her forehead. She adjusted her eyeglasses and read the information again.

"He's been a resident in Spencer for the last four years," David said. "He's registered with the county—"

"So I see." The corners of her lips turned upward. "If he's elected mayor of Spencer, will he do anything about that speed trap on Lake Shore Drive?"

"That's not a speed trap," David said.

Cocking his head at David, Gnarly uttered a low, guttural noise.

Edna frowned.

"Look," David said. "I know the speed limit along that stretch of Lake Shore Drive used to be thirty-five, but then all those big houses went up, and the residents petitioned to have it lowered to twenty-five for a good reason: there are a lot of kids in that neighborhood. It would be unsafe to raise the speed limit back up to thirty-five."

Edna's frown deepened.

"But," David said, "Gnarly would suggest that instead of taking Lake Shore Drive, you take Spring Road, which runs parallel to Lake Shore."

"That would be a longer route."

"Yes, it would be longer," David said. "But only by about two miles. Since it's more rural, the speed limit is forty-five. You can travel Spring Road in less time, and it comes out only a quarter of a mile from where you come out when you take Lake Shore." He sucked in a deep breath. "That's what *Gnarly* would suggest."

She regarded David for a long moment before saying, "*Gnarly* has a lot of sense." With a flourish, she stamped the application with an "approved" stamp and handed it back to David. "He's got my vote."

Well, that's one vote! Trying hard not to dance out of the office, David led Gnarly out the door. Once they were out of sight, Edna took her cell phone out of her bag and searched her contacts for a phone number. The call was picked up on the second ring.

"Got anything interesting, Edna?"

"Oh yeah," Edna said. "You'll never believe who's running for mayor of Spencer, Maryland."

Once Gnarly's application to run for office had been officially approved, David felt that it was time for a celebratory breakfast—including a danish for the new mayoral candidate. Upon returning to Deep Creek Lake, David pulled his cruiser into Beagle Bailey's Bagels for a hot cup of coffee. The summer weather was pleasant enough that he and Gnarly could sit out on the deck along the lakeshore.

David and Gnarly had just bitten into their breakfasts when a familiar call made the hair on the back of David's neck stand up on end. His ears perking up, Gnarly wagged his tail.

"Hey, look, Hap! It's Gnarly!" Two elderly men rushed over from the outdoor service counter where they had gotten their coffees and breakfasts.

Bernie Stein and Hap Goldman had been best friends since childhood, and the pair was a fixture around Deep Creek Lake. The two men had run a fix-it business for as long as David could remember. They ran their business out of Hap's garage. They spent most of their time in Hap's man cave, drinking beer and watching sports on television. In spite of their less than polished appearance, Bernie and Hap were the local go-to guys for general repair work or small construction jobs. David suspected that that was because they were as entertaining to watch as they were skilled in repairs.

Always grinning his wide, toothless grin, Hap let Bernie do all of the talking—which he did a lot of.

"How're you doing, Gnarly?" After giving the German shepherd a piece of crust from his egg sandwich, Bernie plopped down in a chair at their table. "Are you meeting a date for breakfast?"

"Actually, he's eating with me," David said.

Startled, Bernie looked up to see that David was sitting across from him. "Oh, sorry, Chief. I didn't see you there."

Carrying a bear claw, Hap took a seat at the table. With a wide grin, he nodded a hello to David before giving a bit of his pastry to Gnarly.

"So what's happening, Chief?" Glancing around the outdoor café, which was nearly empty due to the lull between the breakfast crowd and the lunch crowd, Bernie asked in a low voice, "Have you got someone under surveillance?"

"No," David replied. "Gnarly and I were just going back to the police station after taking care of some business at the board of elections." Watching how Bernie and Hap were petting Gnarly, who was inching closer and closer to their food, he said with a sly grin, "Gnarly's running for mayor."

Bernie's and Hap's eyes grew wide. Both of their jaws dropped open.

"Really?" Bernie asked.

"It's official." David nodded his head. "He's running as an independent."

"Well, I'll be." Wagging a finger across the table at David, Bernie said, "You know, I think Gnarly would make a fine mayor—especially compared to those two knuckleheads already running. For one, Gnarly's *honest*—"

Seeing an opening, Gnarly snatched Bernie's egg sandwich from the table and wolfed it down.

Suppressing his laughter, David agreed with a nod of his head.

"Hap and I would love to help. Who've you got running his campaign?"

"Running his campaign?" David asked.

"You have to have a campaign manager," Bernie said.

Hap was nodding his head vigorously.

"But it's only a small-town race," David said.

"Does Gnarly have a website?" Bernie asked. "Is he on Facebook and Twitter?"

"Twitter?"

Bernie jumped up in his seat. "Gnarly's not on Twitter! How do you expect for him to win if he's not on Twitter? Tell me that he's at least on Instagram!"

Hap's toothless mouth hung open in what appeared to be disbelief.

Bernie waved his hands. "Let's not panic." He looked down at Gnarly, who had finished the sandwich and was licking his chops. "We can fix this, Gnarly. Hap and I will take over as your campaign managers." He turned his attention back to David. "What kind of budget does Mr. Faraday have for the campaign?"

"Mac? Campaign budget?"

"Well, as loaded as Mr. Faraday is, I'm sure he'll have a big enough budget for Hap and me to get the job done right." Seeing that his plate was then empty, Bernie stood up. "Man, this sure was an exciting breakfast. I don't even remember eating my sandwich. Come on, Hap, we've got a lot of work to do. We got signs to make and to book some billboards. Plus we need to put the word out online."

Chattering away about the work that they had to do, Hap and Bernie trotted away—leaving Hap's bearclaw for Gnarly to wolf down.

The mention of Mac Faraday's name made David swallow. He didn't consider his registering Gnarly to run for mayor to be a big issue that he should tell Mac about. "Campaign budget? Signs? Billboards? It's just a small-town mayoral race." Looking down into Gnarly's brown eyes, David cocked his head. "I mean, like, how big of a campaign could this become?"

Spencer Manor

Turning the SUV right onto Spencer Court, Archie Monday glanced over to her husband, Mac Faraday, who was asleep in the passenger seat. They had spent the last three weeks cruising up and down rivers in Europe, eating glorious gourmet food, drinking fabulous wine, and even spending some nights in romantic castle getaways.

Thankfully, Mac hadn't started to feel sick until the last day. It had started the usual way. He'd woken up with a sore throat and had been coughing. By the time they'd boarded the plane at Heathrow Airport, his voice had become raspy. He'd been flushed with fever and unable to stop coughing when they'd landed in Dulles. Two hours later, upon landing in a private jet at the airport in McHenry, Mac was full-fledged sick.

Archie patted his knee to wake him up. "Honey, we're home. We'll just get you to bed and unpack tomorrow."

Clearing his throat, Mac rubbed his face and sat up in his seat. "Sounds good to me."

As she approached the stone pillars marking the entrance to Spencer Manor, which was located at the end of Spencer Point, Archie brought their SUV to a halt. Media vans were lined up on both sides of the road. Upon seeing the black SUV, journalists with camera operators hurried forward to escort the vehicle up the circular driveway and to the front of the stone-and-cedar mansion.

"This does not look good," Mac said when he saw the journalists jostling for the best position from which to ambush him when he climbed out of the SUV.

A homicide detective who had had more than twenty-five years of investigative experience under his belt when a sudden inheritance from the birth mother he had never known had thrust him into high society, Mac was ready for everything—

except for a media ambush while he was suffering from a high fever.

Immediately, a pack of microphones was stuck in his face.

"Mr. Faraday," a middle-aged woman asked, "is Gnarly pro-choice or pro-life?"

"Huh?" Mac covered his mouth and coughed.

"Would you say Gnarly leans more to the left or to the right?"

Thinking about the times when he'd walked the German shepherd, Mac replied, "Usually he keeps to the right."

"So he's a conservative!" one of the journalists said.

"Conservative?" Mac asked.

"But he *claims* to be running as an independent," another journalist said.

"How does Gnarly feel about gun laws?" yet another asked. "Does he believe in protecting the Second Amendment? Is he going to support the Constitution?"

"I think," Mac said. "We never really talked about—you do realize Gnarly's a *dog*."

Thrusting herself between Mac and the journalists, Archie asked, "What's all this about?"

"The voters have a right to know Gnarly's platform so that they can make informed choices when it comes time to vote," the first journalist said.

Archie and Mac exchanged long looks during which a young female journalist asked, "As a dog, does Gnarly feel that cats and dogs have equal rights? Does he intend to propose that dogs who identify more with cats be exempt from leash laws?"

"And cats who identify more with dogs will be required to wear leashes," Mac said with a laugh that turned into a coughing fit.

While patting her husband on the back, Archie asked, "What office is Gnarly running for?"

"Mayor of Spencer," the journalists replied almost in unison.

"Mayor!" Mac's voice sounded like a foghorn. "He's never even voted!"

Chapter Three

"How long did you work for Robin Spencer?" Dallas asked Archie while they watched Gnarly and Storm chase each other in and around the floral gardens surrounding Spencer Manor.

In the summer season, the gardens were in full bloom, creating a multicolored glory. Even with all of the foliage, they could see camera operators perched on top of the stone wall bordering the Spencer estate so that they could record the mayoral candidate frolicking about his home.

Upon spotting Gnarly's nemesis, an overweight squirrel that Archie had named Otis, the two dogs partnered up and began what resembled a tag-team competition to chase him high up into a tree. Displeased about being outnumbered, Otis cursed down at them in his squirrel tongue. Standing up on her hind legs with her front paws on the base of the tree, Storm seemed to be weighing how difficult it would be to climb up after him.

Smiling at Gnarly's delight over making a new friend, Archie said, "Ten years."

"And you were her research assistant—"

"And editor."

"That was before—"

"Before what?" Archie jerked her head to look in Dallas' direction.

Seeing that she then had Archie's full attention, the corner of Dallas' lips curled with pleasure. "Nancy Braxton was Patrick O'Callaghan's prime murder suspect back 'bout twenty years ago."

Dallas sensed that eventually, if Archie let her guard down, she would be a fun person—maybe even a friend to her. She thought that there had to be a fun and loyal friend behind that wall. Otherwise, David wouldn't have valued Archie as though she were the sister he'd never had.

Archie wasn't David's only friend who held a grudge against his new love.

Things would have been different between Dallas and Archie if she had met David under different circumstances. As it were, fate had Dallas cross David's path days before he was to marry Chelsea, Archie's good friend. As a matter of fact, Archie was to be Chelsea's matron of honor, which made it her job to deliver the shocking news to David that Chelsea had called off the wedding.

A man of honor, David was planning to keep his commitment to Chelsea, even though he loved Dallas. So why, Dallas quietly fumed, did some of his friends blame *her* when it was *Chelsea* who ran away with another man?

For some reason, in spite of the facts, Archie saw Dallas as *the other woman* who played an active role in breaking up the couple.

"Robin never did like Nancy Braxton," Archie said. "I assumed it was because Braxton is an arrogant bitch. Robin never had time for rude people. What was the victim's name?"

"Sandy Burr."

Dallas watched Archie's emerald eyes narrow in thought. She brought her long, slender hand to her head to scratch her ultrashort blond hair with her finely manicured pale-pink nails. The hue on her fingernails matched the toenails of her bare feet, both adorned with toe rings. Every time she saw Archie Monday, Dallas was struck by her polished appearance—even when she had bare feet. Archie Monday might have been a rich man's wife, but she was no shoe hound. The few times Dallas had been at Spencer Manor for dinner parties, she'd found Archie Monday dressed in the latest styles with rubies dripping from her ears—and with bare feet.

Even though Dallas Walker was the daughter of a Texas billionaire, she had been born and raised in the outdoors, getting her hands dirty and learning how to hold her own against cattlemen and ornery quarter horses.

Unlike Archie Monday, who never had a hair out of place and kept her nails clean and manicured, Dallas Walker wore her brunette mane long and loose down to the middle of her back and kept her fingernails unpolished and trimmed short. Women with long acrylic nails had no place on Buddy Walker's Ranch.

"Sandy Burr does sound familiar," Archie said. "Tell me a little about the case."

"Found with his wrists slashed at the Lakeside Inn. The last person he was seen 'live with was Nancy Braxton." She quickly added, "He was an investigative reporter who found irregularities in how Braxton Charities awarded research grants."

"I've heard about that case," Archie said with certainty. "It was murder. I remember it now. The slashes in his wrists had been made from the left to the right—on both wrists. If he had sliced his own wrists, one slash would've been from the left to the right, and the other one would've been from the right to the left."

"That's right." Dallas nodded her head in agreement. "Because he would 've had to switch the blade from one hand to the other."

Whirling on her heels, Archie crossed the deck to the door. "Robin wasn't involved in the case—she might have been out of town at the time," she said over her shoulder. "If she did any research on the case, there will be a folder for it in her file cabinet down in the study."

As soon as the door was open, Storm and Gnarly raced up onto the deck and practically knocked Dallas over in their furor to get inside. While Storm followed Archie downstairs to the study, Gnarly galloped into the living room to join Mac and David.

"I never noticed that about you before," Mac said to David when Gnarly leaped over the back of the sofa and landed on the cushions next to him. Mac had changed into his pajamas and a bathrobe and had taken a dose of medicine for his cough, flu, and sore throat.

"Noticed what?" David said, chuckling where he was sitting across from him. "You look like hell, and you sound worse."

"That you're crazy. What sane man nominates a *dog* to run for mayor?" Mac pulled the afghan from where it was draped across the arm of the sofa so that he could warm the chill that was sending shivers up his back and across his shoulders.

"I was making a political statement. All I intended to do was get Gnarly's name on the ballot. So many people in Spencer are furious with the direction this town has gone in. Mayor Gannon doesn't give a darn."

"I think our current mayor just got tired of fighting with Clark," Mac said. "That's why he's retiring. He's sick of it."

"Everybody I talk to," David said, "dislikes the nominees. They need another option. An independent who can't be intimidated and who doesn't feel obligated to toe any party line. Who will simply do the right thing no matter who it ticks off."

"Then why not *you?*"

"I may be crazy, but I'm not insane."

Mac gestured at Gnarly, who was looking from one of them to the other. "In all honesty, I can't in good conscience vote for someone who drinks out of my toilet."

"Everyone knows Gnarly. Everyone loves Gnarly." Seeing Mac cock his head at him and arch an eyebrow, he corrected himself. "Almost everyone. I think that most of the people in this town, when they see Gnarly's name on the ballot, will vote for him simply because they don't want to vote for Clark or Braxton. It won't be a huge percentage, but hopefully, it'll be enough to embarrass the two parties into asking themselves why so many voters are so angry."

"And what about this?" Mac pointed at the collection of news journalists perched on the stone wall like a flock of birds.

"I had nothing to do with that."

In spite of his best effort, David was unable to avoid Mac's gaze. Almost fifty, Mac was fifteen years old than he was. From his tall slender build to his dark hair with a touch of gray, Mac had dipped generously from their father's gene pool. Often, David was struck by how many traits Mac had inherited from the father he had never met—like wordlessly extracting a confession simply by glaring at him with those penetrating blue eyes.

"It must have been Bernie and Hap," David said in a low voice.

"Bernie and Hap?" Mac sprang upright on the sofa. "How did they get into this?"

David wiped beads of sweat from his forehead. "They're Gnarly's campaign managers."

Mac's cursing could be heard downstairs in the study, where Archie was searching through the folders in a file cabinet kept in a small room about the size of a walk-in closet. The musty file room was coated in a thick layer of dust.

When Dallas sneezed, Archie blessed her. "I so rarely use this room that I keep forgetting to dust it."

"I'm surprised you don't have a housekeeper."

Archie knelt down to check the bottom drawer. "We tried. Problem is finding someone who suits Gnarly. Either he doesn't like her, or once she gets a look at him, she runs away screaming like a little girl. Our last applicant refused to get out of her car. As soon as Gnarly ran down off of the front deck toward her car, she did a U-turn and fishtailed out of the driveway. That was when we decided to hang it up." She removed a thick folder from the drawer. "I think I found it."

Dallas followed Archie into the study.

The late Robin Spencer's famous mysteries had been penned in the most cluttered room in Spencer Manor. Built-in bookshelves containing thousands of books collected over five generations took up space on every wall. Robin had left her son first editions of all of her books. First editions that famous authors had personally inscribed to her and books for research into forensics, poisons, criminology, and the law also lined the shelves. Once every inch of bookshelf space had been taken, the writer had taken to stacking books on her heavy oak desk and tables and in the corner.

Portraits of the Spencers' ancestors filled the space not taken up by books. Some portraits had been painted in the eighteenth century. Others portrayed ancestors in fashions from the turn of the nineteenth century and throughout it.

The most recent portrait was a life-size painting from the 1960s of a young Robin Spencer dressed in a white, strapless formal gown. When he had first seen the picture, Mac had been taken aback by how much Robin resembled his grown daughter, Jessica, who was married to a naval officer and living in Great Falls, Virginia.

Archie set the folder on the desk, where Storm was sitting, opened the folder, and scanned a few lines of notes resting on top of the pile of reports. "Here we go. This is it. Sandy Burr. Investigative journalist." Aware of Dallas' chosen profession, she asked, "Are you sure you want to look into this?"

"If Nancy Braxton really did kill someone 'cause he was investigatin' her charities, wouldn't you like to know 'bout it before she becomes your mayor?" Dallas picked up the report resting underneath the notes. "Robin Spencer got a copy of the police report."

"It pays to have friends in high places." Archie checked the date at the bottom of a page of the notes. "Robin started researching this case about fifteen years ago." She scanned through the notes. "'Journalist travels to an out-of-the-way resort town to investigate dirty dealings within an international charity foundation and ends up dead in a bathtub with both of his wrists slashed. Charismatic and sexy police detective is determined to investigate the case as a murder in spite of the pressure from higher-ups to close it as a suicide.'"

"Sexy and charismatic?" Dallas grinned.

"Mac's birth parents had a complicated relationship." Archie continued reading. "'Case is taken from the detective and closed. But the detective's integrity makes him refuse to back down'—Robin used this case for *Cause for Murder*." She went to the bookcase and perused the titles until she found one of Robin Spencer's first editions and removed it from the shelf. "Oh, this was a great one," she said with a smile. "Of course, I thought all of Robin's books were great."

"What dirty dealin' was the journalist investigatin'?" Dallas asked.

"Money laundering," Archie said. "In *Cause for Murder*, a wealthy businessman with mob ties marries a socialite. He then sets her up with this charitable foundation. She hobnobs all over the world, soliciting donations to the foundation from some of the world's rich and powerful. In turn, the foundation disburses the money to the charities underneath it."

"Just like Nancy Braxton does," Dallas said.

"Don't get so excited," Archie said. "Robin would sometimes base her books on real cases, but then her imagination would let loose, and she'd take off in other directions. Just because this foundation was crooked doesn't mean that Braxton Charities is."

"If it's clean, why did its members kill Sandy Burr? How is the foundation in the book crooked?"

"Remember, the wife's husband has mob ties," Archie said. "The foundation he sets up for his wife is really a money laundromat for the mob. Dummy charities are set up for bookies, drug dealers, and arms trafficking." She shrugged her shoulders. "They give bribes to cops and prosecutors and judges. Dirty money is filtered through the foundation and deposited into the accounts of the phony charities, which are really offshore bank accounts for the mob."

"I can't believe a charity could get away with that," Dallas said. "Wouldn't someone realize that those dummy charities don't exist and get suspicious 'bout mobsters donatin' so much money to charity?"

"In Robin's book, this foundation is huge and famous. Plus it does have legitimate charities under it." Archie hugged the book to her chest. "That being the case, when people see the organization listed on an account during an investigation, they never think anything about it. The foundation has an inside man whose job is to separate the legitimate donations from the dirty money." She looked down at the book she was clutching. "Can I trust you to give this back to me?"

Dallas looked at the book that Archie was holding out to her. "Is it available as an e-book?"

Nodding her head, Archie uttered a sigh of relief.

"I'm not the enemy, Archie," Dallas said while checking a text on her cell phone. "I know you don't like me—" Abruptly, she uttered a curse at what she had read on the screen of her phone and ran out of the study. Barking, Storm scrambled out of the chair and ran after her. At the bottom of the stairs, Dallas yelled up to the living room. "David! Mac! You're gonna to see this!"

Archie ran up behind her. "What's going on?"

Dallas thrust the phone into Archie's hands. "Look at this!" After reading the text message, Archie led the way into the home theater, where she clicked through the buttons on the television to take them to the home page of her Internet browser.

With Gnarly leading the way, Mac and David galloped down the stairs to ask what had gotten Dallas so excited. Gnarly and Storm jumped up onto two chairs and lay down to see what Archie was bringing up on the screen for them to watch.

"A friend of mine with ZNC in New York just sent me this link," Dallas said. "It's all over the news!"

Abruptly, Gnarly's face and a red, white, and blue background filled the wide-screen television. Upon seeing Gnarly's face, Storm let loose a round of loud barks until Dallas shushed her.

The presidential march floated from the speakers. In block letters on the home page were the words "Don't Give a Paws! Vote for Man's Best Friend for Mayor! Gnarly!"

"He's got a website?" Mac turned to David. "How much does it cost to set up a website?"

"Maybe it's a freebie," David said in a hopeful tone.

"Oh," Dallas said with a smile, "it gets better." Pointing the remote at the television, she pressed a button.

A video scanning the tranquil lakeshore late at night filled the screen. There were porch lights and dim lights shining on the homes around the lake.

"It's three a.m. on Deep Creek Lake, and your children are home asleep," the smooth, low, masculine voice of the narrator said as the scene dissolved to a child tucked safely in her bed.

"Oh, Lord, tell me it isn't so." Covering his face with his hands, Mac sank down into a chair.

The narrator continued: "But a phone is ringing at Spencer Manor. Something is happening. Your vote will decide who will answer that call. Will it be someone who knows the area's leaders, whose loyalty has been tested, and who you can trust to do the right thing for the right reasons? It's three a.m., and your children are safe and asleep. Who are you and your family going to entrust with your safety? A politician or someone with integrity who has stood the test of time? Someone with loyalty embedded in his DNA? Someone who has been known for generations as 'man's best friend'?"

The scene shifted to a mother closing a bedroom door while the narrator asked, "Who do you want answering that phone?"

The scene then cut to a picture of a phone and a dog paw slapping the receiver off the hook, and it was followed by a picture of Gnarly—looking seriously pensive.

Seeing Gnarly's face, Gnarly and Storm sat up in their seats and barked loudly as if to applaud the commercial.

"Well," David said, "the ad is true. Dogs are man's best friend for a reason. I can't tell you how many canines have given their lives in law enforcement and the military. Can you see Bill Clark giving his life for anyone?"

In silence, Mac stood up from his seat and turned to David. He opened his mouth to speak, but before any words could escape from his mouth, Mac fell face first to the floor.

The Next Morning

Mac woke up to Archie's voice. Lying next to him in their bed, she was speaking softly into the phone.

"He's okay, Jessie," she said. "Luckily, David was here to take care of him while I called nine-one-one. He came to, like, two minutes later and insisted that we cancel the EMTs."

Shaking his head to clear the fog from his brain, Mac coughed, raised his head from the pillow, and saw that he was in their master suite. Gradually, he remembered the events of the day before—he had started feeling sick, then he'd arrived home from Europe, and had been ambushed by the media asking about—*no, that had to have been a dream.*

His last clear memory was of watching a political commercial. *Must have been a hallucination.*

"I think he's awake," Archie said to Mac's daughter, Jessica, over the phone.

"I'm awake." Mac was surprised by his own voice. The words came out as a croak. He extracted his arm out from under the covers to hold out his hand for the phone, which Archie placed in it. "Hey, Jessie, how are you doing?"

"Better than you," Jessica Faraday said with a smile in her voice. "I heard you fainted like a girl yesterday."

"I did not faint like a girl. I stood up too fast and passed out."

"You need to see a doctor," she replied. "You were just in Europe. There's no telling what you picked up or where you picked it up."

Jessica Faraday, who was in her midtwenties, was Mac's only daughter. The only grandchildren of Robin Spencer, she and her brother, Tristan, had both received multimillion-dollar trust funds after Robin's death. Mac was proud to see that while Jessica enjoyed the luxuries that her inheritance afforded her, including a mansion tucked away in Great Falls, Virginia, she still kept her feet on the ground. After a couple of years of making the high-society circuit, she'd settled down and gotten married and was then returning to school for a doctorate in forensics psychology.

Tristan was even more grounded than his sister and father. Calling himself a "professional student," Tristan rented the guesthouse at his sister's estate and attended George Washington University. He had only recently purchased his first car. The last Mac heard, he was studying cybersecurity. The time before that, he'd been pursuing a double major in natural science and computer science.

"It's the flu," Mac said. "I think my fever has already broken. How are things in your neck of the woods? Has Murphy come home yet?"

"No," Jessica replied.

Even in his weakened state, Mac picked up on the forced upbeat tone of her voice. "How long has your husband been gone this time?"

"Ten days," she replied.

"With no communication from him." Mac's tone was disapproving. He didn't like his daughter being frightened about her husband's well-being. "What if—"

"Dad, I went into this with my eyes open," Jessica replied. "You don't like Murphy's worrying me when he goes on these missions and is gone without my knowing where he is or if he's dead or alive. Well, I don't like your worrying Archie when you're sick and refusing to see a doctor. So there!"

"Doc called last night," Archie said in the direction of the phone so that Jessica could hear her. "She's coming out to take a look at him."

"Doc is coming to look at me." Mac threw back the covers and swung his feet to the floor. Feeling slightly dizzy, he paused at the edge of the bed. He could feel Archie watching him. If he so much as stumbled, she would tackle him, shove him in the car, and drive him to the emergency room.

"Are you drinking plenty of fluids?"

A water glass on the night table told Mac that he was. Carefully, he pulled himself up to his feet and made his way to the window seat that looked out across the gardens and the circular driveway below.

"How does your stomach feel?" Jessica said, continuing to bombard him with questions.

"It's not my stomach as much as it's my head and chest," Mac said with a chuckle. "I have never had such funky dreams in my life." Grateful that he'd made it to the window seat without stumbling, even if he hadn't made it in a straight line, Mac plopped down onto the cushion. He saw Archie cocking her head at him with suspicion in her eyes.

"Why kind of funky dreams?" Jessica asked.

"I had this dream that Gnarly was running for mayor—"

"Mayor?" She laughed. "Good one, Dad."

Chuckling at such a bizarre dream, Mac pulled back the curtain to peer out at the garden. "Mayor of Spencer."

"Is that legal?"

"It was in my dream." Sensing some commotion toward the entrance of the estate, Mac leaned over to get a closer look. He spied a mob of paparazzi packed in between the twin stone pillars marking the entrance to the driveway. Their cameras were firing on all cylinders in the direction of the flower bed in the center of the circle.

What are they doing? What are they taking pictures of?

"How would he participate in a debate?" Jessica asked.

"I have no idea." After climbing up on his knees and pressing his face to the window, Mac found the subject of the photographers' excitement.

A yard sign was stuck in the edge of the circular flower bed so that it could be clearly read out on the street. The sign had Gnarly's face and the words "He's not snarly! Vote for Gnarly!" on it.

Lying in a sphinxlike pose under the sign, Gnarly regarded the mob with curiosity, his ears standing tall and proud while the paparazzi snapped away.

"Dad, are you there?"

"It wasn't a dream?" Mac said. "He's really running for mayor?"

"He's not just running," Archie said. "Polls have Gnarly at thirty-seven percent. Clark and Braxton are tied at twenty percent each. Gnarly is winning."

"Dad, are you still there?"

Mac handed the phone back to Archie.

"I think he got out of bed too soon," Archie told Jessica.

"That's for sure." Mac stumbled back to the bed and pulled the covers up over his head. "Wake me up when the election is over."

CHAPTER FOUR

Schaarbeek Neighborhood of **Brussels, Belgium**

Murphy Thornton yearned for daylight.

It was not something that he had thought about missing until after several days, or, rather, nights, of only moving about and working in the dark—not unlike a vampire.

Vampire.

In the back of the van making its way through one of the more depressed neighborhoods in Brussels, he smiled at the thought. During this mission, he had taken on the role of a vampire—moving about only at night with those who thrived on sucking the life out of those who lived in the daylight.

"What're you grinning about, Thornton?" For a few seconds, Donald Wiley's bald head shone in the light of a streetlight that the van was passing. Even the brute of a man's bald head seemed to have muscles.

Not wanting to come across as philosophical, Murphy leaned back against the cold wall of the van's interior and shrugged his shoulder. "A few hours from now, the sun will be up, and it will be a whole new day."

"Miss the sun, Thornton?" Seth Monroe asked from where he was sitting behind the van's driver. When Murphy didn't answer, he chuckled.

Considering that the two marine majors were at least ten years older than the young navy lieutenant and that they possessed more than twice the experience that he did, Murphy should have guessed that they would know what he was missing. The only thing he missed more was his wife. It was hard being away from Jessica and harder to not be able to communicate with her in any way, shape, or form—not even through a text from an untraceable cell phone, which could've made her a possible target for one of his enemies.

"ETA, five minutes," Monroe said. "Suit up."

Murphy pulled the ball cap down tight to cover his auburn hair. For this mission, he had let it grow out from his military cut, and it had taken on a slight natural wave. He had ceased shaving in order to grow an unkempt beard and a moustache. He'd also covered up his striking blue eyes with dark-brown contact lenses that had taken him days to get accustomed to.

He patted his outer thighs to ensure that he had a semi-automatic on each hip and then checked that he had a thirty-two-caliber semiautomatic in an ankle holster on one of his ankles. He was wearing a fighting knife on his other leg. His last weapon was a hand grenade that he had tucked into the pocket of his jacket. He had other goodies in his other pockets.

Across from him, Wiley was pulling a skullcap down over his bald head. He was clean-shaven from the top of his head down to around his chin. He zipped his army fatigue jacket all the way up to his chin. He usually had a hard-core demeanor, but in a matter of seconds, Murphy saw it become a shade harder—so hard that a shudder went down his spine when he looked at him.

He was not a man Murphy would've wanted to cross.

"What's the code word?" Monroe asked the team, which included a driver, who was in the front seat of the van.

"Snow," they said in unison.

The van made such a sharp left turn into an alley that Murphy almost lost his balance. Then it came to a halt. In French, the driver announced that they had arrived.

Monroe checked the time on his cell phone. "We have fewer than fifteen minutes. If we aren't out of here by the time the Syrians arrive, we're going to have a war on our hands. Is that clear?"

"Crystal." Murphy rose to his feet, picked up a duffel bag, and slung it onto his shoulder. "We go in, grab our target, and leave before the real Syrians arrive. No sweat."

In French, Monroe went over the instructions with the van's driver while Murphy and Wiley climbed out of the back. As soon as Murphy's feet hit the ground of the filthy alley, he was aware of eyes watching them from the back door of the dilapidated row house next to them. He didn't miss the machine gun the doorman was clutching with both of his hands.

Opening his army jacket, Donald Wiley displayed his own automatic weapon. Murphy held the back door of the van open so that Monroe could jump out of it. With Donald taking the lead, the three men stepped up to the door.

In French, Wiley announced that they were the team from Syria that had been sent to deliver the materials needed for their latest batch of explosives. "We're to meet with Salah al-Hazmi," Monroe said in a firm tone. "We notified him that we were coming early. Interpol is on our ass. Need to get out of country."

The guard looked over all three of them before disappearing from the door. After a loud discussion in Farsi, the guard returned to lead them into a squalid kitchen. Food in takeout containers littered the table and counters. The guard closed the door behind them while a slender man with dark hair and a long, ragged beard stepped into the kitchen. He was wearing a gun on his hip. With a jerk of his head, he directed them into the other room.

With Wiley leading the way and Murphy taking up the rear, they filed into what had been a dining room in a previous life. It was then being used as a bomb factory.

Upon seeing them enter, a rail-thin man with wild hair and a long, scruffy beard with bits of forgotten food in it stood up. "Rafael Cannon?"

Monroe stepped forward to offer his hand. "Al-Hazmi. Good to finally meet you." He took in the assortment of explosives that they were putting together. "I see that you have been very busy."

Salah al-Hazmi smiled with pride. "We do have a deadline. We refuse to let anything keep us from completing our mission." His eyes flickered from Monroe to Murphy, who had stepped up to the table for a closer look.

"Even a spy." Monroe sidestepped to block Salah's view of Murphy, who had slipped a tiny device under the tabletop.

"Not even a spy," Salah said with a cold tone.

"Where is he?"

"We have him down in the cellar with the rest of the rats."

"Bring him to us," Monroe said.

"But—"

"We are taking him back with us," Monroe said. "The council intends to make an example of him."

"But we captured him," Salah said with a pout.

"And in the last ten days, have you extracted *any* information from him?" Monroe asked.

Salah looked around the room at his half dozen men.

During the long silence, Murphy was aware of the ticking of the clock. Each tick signaled the expected arrival of this terrorist group's real leaders. Pretending to admire a shrine that had been set up on a table under a window, he rubbed his fingers along the edge of the tabletop, leaving yet another surprise gift for the murderous group.

"According to our information, this spy has been in *your* midst for the last nine months," Monroe said with displeasure. "And you didn't even suspect him." He grabbed Salah by the throat. "You allowed him to work his way up to your top ranks. There's no telling how much information he's passed on to the infidels."

"But we did capture him." With a flicker of his eyes, he ordered two of his men to fetch their prisoner. Like well-trained dogs, they ran into the kitchen. Murphy heard them scurry down a flight of stairs to the basement.

"Only after *we* told you to." Monroe shoved Salah so hard that he fell back onto the table, scattering some of their bomb-making materials. "You're lucky we're not going to take you back to our home base to have you executed alongside him."

Murphy saw fear come to Salah's eyes before the two men dragged a beaten, bloody young man into the room and dropped him at Monroe's feet. The young Iraqi's clothes were nothing more than bloody rags. One of his eyes was swollen shut. Murphy could see that his nose was broken. His bloody feet were so raw that he couldn't walk.

Fury made Murphy reach for one of the weapons on his hip. He saw Wiley do the same.

"Very good," Monroe said when he found his voice. He nodded his head in Murphy's direction. "Give them the supplies they ordered."

Murphy placed the duffel bag on the table and unzipped it. Like children getting a present, Salah's men searched through the contents to find the materials for the sophisticated explosives that would be detonated remotely using a public Wi-Fi signal.

With a wave of his hand, Monroe ordered Murphy and Wiley to pick up the bloody, broken man and carry him off to the van.

"Murph—" he said, regaining consciousness and noticing Murphy, who was laying him down in the back of the van.

"Hey, Tawkeel." Murphy patted his shoulder. "No man left behind."

"We've got company," Wiley said.

A pair of headlights bathed their van in light as an SUV pulled up behind them.

"Oh, oh," Wiley said. "I think those are the Syrians...the *real* ones."

All of the men drew their weapons.

"Let's get out of here!" Monroe said to the driver, who hit the gas.

Two men piled out of the approaching vehicle and fired at them with machine guns. They hit the floor in the back of the van while it raced down the alley in an effort to escape the hailstorm of bullets.

"Time for the big finish, Murphy!" Wiley yelled.

Grasping the remote in his pocket, Murphy sat up from where he had thrown himself over Tawkeel's broken body. "We need to get farther away, or we'll get caught in the blast."

Firing his automatic weapon out of the shattered rear window, Monroe said, "If you don't detonate it now, we're gonna be dead anyway!"

Pointing the remote at the Syrian terrorists, Murphy pressed the button, detonating the tiny explosives that he had left all over the room in their bomb factory and the explosives that they had sewn into the lining and secret pockets of the duffle bag that Murphy had generously given to them.

With a single press of the button, the terrorist hideout and group and the leaders who had traveled from Syria to oversee their deadly operation went up in an explosion that was felt throughout the neighborhood.

The force of the blast hit the rear of the van, causing it to buck. The men in the back fell backward.

Catching his breath, Murphy rose up onto his elbows and saw the house they had just left and the Syrians' SUV engulfed in flames. Next to him, his friend Tawkeel lay unconscious. "It's over, my friend. Time to go home."

Chapter Five

Archie was thankful that Mac was not like a demanding child when he was sick. Instead, he sacked in as best he could after coughing all night, which had left him exhausted. After showering and dressing, she went downstairs to the kitchen to see if she could find some breakfast that would interest him only to discover Dallas' Belgian shepherd curled up with Gnarly on the love seat, a piece of furniture that he had declared was his.

"Storm, what are you doing here?" Archie asked as if the dog could answer.

"Snuggling with Gnarly," Dallas replied from where she had made herself at home at the dining room table. She had spread out the various reports from the case file that Archie had shown to her the day before. With a mug of coffee and a slice of toast on a saucer next to her hand, she was working away on her laptop.

At the top of the steps leading down into the dining room, Archie planted her hands on her hips. "How did you get in here?"

"I used your key," Dallas said over the top of her coffee mug before taking a sip.

"*My* key! Where did you get it? Did *David* give it to you?"

"David would never do that," Dallas said. "I think he's a little afraid of you. He says you're a crack shot. So am I. My pappy taught me to shoot when I was knee-high on a coyote. We should go to the shootin' range sometime. How 'bout next week?"

Archie bit off her words. "Where did you get our key?"

"I got it out of that phony rock that you have planted in the garden next to the sidewalk."

Archie held out her hand in a silent order. After Dallas dropped the key into her palm, Archie snapped her hand shut. "And Gnarly didn't bark, because he knows you," she said while tucking the key into her pocket.

"He really likes Storm."

Archie turned around in time to see Gnarly and Storm licking each other's snouts.

"That means you have to like me," Dallas said. "We're kind of related."

Wordlessly, Archie glared at her from across the table.

Showing no sign that she was intimidated, Dallas held up her mug for Archie to see and shot her a toothy grin. "The coffee is fresh, my friend."

"I'm not your friend." Archie stormed through the swinging door leading into the kitchen.

"Oh, but you will be," Dallas said while turning back to her laptop. She raised her voice a notch to call to her in the kitchen. "Fiona Davis is dead."

The swinging door swung back open. Archie hurried back out. "Dead?"

"Buzzard bait."

Archie paused. "Who's—"

"The witness who had dinner with Sandy Burr when he ate his last meal," Dallas said. "She committed suicide six weeks later, which I find interestin' 'cause Burr's murder was meant to look like a suicide. Maybe Nancy's hired gun learned from his mistake, and Fiona didn't really kill herself."

Warming her hands on the hot coffee mug, Archie lowered herself into a seat across from Dallas. "Did she leave a note?"

Dallas slid a report across the table to her. "I guess Robin Spencer wondered the same thing. There was a copy of the police report in that folder you gave me. Fiona did leave a note sayin' that she couldn't stand the grief any longer. Her momma had died the month before—*after* Burr's murder, I might add."

Archie read through the police report. "She took a whole bottle of migraine medication. Then she got sick, threw up, passed out, and drowned in the toilet."

"One of her friends found her in the bathroom with her head in the toilet." Dallas shook her head. "That's not how I want to be found when I trade in my guitar for a harp."

Archie flipped through the pages to find the medical examiner's report. "Cause of death is drowning." She slid the report back across the table to Dallas. "Bull! She was murdered." She went into the kitchen.

"Then I was right. It wasn't suicide." Dallas followed Archie into the kitchen, where she was taking yogurt out of the fridge. "The police called it a suicide because Fiona's friends and family told 'em that she was distraught 'bout her momma passin'."

"Maybe she was depressed." Archie ripped the lid off of the yogurt. "But there's no way she drowned in a toilet without help."

"Come on," Dallas said. "I've heard of people gettin' drunk and passin' out after tossin' their cookies and then drownin' in a toilet. It ain't pretty—"

"Name one person who *actually drowned* in a toilet."

When Dallas didn't have an answer, Archie pushed past her and led the way to the half bath located down the hallway from the kitchen. Opening the door, she gestured for Dallas to go inside. "Get down on your knees, and pretend to throw up in the toilet."

Looking her up and down, Dallas said, "You do it."

"I already know why it's impossible. You'll understand what I'm talking about if you see it yourself."

Unsure, Dallas bundled her long hair into one of her hands to hold it back and, feeling silly, lifted the toilet seat and knelt down in front of it.

"Now," Archie said. "When you throw up, you get up onto your knees and put your head over the toilet, right?"

"You really do hate me, don't you?"

"I'm showing you how Fiona couldn't have accidentally drowned in the toilet. Put your head down into the toilet. You don't have to put your head in the water."

Uncertain, Dallas rose up onto her knees, clutched the sides of the toilet, and lowered her head down toward the water.

"Good," Archie said. "Now, what'll happen when you pass out?"

"I'll lose my grip on the toilet." Dallas dropped her hands down to the floor. Pushing up, she tried to drop her head into the toilet as best she could without actually touching the water. Allowing her body to go limp as if she were unconscious, she slid away from the toilet and slumped down onto the floor.

Standing above her with her arms folded across her chest, Archie grinned. "Get my point?"

"What's going on in here?" Mac asked from where he was leaning in the open doorway. Dressed in his bathrobe, he looked as sick as he felt, and there were dark circles under his eyes. "Archie, are you trying to drown David's girlfriend?"

Accepting Archie's hand to help pull her up, Dallas said, "Archie and I are researchin' the case of a supposed suicide victim who drowned in a toilet."

Mac shook his head. "You can't accidentally drown in a toilet, and you can't commit suicide by drowning in a toilet without help. The way the toilet is constructed, the body acts as a counterweight. As soon as the victim passes out and his or her body goes limp. Their own bodyweight naturally drags the victim's head up and out of the water."

"But I could have sworn that I heard of people drownin' in—"

"Cause of death is not drowning," Mac said. "Yes, people have died in the bathroom from drug overdoses or alcohol poisoning. They passed out after throwing up and their bodies are found on the floor in front of the toilet—not with their heads in the bowl.

"I was right. She was murdered."

From the bathroom doorway, Mac watched Dallas rush into the dining room with the enthusiasm of a child. In silence, he turned back to Archie, who was lowering the seat back onto the toilet. A slow grin came to his lips.

Seeing the grin, Archie said, "I still don't like her."

Spencer Police Department

David practically got rear-ended when he screeched his cruiser to a halt after turning onto Lake Shore Drive and finding "Don't Give a Paws! Vote for Gnarly!" signs at every corner and in every yard along the lakeshore.

Guess Bernie and Hap are out to earn their pay—whatever it may be.

At the police department, he found four signs, one on each side of the driveway at each end of the police department's property. Bernie and Hap were in the process of erecting a huge wooden sign with Gnarly's face on it directly below the lighted sign identifying the police department.

Upon seeing the police chief's cruiser, Bernie and Hap stopped pounding the sign into the ground and turned to wave enthusiastically at him. "Hey, Chief!" Bernie shouted.

Slowing down, David read the bold block letters across the top of the sign. The sign read, "Endorsed by the Spencer Police Department." After parking, David strolled over to where Bernie and Hap were bursting with pride.

"What'd you think, Chief?" Bernie asked. "You'll never believe how this campaign has taken off. Our phone is ringing off the hook at Gnarly's campaign headquarters with people asking for signs, and they're throwing money at us like crazy."

Hap was nodding his head up and down so fast that he looked like he a bobblehead.

"Gnarly's even got a commercial," Bernie said. "It went viral on the Internet. As of this morning, it had gotten five hundred thousand hits. Hap's granddaughter made that commercial and a couple more for Gnarly, too. Smart as a whip, she is. She won the elementary-school spelling bee last year. Went all the way to the state capital."

Hap stepped up his head nodding.

"What does Gnarly's schedule look like?" Bernie asked.

Tearing his attention away from where Hap was nodding his head as though he were about ready to take off, David said, "Schedule?"

"People want him to go speak to their groups," Bernie said. "They want to know where he falls on the issues."

"He's a dog," David said.

"Yeah, we've been pretty transparent about that." Bernie pointed to the sign between Hap and him. "As Gnarly's campaign manager, I strongly encourage him to get out there to meet the voters. He needs to be shaking paws and licking babies, or people are going to think that he's hiding something."

Slowly nodding his head, David stepped back from them. "I'll get back to you two on that." He was halfway across the parking lot of the police station before he realized that Bernie had mentioned a campaign headquarters and phones ringing off the hook.

No, it can't be. People can't be serious.

Shaking his head, he pushed his way through the front door to enter the police station. "Who authorized our department's endorsement of Gnarly for mayor?" David asked while picking up his mail from the reception desk.

Tonya jerked a thumb in the direction of Bogie, who was watching a press conference with the rest of the officers in the department.

Without turning around, Bogie said, "We took a vote at roll call this morning. It's unanimous. Gnarly's our guy for mayor."

"He's got more loyalty and trustworthiness in his dew claw than both of those knuckleheads have in their whole bodies combined," Tonya said. "I just heard from Jeannie at the fire department. They're endorsing Gnarly, too. Who knows? I may even register to vote this year."

On the television screen, Nancy Braxton was raging. "Shame on you, Chief O'Callaghan!" She wagged her finger at the cameras. "Shame on you for making a mockery of this election! The position of mayor, whether in a major metropolitan or a small resort town, is a serious job. It is not a joke, and you, the chief of police, should know that better than anyone else. Nominating a dog for mayor is not only inappropriate but also insulting!"

"Especially since Gnarly's beating her pantsuit off," Tonya said with a laugh.

David turned to her. "Gnarly is beating her?" He threw his head back and laughed. "That's better than I thought."

"He's beating Bill Clark, too," Bogie said. "As of this morning, Gnarly is polling at forty-two percent, while Clark and Braxton are tied at seventeen. Gnarly is twenty-five points ahead of both of them. That's why they're so mad."

Abruptly, the door flew open, and Marilyn Newton breezed in. An attractive woman in her forties, Marilyn did not look at all like what she was—which was a middle-aged churchwoman. She looked more like a middle-aged heiress—which was also what she was.

"Is Chief—" she said to Tonya, and then she saw David. "Chief O'Callaghan, I am so glad to see you."

Before David could stop her, she rushed over as fast as she could in her high heels to hug him. "I just had to come over to give you the news. We all heard about Gnarly running for mayor—well, how could we not hear about it? Nancy Braxton about had a stroke at the chamber of commerce breakfast this morning when she found out that Gnarly is leading her in the polls."

"I thought you said last year that you were going to run for mayor," Tonya said.

"Oh, I'm sure I did," Marilyn said. "As a matter of fact, Twerpie's party leaders—"

"Twerpie?" Officer Fletcher interjected to ask.

"Bill Clark," Marilyn said. "He's a twerp so I call him Twerpie. Anyway, his party asked me to run against him in the primaries because I'm a woman, and Nancy Braxton wouldn't be able to play the gender card against me. But I turned them down."

"You didn't want to lower yourself into all that mudslinging?" David asked.

"That's one reason." Marilyn waved her hand to show off her elegantly painted fingernails. "The Tuesday morning meeting with the town council conflicts with my standing appointment with my manicurist."

"And you couldn't change your manicure appointment?" Tonya asked.

"The only other time she has available conflicts with my yoga class," Marilyn said. "Now, I could change to the Tuesday-and-Thursday yoga class, but then that would interfere with Poo's therapy sessions, and there's no way that I could touch that." She frowned. "Poo doesn't like change."

"Your dog is in therapy?" Bogie asked.

"To treat his sleepwalking. A few months ago, Poo wandered away from home during the night. Richard Bailey found him asleep in the front seat of his Mini Cooper."

"That must have been a shock," Bogie said. "Finding a one-hundred-eighty-pound Newfoundland dog squeezed into the front seat of a compact car like that."

"Not as big of a shock as it was to find that while Poo had been climbing into it, he'd disengaged the emergency brake. The car then rolled down the hill and landed in Reese Hardy's swimming pool, which woke Poo up. It was terrible. You know, they say that you're never supposed to wake up a sleepwalker."

"How do you know Poo was sleepwalking?" David asked. "Why not assume that Poo wandered off and climbed inside the car while he was wide-awake?"

Marilyn's eyes grew big. "Chief O'Callaghan, Poo would have never considered doing such a thing while he was wide-awake and in his right mind. He's a good dog." With a wave of her hand, she said, "Speaking of good dogs!" She proceeded to dig into her purse. "After Nancy Braxton had her cow at the chamber of commerce, I went running over to the church as fast as my Mercedes could go—" Aware of the police officers surrounding her, she corrected herself, "I mean, as fast as my Mercedes could go while staying within the speed limit."

"Of course," David said with a grin.

"And we had an emergency meeting of the ministry councils of all of the churches in Spencer and voted unanimously to endorse Gnarly Faraday for mayor." With a flourish, she held out an envelope to David. "Nancy said that you were the one who nominated Gnarly to run as an independent, so I assume that you're the one I should give this endorsement to."

Stunned, David stared at her.

Bogie clapped his hands together. "That means Gnarly won the evangelical vote!"

"How could he not?" Marilyn said. "With a choice between a pathological liar and an arrogant blowhard—"

"O'Callaghan!" Bill Clark said while coming through the front door.

"Speak of the devil!" Spinning on her high heels, Marilyn threw out her arms. "Twerpie! If it isn't Spencer's very own bombastic boob."

"Marilyn Newton," Bill said, pronouncing her name with disdain in every syllable. "I should have known that you'd be somewhere behind all of this."

"And once again, you're wrong," Marilyn said. "As much as I would *love* to take the credit for blocking your attempt to put one last nail into Spencer's coffin, I can't. As a good Christian woman, I can't lie—unlike you and your friends on the town council."

"Then what are you doing here?" Bill asked with a hint of worry in his tone.

"Maybe I'm telling your opponent about your deep, dark, dirty secret," Marilyn said with a mocking, evil grin. "So that he'll be properly armed with a missile to fire in your direction if you should choose to try any of your infamous dirty tricks during the election."

David saw a wave of worry cross Bill's face before he regained his composure.

"Worried, Twerpie?" Marilyn giggled. "You should be."

"Gnarly just got the evangelical vote," Tonya told the candidate.

"Well, he won't have it for long." Bill stepped up to David. His mouth curled up in a snarl. "You think you're so clever."

"Based on the polls, the voters are more clever than I thought," David said. "Given the choice between you and a dog, they're voting for the dog."

"We'll just see about that after tomorrow night."

"What's tomorrow night?" Bogie asked.

"The debate." The candidate chuckled. "Since you so rudely interrupted our last mayoral debate—well, we're going to finish what we started. Since Gnarly is now a candidate, it'll be his chance to let the voters know where he stands on all of the issues. Tomorrow night. Eight o'clock. Spencer Inn. See you then."

Taking in the fallen faces of all of the officers and the angry glares from Marilyn and Tonya, Bill Clark left the police station with a bounce in his step.

"Well," Officer Fletcher said. "It was fun while it lasted."

"What do you mean, 'fun while it lasted'?" Marilyn threw up her hands. "That's what he expects! Did Moses back down when the pharaoh doubled the Hebrew slaves' work after he told him to let his people go? Did America roll over and play dead after the Japanese bombed Pearl Harbor? No! These are crazy times, and politicians and the media have turned things upside down so that voters care most about how much free stuff a politician promises them even when they *know* that he's a bold-faced liar—"

"All I wanted to do was make a point about the couple of knuckleheads the parties have stuck us with," David said.

"And you are making a point," Marilyn said while jabbing a manicured nail into his chest. "If you weren't, do you think Twerpie and Nancy would be so upset?"

"Gnarly can't participate in the debate," David said.

"Why not?"

"Duh! He's a dog," David said.

"Dogs have been acting in movies since Rin Tin Tin first appeared in them," Marilyn said. "They rescue people from drowning and dig them out of collapsed buildings. They serve in law enforcement and in the military. God will find a way for Gnarly to participate in that debate and win!" With a wave of her hand, she spun around and headed for the door.

"Wait a minute," David said. "Clark looked very worried when you mentioned his dirty little secret. What is it?"

Placing a hand on her hip, Marilyn giggled at the faces of the police officers around the squad room waiting for her response. "You mean you don't know?"

"If we knew, it wouldn't be a secret," Tonya said.

"That's very true," she said. "I never thought about that. I knew it was a secret, but I thought everyone knew about it—in which case it wouldn't be a secret."

"But we don't know about it," Bogie said. "So it is a secret to us."

"But if I tell you, it won't be a secret."

"It will still be a secret if we don't tell anyone," David said.

"If you don't tell anyone, what good will knowing about it do you?"

"Just tell us!" David said.

"Okay," Marilyn said with a shrug of her shoulders. "Bill Clark killed his own mother."

"How did Fiona's mother die?" Archie asked Dallas. The two women were sitting at the dining room table with folders, and their laptops were humming away.

Curious about what they were doing, Mac came out of the kitchen with a glass of orange juice and watched them work.

"Took a header down a flight of stairs," Dallas said, pointing at a section of the case file on Fiona Davis' suicide. "Bashed her head in. She was fifty-three years old."

"That was probably murder, too," Archie said.

"Maybe Fiona knew too much 'bout Sandy Burr's murder, and the killer was tryin' to silence her by killin' her momma. Then that upset Fiona to the point that the killer thought that she was gonna spill the beans, so he had to silence her."

"Murderers aren't that complicated," Mac said. "If your suspect killed one man, then he was already capable of murder. If he wanted to keep this Fiona quiet, he'd kill her. He wouldn't take a detour to the inevitable by killing her mother."

"Maybe Fiona was blackmailin' the killer, and that was why she was murdered," Dallas said.

"And her mother's death really was an accident?" Archie asked.

"We're *sure* that Fiona was murdered." Dallas leafed through the pages of the case file. "Accordin' to the witness statements here, she was really close to her mother. Her suicide note said that she couldn't go on livin' and that she wanted to be with her momma. But if it's impossible to drown yourself in a toilet, it had to have been murder. Guess I'm gonna be talkin' to the Gettysburg police."

Mac sat down on the steps of the sunken dining room and sipped his orange juice. "What murder did this Fiona witness?"

"Sandy Burr," Dallas said. "An investigative journalist lookin' into Nancy Braxton."

"Dallas seems to think that Braxton either killed him or had him killed because he was nosing into some irregularities about Braxton Charities," Archie said.

One of Mac's eyebrows rose up in an arch. Curious about what Mac was imbibing, both Gnarly and Storm scampered across the living room and sat on the top step to sniff at the juice glass from over his shoulder.

"This isn't the first time I've heard of some questions about Braxton Charities," Mac said while pushing both of their snouts out of his glass. "Back when I was working homicide in DC, I heard rumors about some unsavory movers and shakers, both politicians and special-interest groups, who were very tight with Braxton Charities. But there was never anything concrete."

"Maybe Sandy Burr got too close, and that was why Nancy Braxton turned him into buzzard bait," Dallas said.

"How was he killed?" Mac asked.

"Slashed wrists at the Lakeside Inn," Dallas said. "Your dad and Bogie started the investigation. Braxton was the last one seen with him."

"And the woman who drowned in the toilet?"

"She had dinner with the victim hours before he was killed," Archie said.

"But that was before he had a sit-down with Nancy Braxton," Dallas said. "Fiona saw the two of them together in the lounge on her way out for a walk. She must've seen somethin' that made Braxton want to have her killed."

When a cell phone buzzed, Archie and Dallas both grabbed their phones. "It's mine," Archie said with a laugh.

"It's David." She shot a cocky grin across the table to Dallas while bringing the phone to her ear. "Hey, you'll never guess who I'm sitting across from."

"My dear Dallas," David said. "I tried to call Mac, but his phone went straight to voice mail."

After explaining that they must have forgotten to charge his phone, Archie handed the phone to Mac, who had to push Storm's snout away from where she was licking his ear in order to hear David. "What's up?"

"Gnarly has been invited to a debate. Tomorrow night. Spencer Inn. Eight o'clock."

Everyone waited in silence while Mac turned his head to look at Gnarly, who was eyeing him back.

"I know you think it's silly, but Bogie and I have been thinking about this," David said. "As his owner, you're his representative. You'll bring Gnarly to the debate, and you'll answer the questions for him."

"Oh," Mac said, chuckling. "You want me to channel Gnarly for the debate."

"Not exactly channel—"

"Will Nancy Braxton and her crew be there?"

"Of course."

"I'll do it," Mac said. "Hopefully, I'll be over this flu by then, and if I am, I'll do it."

"You're not mad?"

"I'm too sick to be mad." Mac hung up the phone.

"You're going to debate Bill Clark and Nancy Braxton?" Archie asked.

"If I'm alive." Every part of his body aching, Mac pulled himself up to his feet. "And while I'm debating Nancy Braxton, you two can snoop around to see if you can find out who killed Sandy Burr and that witness. The last thing Spencer needs is a dirty, rotten killer for a mayor."

CHAPTER SIX

Garrett County Sheriff's Department, Oakland, Maryland

In his office at the end of the hallway that led away from the squad room, Christopher Turow, the sheriff, was up to his eyeballs in statistical quarterly reports for the county commission. Looking out the window, he saw that it was a bright, sunny day.

Guess I could go out on patrol.

His eyes fell on an old family photo of his daughter, who'd been only five years old when the photo had been taken, and his late wife, Belle. Suddenly, the bright, pretty day reminded him of the last day they had spent together as a family, before Belle had gone off to Iraq and come back in a box.

Suddenly, the sunny day made the big, muscular chief law-enforcement officer feel solemn.

The sound of a deep bark followed by a familiar ruckus outside of his office granted him a reprieve. Recognizing the bark, a grin came to the sheriff's lips. He wasted no time in getting up from his desk and opening the office door—just in time to see Gnarly on his leash pulling Police Chief

O'Callaghan down the hallway. The German shepherd clawed his way across the tile floor to get to the sheriff.

Sheriff Turow dropped to his knees. "Hey, Gnarly! How's my boy?"

David dropped the leash, allowing Gnarly to gallop to the sheriff, who took the dog into a bear hug. The former army officer allowed Gnarly to lick him all over his face before he stood up.

"How're they treating you in Spencer, boy?" the sheriff asked.

"We're spoiling him rotten," David said.

"As you should be." Leading Gnarly into his office and behind his desk, Turow said, "Hey, Gnarly, I've got something for you. I found it while cleaning out the garage and re—" His voice trailed off. Wiping his mouth, he opened the bottom drawer of his desk and extracted a stuffed squirrel from it.

Upon seeing the toy, Gnarly practically knocked the sheriff out of his chair and then clutched the toy in his jaws.

Sheriff Turow laughed when Gnarly took the toy out from behind the desk and trotted over to show it to David. When the police chief reached for the squirrel, Gnarly jerked it away. Shaking his head, Gnarly turned around in circles until he got dizzy and plopped down onto the floor—much to David's and Sheriff Turow's amusement.

The sheriff cleared his throat. "I knew he'd like that."

"Where did you get it?" David asked.

"I was going through some old boxes in the garage," he said. "You know. Spring-cleaning. Trying to put the past behind me and move on." Looking down at where Gnarly was licking the toy, he smiled softly. "Hard sometimes."

Glancing over at the family photo on the table next to the window, David remembered that Sheriff Turow was a widower. The sheriff never talked about his wife, though David recalled his mentioning the year before that she had died while serving in the Middle East.

"Now," David said, "with Dallas, I can't imagine going on if something happened to her."

"What's the alternative, especially when you have a child together?"

With the squirrel in his mouth, Gnarly got up and went around the desk to lay his head in the sheriff's lap. Happily, Turow stroked the top of the dog's head while he chewed on the toy.

"I know that this was before your time," David said, "but I was hoping that you could look into the county's case files to see if the sheriff's department has any information about Ida Clark's death. She was Bill Clark's mother."

"The Bill Clark who's on the town council in Spencer?" Sheriff Turow asked. "Who's running against Gnarly for mayor?"

"You heard about that?"

"Heard about it? I donated two hundred dollars to his campaign fund."

"To Clark's?"

"Hell, no!" the sheriff said. "I donated to Gnarly's campaign." He leaned across his desk. "What do you need? Are you looking for dirt on Clark?"

"Maybe," David said. "I heard a rumor that Bill Clark killed his mother."

Sitting up straight, Sheriff Turow furrowed his eyebrows. "His own mother? I'll admit the guy is an a—number one jerk, but murdering his own mother?"

"Back in school, I was friends with his younger sister, Lisa," David said. "She joined the army. I joined the marines. Sometimes we'd get together when I was stateside between tours." He swallowed. "Unfortunately, she died. But after hearing this rumor today, I did a little bit of digging. Bill

Clark was the oldest of three children. Lisa was his sister, and they had a younger brother named Leroy. Their mother, Ida, was a local society matron. She came from money. Her husband, Bill's father, had worked in finance and real estate and had left her millions of dollars. She spent her time doing volunteer work with the social clubs. Leroy was a drunk and eventually took off somewhere. Lisa joined the army, and Bill—well, we know what happened to him."

"Get to the murder, O'Callaghan."

"A little over a dozen years ago, Ida Clark died in her home, supposedly in her sleep," David said. "It was about eight months after Lisa died."

"Before either of our time," Sheriff Turow said while smiling down at Gnarly.

"I went through the county's records, and this is what I was able to piece together," David said. "Bill Clark found her body. The sheriff at the time, Clark's father's old friend, did nothing more than write up a report. I found no record of any investigation. There was no autopsy. The death certificate was signed by the family doctor, another one of Clark's old friends, and Ida was at the funeral home and cremated within twenty-four hours of Bill's finding her body."

"What was Clark's motive for killing his mother?" Sheriff Turow stopped petting Gnarly to look over at David for his answer.

With a grin, David rubbed his fingers together. "What else? Money. That, power, and sex mean everything to Bill. I found in the court records that after his mother's death, Leroy contested Bill's handling of the estate. Leroy claimed that Bill, the executor of their mother's estate, which was worth millions, cheated him out of his share of the inheritance."

"Sounds like something Clark would do."

David was nodding his head. "Bill and Leroy never got along. Bill was his father's favorite. Ruthlessly ambitious. Lisa told me that he was just like their father." Sitting forward, he scratched behind his ear.

"What is it?"

"Lisa and I got pretty close in Washington before she got killed." Pausing, David rubbed his hands together. "She told me some family secrets."

"Any of those secrets point to a motive for murder?"

"Bill was very jealous of Leroy."

"Why would Bill Clark, a very successful businessman who's worth millions, be jealous of a drunk?"

"Because his mother always liked the drunk more," David said. "Lisa told me about this one incident…after their father had passed away. There was a signet ring with the family crest on it, and their father had always worn it on his pinkie. The family tradition was for it to go to the first-born son. Well, Leroy had been gone for over a year before their father died. He showed up right before the viewing at the funeral home. As soon as Ida saw Leroy, she took him to a back room at the funeral home. Lisa assumed that it was to say hello, because no one had seen or heard from Leroy in over a year. A little bit later, Bill saw that Leroy was wearing the signet ring on his pinkie. Well, Bill went nuts. Right there at the viewing…in front of everyone. Lisa told me that in all fairness, Bill should've gotten the ring. Their father had wanted him to have it. But their mother said that because their father had been so hard on Leroy, she felt sorry for him, so she decided on her own to give it to him."

"So," Sheriff Turow said, "Bill Clark could have killed his mother, who had denied him her love and his birthright, the ring. Then, to take it a step further, he delivered payback to his baby brother by cheating him out of his share of the family inheritance."

"I know that it sounds devious even for Bill Clark." David shrugged his shoulders. "The lawsuit was dropped after Leroy Clark got drunk and drove his truck into the lake."

"At which point Bill Clark got all of it," Sheriff Turow said.

"Exactly. Lisa had told me that she was worried because her mother mentioned that Bill kept suggesting that she put his name on her bank accounts. Ida herself asked Lisa if she thought that that would be a good idea. She didn't know how to tell her mother that she shouldn't trust her own son. Well, she told me that less than a year before Ida Clark died."

"If Bill Clark got his name on his mother's bank accounts and was the executor of her will, he could've legally embezzled the money in her accounts," Sheriff Turow said.

"Then after killing her, he could've claimed that the amount in her accounts was all there was," David said. "Maybe when Leroy contested that, Bill Clark had him killed so that no one would discover the embezzlement."

"You really don't think that Bill Clark has a moral compass, do you?"

"Not really," David said. "Think you can do some poking around for me?"

With a whine, Gnarly held up his paw to shake the sheriff's hand.

Shaking his paw, Sheriff Turow said, "Of course—anything for a friend of Gnarly's."

After leaving the sheriff's office, David called Archie to check on Mac. When David had stopped by Spencer Manor to pick up Gnarly, Mac hadn't eaten anything and had claimed that he simply wasn't hungry. He had spent the day in bed, dozing in between coughing fits. Archie requested that David pick up the takeout pizza that she had ordered.

The parking lot of Carmine's Pizza, one of the most popular Italian restaurants for local residents, was packed with vehicles when David arrived. Since it was too early for the peak dinner hour, David surmised that a party or an event was taking place in the banquet room.

"Stay in the cruiser," David said to Gnarly while slipping out of the driver's seat.

Leaving his toy squirrel on the front seat, Gnarly leaped out of the open passenger-seat window and beat David to the entrance.

"You listen so well," David said sarcastically before opening the door to allow Gnarly, who was clad in his service-dog vest, inside.

Behind the checkout counter, Carmine Romano greeted them with a broad grin. "My main man, Gnarly!" He rushed out from behind the counter and held up both of his hands. "Give me ten!"

Laying his ears back, Gnarly trotted over to the jolly Italian and jumped up to touch both of his paws to his hands. After rubbing Gnarly's side, the restaurant owner grabbed a jar of garlic sticks from the counter and fished one out of it for him.

Despite the loud greeting, David could hear Nancy Braxton's grating voice in the banquet room off of the main dining room.

"*When* I am mayor, we are going to have a police department that's *serious* about protecting Spencer—*including* our people."

Carmine chuckled upon seeing David cringe. "Can you imagine listening to that for the next six years?"

"If she gets elected, I'm moving to Canada," David said.

"I'll go back to Chicago," Carmine said. "Worse, can you imagine listening to her day in and day out? Guess that's why her hubby spends all of his time otherwise engaged." He jerked his thumb over his shoulder, indicating the bar in the lounge.

Cocking his head to look beyond Carmine, David recognized Nathan Braxton, who was sitting at the bar next to a slender young woman with long, lush auburn hair. The husband of the mayoral candidate was blocking David's view of the woman's face. However, he was able to get a good view of her long legs and her ultrashort, form-fitting dress. David was also able to see Nathan's hand, which was resting high up on her bare thigh.

"And his wife is right on the other side of the wall?" David asked. "Does he have a death wish?"

"Those two are all lovey-dovey when they're in front of the cameras, but offstage?" Carmine rolled his eyes. "You should have seen them an hour ago. Mr. Octopus—"

"Octopus?"

"That's why I'm running the cash register instead of cooking my secret pizza sauce in the kitchen," Carmine said. "When Braxton got here, he wouldn't keep his hands off of my host—until she fed him a fistful of knuckles to the throat. I sent her back to work in the kitchen, where we have plenty of knives that she could use to defend herself. Guess Braxton decided it was safer to redirect his attention to Mrs. Clark."

"Clark?" David jerked his head back to look into the lounge and saw the woman reach for her martini. She was indeed Cassandra, Bill Clark's third wife. They had been married for less than a year.

"It's true," Carmine said. "Politics does make strange bedfellows."

"Does Nancy Braxton know about this?"

Carmine shrugged his shoulders. "Politicians aren't like regular folks. That's why I'm wearing this every day until the election." The restaurant owner unbuttoned his white cook's jacket and opened it up so that David could see that he was wearing a blue T-shirt with Gnarly's face on it. Gnarly's name was scrawled across the top of it. In block letters below it were the words "He's Not Snarly! Vote for Gnarly."

"Where did you get that?" David asked.

"I got a whole case of them for free when I donated the use of my sign out front to Gnarly's campaign." Then in a whisper Carmine said, "Braxton had already scheduled her event when I found out that Gnarly was running. As soon as Braxton is off of the property, it'll be 'Gnarly for Mayor' from here on out." He gave Gnarly a thumbs-up. "You've got our vote, dude."

"Is this Gnarly?" A young woman clutching an excited little boy's hand had come out of the banquet room.

"The one and only!" Carmine said, and then he bent over to talk to the little boy. "Do you want to meet Spencer's next mayor?"

The boy answered by throwing his arms around Gnarly, who licked his face. His mother whipped out her cell phone to snap pictures of them. When Carmine offered to take her picture with Gnarly, she gladly accepted.

Hearing the boy's shrieks, some patrons looked over to see what was happening. Three teenage girls screamed and ran over with their cell phones to start snapping selfies with the local celebrity. Before David could realize what was happening, the canine mayoral candidate was being mobbed by restaurant patrons—and loving every bit of it.

Cell phones were thrust into David's and Carmine's hands so that they could take pictures of Gnarly with single voters, couples, children, and even a group of smiling women wearing "Change Spencer with Nancy" T-shirts.

David was snapping a picture of Gnarly "kissing" twins whose mother was holding one of them in each arm when Nancy Braxton's shrill voice sent a shiver up his spine.

"What the *hell* is going on here?" She shocked David so much that he dropped the phone.

The mayoral candidate had come out of the then-empty banquet room to see who had stolen her audience.

A young woman who David recognized as Carmine's special-event coordinator made the mistake of stepping up behind Nancy Braxton with a martini glass containing a purple drink. "Ms. Braxton, I think we finally got your drink right. I made it myself."

Uttering a loud vulgarity, Nancy Braxton slapped the drink out of the coordinator's hand, which sent the purple beverage flying. It drenched the restaurant employee's face and neck and the front of her blouse.

A gasp went up throughout the restaurant.

Behind Nancy Braxton, Cassandra Clark scurried into the kitchen while Nathan Braxton smoothed his hair and straightened his suit to assume the image of a supportive husband before coming out of the lounge.

Muttering curses, Carmine ushered his tearful employee out of the room.

Oblivious to her rude behavior, Nancy directed her attention toward David. "I am *sick* and *tired* of you and your candidate *stalking* me!" She emphasized each word by shaking a finger at him.

"*Stalking* you?" David said with an involuntary chuckle. "Seriously?"

With her fists clenched, she moved toward them only to have her path blocked by a pudgy man in a gray suit and a red tie. "Don't, sis," he said in a low voice. His eyes darted around to indicate that they were in a public venue. "*Now* is not the time."

Nancy's eyes bulged, causing David, who thought that she might completely lose it and come after him with her claws, to lay his hand on his gun. "Who let him and that dog in here?" She slapped the man in the suit. "This is all your fault, Hugh!"

"Listen to your brother, Ms. Braxton," Erin said as she wedged herself in between the enraged politician and Hugh. "Let's just go back into the banquet room and finish your speech."

"You should do what Erin said to do." Nathan had casually joined the group surrounding Nancy.

Determined to have the last word, Nancy said, "You've made the wrong enemy, O'Callaghan. My political enemies have been trying to silence me and take me down for thirty years because they know that when I get into power, I will eliminate them all." She thrust a finger in his direction. "You are just one more player in a long line of players in this vast conspiracy—"

Abruptly, Erin and Nathan grabbed Nancy and tried to drag her back into the banquet room.

Nancy pulled away from them and said, "By the time my political machine is through with you and your little dog, every single bone in every single closet will have been dragged out into the town square for everyone to see."

"If they want to dig up Gnarly's bones, go right ahead," David said. "Just be sure to put them back after your photo op, because Gnarly hates it when people move his bones."

As if to voice his agreement, Gnarly barked—which prompted a laugh from those watching the exchange.

"You're going to regret even thinking of messing with me," she said while brushing Nathan's hand off of her shoulder.

"Erin, get her out of here," Nathan said.

"Are you going to deal with me the same way you dealt with Sandy Burr?" David asked.

The mention of Burr's name propelled Nancy Braxton backward.

Hugh's double chin quivered. "We have no comments about something that is part of ancient history."

"I'm sure Burr's family doesn't consider it ancient history." David enjoyed seeing the color fade from Nancy Braxton's face as her assistant ushered her back into the banquet room. Meanwhile, her brother urged everyone to return to the room so that Nancy could resume the speech, and then he thrust his chubby finger into the police chief's face.

"You know full well that the state police investigated Sandy Burr's death and closed it as a suicide. She was not charged with anything. So if you as much as even mention his name again during our campaign and insinuate that she had anything to do with his death, we will sue you for slander and defamation of character."

"What did Sandy Burr uncover during his investigation?" David asked.

"Like my sister said, you've made a big mistake, Chief. Because when it comes to digging up dirt, we're not only able to dig deeper than anyone else but also to make it ourselves," Hugh said.

"Which is precisely why the more voters see of today's politicians, the more they like their dogs."

"You should have seen her face, Mac." Sitting in front of the fireplace in the master suite, David was watching Mac try to stir the bowl of wedding soup resting on a bed tray. After learning that Mac was sick, Carmine had insisted on sending a bowl to him, claiming that it was a surefire cure for everything.

Afraid that the soup was going to spill, David picked up the tray from the bed and held it over Mac while he had a coughing fit. After he had finished, David shook his head. "If you cough any harder, you're going to cough up a kidney."

"I'll be better tomorrow." Mac took the tray from him. "Do you think Nancy Braxton killed Sandy Burr?"

"She's definitely guilty of something." David went back to his seat in the sitting area. "She and her group are scared to death that his murder will come back up to bite her in the butt during this campaign."

Since Mac and Archie were eating their dinner in bed, Gnarly was staying a respectable distance away from them. Instead of begging, he opted to be generously petted and perched between David's knees.

"But the state police hijacked the case and closed it as a suicide," Mac said. "That means that there's nothing we can do—unless we can uncover new evidence that proves that it was murder."

"Why wouldn't the state police have noticed that both of Burr's wrists had been slashed from the left to the right?" Archie asked. "He didn't switch the blade to the other hand to slash the other wrist, which means that he didn't slash his wrists himself." Archie was curled up on the other side of their bed. She folded a slice of pizza in half and bit into it.

"I'm sure they did," David said. "They hijacked the case because Dad had zeroed in on Nancy Braxton as a prime suspect, and her party bosses couldn't allow her to go down, because she gave them a lot of money—and still does."

"We're going to need a ton of evidence that will be impossible to spin if we're going to bring Nancy Braxton down, especially with all of the power backing her." With a defeated sigh, Archie shook her head.

"She won't have any of that backing if Gnarly wins the election." David emphasized his statement by clasping both sides of Gnarly's head. Seeing that he was the center of attention, Gnarly sat up straight with his tall ears erect, projecting a commanding presence.

"I'm sick of seeing people like her and Clark thinking that laws are for peasants, and I'm sick of party bosses confirming that belief by protecting them all for the sake of grabbing or holding onto political power," Mac said.

"Well, I should be going," With a tired sigh, David stood up. "I'm meeting Dallas for dinner at the Lakeside Inn."

"Lakeside Inn?" Archie grinned. "I wonder who picked that place."

"She did." David cocked his head at the wicked grin that had crossed Archie's face. "Judging by your expression, I would think that you two have been conspiring against me. But since you two don't like each other—"

"No, I am not warming up to Dallas," Archie said with a firm shake of her head. "She asked me if Robin had any information on the Burr case, and I checked Robin's files. That's it. We have a purely professional relationship. No friendship at all."

Behind her, Mac was slowly shaking his head.

"Not even just a little bit?" David pressed his thumb and forefinger together.

"She's very...loud," Archie said.

"I know," David said, "and I kind of like that. It's refreshing. Up until now, every woman I have been involved with was—"

"Pretentious," Mac said. "Behaving in accordance with how our culture says you have to behave. It's low class to dry your sheets on a clothesline and Spencer can't tolerate low class. So if you're into clotheslines, you need to either get out of town or hide your air-dried laundry in the closet."

"And it's not mayor-like to get a fresh drink of water out of the toilet," David said as Gnarly, licking his chops, came out of the master bathroom. "Dallas doesn't put on any airs for anyone."

"I'm sure being Buddy Walker's daughter had everything to do with that," Archie said.

"If you ask Dallas, she'll tell you she's a rancher's daughter, not the daughter of a Texas billionaire." David went on to ask, "What did you and my loud girlfriend uncover?"

"A second witness," Archie said. "The bartender saw Burr meeting with Nancy Braxton in the lounge less than two hours before the time of death. He still works at the Lakeside Inn and is now the manager."

"I guess it's going to be dinner and a show."

CHAPTER SEVEN

Nestled along the shore of Deep Creek Lake, the Lakeside Inn was a midpriced hotel with only four floors, a lobby, a sitting area furnished to serve guests a free continental breakfast, and a restaurant lounge that served traditional all-American meals that were both tasty and inexpensive.

Since summer was in full swing, the hotel's parking lot was filled with cars and SUVs. Vacationing families with young children flitted in and out of the front doors. Most of the children were scurrying down the walkway to the hotel's private beach.

Taking in the family atmosphere as she climbed out of the passenger side of her maroon truck, Dallas felt slightly over-dressed in her straight-leg jeans, high heels, and rose-colored silk blouse. "Guess I've gotten too used to the Spencer Inn."

Joining her in front of the truck, David took her hand. "You're not supposed to fit in with the tourists. You're an investigative journalist, and your subject will take you more seriously if you look professional."

Noticing that David had changed out of his police-chief uniform into jeans and a blue polo shirt, she said, "If we want him to take us seriously, why aren't you wearin' your badge and packin' your side arm?"

David escorted her through the front entrance and into the lobby. "My department can't reopen the Burr case until we have new evidence. Until then, the only role I can play during your interview is that of your supporting boyfriend. So when it comes to introductions, don't mention the name 'O'Callaghan' or say anything about my being with the police." Then he whispered, "By the way, I'm always packing." He winked at her.

Pulling him in close to her, she whispered in a husky voice, "And here I thought you were just happy to be with me."

He slipped his arm around her waist and ushered her into the hotel, through the reception area, and into the lounge. Since most of the hotel guests were families with children, the lounge's busy dinner hours were early, between five and seven o'clock. Since it was close to seven-thirty, busboys were still in the process of cleaning up a half dozen large tables, some of which had high chairs around them. There were three older couples dining at smaller tables along the window that provided a view of the lake outside.

"You can sit anywhere," the bartender behind the bar said. "The server will be right with you."

David and Dallas took a table for two by the fireplace, away from the other patrons so that they could talk without being overheard. As was his custom after spending years in law enforcement and in the military, David positioned his chair so that his back was to the wall and he had a clear view of everyone and all of the exits.

By the time the server, a pretty, young woman named Leeza, arrived, Dallas had shifted to her chatty investigative-journalist persona; her intention was to charm the server into putting in a good word with the hotel manager for her.

Everything seemed to go as Dallas had planned. Dallas and Leeza hit it off, and it didn't hurt that Dallas' date was so attractive that the server paid special attention to their table. David returned her attention by flirting with her, and Leeza was more than receptive when Dallas moved in for the kill.

"Does Caleb still work here?" Dallas casually asked when Leeza was clearing their plates after they had finished their dinners. Dallas had had a large prime rib, and David had eaten fish.

"Do you mean Caleb Montgomery?" After Dallas confirmed that that was whom she'd meant, Leeza grinned. "Sure. He's the hotel manager."

"Really?" Dallas replied with a wide grin. "Maybe he's the one I'm talkin' about. He used to be a friend of my momma's. The Caleb I'm thinkin' of was a bartender."

"That must have been quite a few years ago," Leeza said. "From what I understand, Mr. Montgomery has been managing the Lakeside Inn ever since the owners renovated it."

David's eyebrows furrowed. Leeza had jogged his memory and reminded him of the old hotel, which had undergone an extensive renovation several years earlier. He vaguely remembered that the hotel had been mowed down and that a new one had been built onto the foundation. Had that been before or after Sandy Burr's death?

Unbeknownst to her, Leeza answered his question. "I remember hearing that Mr. Montgomery was the bartender before the hotel changed hands."

"That's quite a promotion." With an arched eyebrow, Dallas cocked her head in David's direction. "Is Mr. Montgomery working tonight? I'd really like to say hi and to see if he remembers my momma."

After saying that she would go fetch him, Leeza rushed off.

As soon as she was out of earshot, Dallas leaned toward David. "I wonder who gave the bartender such a plum promotion and what he did—or didn't do—to earn it."

"Are you thinking that Nancy Braxton paid Caleb Montgomery for his silence by buying the hotel and promoting him to manager?" David nodded his head in the direction of the doorway. "We'll find out soon."

An exceedingly tall man with curly salt-and-pepper hair sauntered into the lounge. After Leeza pointed Dallas and David out to him, he strolled over with a wide grin on his face and offered Dallas his hand. "Leeza said you asked to see me. She said your mother was an old friend, but—"

Dallas grasped his hand. "Actually, I was lyin'. I'm Dallas Walker, and I came across your name while investigatin' the Sandy Burr murder. I understand that you were one of the last people who saw him alive."

The smile dropped from Caleb Montgomery's face. He extracted his hand from Dallas' grasp so fast that one would have thought that she had some sort of disease.

"I'm afraid your information is wrong, Ms.—what was your name?" Caleb Montgomery looked from Dallas to David.

David sensed a spark of recognition in the hotel manager's eyes. He should have known that the odds that Caleb wouldn't recognize the small-town police chief were extremely low.

"My name is Dallas Walker," she said. "I'm an investigative journalist."

"Well, I refuse to be a part of your investigation."

"Accordin' to my research and sources," Dallas said despite his objection, "you tended bar the very night that Sandy Burr died, and he was in the lounge from shortly before five o'clock until well after eight. Witnesses said that there was hardly anyone here, so you had to have noticed him."

"I didn't," Caleb said. "I didn't see or notice anything."

"In the statement you gave to the police on the day Sandy Burr's body was found, you said not only that you noticed him but also that you noticed the woman he met after dinner for drinks—"

"I think it's time for you to leave," Caleb Montgomery said in a firm—and threatening—tone. "You and your friend—and if you're both smart, neither of you will come back. We don't need your business."

"But also that you noticed the woman he met after dinner for drinks was Nancy Braxton," Dallas said, finishing her thought.

But Caleb Montgomery had hurried across the lounge and gone out the door.

"He remembers everything," David said in a low voice.

"Dirty, rotten liar," Dallas said. "I hate liars."

Great Falls, Virginia

Located in the rugged woods lining the Potomac River, Great Falls, Virginia, offers its residents the best of both worlds. The area just outside of the capital beltway is rural enough that it offers an escape from the tensions of city life but close enough to that city life that one can partake of the electrifying excitement of Washington, which is only a few minutes away on Georgetown Pike.

Tucked back behind a security fence with an automatic gate and hidden behind thick trees, the Faraday-Thornton estate took up seven acres of woods and rocky trails at the end of which was a fast-flowing section of the Potomac River.

The Faraday-Thornton home consisted of a sprawling gray-stone six-bedroom mansion with white trim. Jessica's younger brother, Tristan, was renting the two-bedroom guesthouse located at the end of a wooded path while his Georgetown brownstone was being renovated.

The sun had given way to nightfall. High in the sky, a full moon cast a golden glow in the darkness when Murphy pressed the remote button to open the garage door and then parked his motorcycle in its spot in the six-car garage.

After turning off the bike's engine, Murphy took off his helmet and ran his fingers though his hair and over his scalp.

"Welcome home, Murphy. Would you like me to close the garage door and turn on the security system?"

Grabbing his weapon on his belt, Murphy almost fell off his bike as he searched for the owner of the low, throaty, sensual voice that was not unlike that of James Earl Jones, a.k.a. "Darth Vader."

"Nigel," Murphy said when he remembered to whom the voice belonged.

"Yes, Murphy?" the voice of their state-of-the-art smart home's speaker said. "Do you want me to close the garage door and turn on the security system, or would you rather do it yourself?"

"Yes, close the door and turn on the system. Thank you, Nigel." Murphy asked himself why he couldn't keep from saying "please" and "thank you" to a computer.

The garage door proceeded to close behind him. Before it clicked into place, Murphy heard the beep of the garage's security system, which indicated that it had been activated.

Mentally, he counted down the seconds until he would be in her arms again.

As soon as Murphy's feet hit the path leading up to the main house, Nigel, clued into his movement by the motion detectors that had been placed around the property's perimeters, turned on the outdoor lights to illuminate his way to the side door. Except for the lights that Nigel had turned on for Murphy, the house was dark.

After a week and a half, she must have given up on waiting up for me every night.

In his excitement, Murphy's hand shook while he unlocked the door, pushed his way inside the mansion's two-story foyer, and pressed his thumb against the security panel inside the door. After scanning his thumbprint and verifying that he was indeed Murphy Thornton, the system beeped.

"Welcome home, Murphy," Nigel said again.

That time, Murphy remembered to whom the voice belonged. "Good evening, Nigel. Where's Jessica?"

"She is upstairs in the master bath, Murphy," Nigel said.

"Honey, I'm home!"

Murphy took the steps two at a time up to the second floor while Nigel continued: "The temperature of the water in the whirlpool tub is one hundred seven degrees. The jets have been running at top force for ten minutes. The music Jessica requested was a party mix of the top-forty hits on shuffle."

Murphy heard the television playing in the downstairs game room. Anxious to see Jessica, he put off saying hello to Newman, the couple's mixed-breed couch-potato dog. Predominantly a Bassett hound, the overweight short-legged canine spent all of his time in a worn, discolored recliner from Murphy's old apartment. He watched television twenty-four-seven.

However, Spencer, Jessica's pure-bred Shetland sheepdog, was not going to miss out on a chance to welcome the master of the mansion home. Her long, thick fur had a bluish tint to it that matched her blue eyes. The young shelty met him at the top of the stairs and leaped into his arms.

"How's my furry Candi girl?" Murphy buried his face, which still donned more than a week's worth of stubble, in her fur. While the dog's official name, Spencer, had been given to her by Jessica, Murphy called her "Candi." Setting her down, he ordered her to take him to Jessica.

With no hesitation, Spencer raced across the master suite with Murphy directly behind her. He threw open the bathroom door and heard Jessica loudly and enthusiastically singing a popular song by a female pop singer about a girl who wanted a boy to call her...maybe. The roar of the whirlpool tub's jets accompanied her song.

Awed by the sight of not only her but also the entire scene, Murphy stood in the open doorway.

The bathroom was dimly lit, and there were scented candles all about it. A glass of wine was resting on the counter next to the tub. In the round, sunken whirlpool tub, Jessica was soaking up to her chin.

The music from the central sound system, which was also a part of their smart home and monitored by Nigel, was on at full blast.

With her violet eyes closed, fully enthralled in her fantasy of being a pop star, Jessica Faraday Thornton was waving her arms and hands over her head and belting out the song about a girl giving her phone number to a boy whom she had just met.

Cocking his head at her, Murphy realized that this was a first in their marriage. Never before had he heard Jessica Faraday sing. His lips curled up in a smile while he listened to her. She sang really...badly. Loudly. Passionately. And very off-key.

Well, no one's perfect.

Unable to wait any longer and wanting to put an end to Jessica's singing before she had all of the dogs in Great Falls howling, Murphy pulled his shirt up and over his head.

111

Leaving a trail of clothes behind him, he made his way to the tub.

Murphy slipped into the tub and covered her mouth with his to squelch any possible objection to him interrupting her private concert.

The unexpected contact caused her to shriek. Her eyes flew open. In the moment of flailing, the wine glass toppled over, the wine flew out of it, and the glass broke.

"Murphy!" Instantly, she threw her arms around him.

"I've missed you so much—I can't even begin to say how much," he said into her ebony hair that usually fell in a dark wave to her shoulders. For her bath, she had twisted it and piled it up on top of her head.

"Tell me later. Come here!" She wrapped her arms around him and kissed him with all of the passion that had been building up for the last eleven days.

CHAPTER EIGHT

As the final image of the horror movie cut to the closing credits, David looked down to where Dallas was resting her head on his bare chest. Her arm was draped across his stomach. In the dim light of his master bedroom, it was difficult for him to see whether she was asleep.

"Now that leaves me as confused as a goat on Astroturf." She pulled the comforter up to cover her naked body.

As if to voice her agreement, Storm uttered a deep sigh from where she was sleeping in a dog bed in the corner of David's bedroom.

It took him a full minute to decipher the meaning behind Dallas' statement, and during that time, she lifted her head from his chest and pushed some unruly strands of hair out of her eyes. "I didn't understand that endin' at all. Why was that guy standin' in the corner? And what was his name again?"

David chuckled. "If you'd watched the first half of the movie instead of"—with a wicked grin, he pumped his eyebrows up and down—"you'd understand the ending."

She climbed up on top of him. "Hey, I didn't hear any complaints from you."

"I'd already seen the movie." He wrapped his arms around her. "You hadn't, which is why we were watching it in the first place." He pulled her in close to kiss her.

"Why don't you just tell me what I missed?" she whispered.

"Forget the movie." Grabbing her, he rolled her over and landed on top of her. Giggling, she pretended to fight him off until he managed to pin her down by the arms, and then he gave her a deep kiss. She had just given in to his passion when the cell phone on the nightstand rang.

With a groan, David dropped down on top of her.

"Can't you—"

"Not when you're the chief." David crawled to the other side of the bed and grabbed the phone from the nightstand. "O'Callaghan."

Dallas' deep sigh of disappointment lured Storm out of her bed so that she could offer her a consolation cuddle.

"I'll be there in twenty minutes." David threw back the covers and climbed out of bed.

"Where're you gonna be?" Sitting up, Dallas watched him take a fresh pair of underwear from the dresser.

"The Braxtons' estate," he said while putting on his briefs. "There's been a shooting."

"A shootin'?" Dallas threw back the comforter and climbed out of the bed. "At the Braxtons' estate? As in Nancy Braxton's?"

In the midst of getting dressed, David stopped when he saw Dallas throwing on the clothes that she had tossed around the bedroom before they'd settled in for the movie. "What are you doing?"

"I'm comin' with you, sugar."

"Whoa!" David held up both of his hands, which were then holding his clothes. "Hold your horses, Lois Lane!"

Half-dressed, she looked at him with narrow eyes, daring him to tell her that she couldn't go with him.

"We need to set some boundaries," he said. "I'm the chief of police."

"And I'm an investigative journalist."

"I do not discuss open investigations with the media," he said while stepping into his pants. "I can't. And the people in this town aren't going to trust me if I go blabbing about their personal business to my journalist girlfriend."

"I'm not askin' you to blab to me," she said while zipping up her pants. "You don't have to tell me anythin'. I'm just gonna go along and do what I do best."

"Which is?"

"Snoop." She tossed him his keys. "You drive."

"Yeah, I'll drive, but I'm not taking you," he said while she stepped into her shoes. "I can't show up to investigate a shooting with the media in my cruiser."

Offering no response, she picked up her cell phone and purse from where she had tossed them onto a chair.

"Did you hear me?"

"Yes, I heard you." She shrugged into her blouse "You're not drivin' me. That means I have to drive myself." She kissed him. "Your barn door's open and the mule's tryin' to run."

"Huh?"

She pointed down to where he hadn't zipped his fly. Then, with her silk blouse not yet buttoned, she ran out the door. "See you there, lover."

He heard the clatter of her heels racing down the stairs.

"Come on, Storm! You're ridin' shotgun!"

With only one bounce in the center of the mattress, Storm flew over the king-sized bed and raced out the door and down the stairs.

"I can feel myself getting into trouble," he said while zipping up his pants.

The Braxtons' mansion was located halfway up Spencer Mountain. Tucked up against the heavily wooded mountainside, it provided a broad view of the lake below and the valley beyond. A gate prevented unwelcome guests from wandering up to the front door of the stone mansion that had been designed to resemble a palatial European estate.

One Spencer and one Garrett County sheriff's cruiser were stationed on either side of the stone pillars marking the end of the driveway to keep the curious out. Knowing that the odds were that she wouldn't be allowed to pull her truck up into the driveway, Dallas parked off to the side of the road and, leaving Storm in the passenger seat, trotted up the Spencer police officer whom she recognized as Officer Zigler.

The young officer greeted her with a polite grin. "Hi, Dallas."

After returning his greeting, Dallas craned her neck and saw that both an ambulance and an EMT vehicle were inside the gate. "David told me that there'd been a shootin'. Was it Nancy Braxton?"

Officer Zigler and the sheriff deputy exchanged looks.

"David told me to meet him here," she said. "He'll probably have an easier time of findin' me if I wait inside."

"Nice try, Dallas." Bogie's deep voice in the darkness caused her to jump. She located the deputy chief, who was leaning against one of the stone pillars. "Chief called ahead and told us not to let you in."

"Sorry, Dallas," Officer Zigler said. "Chief's orders."

"Why that—" she said, and then she sputtered, trying to find the right words to express her disgust, until she felt a friendly swat on her rump.

David passed her on the way inside. "Better luck next time, lover."

Bogie fell into step beside him, and they made their way up the driveway to where the EMTs were wheeling a gurney out of the mansion.

"You can't expect me to sit in the car like...some...*child!*" she said, calling after him.

Turning around, David made a broad shrugging motion. "If you don't want to do that, go home and watch the first half of the movie."

With a growl, Dallas spun around on her heels in time to see the sheriff's cruiser pull up and park behind David's vehicle. While she watched, Sheriff Turow got out and made his way to the driveway, stopping to greet Storm, who had stuck her head out of Dallas' truck and was wagging her tail. "Well, who might you be?"

Seizing the opportunity, Dallas trotted up to him. "Sheriff Turow?" She offered him her hand. "We've howdied but we haven't shook yet. I'm Dallas Walker. Police Chief O'Callaghan's girlfriend. This critter's name is Storm."

Grinning at her and the dog, Sheriff Turow said, "I assume David is inside already?"

"Sure is," Dallas said. "Gettin' the lowdown on what happened. Since they called out the big guns, I guess this ain't just some petty crime."

The sheriff made his way up the road to the Braxtons' driveway. "It's never a petty crime when someone gets shot."

"Who got shot? Ms. Braxton? Or was she the one who did the shootin'?"

With a slim grin, Sheriff Turow stopped and turned to her. "Chief O'Callaghan won't give you a clue, will he?"

Her bottom lip came out in a pout. "He says he can't comment on an open investigation—especially to the media."

"And you're an investigative journalist."

"Freelance," she stressed. "So I'm not really—"

"I've seen your blog," he said. "You're a journalist, and I can see that you have a lot of your mother's talent...and tenacity."

"Nuts don't fall far from the tree in the Walker clan," Dallas said with pride. Her grin turned wicked. "Pappy used to say that that's why our family is so nutty."

"I've heard about Buddy Walker's sense of humor," the sheriff said, chuckling.

"Did David tell you that I was named after the city I was conceived in?" She smiled. "I was conceived in Dallas, Texas. My brother's name is Phil, and he was named after Philadelphia."

Sheriff Turow let out a deep, hearty laugh. Seeing that she had broken the ice, Dallas asked, "So you'll help me, Sheriff?"

After glancing in all directions, the sheriff lowered his voice. "Victim is Nancy Braxton's assistant. Erin something. She walked in on an intruder. Police are searching the house and grounds for him now. My department was called in at the request of Nancy's brother because your boyfriend nominated Gnarly to oppose her on the ballot for mayor. The family fears that he has a conflict of interest with the case. You didn't hear it from me."

"Thanks, Sheriff," she said with a broad grin. "You're a peach."

"That's what they all say."

"We've been searching the house and the grounds for the gunman," Bogie said to David as he made his way up the driveway. "But we haven't found any sign of the shooter."

"Who's the victim?" David paused to observe the ambulance pulling away. Beyond the gate, Dallas' truck took off to follow the ambulance. Shaking his head, he surmised that she was going to tail it to the hospital to gather information from the EMTs or, if she got lucky, from the victim.

"Erin Devereux," Bogie said. "Nancy Braxton's executive assistant. She took a bullet to the shoulder. She was conscious and talking when we got here. Said she couldn't sleep, so she decided to do some work. She realized she'd left a folder in the study. She walked in on what must have been a burglar."

"Did she give you a description?"

With a shake of his head, Bogie explained that Erin had said that it had happened too fast. "She told me that she didn't even remember seeing the gun before she felt the bullet."

Sheriff Turow stepped out of the shadows cast by the bushes lining the driveway. "I met your new girlfriend, O'Callaghan."

"And I'm sure she pumped you about the shooting," David said. "You didn't tell her anything, did you?"

With exaggerated innocence, the sheriff said, "Me? No!"

"That woman could charm a rattlesnake." Realizing what he'd said, David drew in a deep breath. "Did I really just say that?"

Chuckling, Bogie shook his head. "You've been hanging around Dallas much too long, Chief."

"Are you taking the lead on this case, Turow?" David asked the sheriff.

"The Braxtons want me to. Ms. Braxton is convinced that the root of this attack is dirty politics from one of her opponents."

"Seriously?" David replied. "Who would kill to become the mayor of a town with a population of fewer than a thousand people? That's crazy."

Bogie was shaking his head. "Not really. A lot of our seasonal residents are movers and shakers from Washington, DC. An ambitious politician who knows how to network can make contacts here in Spencer who will launch him or her into a juicy position in Washington."

"Ambition is a very common motive for murder," Sheriff Turow said in agreement. "And we all know how badly Gnarly wants to be mayor."

"Yeah," Bogie said. "He'd say or do anything to get votes. I saw on Twitter today that he promised to repeal the leash law on day one after getting into office."

"Really?" David asked. "You saw that? When did Gnarly get on Twitter?"

"Don't know, but he's got a hundred thousand followers already. I'm following him."

"Me, too." Sheriff Turow patted David on the back. "I'll keep you and your department in the loop, Chief."

Inside the home, they found that Spencer's police officers and Sheriff Turow's deputies had separated those staying at the estate. Nathan Braxton was playing pool in the game room on the ground floor. Nancy Braxton's brother, Hugh Vance, was having a stiff drink in the living room. There was a housekeeper cleaning out the refrigerator in the kitchen.

David and Sheriff Turow stopped to study the security keypad on the wall inside the foyer. The system was on standby—meaning that the alarms on all of the doors and windows had been deactivated so that people could come and go without setting them off.

"Was the system on at the time of the shooting?" David asked Bogie.

Nodding his head, the deputy chief said, "I talked to the security monitoring company. It went off after the shooting when the side door off of the dining room was opened. Nathan Braxton confirmed that the alarm went off *after* he heard the shot. Then he looked out of his bedroom window and saw someone running off into the woods."

"That terrain is steep and rough," David said. "If you're not familiar with the area, it's practically impossible to make it in the dark. If you trip over a rock, you'll fall straight down and break your back—or worse."

"So it was a local who knows the mountain," Sheriff Turow said.

"But the system didn't go off to signal that someone had broken in," Bogie said. "Plus the system log doesn't show that anyone put in a code to turn it off until after the call to nine-one-one."

"That means that the perp was inside before the security system was turned on, or he or she was able to bypass it somehow," David said. "Since this is your party, Sheriff, where do you want to start?"

"Let's start with the scene of the crime," Sheriff Turow said. "The study."

"Where's Madam Braxton?" David looked up the stairs that led to the bedrooms and then through the open doorway that led to the rooms on the main floor. "I expected her to be here running the show."

Bogie turned around. "Believe it or not, she's upstairs asleep…according to her husband."

"Asleep?" Sheriff Turow asked.

"My wife was very upset about the break-in," Nathan Braxton said as he made his entrance from the stairs at the back of the foyer. He was followed by a sheriff deputy. "Erin has been Nancy's assistant for three years. They have formed a close bond. My wife was so distraught that we had to give her a sedative."

"And yet she thinks she's strong enough to lead a whole town," David said.

"That attitude is why we requested that Sheriff Turow lead this investigation," Hugh Vance said as he charged out of the living room. In one hand he held a drink, and he pointed an accusatory finger at David with the other. "Why are you even here?"

Sheriff Turow turned to face Hugh. Stepping into the man's space, the sheriff commanded Hugh to back down with sheer force. "This break-in and shooting happened in Spencer, Maryland. It would be impossible to conduct this investigation without the involvement of their police force. Per your request, I will lead this investigation—which means that I'm in charge." The sheriff turned his attention to the men in the foyer. "Now let's see where the shooting happened."

Bogie led them to the room at the end of the hallway off of the foyer. The Braxtons' study appeared to be more of a trophy room, with its glass cases displaying Nathan Braxton's many athletic awards and pictures of him with famous people. Across the room, the executive desk rested a few feet from the glass doors that led out onto the patio—the doors through which the assailant had fled, according to Erin. The door had been closed by the police.

Surrounded by discarded bandage wrappers, a pool of blood was drying on the floor in front of the desk.

Aware that Nathan Braxton and Hugh Vance were watching them from the doorway, David crossed the length of the study and stood over the spot where the EMTs had treated the shooting victim. Squatting down to examine the blood spatter, he noted that she had almost crossed the entire length of the room before she'd been shot.

"Has the gun used to shoot Ms. Devereux been located?" Sheriff Turow asked Bogie.

"Shooter must have taken it with him," the deputy chief said. "No shell casing was found either."

"Either he took that with him, too," Sheriff Turow said, "or it was a revolver."

"The shooting happened at what time?" David asked.

"Nine-one-one call was made at eleven forty-two," Bogie said.

"I called after I heard the shot, and we found Erin," Hugh said.

Rising to his feet, David turned around and noticed that the desk had been cleared of everything but an inbox with a few folders in it. "What was Ms. Devereux doing here in the study so late?"

"She said that she came in to look for a folder," Bogie said, pointing to the inbox.

"Erin does a lot of work here in the study," Nathan said. "She and Hugh use the desk and the printer or whatever. Erin goes everywhere with Nancy, but when she works here at the house, she uses the study. She did some work after dinner, and I guess she forgot a folder that she needed. She was coming to get it and walked in on a burglar."

"Shouldn't you be outside looking for this animal?" Hugh asked.

Taking note of Hugh, who was glaring at him from the study's doorway, David turned around to face the glass doors that filled the wall. The doors led out to the patio. "Did Erin say where the shooter was when he shot her?"

"She was right where you're standing, Chief." Bogie then pointed to the doorway. "The shooter was over by the door."

"So she didn't walk in on him," David said. "She'd entered the room and walked all of the way across it before he shot her from the door."

"*He* walked in on *her*," Sheriff Turow said.

"The room was dark," Nathan said. "Maybe the burglar was hiding in the room, and when she got all of the way across it, he jumped out and shot her."

David took note of the light switch on the wall by the doorway, but he chose to say nothing. "Then after the shooter shot Erin, he ran across the room, practically jumped over the woman he had just shot, went out the door to the patio, and ran into the thick woods on the mountainside."

"That's exactly what happened," Nathan said.

David waited until they were outside and walking down the driveway to their cars to ask the sheriff a question. "Any sign of the shooter or the gun yet?"

"None." Sheriff Turow paused while David opened the driver's side door of his cruiser.

"You won't find either," David said.

Dallas knew that she wasn't going to get any information about the shooting by cooling her heels in the hospital's waiting room. She needed to make a connection. Privacy laws had really put a damper on using hospital employees as a source of information.

By a great stroke of luck, she caught up with the two EMTs who had treated Erin Devereux's gunshot wound and had actually been at the crime scene not long after the shooting had taken place. Seeming to admire the way Dallas filled out her jeans, one of the EMTs gave her more than a passing glance when they were leaving the break room after she greeted him with a friendly smile and a hello.

"Y'all just brought in that lady who got herself shot in Spencer, didn't you?" Dallas added an extra dose of Texan charm to her drawl. "Do you get a lot of shootin's in Spencer? It seems like such a nice little town."

"No more than in any other place." The young man with extra broad shoulders had taken note of her accent. "You're not from around here, are you?"

"My, you are observant." She offered him her hand to shake. "I'm Dallas, from Dallas, Texas."

As usual, that was enough to break the ice with the two men.

"Did she tell you who shot her?" Dallas asked them.

"A burglar," they said.

"And, man!" the younger of the two said, chuckling. "She was *mad*!"

"Of course she was mad," Dallas said. "She got shot. I'd certainly be in a horn-tossin' mood if someone put a bullet in me."

"Nah," one EMT said. "She was mad at the folks she was staying with."

"You mean Ms. Braxton?"

"*Ms.* Braxton?" He shook his head. "I didn't see any women there."

The older EMT interjected. "Nathan Braxton. The football player. She was mad at him and at the other guy. She was cussing at them—"

"What was she cussing about?" Dallas asked.

"Maybe she blamed them for not having the security alarm on," the older EMT said. "Look, we were trying to save her life—not that it was a life-threatening injury, but any gunshot wound can be. We weren't paying attention to who was saying what to who."

"But she was mad enough to call her lawyer," the younger EMT said. "She insisted on bringing her purse with her, and while we were in the ambulance, she called him."

"Her lawyer?" Dallas asked. "Are you sure?"

The older EMT nodded his head. "You'd be surprised by how often that happens—people calling their lawyers from the back of the ambulance on the way to the emergency room."

"Smells like a lawsuit," Dallas said. "Or maybe a shakedown."

After saying that they had to get back on duty, the older EMT tore his young partner away from Dallas, and they headed out of the emergency exit. As they were going out the door, a slight man in an expensive suit stepped inside.

Recognizing George Ward, Dallas ducked into the snack bar just in time to avoid being seen as he made his way to the recovery unit.

Lawyer, my butt. She called the head of Nancy Braxton's political party. Now, I wonder what that's about. Is he a friend, a foe, or a partner in crime?

CHAPTER NINE

Great Falls, Virginia

In the master suite, Spencer, a.k.a. "Candi," inched across the width of the king-sized bed toward the sleeping man. The blue-eyed shelty uttered a soft whine and pawed at his arm.

There was no movement.

She stretched toward him. Sticking her snout close to his ear, she sniffed his dark hair, which, in the last couple of weeks, had grown long enough to curl slightly at the ends. Moving on to his jaw, she touched his beard with her little pink tongue as if to check out the new addition to his face. In the year that he had been married to her master, Murphy had never had a beard before. Not particularly liking the feel of its scruffy texture on her tongue, she settled for licking the inside of his ear.

Jerking his head away from the tickling sensation in his ear, Murphy sat up and looked over to the other side of the bed, where the blue-colored shelty was wagging her tail and grinning up at him.

Not having the energy to open both of his eyes, Murphy looked down at the dog with only one eye open. "Where's your mother?"

"Here I am!" Clad in a short, sheer lilac robe, Jessica sashayed into the bedroom. She was carrying two mugs. One contained her coffee with gourmet cream and sugar. The other had green tea—unsweetened.

After planting a long kiss on Murphy's lips, she handed him the tea.

"Who made the tea? You or Nigel?" Murphy asked.

"Nigel," she said. "He heats the water to the perfect temperature so that your tea can seep."

"Yeah, but he doesn't put in that dose of love that only you can supply."

"Well, I'm just going to have to serve that love to you as a side dish." Jessica plopped down into the bed next to him.

In silence, they sipped their drinks. Finally, she set her coffee mug aside and slid over to rub her hand across his jaw. "I missed you."

"Like the beard?"

"I don't know." She studied his appearance. "You have such a handsome face."

After taking a sip of his tea, he set the mug on the nightstand. Then he pulled open the drawer of the nightstand and took out his wedding band, which he had to leave behind when he went on a mission. The risk of anyone tracing his wedding band back to her was too high. He took a moment to admire the ring and the commitment it represented before rolling over to wrap his arms around her. Taking in a deep breath, he took in the sweet scent of her body and the warmth of her flesh in his arms.

Content, he smiled and looked into her eyes.

"Now I know why I don't like your beard. It covers up your dimples." His dimples, which were deep in both of his cheeks, were the first things that had attracted her to him. With a wave of her hand, as though she were a queen speaking to her servant, she said, "Off with your beard!"

Murphy climbed out of the bed and bowed deep at his waist. "Your wish is my command, my dear buttercup."

Taking in his naked bottom while he marched off into the bathroom, Jessica fell back onto the bed in laughter. "I didn't mean now!"

"Nah," he yelled over the water running in the sink. "It needs to come off anyway before I go back to work."

"But don't you have some home-leave time?" She climbed out of the bed, picked up her coffee mug, and joined him in the bathroom. "You always get time off after a mission."

"This time I get a week off." Murphy splashed warm water onto his face to moisten his beard.

Knowing that he would be unable to go into details about the mission he had been on, Jessica gently asked, "How did this mission go?"

Images of Tawkeel's broken body flashed through Murphy's mind. *There but for the grace of God go I.* Angry at what the terrorists had done to his friend and sickened by the knowledge that the same thing could happen to him if a mission ever went sideways, he clutched the sides of the sink.

"Murphy?"

He stood up straight. "Fine." He took his shaving supplies out of the cabinet. "It was a rescue mission."

Jessica was surprised by that information. Murphy never discussed his missions.

"You've met Tawki."

Jessica had met Tawkeel Said, who they called "Tawki," when he had helped save her life during a home invasion at their previous home. It turned out that the Iraqi had known Murphy's father, Joshua Thornton. Joshua had helped Tawkeel and his family escape from Iraq when Tawkeel was a child.

"We haven't seen him for a long time."

"Nine months," he said. "He's been on a mission. Deep undercover. Someone outed him and his handler. His handler was tortured to death, and Tawki would have been killed if we hadn't gotten to him in time."

"Is he okay?"

Murphy sank down to sit on the side of the tub. "Those animals tortured him for over a week. He's—" He swallowed. "But he refused to tell them anything, and we got him out alive."

"That's good." She nodded her head. "He's going to be okay, right?"

Murphy uttered a deep, cleansing sigh. "Thing is…Jess, they're saying that *he* blew his cover. But *our* intel going into this mission and tracking him down proves that he didn't."

"Maybe his handler blew it," Jessica said. "You said he was tortured to death."

"Tawki was grabbed the day *before* his handler was captured." Because he had gone that far already, Murphy rattled on. "The agency that Tawki was working for was going to leave him out there—let him die. Because he was deep undercover, they said that they couldn't risk losing any of their people by going in to get him. When word reached the Phantoms, we couldn't leave him there."

"Because Tawki is your teammate," Jessica said with understanding. "A fellow Phantom."

"We followed the intel trail all the way to him. Those around him were good and solid. His cover in that country was secure. The word about the fact that Tawkeel and his handler were spies came from those at the top of the organization he'd infiltrated—from people Tawki had never even met."

"How could they have known?"

Murphy raised his eyes to meet hers. "Someone told them."

"Who?"

Anger seeped into his tone. "Someone in Washington."

David practically drove over the curb when he pulled his cruiser into the first empty space in the emergency room's parking lot. After slamming the SUV's door shut, he sprinted through the doors and looked around for Archie or Bogie, who had met the emergency crews at Spencer Manor when the call that Mac Faraday had collapsed and was unconscious had come in.

Recognizing the police chief, the receptionist pressed the security button to allow David through the doors of the reception area. He found Bogie sitting next to Archie in the waiting room. Donning his service-dog vest, Gnarly was sitting next to Archie with his head in her lap.

"Archie, how is he?"

Blubbering, she sprang out of her seat and threw herself into David's arms. He held her tight while she cried into his shoulder.

Seeing that Archie was too frightened to speak, Bogie said, "Mac has a fever of one hundred and three, and his breathing was shallow when the EMTs got there. They got him on oxygen. Doc went to find out more. Last we heard, they'd taken him to X-ray his lungs."

"I should have made him come to the hospital when he passed out the other day," Archie said. "This is all my fault."

Extracting her from his arms, David grabbed Archie. "Don't even think like that. It is not your fault. I was there too when Mac passed out. He *refused* to go and *insisted* that we cancel the EMTs. If it's anyone's fault, it's mine. I should have hog-tied him, thrown him in the back of the cruiser, and driven him here."

"That's why they say doctors should never treat family," Dr. Dora Washington said as she turned the corner and entered the waiting room.

Upon meeting Garrett County's medical examiner, one's first impression would be that the stunning woman in her early forties used to be a high-fashion model. With her flawless figure and blue-black hair that she always wore in a silky ponytail that spilled down her back, she looked more like she belonged on the cover of a fashion magazine than cutting up dead people in the morgue. Some would be further surprised upon discovering that the beauty was sixty-five-year-old Bogie's steady girlfriend.

"What have you found out, Doc?" Bogie asked her.

"They were bringing him out of the X-ray and taking him to an examination room when I left the doctor," she said. "He's coming around. Besides the fever, Mac's dehydrated. They've been pumping him full of fluids."

"Is it pneumonia?" Archie asked.

Doc nodded her head. "They're waiting for the results of the blood tests and the X-rays of his lungs to confirm it. They're really worried about his fever. They're going to keep him at least overnight and work on getting it down."

"Pneumonia?" Archie said. "That could...People *die* from pneumonia."

David wrapped his arms around her. "Mac's not going to die." He eased her over to a chair so that she could sit down. Once she was in her seat, Gnarly climbed up to lick the tears on her face.

Doc sat on her other side. "You need to have faith, Archie. Mac is a strong, healthy man. He's fighting this, and he's going to beat it."

"We're all praying for him," Bogie said.

"He was coughing all last night," Archie said. "I was actually a little mad at him for not going to the doctor, and he said that he was going to stay in bed this morning so that he'd have the strength for the debate—" She gasped. "The debate. Mac won't make the debate."

"Don't worry about the debate," David said. "Getting Mac well is more important."

"But someone has to take Gnarly, and—"

"I'll take Gnarly," David said. "I can channel him and handle the debate."

Bogie and Doc exchanged glances. With a flicker of Doc's eyes, Bogie captured her wordless order. David was Mac's half brother. Since Mac's arrival in Deep Creek Lake, the two had formed a close brotherly bond. Sure, David could've gone to the debate, but he would've been consumed with worry the whole evening.

"That's a no-go, Chief." With an air of authority that dared David to argue with him, Bogie snatched up Gnarly's leash. "*I'll* take Gnarly to the debate. Archie and Mac need you to be here."

"But I'm the one who started all of this. I nominated Gnarly," David said.

Bogie's hand shot up. "We're all in this together."

By midmorning, Dallas had arrived at the waiting room with a bag of chocolate truffles and three mocha lattes.

Holding out the open bag of truffles to Archie, she said, "My momma used to say that when you feel lower than a gopher hole, sit back, eat a fistful of chocolate, and let God do all of the heavy liftin'."

The two women's eyes met when Archie reached into the bag and took a handful of truffles. A soft smile came to her lips. Mouthing a thank-you, she leaned against David, who was sitting next to her, and sipped her latte. Taking a seat across from them, Dallas took a sip of her latte and then went about carefully unwrapping a truffle.

"Archie! David!" someone said in the doorway next to the reception area.

Dallas' first thought upon seeing the stunning brunette with striking violet eyes and thick, ebony hair that fell in a single wave to her shoulders was that she was Robin Spencer come to life. She was almost a perfect duplicate of the woman in the portrait over the author's desk. She was dressed in skinny white jeans, flat shoes, and a lilac-colored sleeveless top with a plunging neckline that accentuated her feminine curves.

Then Dallas saw a man with dark-auburn hair two steps behind her. He was tall with long, lean muscles and a square jaw. His blue eyes sparkled when he smiled and greeted them. The only things brighter than his eyes were his smile and the deep dimples in both cheeks.

"Jessie!" Archie jumped from the sofa and took the young woman into a tight hug.

"Mac's daughter and son-in-law," David told Dallas in a low tone. "They must've driven in from Washington as soon as Archie called them."

"I told you that you didn't need to come," Archie said to Jessica Faraday while leading her into the waiting room, where David immediately hugged her.

As soon as Archie had released Jessica to David, she turned to Murphy, who took her into his arms. "I'm so glad you're home safe and sound, Murphy," she whispered into his ear. "We all worry about you. When did you get home?"

"Last night."

"We had to come." Seeking comfort, Jessica wrapped her arms around Murphy's waist and rested her head on his shoulder. "Dad sounded so bad yesterday. How is he?"

"He has pneumonia," David said. "His fever has come down a little. They want to keep him overnight for observation and are setting up a private room for him. If they get a handle on his fever, he can go home tomorrow."

"That's good," Murphy said. "Then they're optimistic about him going home."

Grasping Dallas by the hand, David led her forward to introduce her. "This is Dallas Walker. I believe you already heard about her from your dad and Archie."

"You like chocolate." Jessica took note of the bag of truffles in Dallas' hand. "I see we're going to be good friends."

"Well, then don't be shy, darlin', help yourself." Dallas thrust out the open bag for Jessica to grab a handful of candy.

While Jessica unwrapped one of the chocolate delicacies, David asked, "Did Tristan come with you?"

"He's pet sitting," Murphy said.

"Tristan's working on an important presentation to apply for a fellowship to Oxford," Jessica said. "He's been completely immersed in the dark web studying cybersecurity…Or is it astrophysics?" She turned to Dallas. "My brother prides himself on being a renaissance man." She asked Archie, "Can we see Dad?"

After Archie explained that Mac was only allowed two visitors at a time, Murphy insisted that she and Jessica go to see him and leave him with David and Dallas. After Jessica linked arms with her stepmother, she and Archie trotted down the hallway to Mac's room.

"Was your mission successful?" David asked Murphy in a low voice. He noted the longing in Murphy's expression as he watched his wife depart down the hallway.

When he turned around to answer David, Murphy saw the news on the television mounted on the wall. The image on the news was that of a house in Brussels that had been blown up two nights before. The closed captioning reported that witnesses had reported hearing gunfire shortly before the explosion. Ten men were dead. The authorities indicated that the house had long been suspected of being a headquarters for a radical Islamic group with ties to terrorists in Syria.

Dallas followed Murphy's gaze to the television screen. "They're all dead," he said before a grin came to his lips.

"Murphy?" David said, and then he repeated his question.

"Yes. It was a successful mission." Murphy tore his attention away from the television. "I'm sorry. I haven't gotten much sleep this past week."

"Hey, O'Callaghan," Sheriff Turow said from the doorway. With a jerk of his head, he invited them to the dining hall for a quick lunch. "I haven't had breakfast, and I'm starving." He led the way down the corridor. After getting an update on Mac's condition, they each got sandwiches and chips and then took a table in the corner of the hospital's dining hall.

A pescatarian, or a vegetarian who ate fish, Murphy got a bottle of water and a salad with tuna fish sprinkled on it.

The sheriff was pouring his soft drink into a glass when David asked if they'd found the burglar or the gun used to shoot Erin Devereux at the Braxtons' estate the night before.

With a shake of his head, the sheriff took a sip of his drink. "And we haven't been able to talk to Nancy Braxton yet either. Of course, the media has gotten wind of the shooting." He shot a glance in Dallas' direction.

"I haven't reported anythin'," Dallas said. "I'm waitin' for the whole story before I go public, and I think there's more to this shootin' than meets the eye."

"Reported?" Murphy looked at Dallas like she was the enemy. "You're—"

"An investigative journalist," she said.

David waved his hand for the sheriff to continue. "What do you think happened, Turow?"

"There's certainly something going on," the sheriff said. "Nancy Braxton has not made a public statement."

In silence, Dallas watched Murphy eat while David spoke.

"Normally, she'd be all over this. She'd be right in front of those cameras, shrieking about crime and guns and needing more laws and bigger laws and bull like that. But sedated? That is in complete conflict with the position she's running for and totally out of character."

"Maybe she needs time to get her story straight," Sheriff Turow said. "That's what I'm thinking."

"Maybe it's a publicity stunt," Dallas said. "The EMTs who brought Erin Devereux here told me that she made a phone call from the back of the ambulance before they made it to the hospital."

"She must not have been that badly hurt if she had enough wits about her to make a phone call from the back of the ambulance," Sheriff Turow said.

"She was treated and left before sunrise," Dallas said. "And guess who drove her? George Ward, the chair of Nancy's political party."

"And he was still there when I went by this morning," Sheriff Turow said. "He said he was helping Nancy Braxton prepare for the debate tonight."

"She'll be well enough to go to the debate, but she's not well enough to talk to the police about a shooting at her home," David said.

"I'm beginning to agree with your girl Dallas that this is a publicity stunt," Sheriff Turow said.

"Well, if it is, I have faith that you'll do the right thing. After all, this is your party, not mine," David said.

"No one calls out my people to investigate violent crimes just for the sake of a headline." Finished with his lunch, the sheriff sat up tall and gathered his paper plate and wrappers.

"Speaking of violent crimes, about that other case we talked about—"

"Another case?" Murphy asked. "What is Spencer's crime rate?"

"Enough comments from the peanut gallery," David said before urging the sheriff to continue.

"What other case are you talkin' about?" Dallas asked David. "Did you invite the sheriff into our investigation of the Sandy Burr murder?"

"What's the Sandy Burr case?" Murphy asked.

"Finish your salad," David said to Murphy.

"He'd better not be investigatin' the Burr case," Dallas said. "Because that case is mine."

"What about the Sandy Burr case?" Sheriff Turow asked them. "When was he killed?"

"You yourself said that it was up to me to get new evidence in order to open up the case again," Dallas told David.

"And I meant it."

"Then why did you invite the sheriff to join our rodeo?"

"Before I join any rodeo, I need to know what bull I'll be riding," the sheriff said. "Are you telling me that there's another murder?"

"No," David said before correcting himself. "Yes. But it's not an official case, because it was closed as a suicide. Dallas is investigating it and trying to dig up enough evidence to prove that it was murder so that we can reopen the case."

Sheriff Turow waved his hands for them to stop. "Can we talk about one murder case at a time, please?"

"I asked Turow to look into an old case involving Bill Clark," David told Dallas.

"You mean that the *other* candidate is also involved in a murder?" Dallas asked louder than they wanted her to, prompting David to shush her.

"What did you find out about Bill Clark?" David asked.

"There are a lot of people in and around Deep Creek Lake who believe that the rumor you heard is indeed a fact," Sheriff Turow said. "And for good reason, as there was no investigation, no autopsy, an instant cremation—"

"Smells like murder and a cover-up to me," Murphy said.

"Me too," Dallas said.

"But it isn't," the sheriff said.

"It isn't?" David was unsuccessful in keeping the disappointment out of his tone.

"Frankly, the way it looks, I'm surprised that it didn't come up in Clark's campaign." Sheriff Turow let out a deep sigh. "But I had a heart-to-heart talk with the doctor who signed the death certificate, and he really didn't want to admit what had happened—but when he became aware of where I was going with the case, he admitted that we were right about there being a cover-up. They weren't covering up what we thought they were covering up, though."

"What were they covering up?" David asked.

"A suicide. Ida Clark had late-stage cancer. She didn't tell anyone and swore the doctor to silence because she didn't want pity from her friends. Only Bill and the doctor knew. She was diagnosed the month after her daughter, Lisa, died. She was depressed and told her doctor that she was ready to join her late husband and daughter. He told Bill, who tried to keep an eye on her—his brother, Leroy, was never around. Bill found her dead. She had taken a whole bottle of pain pills. They didn't want the shame of her committing suicide, so they covered it up to make it look like natural causes."

Dallas was suspicious. "Suppose the doctor made that up to cover up—"

"He broke about a dozen privacy laws by showing me Ida Clark's medical file, which had notes about the cancer in it," the sheriff said. "I don't like Bill Clark either. I believe he's a pompous ass, and he could be capable of murder, but he didn't kill his mother."

"But he did cheat his brother out of his half of the inheritance," David said. "How many months did Ida Clark have cancer before she killed herself? I can just see it. Manipulating his mother, Bill Clark convinced her that for her sake, she should put his name on all of her bank accounts—just in case something happened. And all of the while, he was planning to claim that that money was his, not part of her estate, which had to be split with Leroy."

"Bill Clark has no moral compass," Sheriff Turow said. "We already know that. But what he did was not illegal."

"Leroy Clark did file a suit against his brother," David said. "Luckily for Bill, Leroy was killed when he got drunk and drove that truck into the lake."

"Knowing what you were going to ask next, O'Callaghan," the sheriff said, "I looked into that, too. Leroy's blood-alcohol level was point seventeen. He was drunk. He'd had a string of DUI arrests, and his license was suspended when he had that accident the killed him. Even if he hadn't died, he would have had an uphill battle to prove that his mother had intended for him to get half of the money in those accounts that had Bill's name on them." He shook his head. "Sorry, O'Callaghan, but if you want to nail Clark for the bastard he is, this isn't the case to do it with."

CHAPTER TEN

Having grown up in Deep Creek Lake, Bogie was well acquainted with the ways of the local elections. He had been to many debates. Almost always, the same crowd showed up: those who were invested in local legislature and those who maybe weren't so invested in it as much as they were curious about it. Most everyone else would stay home and find out what had happened the next morning while picking up breakfast at Beagle Bailey's Bagels.

This election was different. Over the last dozen years, Bogie had seen a change in Spencer.

Decades before, the year-round rural population had outnumbered the seasonal residents in the lakeside-resort area.

Gradually, all of that had changed. More big-city residents with fat bank accounts were moving into Spencer, building bigger homes along the lake and on the mountain, and bringing their big-city ideas, laws, and regulations with them.

The rural populace didn't see it happening. One new Spencer resident after another ran for and was elected to a seat on the town council—until they outnumbered the lifetime residents. While some dived into local politics with a sincere desire to help the community, others did so because of a personal quest for power.

Bill Clark, who had moved to Spencer from Oakland after his mother's death, was the cream of the crop. Bill had arrogantly bullied the current mayor into submission with every motion that he'd forced through the town council. With each new legislation, Clark would declare that they had taken yet another step toward bringing Spencer into the twenty-first century.

In silence, the year-round local residents of Spencer stewed with every change made to their town—and to their way of life.

The clothesline ban was the straw that broke the camel's back.

Even so, Bogie had not been expecting the circus-like atmosphere he walked into when he led Gnarly into the Spencer Inn's lobby. He found it packed with seemingly every resident of Spencer, the mayoral candidates, their supporters, and the media.

"How does your client feel about immigration?" a cable-news anchor asked Bernie and Hap, who were wearing their best Sunday church suits.

"Oh, Gnarly is totally understanding about the immigration issues," Bernie said. "After all, his own parents emigrated from Germany."

Trying to duck out of sight of the cameras, Bogie positioned himself in front of Gnarly and turned to go down the hallway leading to one of the banquet rooms where the debate was to take place—only to find himself face to face with Dallas Walker.

"Where do you think you're going?" she asked in a teasing tone.

"The debate."

"They had to move it to the grand ballroom downstairs," Dallas said, pointing to the floor beneath their feet. "Three times more people showed up tonight than the other night." She knelt down to scratch Gnarly behind the ears. "And they all came to see you, handsome."

"They also came to hear his positions on the issues," Bogie said. "Wish me luck."

"Oh, you'll have them eating out of the palm of Gnarly's paw," Dallas said with a wave of her hand. "Hey, Bogie, can you answer a question for me?"

"Well, that's what I came here to do tonight. Guess I can warm up by answering yours. Shoot. What do you want to know about? Gnarly's position on birth control? Immigration? Abortion? He's pro-life, by the way."

"Murphy Thornton."

"Mac's son-in-law?" Bogie shrugged. "I didn't know you even knew him."

"Met him today," Dallas said. "He and Jessica came out to see Mac. What does Murphy do?"

Worried that David's new girlfriend was becoming interested in the handsome younger man who happened to be married to Mac's daughter, Bogie asked, "Why do you want to know?"

"Everyone was very excited and relieved to see that he was safe and sound," Dallas said. "David had told me before that he was in the navy."

"Lieutenant stationed at the Pentagon," Bogie said.

"As relieved as they all seemed to be," Dallas said, "I get the impression that he's not your average pencil pusher stationed behind some desk in DC. Is he special ops? SEAL? Come on. You can tell me."

Bogie let out a chuckle. "Dear, dear Dallas. Seriously? Now, if Murphy were with some sort of covert special ops in the navy, do you really think I'd know? Why would they tell me?"

"Look! It's Gnarly!" someone nearby said. An audible roar echoed through the lobby. An instant later, Gnarly was mobbed by the crowd. As hard as Bogie tried to hold on to him, he felt the leash slip from his hands, and like a log on a raging river, Gnarly slipped away in the mob of enthusiastic voters flowing down the hallway.

"I am getting my butt kicked by a *dog!*" Nancy Braxton said as Dallas made her way down the hallway to the conference room where the mayoral candidate and her campaign team were prepping for the debate. "I knew most of the local yokels in this burg were morons, but a *dog* for mayor? He can't even sign a piece of legislation."

"Actually, Ms. Braxton, he can," Erin said. "He'll put his paw on an ink pad and then press it onto the signature line." There was a tension-filled silence during which Dallas assumed that Nancy was firing a deadly glare. "I heard one of the experts answer that very question on one of the news channels."

"Whose side are you really on, Erin?" Nancy Braxton's tone was so low and threatening that Dallas felt a cold chill go both up and down her back.

Erin's voice shook. "Yours, of course, Ms. Braxton."

"Then why are you even suggesting that that damn flea-bag could possibly be mayor?" There was a loud crash inside the room as something hit the wall. "It's my turn! My turn! My turn!"

"Nancy—" a male voice said. The voice was cut off by the sound of someone's face being slapped.

"George! You traitor! You promised me! This race, it's my turn to win!"

"And you can win," George said. "All we have to do is discredit Gnarly."

"How can a dog be discredited?"

"He's a *German* shepherd."

"So!" Nancy said with a scoff. "Everyone knows that."

"German," George repeated. "Not *American*. German."

Nancy let out a girlish squeal. "If he's German, then he's not American, which means he's not qualified to run for office!"

There was an evil tone in George's laughter. "We'll demand that Gnarly produce his birth certificate to prove he's an American citizen."

"Do they even issue birth certificates for dogs?" Nancy asked.

"No," George answered with a wicked laugh. "So they *can't* prove he's an American citizen."

A shout inside the room caused Dallas to jump away from the doorway and search to see if anyone had discovered her eavesdropping. Seeing no one and recognizing that the shout had come from Erin, Dallas tiptoed back toward the doorway. She then heard Erin excitedly announce a discovery that was going to turn Nancy Braxton's campaign for mayor around.

"Man, you will not believe it! They say that everyone has skeletons in their closet—but, man! A dog?' I thought. What kind of dirt could a dog possibly have in his closet? But I went digging—"

"You got something on Gnarly?" George Ward asked.

Erin's voice moved closer to the doorway. Dallas thought that she was possibly taking center stage for her announcement. "Man! Did I ever! One of my sources just came through!"

The slam of the door cut Dallas off from the news.

Unable to hear the gem of news they had uncovered, she snatched her cell phone from her bag and ran for the stairwell.

David picked up her call on the third ring. "Hey, darling, are Bogie and Gnarly ready for the debate?"

"Maybe not," she said while running down the stairs to the grand ballroom. "What skeleton does Gnarly have in his past?"

"What skeleton?"

"The one he's been hidin' in his closet." She slipped through the door to enter the corridor, which was filled with potential voters anxious to see the new candidate in action. Many were wearing "Vote for Gnarly" shirts and hats. "Nancy Braxton's team has been digging into Gnarly's past and found something that has her very excited. What is it? I need to give Bogie a heads-up."

David stammered. "A few stints as a pickpocket, a couple of purse snatchings, some shoplifting, and a misdemeanor cat burglary—but no one pressed charges. And there's that dishonorable discharge from the army, but they won't discuss that with anyone."

"Dishonorable discharge?"

"But even I haven't been able to uncover what that was for. How could Braxton find that out? I mean—Gnarly's a dog. What could he have done?"

"I have a feeling we're about to find out."

In his private room at the hospital, Mac Faraday was in a drug-induced sleep. Oxygen tubes had been stuck up his nose to help him breathe.

As she sat next to his bed, Archie stared at Mac, watching for any sign that he was getting better or worse. David and

Jessica were sitting at the foot of the bed. Murphy was asleep in a chair in a corner of the room.

After overhearing David's discussion and seeing the concern on his face, Jessica watched him disconnect the call and look down at the phone in his hand as if it would provide the answers he needed. "What's wrong? Bad news from Dallas?"

"Maybe," David said in a low voice. "One of Gnarly's opponents has dug up something from his past that could be used to smear him."

"What? What could Gnarly have in his past?" Jessica asked.

"Everyone knows he's a thief," Archie said. "Must be from when he was in the army."

"But that's classified," David said. "I tried to find out what he did to get a dishonorable discharge, and I couldn't. How could they have done it?"

"It's politics," Jessica said. "If the bosses want their candidate to win badly enough, all they have to do is go up the line to their big bosses on Capitol Hill and ask them to open up the file."

"Well, we need to find out what's in Gnarly's past so that we can head this off," David said.

"I'm way ahead of you." Jessica jumped up out of her chair and crossed the room. She bent over Murphy and kissed him on the cheek. He stirred and let out a pleased moan at the touch of her lips. "Wake up, sweet cheeks. It's time to go to work."

Off of the stage area in the grand ballroom at the Spencer Inn, Bogie was trying to extract instructions about what to do at the debate from the moderator.

A chubby young woman who had graduated from college with a degree in journalism only a few years before, Salma Rameriz was already the producer of a local news program. Pugnacious and aggressive about her views, she was making a name for herself in the political arena. From the debates he had attended, Bogie was well aware that Rameriz didn't know the meaning of the word "objective" when it came to political debates.

A devoted Nancy Braxton supporter, Salma Rameriz would likely play patty-cake with Nancy during the debate and throw as many knockout punches to Bill Clark and Gnarly as the audience would let her get away with.

"We're going to pick numbers to see who'll go first," Salma Rameriz said to Bogie as they went over the schedule on her tablet.

Kneeling next to them, Dallas was brushing Gnarly from head to toe. Seeming to sense the seriousness of what was about to happen, Gnarly sat up tall with his ears erect—until his snout picked up the scent of a goody in Salma's briefcase, which she had placed at her feet.

Seeing that the moderator was preoccupied with giving detailed instructions to Bogie, Gnarly casually dug around in the bag with his snout.

Ah! He had hit the mother lode! With a shake of his head, he managed to shake the last half of a granola bar from its wrapper and then dropped down to snatch the goody from the floor.

Bogie only caught sight of the misdeed a split second before Gnarly gulped down the snack. When Salma turned to pick up her bag, he let out a call and grabbed her arm. "I have one last question!"

"What's that?" Salma turned back to him just in time for Dallas to grab the wrapper and stick it into her own handbag.

"What if Gnarly has to go pee?" Bogie asked.

"He is housebroken, isn't he?" Salma's eyebrows furrowed. "Then you or one of his people will take him outside if he has to go." Scoffing at what she considered to be a less than intelligent question, she picked up her briefcase and went to the table that had been set up for the two journalists tasked with asking questions of the mayoral candidates.

Satisfied that Gnarly was as handsome as he could be, Dallas rose to her feet.

"Any word from David about what they may have on Gnarly?" Bogie asked her.

She shook her head. "Nothing. But he said that he has a source who might be able to find out for us."

Bogie looked down into Gnarly's eyes. "Old boy, what did you do?"

Sensing that they were worried and that he was the source of their concern, Gnarly's eyes softened. His ears fell back in a plea for mercy.

There was a scurry of excitement as Doc Washington hurried through the crowd to make her way to them. She was carrying a digital camcorder in her hand. "I hope I'm not too late." She kissed Bogie on the lips and knelt to kiss Gnarly on the head. "I'm going to record everything and stream it live to Jessica so that they can see it in Mac's hospital room."

Dallas caught sight of Nancy Braxton and her entourage making their way toward the stage area. Her arm in a sling, Erin was doing the best she could to follow the barrage of orders that Nancy was snapping to her and everyone about her. Suddenly, Erin whirled around and hurried away. Watching her, George Ward paused to look Nancy up and down before casually following after Erin.

A sly grin crossed Nathan Braxton's face when he read a text on his cell phone. He raised his eyes to look through the crowd.

Dallas followed his line of sight over to Bill Clark's camp and saw a young woman flash a grin at him. She acknowledged him with a slight nod of her head before turning and slipping her arm through Bill Clark's arm.

It's true. Politics does make strange bedfellows.

While making his way through the crowd, shaking hands, and taking selfies, Bill Clark barked orders to an excited young blond man who was loaded down with laptop cases, cell phone, cameras, and tablets.

Dallas watched the two men step up to the stage, where they stopped. Then they pressed their heads together and giggled like a couple of schoolboys up to no-good. Their chuckles grew to laughter when the young man pressed a button on his cell phone. He and Bill Clark looked up, directing their gazes toward Nancy Braxton's camp, where Salma was hugging Nancy.

Salma then greeted Bill Clark with a firm, business-like handshake and marched over to her seat, where she checked a text message on her cell phone. As she read it, a frown crossed her face. She looked over to Nancy Braxton's entourage and then turned to settle her gaze on Gnarly.

Dallas swallowed.

The ammo was then loaded, and the weapon, aimed at Gnarly.

CHAPTER ELEVEN

They could tell by the glare in her eyes that Archie had uncovered something unpleasant while writing down Gnarly's registration number. She then ended her call to the veterinarian, and, handing the number to Murphy, said, "I found out how they got their information. The veterinary assistant told me that I was the second one to call today to ask for Gnarly's registration number. *Mac* called around lunchtime to ask for it."

"Oh, yeah," David said with heavy sarcasm. "Gnarly's service record has been foremost on his mind all day." They all looked over to the bed, where Mac was sound asleep.

Murphy dialed a phone number on his phone, a special, untraceable cell phone that he used only for his missions. "What time is the debate?"

"Eight o'clock." David checked the time on his watch. It was ten minutes after seven. "The debate is in less than an hour. Do you think they'll drop their bomb during the debate itself or feed it to the news media?"

"Neither way would be good," Archie said. "Even if it's something minor, with the way the members of the media work, take sides, and push for their own agendas, they'll spin and flip whatever it is and turn it into something it's not—all to promote their candidate."

"And they'll bury Gnarly and his reputation in the process," Jessica said while watching Murphy leave the hospital room to find a quiet place to talk to his commanding officer.

"Dad was right," David said. "Anyone who gets involved in politics has to be nuts to begin with."

Murphy found an outdoor patio where hospital employees could eat with the pleasant surroundings of a floral garden and an employee parking lot. Making sure that no one was within earshot of him, he sat at a picnic table and listened to the phone on the other end of the call ring.

The deep, sultry feminine voice answered on the third ring. "Good evening, Lieutenant. I didn't expect to hear from you today. I thought you'd be immersed in marital bliss with your lovely bride."

"So did I," Murphy said. "But my father-in-law has pneumonia, and we've run into a unique situation. I need a big favor."

"Why type of situation?"

"Do you remember Gnarly?"

"I know Gnarly. He's running to be the mayor of Spencer."

"How do you know about that?"

"I know a lot of things, Murphy," she said. "Gnarly is the front-runner and favored to win."

"Unless some dirt from his past is brought before the media," Murphy said.

There was silence on the other end of the line.

"Do you know what that dirt is?"

"I need to make a couple of phone calls," she said.

The first thing that Mac was aware of was the fresh, cool oxygen filling his lungs. The roar in his ears faded away as he began to hear the voices around him.

"First of all"—Mac was shocked to hear Bill Clark's voice—"I want everyone to know that I never did support the ban on clotheslines."

He heard Archie scoff. "He's such a liar. His name was all over that ban."

"He looks like a snake," Jessica said in agreement.

Confused about what Bill Clark was doing in his hospital room, Mac opened his eyes and looked around.

Archie was instantly at his bedside. "Honey, don't try to sit up. You need to rest."

Mac became aware of the tubes wrapped around his head and the IVs in his arms. "What happened?" Seeing his daughter, he asked, "What are you doing here?"

Jessica took his hand. "Watching Gnarly in his first debate."

"Ah, man, I'm still hallucinating."

David appeared on the other side of his bed. "It's the drugs."

Nancy Braxton's shrill voice leaped from Archie's tablet. "When I'm mayor, I won't repeal the clothesline ban. I'll fix it and make it work for everyone."

There was a mixture of applause and boos for several seconds until one of the journalists asked, "How will you make the ban on clotheslines work for everyone?"

"It's simple," Nancy said. "I'll bring people from both sides together, and we will reach across the aisle to come to a solution that will make everyone happy." Upon hearing doubtful grumbles from the audience, she added, "I've done it before. I was the one who negotiated the release of a hundred hostages taken prisoner by pirates in Somalia!"

"Somalia?" Bogie said in disbelief.

He saw the journalists on the stage furrow their brows. Judging by how her mouth was hanging open with awe, Salma Rameriz was buying every word, which spurred Nancy Braxton on.

"The secretary of state was too busy negotiating with Iran. But my heart went out to the families of the victims who had been snatched from their boats by pirates in Somalia." Nancy furrowed her brow in a well-rehearsed expression of sincere compassion. "So I offered to try to rescue them myself. Because the secretary was afraid that I would be taken hostage, he assigned me a security detail."

Trying not to disrespect the mayoral candidate, Bogie turned away from the audience. Dallas' eyes were wide with disbelief.

"I flew into Somalia." Nancy waved her hand to indicate the plane's flight. "And they told us that there were Somali snipers at the airfield. So when we landed, my security detail surrounded me, and we had to run across the airfield with our heads down, ducking the snipers' fire."

The audience didn't know what to make of the candidate's story. Murmurs of both doubt and admiration rose from the audience.

"Then I had the Somali pirates brought to my hotel suite, where we ate dinner and talked. They told me their problems, and I listened. That's all they needed—someone to listen to them. Then finally, they agreed to let a hundred American hostages go."

"Lady, you have way too many cobwebs in your attic," Dallas said. Shaking her head in disbelief over the fact that the moderator seemed to be buying Nancy's story hook, line, and sinker, she turned away and caught a glimpse of George Ward and Erin, who were engaged in what appeared to be a serious discussion.

Nancy pounded the podium. "When I'm mayor, I will get it done! I am the only candidate here on this stage who can!" She pointed a finger at Gnarly. "No *dog* can work to build bridges so that we can all live together in peace and love!"

"Bigot!"

It started as a single outburst from one voter. Then two more joined in and were followed by four more and then eight more and so on and so on until the whole audience was chanting "Bigot! Bigot! Bigot!"

Her eyes bulging, Salma Rameriz stood up to face down the audience members who had dared to disrespect her favored candidate.

Refusing to back down, Nancy shouted into the microphone. "It's the *truth!*"

"You wouldn't know the truth if it bit you in the butt!" a man in a plaid shirt said, prompting laughter.

With a jerk of his chin toward his officers, Bogie gestured for the Spencer police to quiet everyone down. Wading into the crowd, they managed to settle the audience so that Salma could put forth the next question.

"Gnarly, what is your position on Spencer's law regarding clotheslines?"

Immediately the crowd broke into a chant: "Gnarly! Gnarly! Gnarly!"

Bogie and Gnarly walked up to the podium and microphone. The other two candidates on the stage glared at the audience, angry that the enthusiasm that had been denied to them was being shown for the canine candidate.

Sitting up tall at Bogie's side, Gnarly eyed everyone in the audience as though he were looking for someone. His eyes fell on Sheriff Turow, who was dressed in his sheriff's uniform, and the young girl sitting next to him. A wide grin filled the girl's face. Gnarly's mouth dropped open into a grin, and he wagged his tail.

When the chanting showed no signs of fading, Bogie spoke softly into the mic. Unable to hear him, the audience quieted down. Those who were slower to cease their chant were shushed by their neighbors until everyone was silent.

Once the room was silent, Bogie began his response again. "Sixty-five people in Pakistan were killed by a suicide bomber yesterday."

There was a stunned silence in the room.

"Two weeks ago, one state away, a seven-year-old little girl was snatched right off of her bike while riding twenty feet behind her friend—she was taken in broad daylight. She was found dead three days later, and the killer still has not been caught. He's out there somewhere. Maybe he's in this room right now."

The silence became deafening.

Bogie took the time to allow his words to sink in before continuing. "What would you rather have your police force be doing? Do you want them patrolling for jihadist terrorists who want to blow you up while you're waiting for an ice cream cone, searching for pedophiles who are hunting your children, or remaining on the lookout for illegally hung panties?"

There was a growing unease among the audience.

Bogie cocked his head at them. "Do you know how the whole clothesline mess started?" He pointed across the stage at Bill Clark. "Mr. Clark didn't like looking out of the window of his home and seeing his neighbor's extra-large tighty-whities hanging out on the clothesline that he had across his deck. So rather than behaving like a civilized grown-up and politely asking his neighbor to hang his dirty laundry elsewhere or to do it at another time when he wouldn't have to see it or"—Bogie waved a finger—"Closing his blinds and not looking! Instead, Bill Clark decided to *abuse* his power on the town council and to create a regulation that would suit his own agenda. And that resulted in neighbors snitching on neighbors and police resources—the ones paid for by your taxes—being allocated in what has to be the most foolish manner imaginable."

A roar rose out of the crowd.

Bill Clark was instantly on his feet. "That's a lie!"

"No, it's not!" an overweight man yelled. "You've been bitching about seeing my underwear for years, Clark! I told you every summer to just close your blinds if you didn't want to see them, but no!" He turned around to shout to his friends and neighbors. "Clark told me *last year* that he was going to have clotheslines outlawed so that he wouldn't have to see my laundry hanging out on my back deck."

"If you don't believe me," Bogie said, "contact the secretary of the town council, and ask for the minutes of the town-council meeting in February of this year. They're public record. All you have to do is go to city hall and ask for a copy of the minutes, and you will see who proposed the law banning clotheslines. The name of that person is"—Bogie pointed his finger across the stage—"Bill Clark, who less than ten minutes ago told everyone here in this room that he never supported the ban. If he never supported it, why did he himself propose it in the first place?"

Seeing the audience turn on him, Bill Clark fired off a glare at the young man with whom he had been giggling before the debate. The young man quickly typed out a text on his cell phone.

Picking up her cell phone, Salma said, "Our next question is for Gnarly."

Nancy Braxton was on her feet. "It's my turn! I get the next question first." Offstage, George Ward and Erin gestured for Nancy Braxton to quiet down. A pouty expression crossed Nancy's face, and she stomped one of her feet.

Sucking in a deep breath, Bogie braced for the ambush that he'd anticipated would come his way.

"Do you believe that Gnarly has the temperament to be the mayor of Spencer, a resort town frequented by families, many of whom have young children?"

Bogie let out a sigh of relief. "Why, of course. Why wouldn't he? Everyone here knows Gnarly."

A roar of agreement rose up in the room.

Studying Gnarly, Salma waited for the chorus to die down. "Gnarly does have a history of biting and even killing people."

"In the line of duty," Bogie said. "Gnarly proudly served his country in the military. He's also worked police cases here in Spencer."

"Gnarly has attacked and killed people?" Salma asked.

"So have I," Bogie said. "It's not something that either of us wanted to do, but when it comes to keeping the peace and saving people from the bad guys, we sometimes have to step up to bat and do what has to be done."

"Gnarly is a killer. Is that what you're saying, Deputy Chief Bogart?"

"He's not a killer."

"But he's killed people," Salma said. "If he's killed people, then he is a killer, so can he really be trusted around people—and, in particular, children?"

Furious, Bogie said, "If you don't think Gnarly can be trusted around children because he's killed murderers out to kill innocent people, then I guess you can't trust me around them either."

"Did you ever kill your partner?"

Bogie's mouth dropped open. With a shake of his head, he said, "Huh? Repeat that."

"First Sergeant Belle Perkins," Salma said with no emotion. "Gnarly's handler in Iraq. He killed her in her sleep. Isn't that why he received a dishonorable discharge from the US Army? Because he's a killer dog?"

CHAPTER TWELVE

Spencer Manor

"Mac, I wish you hadn't insisted on leaving the hospital," David said while he and Murphy were helping Mac up the stairs to the master suite.

"What were they going to do to stop me? Arrest me? Put me in jail next to my crazy, homicidal dog?" At the top of the stairs, Mac brushed David's hands away from his arm. "Gnarly is not crazy! Yes, he's a kleptomaniac, and he has issues, but he's not a psychopathic killer. I don't care what that so-called journalist says—he did not kill his handler. I'll never believe it, and I'm going to prove to every single one of them that he didn't kill her."

He turned around to where Murphy was holding his other arm. "You've got all types of clearances, Murphy. There has to be a report somewhere about Gnarly's handler getting killed. Find it!"

"I have a call in to my commanding officer," Murphy said. "She'll let me know when she gets it."

"When she calls back, put her on speaker," Mac said. "I want to know what happened."

"You don't have the security clearance, Mac. That's why they wouldn't tell any of you anything before."

Mac's eyes were blazing when he stepped up to his son-in-law. "I don't give a damn about security clearances. I don't care if I have to go all the way to the other side of the planet. Gnarly saved my life, and he saved David's life—he's always been there for everyone! I want his name cleared. *Now.*" Pushing Murphy aside, he went into the bedroom. The slam of the door echoed through the large home.

David sighed. "I've never seen Mac that mad."

"You've known Gnarly for years," Murphy said. "Do you believe he could've flipped out and killed his handler?"

"I'd believe it of Mac before I'd believe it of Gnarly."

The doorbell rang downstairs.

Noting that it was after eleven o'clock at night, David said, "It's probably the media."

Archie peered through the window to check who was on the front porch before she opened the door for Sheriff Turow and a young girl.

Concerned that the sheriff wanted to lock Gnarly up for being dangerous, Archie said, "Gnarly's not here. We thought the media would be hounding him, so Bogie and Dallas took him to an undisclosed location."

Grinning at Archie's nervousness, the sheriff shook his head and then nodded to Murphy and David, who were on the stairs, and to Jessica, who had come up from the dining room. "No, I didn't come to arrest Gnarly for anything. I know he's not a killer." He ushered the girl forward. "I don't believe any of you have met my daughter, Kelly."

While Sheriff Turow made the introductions, Kelly Turow, who was approximately ten years old, stepped into the living room, where they could see that her eyes were red, and her face stained with tears. All of their hearts went out to her.

A solemn mood fell over the room, and the sheriff said, "Can we all sit down? I have something very important to tell you. Mac should hear this too."

At the top of the stairs, Murphy rushed into the bedroom to urge Mac to join them. Jessica went to the kitchen to prepare a pitcher of iced tea and to get the cake that she'd found in the refrigerator.

Once they were all settled in the living room and Kelly was sitting close to her father on the sofa, Sheriff Turow began.

"Five years ago, just after Kelly had turned five years old, her mother, a first sergeant in the army, was shipped off to Iraq for a yearlong mission. She was killed overseas."

"I can only imagine how awful that must have been," Jessica said.

Sheriff Turow cleared his throat before he continued. "Her name was First Sergeant Belle Perkins."

Hearing the name, they all sat up in their seats.

"That's why Gnarly took to you the way he did," David said. "And why you always give him toys and—"

"I've known Gnarly since he was a pup," Sheriff Turow said. "So has Kelly, though she can barely remember him. I'm sorry. I never really talked to Kelly about this before. I only talked fondly about Gnarly, who we have pictures of in our family album. I took her tonight to the debate—we both felt as proud as parents about his success—and then they said those things. But they're lies, and I felt that I had to tell you. What they said tonight"—his voice began to sound like a growl—"well, Gnarly never would have hurt Belle. Yes, she did die over there. But she was not attacked by a dog. The day before she was killed, she, Gnarly, and their unit were ambushed by Islamic terrorists. Four men in their unit were killed. Belle and Gnarly saved everyone else. On his own, Gnarly circled around and killed two snipers who had pinned them to a wall, and Belle took out two others. She skyped with me and told me about it, and then she said that during the last few days of their mission some really funky things had been going on. They were repeatedly ambushed." He sighed. "I don't have a lot of specific information about how she died or about the actual circumstances of her death, because their mission was highly classified, but the army did tell me one thing." He turned to face Kelly. "Belle was not attacked by a dog, and Gnarly is not a killer."

The cell phone buzzing in his pocket prompted Murphy to get up from his seat and go out onto the deck.

"Do you at least know the cause of death?" Mac asked.

The sheriff looked at his daughter, apparently weighing whether he should answer that question in her presence. "Strangulation. And the commanding officer of the unit decided that since Gnarly did nothing to thwart the attack or to defend his partner, he was a coward, and he had him drummed out of the army."

"Gnarly is not a coward." Archie practically jumped out of her seat.

"Nor is he a killer," Mac said. "Do you have any idea why he didn't defend Belle?"

"I know exactly why." Sheriff Turow looked down at his daughter. "After that ambush and after they got back to the base, Belle found out that Gnarly had been hit. His hip had been grazed by a bullet. She told me—the last time I talked to her—that after we finished talking, she was going to take him back to her tent to treat his wound."

"Because of the remote locations of army missions," David said, "dog handlers have to be able to work on their dogs and to do minor surgeries—they can't get them to a pet hospital."

"Depending on how bad Gnarly's wound was," Sheriff Turow said, "Belle would have had to anesthetize him before stitching his wound."

"In which case Gnarly would have most likely been asleep when Belle was killed," Archie said.

"But all they would've had to do was give him a blood test, and they would've seen that," Jessica said.

"When the military contacted me about Belle's death and Gnarly's being a coward," Sheriff Turow said, "I told them that she'd been operating on him that night, but it was too late. The sedative was out of his system. The CO wrote up a report saying that Gnarly was a coward, and he was released from duty. I tried to find him because I wanted him to come live with us, but his records were sealed. I didn't know what had happened to him and even suspected that he had been put to sleep—until the day I met all of you, and Gnarly jumped out of David's cruiser."

At Turow's reference to wanting Gnarly to live with his family, Archie and Mac exchanged looks of concern.

"Well," Mac said, "looks like we have some work to do. We need to get to the bottom of this, find out who killed Belle, and clear Gnarly's name."

"And bring down the dirty, rotten liars who called Gnarly a killer," Kelly said.

"Yeah!" Archie bumped fists with her.

Murphy came in from the deck. "Sorry I had to step outside. I needed to take a call."

"Any success?" Jessica asked him.

"If you're asking whether I got a copy of Gnarly's military records and his handler's case file, the answer is yes."

Mac pulled himself up off of the sofa. "What are we all sitting around for? Time to get to work."

It was after midnight.

After the debate, Dallas had rushed to bring Gnarly back to David's home on the lake.

Upon seeing Gnarly walk through the door, Storm leaped over the back of the sofa on which she'd been sleeping and met him halfway across the great room. The two shepherds twirled around in unison and headed to the back door, and Dallas let them frolic outside.

Despite the late hour, Dallas did not want to sleep. She was struck by the long, detailed yarn that Nancy Braxton had spun at the debate.

Generally, politicians lie. But that whole thing about flying into sniper fire and negotiating with Somali pirates was not a normal lie. It was downright outlandish.

Who in their right mind would make up something so bizarre? Only a nut.

After making a series of phone calls and sending out e-mails to her connections, Dallas was able to ascertain how much of Nancy's claim was true.

Nancy Braxton had once eaten dinner at a Somali restaurant in Washington, DC, which is where the State Department is—and the State Department is where the secretary of state works. It was entirely possible that she and the secretary had both been in the same city at the same time.

Otherwise, none of Dallas' connections, some of whom knew the secretary of state, had any reason to believe that he even knew Nancy Braxton, let alone that he would've entrusted her with handling negotiations on behalf of the United States.

If such a thing had happened, wouldn't it have made national news?

Dallas decided that the woman was delusional, which begged the question, why would her political party go to such lengths to get her elected to office?

Recalling the look on George Ward's face when he'd heard the yarn, she realized that maybe the party was only then starting to realize the depth of her detachment from reality. Maybe that was the topic of the serious discussion he was having with Erin Devereux. Maybe Nancy Braxton was nuts enough to have shot her own assistant.

A high-pitched scream sent shock waves up Dallas' spine and up out of the top of her head.

Storm!

The gut-wrenching yelp was mixed with an anguished cry for help and accompanied by a screech that Dallas recognized from growing up on a ranch in Texas.

Mountain lion!

Springing out of her seat on the sofa, Dallas snatched up her bag. While digging her hand inside for her semiautomatic, she sprinted to the door and threw it open.

In the yard off of the back deck, she saw that Storm was down on the ground and that a big cat was tearing at the fur on the back of her neck while she was fighting it and wailing. Shaking with anger and terror for her dog, Dallas tried to take aim but was afraid of hitting Storm.

If she was going to save Storm, she had no choice.

Gnarly's growl filled the air as he tore out of the darkness. All Dallas saw was a flash of movement.

The mountain lion had only enough time to leap off of his victim before Gnarly body-slammed him with a hundred pounds of fur, teeth, and claws. The force of the impact made the two animals seem to bounce off of each other, but they reconnected instantly in an all-out battle.

Unable to shoot the mountain lion for fear of hitting Gnarly, Dallas fired her gun into the air, which sent the mountain lion running off into the darkness—with Gnarly hot on his trail.

Dallas ran to Storm, who was lying where the mountain lion had left her and bleeding from the wounds on her neck and back.

"You're okay, baby," Dallas said, sobbing into Storm's sable fur.

Covered in blood, the dog whimpered.

Gently, she picked up the trembling dog and carried her toward the house. When she heard the mountain cat's screeches and Gnarly's snarling barks, she stopped and peered into the darkness—praying that Gnarly would be okay.

CHAPTER THIRTEEN

The closest veterinarian offering emergency services was at Pineview Veterinary Hospital, which was several miles away from Deep Creek Lake. Bogie knew the doctor in charge and asked her to meet Storm at the hospital when David and Dallas arrived, which was in a matter of minutes. While Dallas hugged the bleeding dog in the back of the cruiser, David sped to the hospital with the sirens and lights going.

After taking his daughter home, Sheriff Turow had set up a command center at David's house with every on-duty and off-duty officer available to search for the mountain lion who had attacked Storm and for Gnarly, who had still not returned. It was more than a simple search for a lost dog. The mountain lion had been hunting in a residential community on the lake. He could have very well attacked David's neighbors while they were sitting on their docks enjoying the pleasant night air.

Cursing his pneumonia, which still had him feeling as weak as a baby, Mac could do nothing but wait by the phone for news about his dog, who was frequently a pain in the butt. He was a pain to which he had grown quite accustomed. He couldn't take his mind off of Gnarly.

Dallas had called while Murphy had been bringing up Gnarly's military file on his tablet, a specially configured device on which he could access classified information. Upon hearing the news that Storm had been attacked and that Gnarly had taken off in pursuit of a mountain lion, Murphy had shut it down and volunteered to join the search.

At the dining room table, which was where they were working, Mac turned on the tablet again. "How about if you log in and bring up the file so that I can go through it while you're gone?"

"No," Murphy said after kissing Jessica good-bye.

"But—"

Murphy picked up the tablet and handed it to Jessica. "I'll go through it with you when I get back."

Mac turned to Jessica, hoping that she would reason with her husband.

"Don't waste your time, Dad. Murphy doesn't budge when it comes to national security."

"Sorry, Mac, but those files are classified, and you don't have the authority to look at them," Murphy said. "Nothing personal. I trust you, and I know that you aren't going to go out and sell the information. But…I signed an agreement on my first day at the naval academy and took an oath. I did it again on the day I became a Phantom. Both times I swore that I wouldn't share classified information with anyone, and if I do, I'll be charged with espionage, which is a felony."

"There was a case a couple of years ago where a marine in Afghanistan was charged with and convicted of espionage because he'd texted a warning about a possible ambush to his unit," Jessica said. "One text that contained classified information about his unit's location. He had no other way to warn them about it. He saved their lives. But since he used an unsecured cell phone, the classified information could have been accessed by anyone."

"He violated the security agreement that he signed on the day he was sworn in, which spelled it out in plain language," Murphy said. "Now, that marine didn't get any jail time, but he did receive a dishonorable discharge." He patted Mac on the back. "My CO did clear me to go over the case files with you, but first I need to filter out any classified material that's irrelevant to the case."

After giving Jessica one last kiss and giving Archie a hug, Murphy jogged out the door and climbed into Sheriff Turow's cruiser. After seeing the taillights of their car disappear into the night, Jessica turned away from the living-room window and offered to make Mac a cup of tea.

"I'd rather have a cognac," he said in a sulking tone. He was reminded of when he had a broken leg as a six-year-old and had been stuck on his family's front porch, watching his friends play football.

"You're not drinking with all of the drugs you're on," Archie said in a firm tone that dared him to argue with her.

"Then make a pot of coffee," Mac said to Jessica before turning to Archie. "Where are you and Dallas on the Sandy Burr case?"

"What's the Sandy Burr case?" Jessica asked.

"Sandy Burr was an investigative journalist who was murdered," Mac said. "The last person he was seen with was Nancy Braxton."

"The wacky candidate who claimed that she landed in Somalia under sniper fire?" Jessica said, recalling the outrageous story with a laugh.

"Whose team dug up Gnarly's past, spun it around into a complete lie, and gave it to that so-called journalist, ruining his reputation," Mac said, biting off each word.

Archie lifted one of her eyebrows. The corners of her lips curled with pleasure.

"Daddy," Jessica said in a chastising tone, "wasn't it you who used to tell me that when seeking revenge, you should dig two graves—one for yourself?"

"That witch didn't just expose Gnarly's past," Mac said, "that wouldn't have been enough for her. She lied about it, too. Turow said that Gnarly didn't kill his handler."

"Now that the lie is out there, no one is going to believe the real story," Archie said. "There will always be people out there who will believe that he's a killer."

"She buried Gnarly for political gain," Mac said. "I'm going to bury her the best way I know how. We're going to reopen Sandy Burr's murder case, and we're going to prove that she killed him."

"It's Dallas' case," Archie said. "And right now she and David are on their way to the emergency room with Storm. I don't think she's in the mood to go over the case with you tonight, and she may resent our taking it over while her back's turned."

"Wasn't Sandy Burr investigating Braxton Charities?" With a groan, Mac rubbed his face. "Let's get a list of all of the charities that fall under their umbrella."

Archie's emerald eyes were dancing. "Taking a page from your mother's book, I'll see if I can hack into its bank records to see who it distributes funds to. If Braxton Charities is really a money laundromat, we may be able to locate the phony charities that way." She ran downstairs to the study to get her laptop.

"What do you want me to do?" Jessica asked.

"Make a big pot of coffee," Mac said. "We're not going to rest until Nancy Braxton's political career is dead and buried. And maybe bring back some of those special brownies with the white chocolate chunks in them, too?"

"Sure. Coffee and brownies it is." Pausing at the kitchen door, Jessica noticed that a hint of color had returned to her father's face. Nothing made him happier than having a murder case to focus on.

"Someone's on your tail," Bogie said to Murphy in a loud whisper as they made their way through the thick, dark woods.

Unfamiliar with the area, Murphy had been paired with the deputy chief, and together they were climbing the steep ridge up Spencer Mountain. With LED flashlights, they were sweeping the brush in front of them for fallen branches, trees, and assorted critters.

All around them, near and far, police officers were calling Gnarly's name.

Bogie's warning made Murphy turn around in search of a creature sneaking up on him.

"Dallas Walker." With a chuckle, Bogie resumed his climb up the steep mountain.

"David's girlfriend?" Six feet to the older man's left, Murphy was slowly trekking up the slope and sweeping the ground in front of him for freshly broken branches or dog tracks that would indicate that Gnarly had been there. "Why would she be on my tail? She's with David, and she knows I'm married."

"She's an *investigative* journalist."

Murphy stopped in midstride.

Several feet above him, Bogie stopped and turned around, careful not to shine his flashlight in Murphy's face and blind him with the beam from the LED light. Although he was unable to see Bogie's face, Murphy could hear him laughing. "You said or did something to get on her radar, and knowing Dallas, she won't let up until she gets your story. You know who her mother was?"

"Her father was Buddy Walker," Murphy said. "The late Texas billionaire. Her brother, Phil, is the president of the family's billion-dollar conglomerate."

"Her mother was Audra Walker, the award-winning journalist who was like a dog with a bone when she was on a story. Dallas takes after her. She doesn't seem to have much interest in the family's oil business."

Murphy's voice fell to a whisper. "You didn't tell her about the Phantoms, did you? The only reason you guys know about them is because of that terrorist threat last year."

Bogie's whisper matched his. "Of course I didn't tell her. That's why I'm warning you." Turning around, he resumed his climb up the hill.

"Maybe I'll just tell her I'm a SEAL."

"I already told her that you're stationed at the Pentagon."

"If she knows I'm at the Pentagon, I can't tell her I'm a SEAL. There are no SEALS at the Pentagon. Why did you tell her I'm at the Pentagon?"

"She asked." Bogie shone his flashlight down at his feet.

"Just because she asked didn't mean you had to answer her."

Murphy joined him at a level portion of the mountainside. Without offering a reply, Bogie squatted down to observe the furry object lying in the dead leaves. Upon seeing the bloody tan fur in the light beam, Murphy caught his breath and squatted across from the deputy chief. He swept his flashlight across the animal in search of distinguishing characteristics. He was looking for a tail, paws, or a head that would determine whether it was a cat or a dog. It seemed to take him forever to search through the bloody corpse, and then he located one of its paws.

A cat paw.

Then their flashlights illuminated its neck, which had been ripped open, and its giant head. Murphy and Bogie let out sighs of relief.

"Looks like Gnarly came out the winner in this fight." Bogie grabbed his radio to share the news.

"He could still be hurt—and hurt bad." Murphy rose to his feet and searched the trees around them. "Gnarly, where are you?"

For the second time in fewer than twenty-four hours, David was sitting in a hospital's waiting room comforting someone he loved while someone she loved was being treated.

At one o'clock in the morning, the animal hospital was deserted, except for the vet and her assistant, who were in the operating room treating Storm. She had suffered deep scratches from her head to her tail and had bite marks where the mountain lion had tried to snap her neck.

Praying for her dog, Dallas fought the tears of fright that kept fighting their way to the surface. She alternated between pacing the cold and empty room and allowing David to hold her on the thin, worn sofa.

"I'm never allowin' her outside 'lone again," she said with a sigh. "Mountain lions? I never thought there'd be mountain lions here. We have them in Texas, but here?"

"It's been years since I heard of a mountain lion attacking a dog," David said. "Storm is up on all of her shots, right?"

"Of course," she said. "How 'bout Gnarly?"

"Archie is always all over that," David said while taking his vibrating phone out of its case on his hip. The caller ID indicated that it was Sheriff Turow.

"How's Storm?" the sheriff asked at the same time that the vet came out of the operating room. Dallas sprang off of the sofa to meet her.

Taking in the relief that had crossed Dallas' face and the hug that she was giving the veterinarian, David concluded that the news was good so far. "Did you find Gnarly?" he asked after bracing himself.

"Still haven't found him," the sheriff said. "But Bogie and Murphy found the mountain lion. Looks like Gnarly gave him some serious payback for hurting his girl. Tore him apart."

"I don't believe that," David said. "I have never heard of a dog taking down a mountain lion on his own."

"Neither have I," Sheriff Turow said. "I once heard of a pack of dogs taking down one mountain lion—six on one—and all of those dogs needed stitches."

"Then—"

"You don't know Gnarly very well, do you, O'Callaghan?" Sheriff Turow said. "That dog was trained by the best—my wife. He's not just brave—he's also smart and calculating. He took down two armed terrorists single-pawed. He could put together a plan to take down a mountain lion and walk away."

"Or he took him down and got so badly injured in the fight that he's bleeding out somewhere alone on that mountain," David said.

After assuring David that they would find Gnarly and that he'd be fine, Sheriff Turow disconnected the call. Putting on a brave face, David turned and saw Dallas smiling with tears of relief in her eyes. He took her into his arms and held her tight. "Storm is okay?"

Dallas nodded her head. Sniffling, she said, "She got a lot of stitches, especially on the back of the neck. The doctor said that it's a good thing that she has thick fur. Mostly, the cat was getting mouthfuls of fur. If she were a Doberman, she'd be dead. She's all patched up, and we can take her home in the mornin'." She let out a shuddering breath. "How's Gnarly? Did they find him?"

"They found the mountain lion—dead. But no sign of Gnarly. No one knows where he is or if he's seriously hurt—"

She placed her fingertips on David's lips. "You gave me strength while I was waitin' for word about Storm. Now it's my turn."

They sat down on the sofa and held each other for the rest of the night.

After an hour of studying everything she could find on the Internet about Braxton Charities, Archie had managed to break into Hugh Vance's e-mail account. From there, she'd been able to get the password for the charity's accounting program, which had provided her with a list of donors and the nonprofits to which they'd contributed.

While looking over the list of donors, many of whom were influential and powerful figures in Washington, DC, Jessica said, "Let me make sure I have this straight. These people make big contributions to Braxton Charities, which then turns around and gives the money to various charities under its umbrella."

"Minus twenty percent for *administrative* costs," Mac said.

"Including Nancy Braxton's limousine, chauffer, mansion, summer estate in Deep Creek Lake, servants, and executive assistants," Archie said, "to name a few."

"So some billionaire is looking for a tax break," Mac said, "and he gives one million dollars to Braxton Charities, which has been designated a nonprofit by the IRS. The billionaire gets the tax break. Braxton keeps twenty percent."

"Which is two hundred thousand," Jessica said after doing some quick calculations while refilling their coffee mugs.

"And then eight hundred thousand goes to the actual charities under the umbrella," Mac said.

"Or back to the billionaire via his offshore account," Archie said while searching through the accounting data on her screen. "Most of these charities are legit, but I am finding quite a few listed in Hugh Vance's records that aren't on Braxton Charities' website—and don't have an online presence. So far, the bank accounts listed for each one are located outside the United States."

"What a scam." Jessica took a brownie from the plate she had set in the middle of the dining room table.

"It's exactly like what Robin wrote in her book," Archie said.

"What did Robin write in her book?" Jessica asked.

"An organized-crime syndicate sets up a charitable foundation and has it designated as a nonprofit by bribing the head of the IRS. The mobsters launder the money they make off of drugs and prostitutes and extorting people through this foundation. The dirty money comes out clean on the other side, and the mobsters get a tax deduction, too," Archie said. "I honestly don't see Nancy Braxton rubbing elbows with the mob."

"How about with political movers and shakers?" Mac asked. "Who's on that list of donors?'

Placing her fingertip on the monitor, Archie scrolled through the list while Mac rested his chin on her shoulder. Jessica moved around the table to read the list with her. They pressed their heads together to study the names, taking note of the extensive list of members of congress, senators, judges, and presidential-cabinet members.

Jessica let out a laugh when she saw that one of the donors to Braxton Charities was the director of the Internal Revenue Service. "I wonder how much red tape he tied up Braxton Charities with before approving its application to be a nonprofit."

"My dear daughter," Mac said with a sideways glance in her direction. "I'm thinking that you inherited my suspicious mind."

There was a scratch at the door leading out to the deck.

"George Ward!" Mac said to Archie, ordering her to scroll back up the list.

"Who's George Ward?" Jessica asked.

"He's the state leader for Nancy Braxton's political party," Mac said. "He's basically been shoving her down our throats."

"He donated seventy-five thousand dollars to Braxton Charities," Archie said.

There was another scratch at the door. It was louder that time and was paired with a low bark.

"The state party chair is an appointed position," Archie said. "He's a lawyer in Annapolis. Has some big-name clients."

Out of the corner of her eye, Jessica noticed rapid movements in the direction of the deck. Once again, there was a low bark at the door.

"Hold your horses, Gnarly!" Mac said with impatience in his tone. "I'll be there in a minute!" Looking back at the screen of the laptop, he muttered, "Why is he so damn demanding?" He turned to Archie. "It's your fault for spoiling him."

There was a long silence during which they realized why they had been up all night.

Jessica leaned over to one side and peered around the monitor while Mac looked around its other side. Archie stood up and gazed over the top of it.

Sitting at attention, Gnarly cocked his head at them. He uttered a loud bark at the door, commanding them to allow him into his home. He probably thought that breakfast would've been nice, too. He was covered in dried blood.

Archie and Jessica sprang into action at the same time. Archie reached the door first.

On the other side of the window, Gnarly's face, chest, and mane were covered with blood, but he was obviously in good shape, judging by how he was jumping and clawing at the door. As soon as Archie threw open the door, he ran into the kitchen and gulped down most of the water in his bowl. When he was finished, he stuck his snout in his food dish. Finding it empty, he looked over at the door where Mac, Archie, and Jessica were watching him and trying to determine if he'd been hurt. Gnarly looked down at the empty bowl and then back at them. When they didn't move, the German shepherd sat down and looked once again at the bowl. Then, turning his attention back to them, he barked at them as though he were barking an order.

"Well, as your grandmother used to say," Mac said to Jessica, "as long as you're hungry, you must be okay."

While Archie filled the dog's food bowl, Mac knelt down in front of him to examine him for wounds suffered in his altercation with the mountain lion. The German shepherd was more interested in filling his tummy than in getting first aid.

Jessica grabbed her cell phone and called Murphy to relay the news. She reached him after two rings. "Good news, honeybuns. Gnarly came home, and he seems to be okay."

"Great," Murphy said without humor. "Our news isn't so good."

"Is it Storm?"

"No, she's fine," Murphy said. "Bogie and I had looped around and were making our way back along the lake in your direction when we found something."

"Something?"

"Someone, really."

"Who?"

"Nancy Braxton. She's dead."

CHAPTER FOURTEEN

David O'Callaghan had gotten only a couple of hours of sleep, but that didn't matter. A storm was brewing. It would be impossible to keep the news of the death of Nancy Braxton, a philanthropist and political leader and the wife of the Super Bowl–champion quarterback Nathan Braxton, away from the media. Questions and speculation would certainly fly. It would only be a matter of time before Gnarly's political enemies would discover that he'd been missing at the time of her death, and fingers would be pointed at him.

If it had been any other time, Dallas Walker would have been all over David, wanting to tag along with him to the crime scene, but at the moment, her focus was elsewhere.

By eight o'clock in the morning, the Belgian shepherd was coming out of the anesthesia, and the vet released her. The thick, lovely sable fur around her neck and shoulders and down her back to her shoulder blades had been shaved so that the vet could clean up and stitch her wounds. They had also shaved off patches of fur on both sides of her hips where the mountain lion's hind claws had dug into her flesh after pouncing on her back. Soon, the vet assured Dallas, the dog's fur would grow back and would be as thick and as plush as it had been before the fight. Hopefully, Storm wouldn't have any scars. To keep her from scratching or chewing on her stitches, the vet had fitted her with the cone of shame—a large, white cone collar.

The vet, her assistant, Dallas, and David loaded Storm, who was on a stretcher, into the backseat of David's police cruiser. Dallas climbed in and rode next to her to keep her quiet. As soon as David pulled up in front of his house, Sheriff Turow and a half dozen sheriff deputies and Spencer police officers met them with a stretcher.

Helping Dallas out of the backseat, Sheriff Turow said, "We'll take care of Storm." He took the IV that the vet had sent home with her. "You go get yourself something to eat. Tonya has fresh coffee inside, and we have enough breakfast to feed an army."

"Tonya made breakfast?" David asked with a cringe. Tonya had never made any bones about being able to or liking to cook.

"Catered by the Spencer Inn," the sheriff said. "Mac ordered it for everyone as thanks for spending the whole night looking for Gnarly, who showed up at Spencer Manor just in time for breakfast. Grab yourself something to eat fast, O'Callaghan. Doc Washington is already at the crime scene."

Inside the house, Tonya placed a hot mug of coffee in Dallas' hands. Dallas hadn't realized that they were cold until she felt the warmth of the fresh coffee. "How are you doing, Dallas?"

Watching the men carrying Storm into the house and placing her carefully on the dog bed that had been supplemented with an old comforter for added comfort, Dallas said, "I know you must think I'm silly. After all, Storm is just a dog."

"You're not the least bit silly," Tonya said.

Dallas tore her attention from Storm to look at Tonya, who was smiling softly. "I have four dogs, and I'm closer to all of them than I am to my own children. I keep threatening to leave my house to them."

"Your dogs?"

"They have more common sense and are more self-sufficient than any of my kids."

Dallas was still making sense of that news when David came up on her other side to kiss her on the cheek. He had made a sandwich out of the food that had been delivered by the Spencer Inn and had wrapped it in a paper towel.

"I gotta go, hon," he said. "Nancy Braxton's body was found down the road. Turow and I need to get out in front of this before it hits the news." He cocked his head at her. "Are you okay?"

With a shuddering breath, she nodded her head.

"She probably needs some sleep." Tonya wrapped an arm around her shoulders. "I'm willing to bet she was up all night." She gestured for him to be on his way. "I'll stay with her and take care of Storm. You go do your thing, Chief. Don't you worry. I've got this covered."

Shooting a grateful grin in Tonya's direction, David hugged Dallas and kissed her again before trotting out the door after Sheriff Turow.

Juggling his breakfast as he drove, David followed the sheriff's cruiser along the lakeshore road to a turnoff a little over a mile from his house. The dirt road had been carved through the brush and ended near a makeshift boat launch frequented by small fishing boats. It was off the beaten trail, and only those familiar with the area knew about it. A gravel footpath from the Glendale Road Bridge ran along the lake's shoreline to the cove where David lived.

When they approached the crime scene, they found that some Spencer police officers, led by Bogie, had already strung up crime-scene tape to cut off vehicles' access to the area, which forced David and Sheriff Turow to park behind the medical examiner's SUV on the opposite side of the road.

After making their way down the rutted dirt road, Sheriff Turow and David came upon Murphy Thornton, who was looking surprisingly fresh after spending the night searching through the woods. He was sitting with his legs crossed on top of a tree stump frequently for fishing from the shore. As he texted on his cell phone, he leaned over with an elbow resting on each knee, and he seemed to be effortlessly pressing his knees down flat. Because he was the son of a prosecuting attorney and had experience with criminal investigations, Murphy was sitting away from the crime scene in order to not contaminate it—he was leaving it to Bogie and the local police.

"'Bout time you guys got here," he said with a grin while thumbing away on his phone. "I thought Bogie was going to have to solve this case by himself."

"Don't be a smartass, Thornton," David said while glancing beyond Murphy to where Sheriff Turow was conferring with Bogie and Doc.

"You do know Gnarly's home?" One of his eyebrows arched while he cast David a sideways glance out of the corner of his blue eyes.

David nodded his head. "Turow told me."

"He showed up at Spencer Manor about thirty minutes ago." Murphy jerked his thumb in the direction of the medical examiner. "Doc says Braxton died about seven hours ago, and she's got bite marks on her. Gnarly would have gone right past here to go home, and no one knows where he was when she was killed."

David crossed his arms in a sign of defiance. "Gnarly would not have killed her unless she was coming after him or someone he loved."

"Try telling the media supporting Nancy Braxton that," Murphy said with a grin that indicated that he was playing with the police chief's mind. "Word is already out on social media about Gnarly being missing last night. Once people find out that his political opponent is dead—" He shook his head. "Does Gnarly have an alibi?"

David wanted to slap the dimples off of Murphy's handsome face. Grumbling about how no one had a right to look that good after a night of thrashing through the deep woods, David brushed past him to join Doc, Bogie, and Sheriff Turow where Nancy Braxton was lying face down in the water. Her bare feet and legs, encased in filthy white, silky pajamas, were spread in the dirt and weeds of the shore, and her upper body was resting in the water. Her clothes were soiled with muddy lake water, grass stains, and blood. They were torn, and it looked like an animal had ripped them open to gnaw on her bloated flesh.

Without the medical examiner pointing it out, David saw the bloody wound at the back of Nancy Braxton's head.

"Murphy said that the time of death was around one in the morning?" David asked. "Do you know the cause yet?"

"Not an animal attack," Doc said while shooting a glance in the young man's direction. "Murphy was pulling your leg."

David held up his finger. "Hold that thought." He crossed over to the tree stump where Murphy was still texting away and delivered a slap to the back of his head. Scrambling to keep hold of his phone with one hand, Murphy grabbed the back of his head with the other. "Quit being a smartass."

After David rejoined the group surrounding the dead body, Doc gestured at the bloody wound in the back of

Nancy's head. "I won't know until I open her up, but it could be either blunt-force trauma or drowning or a combination of the two. The bite marks were made by a scavenger hours after she was already dead. See the lack of blood around the bite marks? She's been lying here facedown for a while. You'll notice that the blood drained away from her back, where the bite marks are, and settled in her front and abdomen. Yet the blood from the wound to the back of her head soaked her hair. She was alive when she was struck in the back of the head."

David glanced around where the politician was lying and up onto the shore, looking for a rock with blood on it or for anything else that could've been used as a weapon. Taking note of Nancy Braxton's bruised and scraped, bare feet, he asked if she could have slipped along the muddy shoreline and fallen, hit her head on a rock, and, in a daze, passed out and drowned. "Could it have been an accident?"

With a knowing grin, Doc Washington shrugged her shoulders.

"I know. You need to open her up first."

David saw Murphy bring his cell phone to his ear, opting to cease texting to take a call instead. He unfolded his legs and stood up from the tree stump to move down the footpath and farther away from them.

Rising to his feet, David looked up and down the shoreline. They were at least two and a half miles along the shore from where Nancy Braxton's estate was located, and then her home was another half of a mile straight up a rocky cliff.

Glancing back down at Nancy's lifeless body, David took note of her lack of a bathrobe and slippers. "She could have been dumped here." Squatting down to examine her feet, he said, "She was walking around outside in her bare feet." Freshly disturbed gravel and broken weeds indicated a recent struggle in the same spot where her body had been found. "There was a struggle here recently."

"Based on lividity," Doc said, "she died here."

"What was she doing here in the middle of the night without a robe or slippers?" David asked.

"Good question," Sheriff Turow said.

Finished with his phone call, Murphy approached them.

"Anybody notify her family yet?" David asked Bogie.

"No," Bogie said. "We decided to let you and Turow have all the fun. By the way, no one has reported her missing either."

Murphy cleared his throat. "As much fun as I'm having right now, is it possible for someone to give me a ride back to Spencer Manor? I need to get back to Washington—today."

After directing David to go on to the Braxtons' estate to break the news, Sheriff Turow offered to drive Murphy back.

With a crook of his finger, Murphy led Sheriff Turow and David away from where Doc and Bogie were examining the body. "I just talked to my commanding officer. She read through your wife's case file last night, Turow, and has ordered me back to Washington to take over the case."

"Did your CO find something?" Hope came to Sheriff Turow's eyes.

"She noticed a similarity in Sergeant Perkins' case and a case we're already working on," Murphy said. "That's all I can tell you."

Sheriff Turow eased his police cruiser between two groups camped outside of the entrance of Spencer Manor. On one side of the road, picketers were proclaiming their support of Gnarly. They were donning shirts with Gnarly's face on them that read "I love Gnarly," "Vote for Gnarly," and "He's Not Snarly, Vote for Gnarly." They further made their point by waving signs that read "Innocent until Proven Guilty," and "Vast Human Conspiracy."

On the other side of the road were townspeople demanding that Gnarly be banned because he was a threat to the community. Their signs had Gnarly's picture with blood dripping from his mouth on them.

Journalists rushed from one side of the road to the other with their microphones and cameras in search of newsworthy sound bites.

As the sheriff rolled past the crowds, he saw Bernie and Hap front and center of the pro-Gnarly group with a horde of journalists in front of them.

"We all know what this is," Bernie said into the microphones. "This is nothing more than a vast human conspiracy, and we won't stand for it!" Bernie and Hap shook their fists at the group across the street. The supporters behind them chanted, "He's not snarly! Vote for Gnarly!"

Upon seeing the sheriff's cruiser, journalists shouted out questions about Gnarly killing his handler and about how had he disappeared the night before. They asked whether such a vicious dog with a history of murder should be permitted in Spencer.

"The sad part," Murphy said to the sheriff, "is that since Belle's mission with Gnarly is classified, we're unable to tell the media the truth about what happened."

By the time Murphy and Sheriff Turow climbed out of the cruiser, Bernie and Hap's group had changed their song. "Gnarly! Gnarly! Gnarly!"

When Murphy saw the cameras recording their walk inside, he pulled his ball cap down on his head, adjusted his sunglasses, and turned his back to them.

"You look better than you did last night," Sheriff Turow said, pleasantly surprised to see Mac up and about.

"Nothing like a murder case to get Dad on the mend," Jessica said while hugging Murphy.

"We think we found the dirt on Nancy Braxton's charitable foundation." Mac waved the report so that the sheriff could see it. "It could be what Sandy Burr discovered during his investigation."

"Speaking of investigations," Murphy said, "I need to go back to Washington today."

"Why?" Jessica's question came out as a whine.

"CO thinks she found something in Belle Perkins' murder case," Murphy said. "She wants me to take over the case."

"Will it clear Gnarly's name?" Mac asked.

At the sound of his name, Gnarly trotted down the stairs from the master bedroom. In his mouth, he was carrying the toy squirrel that the sheriff had given him earlier. Upon seeing the sheriff, the dog stopped in front of him and sat down.

"We'll definitely clear Gnarly's name and identify Belle Perkins' killer," Murphy said. "Which leads to a request from my CO." Squatting down next to Gnarly, he petted the German shepherd from the top of his head down his back. "She wants me to bring Gnarly back with me."

"Why?" Even Mac was shocked by the defensive tone in his question. Somewhere in the back of his mind, he feared that Gnarly would not return if he went to Washington.

"Gnarly is a witness," Murphy said to the sheriff over his shoulder. "He was there when Belle Perkins was killed. Dogs' sense of smell is forty times stronger than ours. He was the first one on the scene—before any of the evidence was disturbed."

"Even if he was asleep at the time of the murder," Mac said, "Gnarly could have smelled the killer's scent on Belle, and he could be able to identify him from that scent."

"A couple of members of Belle's unit stated that Gnarly went nuts when everyone entered her tent after he found the body," Sheriff Turow said. "One of the men who knew dogs very well calmed him down. Gnarly was so upset that everyone was afraid of him, so he was crated from then until he arrived back in the States."

"He probably went nuts because he smelled the killer when he entered the crime scene with the rest of Belle's team," Mac said.

"But no one understood that he was identifying his handler's killer." Archie reached out to stroke the dog's ears.

"I'll listen to you, Gnarly." Murphy looked deep into Gnarly's almond-shaped eyes.

CHAPTER FIFTEEN

Considering that he hadn't gone to bed, David found it hard to believe that it wasn't quite nine thirty in the morning when he pulled up to the closed gates of the Braxtons' estate and pressed the security button.

"Chief O'Callaghan?" Erin Devereux said over the speaker.

"Good morning," David said. "I'm here to see Nathan Braxton, please."

There was a pause before Erin responded via the speaker. "If this is about the break-in the other night, Sheriff Turow is handling that."

Preferring a face-to-face conversation to hanging out of the side window of his cruiser and yelling into the intercom, David sighed. "No, this isn't about the break-in. I need to speak to Mr. Braxton. It's important."

"I'm afraid he hasn't come down for breakfast yet."

"Get him up," David said. "Look, if it's more convenient for you, I can come back later with my whole police force, which I'm sure will get the attention of your neighbors and the media."

Instantly, there was a click, and the gates opened.

Her arm in a sling from the gunshot, Erin Devereux met David O'Callaghan in the foyer of the Braxtons' home. "Everyone is getting a slow start today," she said. "We were up late last night after the debate. Ms. Braxton was quite anxious to go over the details of what had come out." The assistant lowered her eyes to peer at David through her long eyelashes. "I'm sorry your candidate got ambushed the way he did." A poor actress, Erin failed to control the curl at one corner of her mouth, which gave away her lack of sincerity.

"I need to see Nathan Braxton as soon as possible," David said. "Can you or one of his people wake him up?"

"The Braxtons don't like to be disturbed when they are sleeping."

"What's the problem, Erin?" Hugh Vance said from the top of the stairs. He was dressed in a pair of white pants that accentuated his wide girth and casual clothes for golf.

"Chief O'Callaghan is insisting on talking to Nathan about something. He says it's important."

Hugh had reached the bottom of the stairs. With a smug expression, he asked, "What is this about?"

"When was the last time you saw your sister?" David asked.

David noticed a long trade of expressions between Nancy's brother and assistant before Hugh decided to answer him. "Last night. Right before we all went to bed. Was it eleven o'clock, Erin?"

"Maybe a little after," Erin said. "Closer to eleven thirty. Why?"

"I'm sorry to tell you this, Mr. Vance," David said in a gentler tone, "but your sister was found down by the lake this morning."

After letting out a high-pitched screech, Hugh Vance covered his mouth with his hands and sank down onto the step.

"She's dead," David said. "I'm sorry."

Erin sat down next to the distraught man and draped her arm across his shoulders. "What happened? How—"

"We're still investigating it," David said. "The medical examiner will be doing an autopsy."

"What was she doing down there?" Erin asked. "I saw her go upstairs to her room right after our meeting to go over the debate."

"I'm sorry to intrude on you at this difficult time," David said, "but I do need to ask all of you some questions."

"Where's Sheriff Turow?" Hugh said, standing up. "Shouldn't he be in charge of this investigation?"

"Since your police department is endorsing Gnarly, you do have a conflict of interest," Erin said. "How do we know you didn't kill her to eliminate the competition?"

"To win an election for mayor in a town with fewer than a thousand residents?" Shaking his head at them, David said, "Sheriff Turow is leading this investigation, and he will be here soon. In the meantime, until he gets here—"

"Erin, what are the police doing here?"

The front door slammed behind Nathan Braxton as he came in. David recognized the expensive suit—it was the same one he had seen on the live stream of the debate. Nathan had removed his tie and had undone the first three buttons of his shirt, but it was the same suit. Based on his slightly rumbled appearance, David doubted that he had been to bed—at least not to the bed in his home.

"Mr. Braxton." David stepped forward and offered him his hand.

Nathan Braxton gave his hand a firm shake. "Did you and Sheriff Turow locate the burglar who shot Erin?" He looked from David to Hugh and Erin.

David swallowed. "It's about your wife—"

Nathan's eyes closed. He sucked in a deep breath. "I guess we should talk in the study."

"I'm sorry to tell you that it appears that your wife has been murdered."

Nathan's eyes popped open. David saw stunned disbelief cross his face for only an instant before Erin rushed forward to hug him tightly.

Hugh's voice was shaking. "She was killed down at the lake."

"What was she doing there?" Nathan asked. "Who?" He directed his gaze at David. "What happened?"

"Oh, Mr. Braxton, I'm so sorry," Erin said. "I can't believe it either. We were all together just last night and were planning for her to win the election."

Sniffling, Hugh slapped his brother-in-law on the back. "We're all in shock." When he tried to lead Nathan into the study, they found David O'Callaghan blocking their path.

"Excuse me, Mr. Braxton," David said. "I know this is a very difficult time, but we do have some questions that we need answered. The sooner we talk, the sooner we'll be able to get to the bottom of what happened to your wife."

"Shouldn't we call our lawyer first?" Hugh asked.

"Yes, you should," George Ward said upon entering through the front door without pausing to knock first.

David was about to ask who had called the state chairman of their political party when Bogie hurried in behind him and ushered the police chief aside. "Talked to the security company. They have security cameras at the front gate, the backyard, and both sides. Motion activated. They're sending us the recordings from last night."

Half listening, David was more concerned about his witnesses comparing notes...and getting their stories straight. "Great," he said to Bogie over his shoulder while breaking up the group. Upon seeing Officers Fletcher and Zigler walk through the door, David directed them to stay with Erin Devereux and told Bogie to get a statement from Hugh

Vance while he questioned the victim's husband in the living room.

As soon as they were out of earshot of the others, David looked Nathan Braxton up and down. "Can you tell me what happened last night after the debate?"

"There's really nothing to tell." Nathan lowered himself down into a wingback chair. "Once the debate was over, Nancy and her entourage came home, and I went to the bar." He looked up at David. "How was she killed?"

"The medical examiner has to finish her exam first. Why didn't you come home with your wife?"

Nathan offered David a small grin. "I'm sure you've heard about my reputation. The womanizing."

"I've heard some stories," David said. "I try not to pay attention to rumors. So many end up being false."

"Most of what you've heard about my womanizing is true," Nathan said with a smile of pride. "Especially those about the Stimulator."

"The Stimulator?"

"When you're married to an arctic ice queen like Nancy, believe me, you need some sort of emotional stimulation," Nathan said. "As soon as Nancy would leave town for one of her many fund-raising endeavors for Braxton Charities, the Stimulator would swoop in to defrost me."

"How did your wife feel about that?"

"As long as she had deniability—as long as she could claim that she didn't know anything about it, and people could half-way believe her—she was fine."

Unable to conceal the doubt on his face, David cocked his head at him.

"Nancy and I had an agreement." Nathan pulled a cigar and a lighter out of his jacket pocket. "She enjoyed the money and the connections that she hoped would grant her access to the power that she was obsessed with obtaining, and that money and those connections came from being Nathan Braxton's wife."

He paused to light the cigar. After a few puffs, he blew a smoke ring and continued. "I enjoyed the company of other women. As long as I was discreet and didn't jeopardize her political ambitions, I could do what I wanted—and she could do whatever she wanted as long as I didn't need to be subjected to the company of her idiot political friends."

"Did you love your wife?" David was surprised by his direct question.

He was even more surprised by Nathan's blunt response. "No." He shrugged. "Nancy was a very difficult person to love. Even worse, she was extremely difficult to like, which is why she had to bribe her political party before it would endorse her—or commit voter fraud for her, if the rumors are to be believed. She had to get elected to an office someplace so that she could live out her fantasy of being queen." He ended his statement in a mocking tone.

"Do you have any proof that your wife bribed her political party or that it committed voter fraud?"

Nathan chuckled before answering him in a whisper. "The legal term is 'donation.' Nancy made sure that large amounts of money went from Braxton Charities to her party. I doubt if it's written down anywhere, but the agreement between those at the top and Nancy was understood."

David peered at the former football star, who appeared to still be enjoying the sports-celebrity lifestyle to the max. Nathan Braxton was an attractive man who kept fit even though he was in his late fifties. "Okay," the police chief said. "About last night. Your wife and her 'entourage' came home, and you stayed at the Spencer Inn. Did you meet the Stimulator at the hotel?"

"She has a name." Nathan reached for David's pen and notepad. "Eleanor Singleton." He glanced up at him. "I assume you can be discreet about this."

"We can't promise anything," David said. "Were you with her the whole time?"

"Even had room service bring up breakfast," Nathan said. "Call Eleanor. I met her in the lounge at the Spencer Inn. The bartender will confirm we were there. He knows both me and Eleanor. After a couple of drinks, we went up to her room—shortly after ten thirty."

David checked her name and phone number and the room number in which she was staying. "How long have you and Eleanor been together?"

"Seven years," Nathan said without hesitation.

"And your mistress is okay with that?" David asked. "Most mistresses would be anxious to get rid of the wife and to move into the number-one slot."

"Not Eleanor," Nathan said. "I take very good care of her. She has a fabulous condo. Clothes. A car. She's free to come and go and to do what she wants—even enjoy the company of other men. She travels—sometimes with me and sometimes without me. She has her own business—interior decorating. She has all of the fun and perks of having a career with none of the strings of a husband and a family to hold her back."

"And you got to escape from a wife who you didn't even like," David said. "If you don't mind my asking—"

"Why did I marry Nancy?"

David nodded his head. "You just told me that you didn't even like her."

"At one time I did," Nathan said. "But then she changed. Nancy was always independent and ambitious. She wanted more than money. Her family had that. No, she had to have power—and she was willing to say or do anything to get it. When I set up the foundation, I did so with the intention of giving her something to do that would make her feel like a top dog—that would let her meet all of these celebrities and politicians and influential people and feel like a part of it. But the more she got, the more she had to have. Until that was all that it was about."

David frowned. "Can you think of anyone who disliked your wife enough to want to kill her?"

Nathan paused to consider his answer. "Anyone and everyone who has ever met her."

Bogie was finishing up his interview with Hugh Vance when David left Nathan Braxton. When the police chief entered the study, Bogie joined him at the doorway. Visibly upset, Hugh was sitting with his head in his hands.

"Anything?" David asked.

"He and his sister were close," Bogie said. "She was the typical bossy older sister. Demanding and difficult. I asked if there might be any disgruntled former employees." He chuckled. "He asked how long I had to listen to the list. Many were former employees of the charity. Most were former assistants who'd worked directly with Nancy. According to him, few lasted a year before Nancy fired them, claiming that they were working in cahoots with her political enemies to discredit her, or they quit, saying they'd rather live on the streets than work for an abusive witch. Erin Devereux is a record breaker. She's lasted three years."

"Wow," David said. "Sounds almost like the mystery isn't who killed Nancy Braxton but why it took so long for him or her to do it."

Crossing the study in Hugh's direction, the police chief said, "Mr. Vance, earlier Erin said that last night, everyone stayed up to go over the debate. Were you part of that meeting?"

"Yes," Hugh said. "We met here." He indicated the study.

"Who was included in that meeting?"

"Nancy, Erin, George, and I," he said. "Nathan had some business that he had to take care of at the Spencer Inn."

David suppressed a chuckle at the reference to "business." "How did that meeting go?"

"Very well." Hugh's voice went up an octave, and his eyebrows shot up onto his high forehead.

"No disagreements?"

Instead of answering him, Hugh stared at his hands.

"Mr. Vance?"

"I guess it doesn't matter now," Hugh said. "Salma Rameriz was here, too." He sighed.

"You didn't mention her being here earlier," David said.

"Because Salma's public persona is supposed to be fair and unbiased," Hugh said.

"Funny—I never thought of her as being anything but *unfair* and *biased*," Bogie said. He was still wounded from the previous night's attack on Gnarly.

"Truth is," Hugh said, "Salma was always a big supporter of Nancy's. They became good friends when Nancy ran for the state senate...and lost. Every time Nancy ran for office, Salma dug up dirt on her opponent and blew it out of proportion to discredit him."

"Like that *lie* about Gnarly killing his handler in the army," Bogie said with a low growl while moving in on Hugh.

"*We* had nothing to do with that." Hugh held up his hands as if to block any blow that might come his way. "That's the thing. Salma thought that we'd sent that story to her and told her to bring it up at the debate, but we hadn't. Yes, Erin had dug up some story about Gnarly sneaking into a four-star general's tent in Afghanistan and eating the steak dinner he had ordered for himself while the rest of the troop was having overcooked chicken—which shows utter disrespect for authority! But that was it!" He waved his hands. "We knew *nothing* about Gnarly killing his handler. But Salma thought that we had sent it! When we got back here last night, Salma was laughing about what a coup we had pulled and congratulating us on getting that story. We thought she had dug it up! Salma told us that Erin had sent her the story!" He mopped his brow. "That was when things blew up."

"How did they blow up?" David asked.

Hugh uttered a deep sigh. "Somehow it got out on social media that Nancy had planted the phony story about Gnarly killing his handler. There were copies of the e-mail that Erin had sent to Salma admitting that the whole story was a lie—only Erin swore that the e-mail hadn't come from her. Then the death threats came in."

"Death threats? What death threats?"

Hugh was nodding his head. "Gnarly's supporters are very devoted to him. We all saw that. They're a bunch of fanatics!"

"I wouldn't call them fanatics," David said.

"Can't you see he's a *dog?*"

"Nancy was a pathological *liar!*" David said.

"At least she didn't drink out of the toilet!"

"Gnarly served his *country!* All Nancy served was *herself*."

Throwing his muscular bulk between the two angry men to hold them back, Bogie shushed them. "Now let's just try to get along." Patting David on the shoulder, he ushered him out of striking distance of Hugh.

"Nancy and her team were not newbies," Hugh said. "They knew that they would have to be very careful in discrediting Gnarly. I mean, you couldn't call out Santa Claus for being a child molester—even if he were—without having to duck bullets from people wanting to shoot the messenger. So Nancy and her team knew right off that when it came to discrediting Gnarly, they would have to make sure that the source couldn't be traced back to them. That way, Gnarly would be out of the race, and Nancy would be standing there clean and mud-free. But it didn't happen that way. Immediately it was all over the Internet that the root of the smear campaign against Gnarly had come from Nancy's camp. Within an hour of getting home last night, Nancy got two death threats, and Gnarly supporters were trashing her on social media."

While David and Bogie were digesting that information, Hugh shook his finger at them. "You need to take a look at those loony dog lovers. They're the ones who killed Nancy. Never did trust dog lovers. They're all nuts. At least you can trust a cat person."

"Did Nancy or anyone on her team have suspicions about who'd planted that story?" David asked him.

Hugh rubbed his chin. "Nancy worked hard."

"That's not an answer. Who did she think planted that story and released the e-mail on social media?"

"She blamed Erin," Hugh said before hurriedly adding, "But that was only because Erin's name was on the e-mail that went to Salma, and Salma didn't notice that it wasn't Erin's real e-mail account."

"Why would Erin have wanted to hurt Nancy politically?" David asked.

"That's the thing!" Hugh flapped his arms. "Erin wouldn't have! Nancy was demanding and particular and temperamental, and Erin put up with all of it because she believed in her. Erin knew enough about politics to see that if the people in Spencer even suspected Nancy of smearing Gnarly, her own ranking would go down."

"Nancy must have had some reason to suspect Erin of doing it," Bogie said.

Hugh slumped. "I wish I could tell you."

David and Bogie exchanged glances, and then the police chief said, "You said earlier that everyone went to bed last night shortly after eleven."

"Around eleven thirty," Hugh said.

David noted that that was the time Erin Devereux had said when he'd first arrived.

"After the second threatening phone call, Nancy slammed down the phone, told Erin she was fired, and stormed up the stairs. At that point, the meeting ended. George and Salma left together."

"What was Nancy wearing when you last saw her?" David asked.

Hugh hesitated before he answered. "A pantsuit. Her red one. The same one she was wearing at the debate."

After thanking Hugh, David and Bogie made their way back to the foyer.

"Am I being biased in thinking that it would be right up Bill Clark's alley to leak that story about Gnarly and make it look like it came from Nancy Braxton's camp?" David whispered to Bogie.

"Not at all. But having done that, Clark wouldn't have had any reason to kill Braxton."

"Unless after her temper tantrum, she realized that Erin had been telling the truth and that it hadn't come from her," David said. "So she decided to confront Clark and expose him."

"In her jammies?"

"I want to see those security recordings as soon as we get them."

His arms folded across his chest, George Ward was waiting for them in the foyer. "Gentlemen, word is already leaking out to the media about Nancy Braxton's passing. We need to make a statement. Is Nancy's death being investigated as an accident or a murder?"

"Right now, we're investigating it as a murder," David said.

"And where is Gnarly Faraday on your list of suspects?"

Stunned, David had no answer.

George Ward's wide grin was smug. "My sources are telling me that Gnarly Faraday is missing—that he has been all night. Now, considering that he killed his handler in the army—"

"Gnarly did *not* kill his handler!" Sheriff Turow said as he entered the foyer.

The force of his voice knocked every ounce of arrogance out of George Ward's body.

With the commanding presence of his position, the sheriff stepped up close to George Ward, invading his space. "I have sources too, and I know for a fact that Gnarly never laid a paw on his handler. Yes, she was murdered, brutally murdered, but Gnarly was never even a suspect. Now, you will cease repeating that lie here and now. From this moment on, anyone who repeats it will answer directly to me, and when I track down the source of that lie—and I will—that person is going to find out what we do to liars in my jurisdiction." He lowered his voice to a harsh whisper. "It ain't pretty. Do you understand me, Mr. Ward?"

"Yes, Sheriff." George Ward cleared his throat. "My sources told me that Gnarly is missing."

"Your sources are wrong. Gnarly is home with his family."

"They also said Nancy that had bite marks on her body."

"Raccoons," the sheriff said while putting on his evidence gloves. "Common scavengers in these parts. They bit her hours after she died."

"My sources said she was found in the lake," George said. "Did she drown? Considering that she couldn't swim, it sounds like it was most likely a horrible accident."

"Could've been," Sheriff Turow said. "But then she died in the middle of the night, and she wasn't wearing a swimsuit. And since you said she couldn't swim—"

While George digested that information, Sheriff Turow gestured up the stairs. "Have you taken a look at her bedroom, O'Callaghan?"

"After you." David gestured for the sheriff to lead the way. "We haven't spoken to Erin Devereux yet."

They located Nancy Braxton's assistant in the kitchen, where Officer Fletcher was keeping her separate from the rest of the witnesses. On the way down the upstairs hallway to Nancy's suite, David brought up Hugh Vance's statement about Nancy firing her the night before, which prompted a loud laugh.

"Ms. Braxton fired me at least once a week."

"From what I've heard, she was very difficult to work for," David said.

Erin paused with her hand on the door leading into her late boss' bedroom. "The best word to describe her is 'abusive.' Practically every morning, we began with this greeting: I would say, 'Good morning, Ms. Braxton.' You'd think that after three years, we would've moved on to 'Nancy.' No chance with Ms. Braxton. She relished her position of authority. So every morning when I saw her, I would say, 'Good morning, Ms. Braxton,' to which she would reply, every morning, 'F you.' Only she didn't say the letter—she said the word."

"*Every* morning?" Bogie asked.

"*Every* morning."

"Why didn't you quit?" David asked.

"Because through Ms. Braxton I met some of the most influential movers and shakers in Washington." Erin opened the door with a flourish. "I had no intention of ending my career while I was still an executive assistant to an arctic ice queen. I fully intended to one day become a mover and a shaker in my own right." She flashed them a broad smile. "Today may be that day."

"You certainly aren't broken up about the death of your boss," David said.

"I think you're going to have to search far and wide to find someone who is sincerely broken up about Ms. Braxton's death," Erin said. "Salma Rameriz may be. She bought every lie Ms. Braxton told hook, line, and sinker. To Salma, Ms. Braxton was God's gift to America."

"Where's your room?" Sheriff Turow asked.

Erin pointed to the room across the hallway. "Ms. Braxton liked to keep me close in case she needed me for anything in the middle of the night. I was on duty with her twenty-four-seven."

"Did you hear her leave last night?" David asked.

With a firm shake of her head, Erin answered that she hadn't. She waited in the open doorway while the sheriff, the police chief, and the deputy chief searched the room.

Inside the bedroom, Bogie pointed out the white silk bathrobe draped across the foot of the bed and the slippers on the floor. The red pantsuit that Nancy Braxton had worn at the debate was draped across a chair by her vanity.

David studied the collection of cosmetics, antiaging creams, and jewelry that, while organized and neatly placed, covered the vanity except for one bare spot on the right side of it. A half-full glass rested in front of the right side of the mirror, and there was a bare area in front of it. Bending over, David was able to make out three perfectly round impressions in the dust pattern around the glass.

He peered under the vanity and found that the wooden trash can was empty except for a fresh white liner. "When does the cleaning lady come clean?"

"Thursdays," Erin answered.

"Which is today," David said.

"She came a bit ago," Bogie said, "and we sent her home."

"So this room hasn't been cleaned in a week, which explains the dust on the vanity." David held out the trash can to Erin. "Who emptied the trash?"

"I guess Ms. Braxton did," Erin said.

David, Bogie, and even Sheriff Turow laughed.

"Try again," David said. "Where is the trash that was in this can, and what was in it?"

"Nothing," Erin said. "If anything was in it, Ms. Braxton—"

"You expect us to believe that an arctic ice queen who lorded her position over everyone would have lowered herself to touch the trash with her own superior hands!" David said.

Bogie was already on his radio ordering the officers and deputies to not let any garbage leave the estate without being searched.

"We're going to find out what you're trying to hide from us, and when we do, you'll be charged with obstruction of justice," Sheriff Turow said.

Erin stood up to her full height. "Do you need me for anything else? If not, I'm going to go call my lawyer now." Without waiting for an answer, she left the room. They heard the clatter of her heels on the stairs.

David moved into the bathroom, where he opened the medicine cabinet. Based on the water glass and the size of the dust rings, he suspected that Erin was covering up medications that Nancy Braxton had been taking. The shelves in the medicine cabinet behind the mirror were filled with pain medicine, over-the-counter sleeping pills, cold medicine, vitamins, and other over-the-counter medicines and hygiene products—except for the center of the bottom shelf, where there was a blank space. Once again, the round pattern in the daily accumulation of household soil indicated a recent removal of the pill bottles that had occupied the space.

"They're hiding something," Sheriff Turow said over David's shoulder while observing the empty bottom shelf. He was holding the bathroom trash can, which, like the one under Nancy Braxton's vanity, was empty.

"Of course they are," David said. "They're politicians. Hiding stuff is second nature for them."

CHAPTER SIXTEEN

"I think Mac and Archie need to have a baby," Murphy told Jessica after they had turned onto the freeway heading east. Perched in the backseat of Murphy's midnight-blue SUV, Gnarly was peering out of the front windshield between them.

The corners of Jessica's lips curled up into a grin. "Why would you say that, honeybun?" Her voice oozed with innocence.

Keeping his eyes on the road, Murphy pointed at the list that Jessica was holding in her lap. "Make sure Gnarly doesn't go outside to play for one hour after he eats so that he doesn't get a bellyache? Be sure to play catch with him for one hour every day, or he'll resort to stealing to alleviate his boredom? No table food? What about the food that he's infamous for stealing?"

"That's why Dad said not to *give* him any table food—because he steals more than enough. They don't want him to get fat."

Murphy jerked a thumb over his shoulder in Gnarly's direction. "That dog is more pampered than I was growing up."

Gnarly turned his head to look at the side of Murphy's head. The dog's narrow eyes betrayed an expression that seemed to indicate that he felt worthy of being so pampered.

Reclining her seat slightly so that she could scratch Gnarly's ears, Jessica said, "Tell me what your CO uncovered about Gnarly's case."

"It's classified."

"Don't give me that classified bull," she said.

"You don't—"

"Yes, I do have a need to know," she argued. "By all accounts, he's my brother." She waved the extensive list concerning the care and handling of the German shepherd. "Can I count on you to make sure that Gnarly doesn't eat any dairy products?"

"Dairy products?"

"He can't have anything with milk or cheese in it," she said. "It gives him gas pains. He's lactose intolerant."

Staring straight ahead, Murphy sat up in his seat.

"I didn't think so," Jessica said. "So I'm going along with you as Gnarly's caretaker on this little mission. Since I'm in, that means that I have a need to know. So start talking."

"I can't just start talking, and you know that," Murphy said.

"Then call your CO, and get her approval to read me in on the case."

Keeping his eyes on the road, Murphy tried to reach into the case on his belt for his secure cell phone.

"What are you looking for?" Jessica asked.

"My cell phone to call—"

"What number would you like me to call, Murphy?" Nigel's voice asked over the SUV's speakers.

Shocked by the unexpected question, Jessica shrieked. "What in the—"

Whirling around in the backseat, Gnarly looked for the intruder and barked.

"You put *Nigel* in the car!" Jessica said after gasping.

"He's very handy."

"Handy like a head-on collision," she said. "Why didn't you tell me?"

"I told Tristan to put him in," Murphy said. "I guess he did it while I was gone. He can make hands-off phone calls, and using my cell phone as a remote, I can have him turn on the engine, adjust the temperature, and open the door for me."

Jessica was glaring at him from her seat.

"Imagine this," he said. "You're at the grocery store. Your arms are full with bags of groceries. It's pouring rain. Using your phone's Bluetooth, you tell Nigel to turn on the car and open the rear compartment so that all you have to do is dump the bags in the back—and he'll even open the driver's door for you. If it's winter, he can have the interior nice and toasty for you—even the seats."

"Will he pull the car up to the curb for me too so that I don't have to wander through the parking lot looking for him?" she asked with heavy sarcasm.

"We're working on that." With the SUV at a stop, Murphy unsnapped his seat belt and climbed out of the SUV, slamming the door behind him.

With the front driver's seat free, Gnarly leaped up to take Murphy's place.

Through the windshield, Jessica saw him hit a button on his secure phone to place a call to his commanding officer—a mysterious woman who Jessica had never seen or met. She didn't even know her name. Murphy called her "CO."

"Murphy? Are you there? What number would you like me to call for you?"

Once again, at the sound of the disembodied voice, Gnarly barked and searched for the intruder.

"According to my audio memory bank, your voice is not a match for Murphy," Nigel said.

"That's Gnarly," Jessica said. "He'll be staying with us awhile, Nigel."

"Should I commit the sound of his voice to my audio database?"

"Yes, Nigel," Jessica said while noticing that Murphy had hung up his cell phone and was returning it to the case on his belt.

"I have now committed Gnarly to my friends and family database," Nigel said. "Gnarly, my name is Nigel. It is a pleasure to meet you. I am here to serve you at your pleasure."

Gnarly responded by cocking his head all the way to one side and looking about him for the source of the voice that then knew his name.

Murphy threw open the driver's side door. Instantly, Gnarly jumped over the center console and into the backseat to allow Murphy to slide into the driver's seat. "Okay, you're cleared."

"Yippee," Jessica said, trying to keep her enthusiasm contained. She and Murphy were going to work on a Phantom case together. She was a temporary Phantom.

"Do you still wish to make a phone call, Murphy?" Nigel asked.

"No, Nigel," Murphy said with a sigh. "I took care of it myself."

"Gives me the creeps," Jessica said. "I love automation, but sometimes I feel like as a society, we're becoming so dependent on it that we're becoming slaves to it. Eventually, we'll end up serving our computers instead of the other way around."

"Nigel just needs some adjusting," Murphy said. "Once your brother fine-tunes him and completely integrates him into everything, you'll love him."

Murphy waited until he had eased back onto the freeway to begin. "Do you remember yesterday morning, when I told you about Tawkeel?" When he glanced over, he saw Jessica nodding her head. "How he had been working deep undercover for nine months on a case and how someone blew his cover?"

"You said you suspected that someone high up in Washington blew his cover."

"Exactly," Murphy said. "Not only was Tawkeel's cover blown, but his handler's was also. His handler ended up dead—tortured to death."

"But that was just in the last few weeks," Jessica said. "Gnarly's handler was killed four years ago."

Murphy held up his finger to silence her. "Four years ago, Gnarly and First Sergeant Belle Perkins belonged to a unit stationed in Iraq near the border of Syria. Shortly before Perkins' murder, a contractor with the Army Corps of Engineers, tasked with surveying the region, was sent to their platoon. His name was Benjamin Frost. Perkins' unit was tasked with escorting this contractor around the area and keeping him safe while he surveyed the remote areas in the desert."

"Doesn't sound like fun and games to me," she said.

"It wasn't. Everything was fine for a couple of weeks," Murphy said. "Then their unit was hit with mortar fire, and two men were killed. They had to relocate. A week later, while Perkins' unit had Frost out in the field, they were hit by two snipers. A couple of men were injured. The unit's CO, Lieutenant Frank Watson, personally charged in like John Wayne and took them both out. He got the Bronze Star for that.

"Then, three days later, they went out again and were ambushed by two pairs of snipers. That's the attack Sheriff Turow told us about."

"They really were determined, weren't they?"

Murphy nodded his head. "Four men were killed. Perkins and Gnarly saved their unit by taking out the snipers. Lieutenant Frank Watson wrote up commendations for both of them."

He continued in a soft voice. "The next day, First Sergeant Belle Perkins was dead, and Sergeant Major Gnarly was shipped home in a crate and dishonorably discharged."

"I still don't understand how that case is connected to Tawkeel's."

Murphy swallowed. "Benjamin Frost was CIA, and he was doing classified work out in the desert. No one in the unit knew that. He was working under an alias. Yet it became abundantly clear that somehow, someone had blown his cover. After that last ambush, Frost slipped out of the camp in the middle of the night and got out of the country. He managed to get back to the States okay. But when the agency investigated the situation, they found that his whole cover had been burned completely. They never did find out who did it."

"Is Tawkeel CIA?"

Murphy's silence answered her question.

"And someone blew his cover," she replied. "Was Belle Perkins CIA?"

"No," Murphy said. "But in her last communication with her husband, Chris Turow, she said that something weird was going on there in the platoon and that some stuff had happened on their last outing that she needed to talk to someone at HQ about. Maybe she realized that Frost was CIA, or she identified someone who was slipping intel to the terrorists."

"Do they know for certain that those strikes on Perkins and Gnarly's unit had to do with the CIA agent? Maybe they were just done by terrorists who didn't like trespassers."

"The strikes stopped as soon as Frost got back to the States."

"What's our first stop?"

"CIA."

She allowed herself to smile. She had never been to the CIA before. "If you don't mind my saying, it sounds like we have more questions than answers."

"Welcome to my world, buttercup."

Being sick had already gotten old. With Gnarly gone, Spencer Manor felt strangely empty, and the phone was ringing off the hook with journalists asking if the German shepherd was a suspect in Nancy Braxton's murder. Archie's e-mail was filled with the same questions.

They had to get out of the house, so Mac got dressed to go to the police station so that he could dive into the investigation whether they wanted his help or not. It could have been pure determination that made him feel 90 percent better, or it could've been the medication and oxygen from the day before.

Still, Archie insisted on accompanying him just in case he needed her. With her laptop and her research on Braxton Charities in hand, she grabbed the keys to her SUV, and they went to the Spencer police department.

At the desk sergeant's desk, Tonya informed them that David had gone home to check on Dallas and Storm and to get a nap. With a toss of her head, she directed them to Bogie's office.

"I hear him on a Skype call with Doc." With a wink, she warned them to knock on his office's door before entering.

"Last week, I walked in on one of their video calls and found Doc giving Bogie a preview of her new lingerie."

"I hate it when that happens," Archie said to Tonya before following Mac to the deputy chief's office.

Bogie invited them into his office, where Doc's image was filling his computer screen. Upon seeing them through Bogie's web cam, she chastised Mac for being out of bed. "You have pneumonia. You aren't going to get well if you're out running around."

"I'll rest after clearing Gnarly's name," Mac said. "Word got out that he was missing last night, and now they're thinking that he's some sort of canine serial killer. Did you finish the autopsy on Nancy Braxton?"

"That's Sheriff Turow's case," Bogie said. "And you don't have to worry about him. He'll bend over backward to clear Gnarly's name."

"The more people working on this, the better." Mac turned his attention back to the medical examiner on the computer screen. "What's the cause of death?"

"Blunt-force trauma to the back of the head," Doc said. "One very hard blow. My guess is with a rock. She had very little water in her lunges. She didn't drown, but she was near death when she fell face first into the water."

"If it was only one blow with a rock," Mac asked, "could she have fallen and hit her head on the rock, making it an accident? Sheriff Turow did say that she had bare feet. Middle of the night. Edge of the lake. She could have slipped in the mud along the shore—"

Doc Washington was shaking her head. "She fell face first. She had abrasions on her knees and hands and elbows. None on her buttocks or back. So she was struck on the back of the head with a rock so hard that it fractured her skull and caused cranial bleeding. As hard as she was hit, she would have been unconscious when she hit the ground. The only reason she didn't drown was because she bled out first."

"One hard blow did that?" Mac asked.

"We're looking for someone who's strong," Bogie said.

"And while Gnarly packs quite a punch with his bite, the killer was not a dog," Doc said with a grin. "Good news, Mac. Our forensics people confirmed that the blood they took off of Gnarly was not human. They also said that the bite marks on the mountain lion do match the impressions that a German shepherd would make."

"Well, if any dog could take down a mountain lion, it would be Gnarly," Mac said. "I just wish he hadn't decided to go missing and take down a mountain lion on the same night that someone he had motive to murder was killed."

"Are there any *human* suspects?" Archie asked.

"Does anyone have any idea of what Nancy Braxton was doing out in the middle of the night in her pajamas without a robe or slippers?" Mac asked Bogie.

"I may have a suggestion of where to look," Doc said. "I found gelatin in her stomach contents."

"Gelatin?" Mac asked.

"The type used for time-release capsules," Doc said. "They take up to thirty minutes to digest. Now here's the interesting part. Since it was apparent that she had taken some medication, I ran a tox screen. There weren't any meds in her system. Her blood alcohol was point zero six."

"So she had been drinking and taking…sugar pills?" Mac asked.

"We found evidence suggesting that she had some pill bottles on her vanity and in her medicine cabinet, but they were all gone," Bogie said. "Her executive assistant is lying about not knowing anything about them."

"She might have thought that she was taking meds when she wasn't," Mac said. "Now we need to find out what she was taking meds for—or thought she was taking meds for."

David rolled over in his bed and felt the setting sun's orange glow on his face. He had told himself that he only needed a couple of hours sleep, which would have made it late afternoon when he woke up. Before lying down to sleep in the heat of the day, he had taken off his shirt so that he could cool off while sleeping on top of his bed's comforter.

Dallas must have turned off the alarm clock.

He opened his eyes, squinted at the other side of the bed, and saw Storm, her sable head framed in the ugly white cone of shame, looking directly at him.

"What—" Before he could finish his question about how she'd gotten up onto the bed, her tongue shot out directly into his open mouth in midsentence.

With a curse, he sprang up in his bed. "Dallas!"

The clatter of her high heels on the stairs told him that she was on her way. A second later, she rushed into the room with her laptop tucked under her arm. "You okay, sugar?"

"How did she get up on my bed?"

"She jumped, I guess."

"The doctor said to keep her quiet and to not let her jump around." David urged Storm off of the bed and into her bed in the corner of the room. "We don't want her tearing her stitches."

Hugging her laptop to her chest, Dallas admired how David tenderly checked to make sure that the cone collar was on right and that Storm hadn't torn any stitches. Bare chested, he was the image of contrast: he was a masculine grown man who was tenderly displaying affection for the injured animal who was completely dependent on them for her well-being after a vicious attack the night before.

Seemingly unaware that she was taking notice of his affection for Storm, David asked, "Did you give her the pain medicine?"

"'Bout an hour ago when I gave her supper."

"Did she eat?" David asked.

Dallas nodded her head. "But the vet said not to give her a lot, because she could get sick so soon after surgery. She was hungry."

"What about the antibiotic?"

"That'll be in another hour." She shot him a wicked grin. "You care 'bout her."

His brow furrowed, David looked up at her. "Of course I do. Why wouldn't I?"

"Last week you said she was conniving and manipulative."

"So's Gnarly, and I nominated him for mayor." Satisfied that Storm was on the mend, David rose to his feet and took Dallas into his arms. "I'm very glad she's okay."

"She's not goin' outside by herself anymore," Dallas said. "From now on, I'm goin' out there with her, and I'll be packin'. Next time someone comes after my Storm, he's gettin' a butt full of bullets."

"I believe it," David said with a chuckle. When he leaned in to kiss her, he noticed that the laptop she had pressed against her chest was then between them. "Are you still working on the Sandy Burr case?"

She offered him a gesture between a nod of her head and a shrug of her shoulders. "And Nancy Braxton's murder."

Rubbing his chin, he realized that he had not shaved that morning. He figured it'd be best to freshen up some before going back to the police department and checking in with Sheriff Turow on the status of the case. He trotted into the bathroom. Leaving the door open, he turned on the water in the sink.

Lying across the bed, Dallas opened up her laptop and called after him. "Doc Washington was streamin' the debate to y'all last night. Did y'all hear that whale of a lie that Nancy told 'bout goin' to Somalia and negotiatin' with pirates for the release of American hostages?"

In the bathroom, David laughed. "Yeah, I heard that." He bent over the sink to splash warm water onto his face.

Dallas stepped into the doorway and leaned against the frame with her arms folded. "Total lie."

"But her supporters really don't care," David said to her image in the mirror. "Right now, her party is more concerned with having someone from the party be the first woman mayor of Spencer. That's why the party leaders shredded about a hundred ballots voting for the other candidate. Sure, the people wanted him, and he was from that party—but his genitalia isn't what's currently trending."

"So to translate," Dallas said, "the possession of a vagina trumps sanity and the wishes of the people."

Spraying shaving cream into his hand, David nodded his head. "I can actually feel our founding fathers rolling in their graves." He went about spreading the cream on his face.

"She was a certifiable loon."

Chuckling, David ran his razor under the water. "I don't think being a chronic liar means that she's certifiable. If it did, more than half of the people in Washington would need to be locked up."

"There's lyin', sweetie, and there's *lyin',*" she said. "Everyone lies for a reason. I've seen you lie to manipulate a perp and to get him to tell you what he knows. I've lied—"

"You lie!" he said with mock shock. He proceeded to shave his face while pausing occasionally to follow her train of thought.

"To sweet-talk my way out of speedin' tickets or to get my way," she said. "People lie to spare someone's feelin's or to cover up bad things they've done or to impress a friend or a perspective friend—and most of the time, those are little white lies that don't hurt anyone, and people know they're lyin' when they tell them. But that's not Nancy Braxton." After reminding herself of her murder, she corrected herself. "Or wasn't her."

David rinsed the cream and the whiskers from the razor. "What was different about Nancy's lie last night?"

"Never happened," Dallas said. "I very simply fact-checked her story with one of my connections in Washington and learned that there was no meetin' with the secretary of state. No detail sent to Somalia. No snipers who shot up that airfield and no meetin' with pirates."

"Everyone knew Nancy Braxton was a liar."

"But it's the reason she lied," Dallas said. "It goes beyond tryin' to strut while sittin' down."

He stopped with the razor in midair. "Huh?"

"Tryin' to impress voters," she said. "Watchin' Nancy last night, I think she really believed some of those things she said."

"She *believed* she went to Somalia and negotiated the release of hostages from pirates?"

Rolling her eyes with deep thought, Dallas said, "I think she *believed* she was worthy of the greatness associated with doing such a great deed. She started lyin' to build herself up in the eyes of voters and those she needed to support her. But then her lies grew and got bolder—"

"Like the Somali-pirates-and-sniper lie," David said.

"Her chronic lyin' was probably enabled by her party and by her supporters, who never called her on them—until it became plain to see that she was a few pickles short of a barrel." She paused to take a breath. "So I did some checkin' with a few of my resources in psychiatry."

"You really believe she was psychologically unstable?" David tried not to laugh.

"I think she was certifiably delusional," Dallas said in a serious tone.

Finished shaving, David rinsed the last of the shaving cream from his face. Contemplating her statement, he patted his face dry and followed her into the bedroom, where she sat on the bed. While they had been out of the room, Storm had jumped up onto the bed and curled up on the pillows.

"Let's say you're right, and Nancy Braxton was emotionally unstable," David said. "Besides chronically lying to make herself seem more important and accomplished than she really was, what other symptoms would she have displayed?"

"Well," Dallas said, "based on what I learned, I believe she suffered from delusions of grandeur."

David sat on the bed next to her. "I've run into suspects with delusions of grandeur. They think they're the president or Jesus Christ or—"

"You don't necessarily think you're someone great or famous or attached to someone who's famous or great," Dallas said. "You can think you're destined to achieve those things. Other symptoms are narcissism—"

"She had that all right."

"Paranoia," Dallas said.

"I think she had that, too," David said. "Okay, so let's say that she had that and that she had maybe been diagnosed by a doctor. Are there meds she could have taken for that?"

"Antipsychotic meds," Dallas said with a nod of her head.

CHAPTER SEVENTEEN

Central Intelligence Agency Headquarters
Langley, Virginia

Because she had dressed casually for travel, Jessica felt un-derdressed when she walked across the great seal on the floor of the front entrance of the Central Intelligence Agency. She especially felt like she didn't belong because she had a hundred-pound German shepherd on a leash.

Before driving through the front gates of the massive compound in the wooded area of Northern Virginia, Murphy had pulled into the CIA visitors' center, where they had all presented identification. Even Gnarly had had the microchip inside his neck scanned to confirm that he had been a military K-9.

Jessica couldn't fight the grin that came to her face when the officer behind the desk gave her a visitor's badge that indicated that she had a limited security clearance. It was better than no clearance at all. The distinction made her feel official and closer to Murphy's prestigious position as a Phantom.

As a Phantom, he'd had extensive clearance granted to him by the Joint Chiefs of Staff, so he already had the necessary badges for entrance into the hub of the nation's secrets. His badge even granted him access to a special visitor's parking space in front of the building's main entrance.

Familiar with the building, Murphy escorted Jessica and Gnarly through the front doors and across the seal toward the security scanners. Sensing that this was not Murphy's first visit to the CIA headquarters, she wondered how often he had walked through those doors, whom he'd visited, and why.

One of the security officers took Gnarly's leash and led him around the gates. Not wanting to miss a trick, they ran a metal detector over the canine and took note of his microchip, comparing the identification number to the one that had been put into the system by the visitors' center.

Yep, it was the same dog. No switch had occurred during the four-minute drive between the visitors' center and the main entrance.

The security protocol was not missed by Gnarly, who Jessica saw stand, sit, and heel like the highly trained canine he had been.

"Beautiful dog," the security guard said with admiration when he handed Gnarly's leash back to Jessica. "I see by his ID number that he's done a couple of tours overseas and trained in multiple areas. Only the smartest dogs can specialize in everything."

"That's what makes him special," Jessica said while stroking Gnarly.

Murphy led them around a wall of windows that looked out onto a courtyard, past a cafeteria, and then up an escalator to a set of elevators. By the time they stopped to wait for the elevators, Jessica was breathing hard. "This place is huge."

Murphy smiled. "This business keeps you in shape, buttercup."

"Hey, I haven't heard you complain about my shape yet."

The elevator doors opened and revealed that it was packed with employees. Noting that it was close to five o'clock, Jessica concluded that they were going home for the day. Many noticed Gnarly.

"Is that a bomb-sniffing dog?" a woman asked Jessica.

"He's multitrained," Jessica said, repeating what the security guard had said when he'd seen Gnarly's profile.

The woman didn't wait around. She hurried toward the exit as fast as she could go.

Once the elevator was empty, Murphy held the door open for Jessica and Gnarly and then pressed the button that would take them to the fourth floor, where he then led them through a maze of corridors before they found the office he was looking for.

Murphy opened the door and held it open so that Jessica and Gnarly could step inside what turned out to be a cozy reception area with an equally small office on the other side of it. The reception desk was empty.

Murphy passed Jessica and Gnarly and stepped into the next office, where a man with a gray goatee and moustache clad in a blue button-down shirt and slacks looked at them with curiosity from behind his desk. Murphy extended his hand to him. "Are you Bruce Hardy, also known as Benjamin Frost?"

The man rose from his desk. "Murphy Thornton?" After Murphy confirmed his identity, Bruce clasped his hand. "You obviously have some juice. It isn't every day you get a call from the director of national intelligence." He looked Murphy up and down, taking note of his casual appearance in jeans and a polo shirt. He sniffed. "Are you working undercover?"

Deciding it would take too long to explain, Murphy said, "Sort of. We have a few questions for you about your last assignment in Iraq—when you were working deep under-cover near the Syrian border."

Clearing his throat, Bruce reached for a tissue from the corner of his desk. "Sure. Whatever you need." Blowing his nose, he gestured for them to sit down in his small office.

When Jessica and Gnarly stepped in, Bruce's eyes grew big at the sight of Gnarly. "That's—" He sneezed. Then he coughed. Gasping for breath, he pointed at the dog. Tucking his tail between his legs, Gnarly tried to back away from the man whose face was turning red before their eyes.

"What?" Jessica said, confused.

"Allergic!" Bruce waved his arms for them to leave.

After gathering up the dog's leash, Jessica took Gnarly through the reception area and out of the office, allowing the door to slam behind them. Out in the corridor, Jessica said, "Well, it's plain to see that *he* didn't kill Belle. He would have died of shock before getting within ten feet of her with you in the same tent."

Inside the office, Murphy rushed to get Bruce a drink of water from the water cooler and handed the paper cup to him. By the time he returned to the agent's desk, Bruce was using an emergency inhaler to regain control of his breathing.

"I'm sorry," Murphy said while waiting for the agent to catch his breath. "I didn't know."

"Well, I don't exactly advertise it," Bruce said. "Outside, I usually do okay. But not in closed spaces with no place for the dander to go except for up my nose." With a chuckle, he sighed.

"Then I guess it's safe to say that you didn't spend a lot of time in Belle Perkins' tent while on that mission in Iraq."

"Belle who?" Bruce wiped his swollen and watering eyes with the tissue.

"Gnarly's handler?" Murphy jerked a thumb over his shoulder in the direction of the door through which Jessica had left with Gnarly. "That was her dog. Sergeant Major Gnarly."

"That was the dog that saved my life?" Bruce sat up in his seat. "At one point during that last battle before I got out of there, I was trying to get to one of the men who had been shot so that I could help him. Just as I got to him, I saw an Iraqi standing not fifteen feet from me. He had climbed up onto the roof of a truck and had his rifle aimed right at me. That dog"—he pointed at the door—"came out of nowhere. He jumped from the ground up onto the hood of the truck and then up onto the roof. In midair, he got both the rifle and the guy's arm in his jaw, and he took that bastard all the way down off that roof and onto the ground. I got out of there as fast as I could crawl." He cocked his head at Murphy. "Why are you asking about his handler and her tent?"

Murphy gazed at him. "First, tell me about what happened after that ambush that killed four soldiers. The official report from the unit says you went missing."

"Of course it does," Bruce said. "I was undercover. No one knew I was CIA. Not even the CO of the unit. As far as they were all concerned, I was Benjamin Frost, a contractor with the Army Corps of Engineers. None of them had any idea of what I was really doing there. But somehow my cover had been blown. When the unit was first attacked, we figured that the terrorist cell had just gotten lucky. They'd happened upon us. But then they kept following us. They would know where we were within one day of our moving. When those four soldiers were killed, I knew I was the real target. As long as I was around, I would be putting every one of those soldiers in danger. So that night, as soon as it was dark, I packed up only what I needed and got out of there."

"In the middle of the desert?"

"I had no idea who had blown my cover," Bruce said. "That cell was getting intel from someone—not from anyone in the camp, though. The only person I regularly communicated with who knew that I was with the agency was my handler, who was stationed in Afghanistan. He drank a lot. Maybe, I thought, he had somehow blown my cover. So I cut off communication with him and went underground on my own. It took me five days of traveling through that desert dressed like a refugee to get to the American embassy in Israel."

"Was it your handler who blew your cover?"

"He swore he hadn't, and the agency could find no proof that he had," Bruce said. "They decided that I had to have blown it somehow." He glanced around the office. "That's why you find me here now. It turns out that my cover had been so widely blown that I can't go out in the field anymore. I am now deskbound." He paused. "What is this about?" he asked again.

"The night you took off from the base camp," Murphy said, "Gnarly's handler, First Sergeant Belle Perkins, was murdered."

"That sweet young woman?" Bruce swallowed. "I had no idea."

"As far as the army was concerned, you'd been captured by the Iraqi terrorists and most likely executed," Murphy said. "The way I found out that you had survived was through the intelligence community. Did you have any sort of relationship with her?"

Bruce gestured to the door through which the dog had recently left. "As you can tell, I didn't. She found out rather quickly that I was allergic to her dog, so she kept her distance. We would exchange pleasantries but always outside, and she would keep her distance. She was understanding like that."

The agent let out a deep breath. "The only time I got near her was that day—after that dog had saved my life by killing that terrorist who'd had me in his sight. I was walking across the camp, and I saw her outside her tent. Gnarly was lying down on the ground, and she was kneeling next to him, giving him a belly rub. I had to thank him—even though I was so allergic. So I went up to them and told her what he had done. My eyes were getting red, but I owed it to him and wanted him to know how much I appreciated it. I rubbed his tummy, and my throat was closing up. Then my hand went across his ribs and down his back, and I saw that he was bleeding. He'd gotten hurt. His hip had been grazed by a shot. She said that she was going to stitch him up. I asked her how he would handle that. She laughed and said that she'd have to give him a sedative to put him to sleep while she did it but that he would be good as new the next morning. That beautiful, smart, and courageous dog got hurt protecting me."

He sucked in a deep breath. "*That* was when I made the decision to get out of there before anyone else got hurt." He cocked his head at Murphy. "And now you say she died. How was she killed?"

"Strangled. Could she have known you were agency?"

"If she did, she never let on," Bruce said.

"Did you see her have any disagreements with anyone in her unit?"

Bruce Hardy fell silent. His face was filled with deep thought as he stared up at the ceiling. He kept his eyes on the ceiling even while he wiped his nose one last time. "There was another woman in the unit, and Perkins didn't get along with her. Rather, the two of them did not get along. You would think that the only two women would form some sort of friendship, but that wasn't the case with those two. I don't remember her name, but she was very butch, and Perkins was more—well, you get the idea. If I recall, Perkins was married. Wasn't she?"

"Yes, she was," Murphy said. "She had a young daughter."

"I'm so sorry," Bruce said with a soft voice before abruptly sitting up in his seat. "I just remembered—that last day, after the ambush, there was definite tension between Perkins and the commanding officer." He snapped his fingers, trying to recall what had happened. "What was his name? Holmes? No." He pointed at Murphy. "Watson! The CO for their unit. I remember hearing them arguing on our way back."

"Do you remember what it was about?"

"She claimed that it was his bad call that had gotten four of their people killed," Bruce said. "He reminded her that he was the CO, and she wasn't. She was really hot about it, though. I thought they were going to get into a physical altercation. The dog was barking. It ended when he had to order her to stand down and to get control of her dog, or he would shoot him. She backed off real fast after that."

"But if Watson was an officer and she was enlisted, there really wasn't much that she could've done about a bad call."

"It was apparent that I was the target of those attacks," Bruce said. "The agency confirmed through intelligence channels that my cover had been blown, and the attacks stopped after I got out of there."

"Maybe somehow Perkins figured out that you were agency, and she was hot because your presence put the unit in danger."

"How would she have known? The CO didn't even know."

"The fact is that your cover got blown," Murphy said. "The Iraqi terrorists knew who you were, what unit you were with, and where they could find you. Someone was communicating with them. You said it wasn't your handler. The only other ones who knew your movements were the soldiers in that unit, and someone in that unit killed Belle Perkins."

"You're thinking she was killed because she identified a traitor inside the unit."

"And the traitor killed her."

"What are you doing here?" David asked upon entering the police station and finding Mac sitting next to an empty desk.

Like two peas in a pod, Mac and Archie were sitting with their heads close together and going over information on the screen of her laptop while he made notes on a computer tablet.

"We're suffering from empty-nest syndrome." Archie had her finger on her screen and was pointing to something that she wanted Mac to type into his tablet.

"The house is too quiet without Gnarly there," Mac said.

"I've noticed that Gnarly hasn't dropped out of the race." David crossed the squad room to see what they were working on, at which point Archie snapped the laptop shut.

"Deniability." She winked at him.

Mac sat back in his seat. "Gnarly's staying in the race. When you mess with my dog, you mess with me. I'm going to wipe the floor with both of Gnarly's opponents."

"One of whom is dead," David said. "I don't think there's anything more you could do to hurt her. What's your excuse for Gnarly's absence?"

"Didn't you see Bernie and Hap's press announcement?" Archie asked.

Carrying a tablet, Bogie stepped out of his office. "You should have seen it, Chief. It was awesome."

"I needed to get a couple of hours of sleep." David took the tablet that Bogie was handing to him. "I was up all night."

"So were all of us," Bogie said with a yawn.

"Go home, and get some beauty sleep, Bogie." David looked his deputy chief up and down. "You could use it."

Bogie gave him a playful punch in the shoulder. "I can still turn you over my knee, kid."

"Well, Mac wrote a brilliant press release," Archie said with a grin. "I can see that he did inherit some of his mother's imagination."

"I simply told the truth...with some embellishments," Mac said with a wave of his hand. "Gnarly's on a secret mission for God."

For a long, silent moment, David wondered whether he should believe Mac. He searched Archie's and Bogie's expressions. Archie broke first. "Smartass," David said.

"You started it." A broad smile filled Mac's face. "We simply said that he went away for a few days to meet with the leaders of his campaign committee to plan how to best proceed during the rest of his campaign for mayor."

"Smooth," David said.

"I lifted it word for word from a press release sent out by one of the presidential candidates after his long connection with organized crime got leaked."

David peered at the image on the tablet that Bogie had handed to him. It was of the front of the Braxtons' mansion from the security gate and up to the front door. "Is this the security recording?"

"Just came in. They sent it to both us and the sheriff's office."

"Did the security cameras pick up anything from the night of the shooting?" David asked.

Bogie was shaking his head before David even finished the question. "I asked the security company already. The cameras were shut off when the alarm system was turned off after the shot. The camera positioned at the rear of the house, focused on the back door didn't pick up anyone going out that back door."

"Really?" David asked while looking over at Mac. "Yet, our witnesses say the shooter went out that door and ran across the backyard and into the woods."

"If they're telling the truth," Archie said, "the shooter may have left through that door after the system and camera was turned off."

"Why have a security system and cameras if you're going to turn them off while the shooter is still in the house?" Mac asked.

"I said *if* they're telling the truth," Archie said.

"Since they're in politics, then it's highly unlikely that they are telling the truth." Bogie gestured for Mac to join David in watching the security recording from the night of Nancy Braxton's murder. The deputy chief pressed the "play" button on the touch screen.

The time on the recording was 11:57 p.m.

The front door flew open, and Nancy Braxton ran out. Her bright-white pajamas shone in the porch light and the lights illuminating the driveway. She wore no bathrobe or slippers. Agitated, she spun around on the porch, lost her footing, and tumbled down the steps. Looking over her shoulder several times, she ran down the driveway and out of the range of the camera.

The recording stopped and then restarted at 12:04 a.m., when Erin Devereux, clad in her nightgown and bathrobe, ran outside and looked around. Apparently calling for someone, she stepped down off of the porch and searched the woods surrounding the house.

"She's looking for her," Mac said. "So they knew Nancy was missing at four minutes after twelve—seven minutes after she ran out of the house."

Erin Devereux went back inside. Minutes later, she returned with Hugh Vance. Both of them were carrying flashlights, which they then used to search the grounds. Then Hugh climbed into his car and drove off. Erin Devereux went back into the house.

The time on the recording read 12:55 a.m. when Hugh Vance's car returned. Slowly, he climbed out of the car and returned to the house. The recording stopped at that point.

"Why didn't they report her missing?" Archie asked.

"What was the time of death?" Mac asked them.

"Between twelve thirty and one o'clock," David said.

"Hugh Vance returned to the house at five minutes to one," Mac said. "Their estate is about five minutes from the murder scene. He could have found her, killed her, and then went back home and gone to bed."

Scratching his head, he asked David to replay the recording. When it reached the point where Nancy Braxton raced out of the range of the camera, Mac told him to pause the frame. "Look at how she came flying out of that house. She was scared to death of something."

Getting his point, Archie said, "She didn't leave quietly."

"There were two other people in that house," Mac said. "Why didn't they hear her screaming bloody murder? It took her assistant seven minutes to go looking for her. Yeah, it's a big house, but still—"

"Better question is, why didn't Nancy Braxton go running to either of them for help?" Archie said.

Recalling his conversation with Dallas, David said, "Because she thought they were out to get her?"

"Were they?" Mac asked.

"Paranoia," David said. "I just thought it was part of Nancy's hyper-self-esteem, but Dallas did some research, and based on the outlandish lie Nancy told last night—"

"About her little trip to Somalia?" Bogie asked with a chuckle.

"Face it," David said. "Nancy Braxton told some lies that were really out there more than once during this campaign."

"She was always a liar," Bogie said. "And she was good at it, too. When your father and I were investigating the Sandy Burr case, ol' Pat said that that woman had absolutely no regard for the truth. That she'd say whatever she had to say to get what she wanted."

"Which was to be queen." David hitched a leg over the corner of one of the squad-room desks. "That is—was—Nancy Braxton's ultimate goal. She believed it was her destiny because she was so superior to us peasants. We all dismissed that as a flaw in her personality. I mean, we've all met narcissists—especially here in Spencer, where overachievers spend their holidays. But suppose it was something more than just a simple personality flaw with Nancy Braxton. Suppose those outlandish lies were actually a symptom of something worse."

"Like a psychotic ailment?" Mac asked.

David was nodding his head. "An ailment that, if it was actually diagnosed by a psychiatrist, could've been treated with antipsychotic meds."

"The empty spaces on the shelf in her medicine cabinet and on her vanity," Bogie said.

"Have we found anything in the trash yet?" David asked.

Bogie shook his head.

"The tox screen found no drugs in her system," Mac said. "But Doc did find gelatin, which indicates that she had taken capsules. Suppose she had been diagnosed as psychotic—"

"Something her campaign would *never* have wanted the voters to find out about," Archie said.

"If someone replaced her meds with sugar pills, eventually, she would have had a breakdown," Mac said.

"According to Dallas' research," David said, "if Braxton had been suffering from a form of delusions of grandeur, paranoia would've been a symptom. Last night, she had a breakdown, imagined that those closest to her were out to get her, and ran off into the night."

"That would explain why she didn't go to her brother or assistant for help," Archie said.

"But then someone did kill her," Mac said, "which proves that just because you're paranoid doesn't mean someone isn't out to get you."

Chapter Eighteen

**The Next Morning—Faraday-Thornton Estate
Great Falls, Virginia**

Jessica loved nothing more than waking up in her husband's arms. Shortly after their wedding, which had taken place fewer than forty-eight hours after they'd first met, the couple had settled into a routine. The many times that Murphy was called away from his "day job" at the Pentagon disrupted it. But upon his return, they would quickly settle back into it.

While Jessica preferred to wake up well after the sun, Murphy rose promptly at five o'clock in the morning to either run or work out in their gym at home. He would finish off with meditation and yoga. When the weather was pleasant, he would do his meditation in the garden behind their home. Afterward, he would shower and then return to bed to gently wake up Jessica with soft kisses and the scent of fresh coffee in a mug on her nightstand.

"My favorite time of the day," she murmured against his chest. She felt so warm in his arms. Those moments were the ones she never wanted to end.

236

"My favorite time of the day is a toss-up between the morning and the evening," he whispered. "Night time is much more—" He searched for the right word.

"Active?" She looked up into his eyes and grinned. "Mornings can be pretty active, too."

His voice was husky. "Prove it, buttercup."

She pushed him back onto the bed and straddled him. Her mouth was covering his when Nigel said, "Tristan has entered the home with an unidentified person. Would you like me to notify security?"

They parted with the same intensity that they would've parted with if they'd been stunned with a cattle prod. Rolling away from each other, they jumped out of opposite sides of the bed. Jessica reached for her lilac silk bathrobe while Murphy yanked on a pair of sweat pants.

"That does it!" she yelled while shrugging into her bathrobe. "Nigel is fired! He's out of here!" She pointed toward the windows looking out across the back garden and the path leading down to the river. "How can we make love with him lurking around and seeing everything that happens? I feel like I'm living with a virtual Peeping Tom who peeps at me twenty-four-seven."

"Tristan and his unidentified companion are now removing items from the kitchen and pantry areas" Nigel said in a tone devoid of emotion. "Would you like me to tell security that you are being robbed?"

"Keep your pants on, Nigel!" Giving up on finding his slippers, Murphy grabbed his nine-millimeter semiautomatic handgun from the drawer of his nightstand.

Since the security system was monitored by the federal government, the last thing Murphy and Jessica wanted was for Nigel to contact security and cause a SWAT team to descend on their home because Jessica's brother and an unidentified friend were raiding their fridge.

"I'm sorry, Murphy, but I am not programmed to carry out that request. As an artificial-intelligence unit, I have no body. That being the case, I have nothing on which to wear pants. Therefore, I have no pants to keep on. Do you have another request to make, Murphy? The unidentified suspect is now in the wine pantry removing three bottles of Talaria wine. Would you like to launch code sixty-six, sir?"

"No!" Fearing that there wasn't enough time to put a shirt on, Murphy ran from the bedroom. "Negative on launching code sixty-six! Do not launch code sixty-six!"

"Where's Gnarly?" Jessica asked, panicked. "Maybe he's the unidentified companion."

They prayed that the unidentified companion in their home wasn't someone who had a gun pressed against Tristan's head and was ordering him to use his security access for unsavory reasons.

His semiautomatic weapon aimed at the floor, Murphy raced down the stairs to the lower level with Jessica directly behind him. As they approached the kitchen, they could hear Gnarly barking.

Jessica's younger brother, Tristan, yelled, "No! No! I give up! I'll do whatever you ask! Just don't—"

Murphy kicked open the kitchen door and flew in with his gun aimed at whomever was making Tristan beg for his life.

"Don't shoot!" With his back up against the refrigerator door, Tristan threw up his hands. Jessica's brother was a proud geek who was tall and lean. A self-proclaimed professional college student, he wore dark-framed eyeglasses.

Upon seeing the back of the woman who was holding the waistband of Tristan's pants out as far as they would go while aiming a can of whipped cream down into them, Murphy lowered his gun's aim to the floor.

When the playful encounter was brought to an abrupt halt, Gnarly stopped barking and sat down. His ears standing tall, he cocked his head at the can of whipped cream. Spencer poked her head out from behind the granite-topped island in the center of the gourmet kitchen. A large Amazon pantry box filled with the food items that the pair of thieves had been pilfering rested on top of the island.

The athletically slender young woman with long auburn hair that fell in a silky wave down past her shoulders turned around from where she had Tristan held up against the fridge to face Murphy and Jessica. She was dressed in a navy-blue tank top and blue jean short shorts. Her feet were bare. Instead of looking guilty about being caught in the act, she looked amused.

"Sarah wanted to show me a trick with whipped cream that she saw in a movie." Tristan snatched the can out of her hand and put it in the box. "I wanted to wait until we got back to the cottage."

"Dad told me you were on a mission out in the field," Sarah Thornton said to Murphy with a bit of annoyance in her tone.

"I was," Murphy said to his younger sister. "I got back the day before yesterday."

"Well, aren't you going to give your baby sister a hug?" Sarah thrust the can of whipped cream into Tristan's hands and ran up to Murphy to give him an enthusiastic hug and kiss. "I'm so glad you're home safe and sound," she whispered into his ear.

"So am I, sis." Murphy set the gun down on the island and peered into the box to see what the couple was stealing from their kitchen and pantry. The three expensive bottles of wine that Nigel had warned them about were among their stolen goods.

After hugging Jessica, Sarah folded her arms and playfully glared at Murphy. "You do realize you missed your own twin brother's graduation. I was there."

"I know. I didn't have any choice in the matter."

"J.J. is your *identical twin.*" Sarah poked him in the chest. "You two even share DNA. You'd said you wouldn't miss J.J.'s graduation from law school for the world."

"Well, I had no choice, Sarah. You'll know what I mean when you graduate from the naval academy. I already talked to J.J. and Dad. I've got some vacation days, and once I get this next assignment done, Jessie and I are going to try to go see J.J."

"Did you give the dogs hollandaise sauce?" Jessica was examining the three dog-food bowls lined up along the wall next to the pantry.

"Actually, it's a cheddar-cheese sauce," Tristan said. "I went ahead and fed the dogs for you—sort of as a thank-you for letting us steal your food."

"Why didn't the two of you just go to the store and buy food?" Murphy asked. "It isn't like you have no money, Tristan."

"Because then I'd have to get in the car and go to the store and buy food and bring it home and put it away." He hugged Sarah. "Sarah only has a few days before she has to report back to Annapolis."

Sarah took the can of whipped cream out of the box. "And we have stuff we wanna do." With a wicked grin, she sauntered to the door and opened it.

Jessica was still staring down at the dog-food bowls from which Gnarly was licking up the very last remnants of the cheese sauce. "Tristan, didn't Dad tell you that Gnarly is lactose intolerant?" There was panic in her tone.

"Yeah, as a matter of fact, I think he did mention that." Tristan picked up the box. "Whatever."

Remembering the events of the last few days, Jessica rushed across the kitchen toward her brother. "Aren't you even going to ask how Dad is?"

Tristan stopped and turned to her. "He's fine and out of the hospital."

"You talked to him, then?"

"No, I've been too busy to call him." Tristan shot Sarah a wicked grin. "But since you're here, I figure he must be out of the hospital. You're not crying, so he must not be dead. Therefore, he must be fine and out of the hospital."

"Looks like deductive reasoning runs in the family," Murphy said.

"Well, our work here is done," Sarah said. "Come on, Tristan. I can't wait to show you this trick." After Tristan went out the door, she turned back to Jessica and waved the can of whipped cream. "I don't suppose you have another can of whipped cream, do you?"

"No," Jessica said with a frown.

With a pout, Sarah left, closing the door behind her.

Murphy and Jessica looked at each other. After a long silence, she said, "I bought that can of whipped cream for *you.*"

"Sarah is always stealing my toys," Murphy said. "We should have let Nigel launch code sixty-six."

"What's code sixty-six?" she asked while filling a mug of hot coffee since she had left the one Murphy had brought her up in the bedroom.

"It's a security system that we're testing out," Murphy said. "It's directly tied into Nigel."

"I thought our security system was patched into a section of the FBI," Jessica said. "If the estate gets broken in to, Nigel will tell us about it and notify the feds, who'll come out with their guns blazing."

With a grimace, Murphy leaned on the granite island with both of his hands flat. Her violet eyes narrowed, Jessica cocked her head at him.

Finally, he said, "Not exactly."

"What do you mean, 'not exactly'?"

"While setting up Nigel, the IT folks really went all out with him. Since Tristan was setting up the smart features, he had some programming ideas for the security features. He met with the cybersecurity team, and they all got very excited."

"How excited?"

"Let's just say that together, they all released their inner Tony Stark." Seeing the question in her eyes, he said, "Tony Stark. *Iron Man.* Jarvis, his artificial-intelligence butler."

"Huh?"

"The way the system is supposed to work, if someone breeches the estate's security system, Nigel will do more than just notify us and the feds. He'll go into defense mode. Code sixty-six."

"If someone breaks in, we'll go into the panic room, and the house will be locked down until the authorities arrive," Jessica said. "Doors and windows will be secured. Everything is bulletproof. Right?"

"If it's only one or two guys, I can take them on," Murphy said.

"We'll talk about that later," she said. "In the meantime, tell me about code sixty-six."

Murphy went over to the kitchen table and sat on top of it. "Okay, Nigel will go on the defensive. Ideally, if the security system is breached out at the fence or the gate, then everything in here and in the garage will be locked down before the bad guys can get here. Nigel will resecure the fence and the gate, and the bad guys will be trapped here until the authorities arrive to take them away." With his hands, he illustrated the bad guys being taken away.

"Good," she said. "Code sixty-six sounds cool so far."

"That's assuming the bad guys are just some common run-of-the-mill house burglars looking to steal our laptops," he said. "However, if Nigel senses the use of force or violence—like if his audio picks up gunfire or the bulletproof windows or walls are shot at—that's when things will get interesting."

"How interesting?"

"Nigel will launch code *ninety-nine.*"

"What's ninety-nine?"

"Nigel will switch from defense mode to *offense* mode and will use lethal force against anyone on the property who he determines is a threat to those listed as friends or family members in his contacts."

Jessica was doubtful. "How could a *house* go on the offensive?"

"It's a smart house, Jessie," Murphy said. "Tristan and the cybersecurity team set it up so that it knows who is in which room." He gestured down at the game room. "Think about it. Nigel knows what shows Newman likes to watch. Newman barely has to change the channels anymore. Nigel knows his schedule and switches them automatically. Nigel can regulate the temperature of your bath water. He makes your latte in the morning without your programming it."

"I don't think Nigel could take out bad guys," Jessica said.

"It's a beta system." Murphy took her into a warm hug. "So it may not even work."

"If it does work, what will it do? What can a house do against a burglar?"

Murphy shrugged his shoulders. "I don't know. You know Tristan and how computer geeks are. It will probably flash a bunch of lights and make a big racket."

"Whatever made you agree to let them install this thing in *our house* when you don't even know what it can do?"

Murphy shrugged. "Chalk it up to a boy and his toys."

"I felt more secure when the only security we had were our guns and our dogs," she whispered into his chest.

"By the way, where's Gnarly?"

"Gnarly is now in the backyard," Nigel said. "I let him out through the patio door off of the game room."

"Why did you do that, Nigel?" Murphy asked.

"Because he asked me to let him out, Murphy," Nigel said. "And Jessica told me to save his voice and to remember that he's a family member, which means that he is cleared to make service requests."

With a growl, Murphy went down the stairs to the game room.

"Would you like me to save Sarah Thornton to your friends-and-family database, Jessica?" Nigel asked.

"Yes, Nigel," Jessica said with a sigh. "How did you know her last name was Thornton? We didn't—"

"I ran her face through the federal facial-recognition program," Nigel said. "Sarah Jane Thornton. Twenty-one years old. This upcoming fall she will be a third-year cadet at the United States Naval Academy. If you would like, I can access her fingerprints from the military database for our records. However, I will still need to scan her retina for the home's security system."

"That's enough, Nigel," Jessica said with a sigh.

"Would you like me to remind her that she needs to renew her driver's license? Her current license will expire in twelve days."

"Sometimes I think you're too well connected, Nigel."

On the lower level of their home, Murphy's Bassett hound mix, Newman, was sprawled out in his own worn chair on which he watched television twenty-four hours a day, seven days a week with breaks only to eat and to go outside via the patio doors off of the game room.

As soon as the blue shelty, Spencer, saw that the door was open, she raced out to play with the German shepherd.

Distracted by a morning news show, Newman refused to budge.

"We should get another dog," Jessica said with sarcasm while handing a mug of green tea to Murphy.

"The next addition to our family is going to be a baby." Murphy draped his arm across her shoulders.

Jessica gave him a soft smile. "We'll talk about that *after* I get my doctorate."

"And now for a breaking-news item," the female host of the news program said. "It seems that one small-town mayoral race in Western Maryland is drawing more national attention than our current national election. The other day, the political front-runner, an army veteran named Gnarly Faraday, a five-year-old German—"

"Gnarly!" Jessica whirled away from the open patio door and scurried across the room to watch the big-screen television mounted on the wall. Murphy was right behind her.

"—ambushed at a debate when the host revealed that the mayoral front-runner was a prime suspect in the murder of his handler, First Sergeant Belle Perkins, who was killed in her tent during the night while serving on a mission in Iraq four years ago."

Looking proper, the news anchor said, "Well, just minutes ago, in an unprecedented maneuver, the US Army released a statement to all news agencies announcing that journalist Salma Rameriz's information was incorrect. The statement from the public affairs office of the US Army says the following."

As she spoke, the words appeared on the television screen.

"While this office and the US Army are unable to comment on the specifics of their investigation into the brutal murder of First Sergeant Belle Perkins, her teammate Sergeant Major Gnarly is not and never has been a suspect."

The screen then showed the news host, who continued her report.

"The statement goes on to reveal that Gnarly's dishonorable discharge was not in any way connected to his handler's death. Sergeant Major Gnarly received his dishonorable discharge as a result of going AWOL. He was hit on the head by a falling beam after rushing into a burning house to save a mother cat and her litter of seven helpless kittens. Due to his injury, he got amnesia, forgot that he was in the military, and ended up being reported AWOL."

"Saving a mother cat and her seven kittens from a burning house?" Murphy doubted that the report was true.

"Not only that," the news host said, "the US Army went on to state that they are releasing Sergeant Major Gnarly's birth certificate, which will prove that he was born in Inwood, West Virginia. This is in response to assertions by some in the anti-Gnarly crowd who claim that the candidate is not eligible to run for political office because he is of German descent. This birth certificate, the US Army says, will put this birther issue to rest. While Gnarly's German bloodline is pure, he is a natural born citizen of the United States, which makes him eligible to run for office."

"But he's still a dog," one of her experts said off-camera.

"The Gnarly campaign is not disputing that." The host turned to her panel of experts. "I have to say, never in my career have I heard of the military releasing a statement so quickly to clear up misinformation about a veteran. Why do you think they released this statement, and how do you think this is going to affect the mayoral race in Spencer, Maryland?"

The first expert, a political analyst from a major news association, chuckled. "Well, I think this is evidence that what goes around comes around. Salma Rameriz was very tight with Nancy Braxton, who was getting slaughtered in the polls by Gnarly Faraday. She was the journalist who broke that misinformation."

"And Nancy Braxton was found murdered yesterday," the host said.

"But my sources are telling me that Braxton's party is looking to bring in another candidate to replace her on the ticket," the expert said. "Even so"—he shrugged his shoulders—"it's not going to do any good, since the army has sent out this press release about Gnarly not being a killer and never even being a suspect."

"Not to mention blowing the whole birther issue out of the water by releasing his birth certificate," the host said.

"Plus the army threw in the fact that his dishonorable discharge was due to a tragic accident while saving a family of cats." The expert laughed. "With all that, Gnarly's favorability ratings are going to go through the roof. His campaign managers might want to consider running him as a write-in candidate for president."

The other expert, a proper-looking man with a big blue bow tie, jumped in. "This statement from the army directly contradicts the information I learned from a source close to the Pentagon who told me that Gnarly Faraday was dishonorably discharged for stealing a steak dinner from a four-star general when he was visiting a platoon in the Middle East."

"According to this release from the army, your source was incorrect," the first expert said.

"Why do you think the army's chief of staff had this statement released to exonerate Gnarly?" the host asked.

"It must have been another canine who stole the general's dinner," the first expert said.

"Gnarly Faraday does have a history of petty theft," the bow-tied expert said, pounding the tabletop. "This candidate has a rebellious nature and a long history of problems dealing with authority figures, which disqualifies him from being Spencer's mayor."

"But he saved a mother cat and her kittens," the first expert said. "With the animal lovers on his side, unless he makes a huge mistake, Gnarly is a shoo-in to become Spencer's first canine mayor."

The expert in the bow tie shook his head. "There are going to be dire consequences if Spencer elects this candidate for mayor. Gnarly is reckless and disrespectful. You know, his kleptomania could be a symptom of a much larger character issue. If you ask me, that whole press release is a lie."

The host jumped in. "In the next hour, we'll be interviewing the mother cat and the kittens Gnarly saved."

With a wide grin, Jessica turned to Murphy. "Your CO got the chief of staff for the army to release that statement, didn't she?"

"What can I say?" Murphy said. "She's a dog lover."

"Remind me to thank her...if I'm ever allowed to meet her."

"Murphy," Nigel said. "Your commanding officer has just arrived at the front gate. She has requested that you meet her out front."

Realizing that he was still dressed only in his athletic pants and that he wasn't wearing shoes or a shirt, Murphy groaned. He could not keep CO waiting.

Seeming to read his thoughts, Jessica said, "Want my bathrobe?" She opened her soft, silky robe.

Murphy opted to hope that CO would be impressed with his firm chest and six-pack abs. While Jessica watched through the living-room window, Murphy went out the front door and walked to where the white stretch limousine was parked at the bottom of the steps leading up to the porch. CO's bodyguard-driver was already waiting at the rear of the

248

car. Taking note of Murphy's bare feet and lack of a shirt, the bodyguard-driver's eyebrows rose up high on his tall forehead. Saying nothing, he opened the door and gestured for Murphy to climb inside.

Trying to appear nonchalant, Murphy made himself comfortable in the seat across from his direct supervisor, a woman with long legs. She was the leader of the Phantoms. Murphy did not know her name. Since she always covered her hair with a stylish hat and her eyes with dark sunglasses, he was unable to give a good description of her. All he knew was that she had the best legs he had ever seen on a woman and a deep, throaty, sensual voice that was unmistakable.

That morning, she was dressed in a white suit with black trim and a matching wide-brimmed hat.

Upon seeing Murphy's casual style of dress—or, rather, undress—she cleared her throat. "I'm sorry if I interrupted anything, Lieutenant."

"You didn't interrupt anything, ma'am. Jessica and I were just getting ready to go to the hospital to see if I could talk to Tawkeel Said about what happened in Brussels."

"Have you briefed Jessica about Tawkeel's assignment in Brussels?"

"I told her only that he had been on assignment deep undercover. I said that his cover had been blown and that he had almost been killed. I did not give her any specifics, ma'am. Did you receive my report about my interview with Bruce Hardy?"

"Yes, I did," she said. "I'm comparing the agents who were on Hardy's team with those who were on Tawkeel's team. It's virtually impossible to get that information from the CIA, even with all of my connections, but I did find out something that is going to turn your investigation into Gnarly's case on its head."

"What's that?"

"Belle Perkins was actively investigating a case for the army's criminal investigation command."

Murphy shook his head. "I worked with her husband. He was well aware of my clearances and knew that I was investigating this case. If she had been working undercover, he would have known it and would have told me."

"He couldn't," she said, "because he wasn't authorized to tell you. That's why it was left up to me. Perkins was a first sergeant in the army, and the US Army Criminal Investigative Command handpicked her and Gnarly to go to Iraq with that unit to investigate a case for them. The army's chief of staff has ordered that a copy of that case file be sent to me. I'll forward it to you as soon as it arrives."

"You're telling me that Gnarly was working undercover." Chuckling at what must have been a joke, Murphy looked over to where Gnarly was sitting on the porch. With his eyes focused on them, the handsome German shepherd cocked his head.

"Gnarly is an extremely valuable dog," she said. "I was told that he was the chief reason that army's CID picked Perkins to work this case, whatever it was. In the very short time he was in the army, he got a reputation for being the most highly intelligent dog in the canine corp." CID stood for the US Army's Criminal Investigation Command.

"If he's so highly trained, why doesn't he do what he's told?"

"Because he's smarter than most people," she said in a matter-of-fact tone. "Even people who are extremely smart can have problems taking orders from someone who they consider unintelligent."

Murphy laughed. "Wait until I tell my father-in-law that. 'Gnarly won't come when you call him because he thinks he's smarter than you.'"

"You can't tell Mac," she said. "Everything I'm telling you about Gnarly is classified. The reason I'm telling you is so that you know exactly what you're dealing with."

She pointed out the window to where Gnarly was hopping around the bodyguard-driver, in an effort to catch one of his feet and untie his shoes. It was the first time Murphy had ever seen the bodyguard-driver smile.

"Gnarly possesses the cognitive ability to examine a situation and to plan and execute a strategy to complete his objective—whether it's stealing the army chief of staff's steak dinner or taking out two snipers who have his unit pinned."

"So Gnarly did steal the general's steak?" Murphy asked with a sly grin.

"Plus the dessert. That dog is as intelligent as any highly trained human agent."

"If he could take out two snipers, then I guess a mountain lion would be a piece of cake?"

"Like stealing a four-star general's dinner."

Struck with a sudden thought, Murphy said, "Maybe Hardy's cover wasn't the one that got blown. Maybe the terrorist group chasing the unit wasn't after Hardy but was after Perkins and Gnarly. The strikes stopped after Perkins was murdered. While everyone assumed Hardy was the target, in reality, it was Perkins."

"That is very possible," she said. "Let's look at that angle. I'll be waiting for your report about your visit with Tawkeel. He's anxious to see you."

Murphy stopped climbing out of the back of the limousine and turned back to her. "Thank you for releasing that statement clearing Gnarly of Perkins' murder and especially for that made-up story about him saving the mother cat and her kittens."

"What makes you think it's a made-up story?"

CHAPTER NINETEEN

David was relieved to see that Mac had more color in his face when he picked him up at Spencer Manor. Not yet 100 percent, Mac was still insisting that he was going to clear Gnarly's name and prove that he hadn't murdered Nancy Braxton.

Despite the official statement telling one and all that Gnarly was not a suspect in Nancy's murder, those who supported the late candidate and some of those who supported Bill Clark believed that the police department was covering something up for their canine candidate, which made for a very intriguing conspiracy theory. Some media outlets had even suggested that the police department had been involved in Nancy's murder so that they could improve the odds of Gnarly being elected.

As far as the police force was concerned, the only way to completely clear Gnarly's name was to find out who had in fact killed Nancy Braxton.

David and Mac arrived at the sheriff's department in time to see many of the deputies in the squad room watching an interview on a cable-news program. The journalist was conducting an interview with a woman and several tabby cats. Mac was about to turn away to go search for Sheriff Turow when he noticed the headline on the television screen: "Cat Family Saved by Gnarly Faraday, Independent Mayoral Candidate."

"You've got to be kidding," Mac said loudly enough that David heard him.

"Gnarly is one busy dog."

"Right before the interview, they announced that PETA has officially endorsed Gnarly for mayor," Sheriff Turow said as he came up behind the two men.

"Sweet," David said.

"Gnarly never saved a family of cats," Mac said in a low voice. "It's all a lie."

"Well," David said, "the media lied about Gnarly killing his handler, and now they're lying about him saving a family of cats. That makes it even."

"I'm with him," the sheriff said to Mac. "I've contacted Nancy Braxton's doctor to ask for a copy of her medical records and a list of what medications she was on so that we can identify what should've been in the capsules she took. He immediately told me to get a warrant. Evidently, Nancy's team and party are circling the wagons to keep us from finding out and making public any unpleasantries about their candidate."

"Even if that information could solve her murder?" David asked.

"They're more interested in their party winning this election," Mac said. "Any word about who Ward is looking at to replace Nancy?"

The sheriff shook his head. "He's in Annapolis for meetings today. He's already arranged for a lawyer to represent Hugh Vance and Erin Devereux. Vance and the lawyer should be here any minute." He checked the time on the television.

"Well, with that in mind, whoever Ward selects for the ballot will also become our candidate for the murder suspect," Mac said.

The desk sergeant entered the squad room with Hugh Vance and a smaller man in an expensive suit. Seeing the sheriff, who had a gold badge pinned to his chest, the lawyer led Nancy Braxton's brother across the room.

"Elliott Curtis," the lawyer said while pumping Sheriff Turow's hand. "I'll be representing Hugh Vance and Erin Devereux in your investigation."

"All we want is to get whatever information we can and to solve your sister's murder," the sheriff said to Hugh.

With a cocky chuckle, Elliott shoved his eyeglasses up onto his nose. "That's what they all say."

Based on the lawyer's body language and tone, the sheriff, the police chief, and Mac saw that he had already determined that they were the enemy.

Since Nancy Braxton's murder had been committed within the town limits of Spencer, David O'Callaghan had an official hand in the case, even though he had relinquished the lead to Sheriff Turow. Appearances didn't usually mean that much to the police chief, but murder convictions meant a whole lot to him. Since Erin and Hugh were claiming that David had a conflict of interest in the case, he knew that a defense attorney could do the same thing when the police nabbed Nancy's killer. David hadn't personally liked Nancy Braxton, but he was not about to let her killer go free.

As a courtesy, Sheriff Turow had invited David to sit in on his interview with Hugh while Mac watched from the observation room. With the case file resting between them, Sheriff Turow and David O'Callaghan were sitting at the table across from Hugh and his lawyer. Both David and the sheriff had notepads resting in front of them. In silence, David allowed Sheriff Turow to take his time checking his notes.

Before long, Hugh Vance began to fidget. From the observation room, Mac watched him bite his fingernails and stare at the two law-enforcement officers on the other side of the table. One leg was twitching. The big-boned, oversized brute of a man was scared out of his wits.

In stark contrast to Vance, Elliott was eyeing both Sheriff Turow and David with disdain—simply because of the uniforms they were wearing and the police shields on their chests.

"Mr. Vance," Sheriff Turow finally said.

Hugh jumped in his seat. "Yes?"

"According to your statement, the one you gave to Police Chief O'Callaghan"—he gestured to David, who was sitting next to him—"and me, you did not realize that your sister was missing until Chief O'Callaghan arrived at your home that morning to inform you that her body had been found down at the lake. Is that not correct?"

A finger in his mouth, Hugh glanced from the sheriff to David and then to his lawyer, who said, "My client stated that the last time he'd seen his sister was when she'd gone up to bed, which was at around eleven thirty the night before."

"That was when he saw her," the sheriff said. "But he failed to tell us that he'd actually realized she was missing less than an hour later, when she ran out of the house and into the darkness—a good six hours before she was found dead."

"Your clients seemed to forget about the security cameras installed around the house," David said. "They recorded Nancy Braxton running out of the house like the devil was chasing her and your client driving off minutes later. He returned close to one o'clock, after the estimated time of death."

"Why didn't your client call the police to report her missing?" Sheriff Turow asked.

"Why did you pretend not to know that she was missing when I showed up to tell you she was dead?" David asked Hugh directly. "When I told you that your sister was found down by the lake, you broke down before I informed you that she was dead."

"That's not true." Hugh told Sheriff Turow, "He's lying."

In the observation room, Mac shook his head in anticipation of the lawyer's next statement.

"Chief O'Callaghan, you asked my client when he had last seen his sister, and he answered that question truthfully," the lawyer said.

"What was she running from when she left that night?" Sheriff Turow asked.

"I have no idea." Hugh Vance shook his head as his lawyer told him not to tell them anything.

Sheriff Turow tried a less direct approach. "We can see that you loved your sister, Hugh. All we want is to find out what happened to her, and I believe you loved her enough to want that, too. She deserves justice. But that's not going to happen if you don't tell us everything you know."

"Was Erin with Nancy before she ran away?" David asked.

"Don't answer that," Elliott said in a sharp tone.

"Why not?" David turned his attention to Hugh. "You are aware that your lawyer is representing *both* you and Erin, right? Think about this. If Erin was the last one with your sister before she left the house scared for her life that night, if she was alone with her, how do you know that she isn't responsible for her death?"

"I told you not to talk to my client," Elliott said.

Ignoring the lawyer, David barged on. "Since Curtis is representing her, too, then how certain can you be that he has your best interest in mind when he tells you not to tell us anything? He's protecting her, too."

"We're through here!" Elliott was out of his seat and gesturing for Hugh to follow him.

"What if she's behind Nancy's murder?" David asked Hugh when he hesitated. "That would mean that your lawyer is telling you to keep quiet in order to protect your sister's killer."

Yanking open the door, Elliott said, "Come on, Vance! We're out of here!"

Hugh stared into David's eyes.

"Now!" Elliot yelled.

Mac held his breath.

Hugh's voice was soft. "Tell Ward thanks, but I want another lawyer."

David and Sheriff Turow sighed in unison.

The slam of the interrogation room's door was heard throughout the department.

Hugh covered his face with his hands.

Plunging ahead, David asked, "Was your sister on any medication?"

"None that I know of," Hugh said. "Why?"

"Standard question," David said. "According to what we saw on the recording from the security company, she was very distraught when she left the house less than an hour before she was murdered."

"Maybe the intruder who broke in the night before and shot Erin broke in again," Hugh said. "Have you thought about that?"

"When I spoke to you on the morning we found Nancy's body, you said that Nancy had fired Erin the night before because she blamed her for leaking that story about Gnarly to Salma Rameriz," David said.

"But it wasn't Erin, because when we checked the e-mail that had been sent to Salma, it was from a different e-mail address," Hugh said.

"Was that before or after Nancy fired Erin?" Sheriff Turow asked.

Hugh hesitated. "Before."

"Why would she have fired Erin if there was proof that she hadn't sent that story to the journalist?" the sheriff asked.

Hugh took in a deep breath. "Nancy could be demanding that way."

"Erin claimed that Nancy fired her on a regular basis," David said. "How did she like that?"

"Nancy was ultrademanding," Hugh said. "Most people called her a bitch. But Erin put up with it."

"Why?" David asked.

Hugh shrugged his shoulders.

"According to the security videos," David said, "Nancy left. Erin came out of the house to search for her and then ran inside to get you, and you drove off after her."

"She was long gone by then." Hugh waved his hands. "I looked all over. Up and down the mountain. Drove past the lake. Even parked and went walking along the footpath and shone a flashlight into the water to see if I could see her—I thought maybe she'd drowned herself. But I couldn't find her. It was so dark. That's why I knew she was already dead when you came the next morning. But I had assumed she killed herself."

"Did Nancy ever show signs of being suicidal before?" Sheriff Turow asked.

"A little." Hugh shrugged his big shoulders.

"Did Erin tell you that Nancy went running out of the house to go kill herself?" David asked.

"She didn't use those exact words." Hugh shrugged his shoulders again. "She came banging on my bedroom door and said that Nancy had flipped out and gone flying out of her bedroom. Erin said she caught up with her in the hall, and Nancy tried to attack her. Then she ran down the stairs and out of the house. Erin kept telling me that Nancy had lost her mind."

"Had she ever lost her mind before?" David asked.

Saying nothing, Hugh looked directly at David. Slowly, he pulled his gaze over to Sheriff Turow. Finally, he said, "No. Never."

In the observation room, Mac looked through the glass to where David was peering over Hugh's shoulder in his direction. Mac could see by David's expression that he didn't believe him either.

While the sheriff and David resumed the interview and asked questions about other potential suspects, like Salma Rameriz or Nathan Braxton's mistress, there was a knock on the observation room's door. The desk sergeant stepped inside. "Mr. Faraday, I didn't want to interrupt the sheriff, but I thought you would like to know that Nathan Braxton is in the reception area and wants to speak to the sheriff or to Police Chief O'Callaghan."

"Did he say what about?" Mac asked while keeping his attention focused on Hugh Vance's demeanor. He'd seemed to relax after his lawyer had left.

"Mr. Braxton says he knows who killed his wife."

The knock on the door woke Dallas up from a deep sleep. It took her a full moment to remember falling asleep on the sofa with her arms wrapped around Storm after David had left for the police station. She had been sleeping so soundly that one of her cheeks was pressed up to her eye, which was resting against the dog's cold, hard plastic cone of shame.

After climbing over Storm to get off of the sofa, Dallas stumbled up the steps and out of the drop-down living room to make her way to the front door. To her surprise, she found Archie Monday on the porch. She was armed with a casserole.

"What's the occasion?" Dallas asked, opening the door.

Archie held out the dish to her. "I made a chicken divan casserole for dinner and happened to have extra chicken. So"—she lifted a shoulder—"it wasn't that hard to just double the recipe. David loves my chicken divan. I thought since Storm is recuperating, you could use a break from cooking dinner."

Dallas shook a finger at her. "Admit it. I'm growing on you."

"No, you're not. It's just that I hate leftovers more than I don't like you."

"Well, if I turned down free vittles, my pap's ghost will come haunt me for a week, so come on in!" Dallas stepped back and opened the door wide for her. "You know where the kitchen is, Ms. Archie. Kick off your shoes, and stay a while." While Archie walked through the door, Dallas saw that she was carrying her laptop case from a strap off her shoulder.

After instructing Dallas in how to warm up the dish when she and David were ready to eat, Archie went over to the sofa to pet Storm and examine her wounds.

"David told me that Gnarly took out that nasty ol' mountain lion," Dallas said. "If he hadn't, I would have hunted him down myself. Did Gnarly get hurt?"

"Just some superficial scratches," Archie said before explaining that Murphy and Jessica had taken him to Washington to investigate the murder of his former handler. "The army put out a statement saying that Gnarly didn't do it."

"Nancy Braxton's and Bill Clark's supporters won't believe that," Dallas said. "They'll believe what they wanna believe, and since Rameriz put it out there that Gnarly is a crazed killer dog, people are gonna cling to that."

Hugging Storm, Archie pressed her face against her shoulder. "Unless Murphy and Gnarly track down the real killer."

Dallas narrowed her eyes and studied Archie. "What role is Murphy playing in this investigation? I thought he was a pencil pusher at the Pentagon."

Caught, Archie stuttered before she said, "Murphy went to the naval academy and has a lot of connections in the military. His dad was a Judge Advocate General officer and knows, like, everybody." She rolled her eyes. "So Murphy should have no problem getting to the bottom of this case."

"Even if his pap was a big wig, does Murphy really have that much pull?" Dallas was doubtful. "I can't imagine the army helping a navy lieutenant who has no official role in a murder investigation."

Instead of answering, Archie opened up her case and extracted her laptop from it. "Mac and I think we found what Sandy Burr uncovered in his investigation of Braxton Charities." She carried the computer to the dining table in the great room. "Want to see?"

"This is still my story, right?"

"Of course," Archie said while powering up the laptop. "I'm an editor, research assistant, and amateur hacker—but don't tell anyone that."

Pulling up a chair so that she could sit next to her, Dallas studied the chart and the notes on the notepad that Archie had taken out of the case. The organizational chart contained names in boxes and a list of amounts of money—including tens of thousands of dollars and even millions—and lines with arrows connecting each box to an amount of money. "Did you find a money trail?"

"Not necessarily anything that would stand up in court," Archie said. "Unfortunately, most of what we found is circumstantial."

"Aren't most cases circumstantial?"

"Yes, but in this case, the parties involved set up an elaborate path involving a lot of money coming and going overseas and through shell companies and phony charities," Archie said. "Plus the people involved are heavyweights, including the director of the Internal Revenue Service."

"He probably helped set up the phony charities, which are complete with a tax-exempt status," Dallas said.

"On the surface, Braxton Charities is a legit nonprofit," Archie explained. "It does have a lot of legitimate charities under its umbrella, and it's given grants to universities for medical studies, to children's hospitals, to homeless shelters—"

"But—"

"But," Archie said, "we believe that it's also a laundromat that enables politicians and special-interest groups to process bribes, kickbacks, and money from extortions."

Archie referred to the organizational chart, at the center of which were the words "Braxton Charities." "Let's say you're a senator from a state where coal is a big industry. The voters expect you to support coal. But a big lobby that wants to shut down coal in order to combat global warming comes to you and wants you to support the Washington crowd. It makes you an offer that you can't refuse."

"If you're as crooked as a barrel of fishhooks, you take the money," Dallas said, "and let your constituents fend for themselves. What do you care? You're now runnin' with the big dogs."

"But if you just take the money, you could go to jail," Archie said.

"Like a bad guy breakin' out of the big house, you've gotta throw the dogs off of your scent."

"And that's where the laundromat comes in," Archie said. "Send the money through enough cycles, and it won't smell like dirty money anymore. In the case of our example, the global warming lobby would make a donation to Braxton Charities, which would then transfer the money into one of its phony nonprofits or even into a shell company. Then the shell company would disburse the funds to the senator for an insanely expensive speech or some consulting he had done for them."

"So the bribe goes from the special-interest group to the charity," Dallas said, "which makes the bribe tax deductible, just like in Robin's book. Then it trickles from the umbrella down to the phony charity or shell company—"

"Which provides some phony service or goods to Braxton Charities," Archie said.

"And from the shell company or phony charity to the dirty senator," Dallas said. "At which point the dirty money is completely clean and practically impossible to trace back to the big interest group."

"Exactly," Archie said. "And for each transaction, Braxton Charities takes twenty percent. Nancy and Hugh, who runs Braxton Charities, were doing that for years. She made the political contacts who needed to have their money cleaned, and Hugh cleaned it for them. We identified some IRS agents, district attorneys, and federal investigators who get monthly payments called 'consulting fees' from various shell companies that are directly connected to Braxton Charities. I managed to trace five back to Hugh Vance, who has multiple bank accounts overseas and a ton of money in all of them."

"Imagine all the dirt Nancy and Hugh have collected on all these people," Dallas said. "No wonder Nancy's party was bendin' over backward to get her elected to somethin' to keep her happy."

Their eyes met.

"And every one of them had a motive to kill her: keeping her quiet," Archie said.

"Sandy Burr was investigatin' Braxton Charities," Dallas said. "He met with Nancy Braxton at the Lakeside Inn and ended up dead by mornin'. Considerin' how much money it looks like they were rakin' in, they wouldn't have wanted to take a chance on Sandy ruinin' their fun."

"Also, with so much money and so many connections, it wouldn't have been hard for them to find someone to do the deed for them."

"And then buy the hotel and make their one witness co-owner."

"Yes," Archie said. "That appears to be what happened. V & M Enterprises is owned by Hugh Vance."

"Is the *M* Caleb Montgomery, the bartender who jumped out from behind the bar and became the hotel manager in exchange for amnesia?" Dallas asked.

"He owns one-third of the Lakeside Inn," Archie said.

"What does Hugh Vance look like?" Dallas asked.

Archie did an image search on the Internet. With effort, they found one image of Hugh Vance posing at an event with his sister and her football-star husband.

A thin grin crossed Dallas' face. "Big guy."

"I'd call him big boned," Archie said.

"Big enough to be called a fat man," Dallas said, "which was how Caleb Montgomery described the man at the bar who was watching Sandy Burr interview Nancy Braxton shortly before he was killed. Can you print that picture?"

"If Vance bought Montgomery off, he's not going to identify him as Burr's killer and put an end to his gravy train," Archie said.

"Maybe not right away," Dallas said. "But if the Lord's willin' and the creek don't rise, we can find a way to make him see things a tad differently."

"Mr. Braxton," Mac said as he stepped into the sheriff's department's reception area and extended his hand. "I'm Mac Faraday. Pleasure to meet you. Sheriff Turow is finishing up an interview and will be right with you."

"Gnarly's owner," Nathan Braxton said with a grin.

As if he had been struck with a lightning bolt of realization, Mac understood the meaning of a complaint Archie had once made about everyone in Spencer knowing her as "Mac Faraday's wife." For over a decade, she had built her own career as an editor, working her way up to editing exclusively for Robin Spencer. Since Robin's death, international best-selling authors and their agents had sought her out to edit books destined to make the best-seller lists even before their releases. Yet in the time it had taken them to exchange wedding vows, Archie's identity had quickly become attached to Mac's.

Mac saw that if Gnarly indeed won the election, the same thing would happen to him. He would become "Gnarly's owner."

"Actually," Mac said, "Gnarly is my dog."

"Is it true—what they said on the news about him rushing into a burning building to save that mother cat and her ten kittens?"

"I heard it was seven," Mac said.

"Hey, Mac!" After seeing their candidate's owner in the reception area, instead of stopping at the welcome counter, Bernie and Hap made a detour over to see him. "Archie said we'd find you here! Where's Gnarly?"

Spotting Nathan Braxton, a football legend, Bernie's mouth dropped open. "You're Nathan Braxton!"

Mac saw Nathan's face transform from that of a regular dude to that of a celebrity. A wide grin crossed his handsome face. "Yes, I am. And you are?"

Bernie pumped the former football player's hand. "Bernie Stein and Hap Goldman." He quickly unbuttoned his button-down shirt to reveal a T-shirt with Gnarly's face on it. "We're Gnarly Faraday's campaign managers. You couldn't ask for a better mayor! Gnarly is brave and has integrity coming out of his ears. Why, just this morning, they reported on the news that Gnarly, with no concern whatsoever for his own personal safety, ran into a burning building to save a mother cat and her twelve kittens! Can you see either of our presidential candidates doing that?"

Clearing his throat, Mac said, "Bernie, Hap, Mr. Braxton is Nancy's hus—"

"Nah, that's okay." To Mac's surprise, Nathan shrugged off his comment. "They're right. Nancy would've never run into a burning building unless it was to save a big bag of money."

"Well, PETA has endorsed Gnarly for mayor," Bernie said. "And as of an hour ago, he is twenty-four points ahead of Bill Clark!" Becoming serious, he led Mac by his arm away from the football player and lowered his voice to a harsh whisper. "Which is why we need to talk to you. Where's Gnarly?"

"I told you," Mac looked from Bernie to Hap, who was on his other side. "You read the statement I released yesterday. He went away for a few days to meet with his campaign leaders to plan how best to proceed for the rest of his campaign for mayor."

"Yeah, that was all well and good to tell the voters," Bernie said. "But then this morning, Hap and I realized"— he gestured to Hap and himself—"that *we're* his campaign leaders. Is Gnarly pulling a double cross on us? Now that we've gotten him national attention, has he decided that we're too small potatoes for him and hired some big-time campaign manager?"

"No, Gnarly would never do that. You both know Gnarly. He is the most loyal per—" Realizing he was about to say "person," Mac stopped. *What am I saying? He's a dog!* "Gnarly would never betray anyone. He almost died rushing into a burning building to save that mother cat and her fifteen kittens. I mean, you saw it on the news."

"And on the Internet," Bernie studied Mac with narrow eyes. "It wouldn't be on the Internet if it weren't true."

Hap nodded his head in agreement.

Mac held up his hand in an oath. "I swear on my mother's grave that Gnarly just needed a couple of days of rest and relaxation. He'll be back in a few days raring to go to beat Bill Clark's butt and become Spencer's mayor."

"Are you sure Gnarly's safe?" Bernie reached over to tap Hap on the arm. "Now that Nancy Braxton is out, that leaves just Gnarly and Bill Clark, and we all know Clark. He'll do anything to get what he wants."

His eyes wide with fear, Hap's head was bobbing up and down.

In a harsh whisper, Bernie said, "Everyone knows Clark killed his own mother."

Mac looked from one of them to the other. "I assure you that Gnarly is completely safe. He's got the best protection available."

"You mean you hired bodyguards for him?"

Looking around to make sure that no one was listening, Mac lowered his voice to a whisper. "I didn't put it in the release because I knew no one would believe it."

"What?"

"The military has reactivated Gnarly. He's on a secret government mission in Washington."

"No," Bernie said.

Hap's mouth hung open. His eyes were so wide that they looked like they were going to pop out of his head.

"What kind of mission?" Bernie asked.

"It's classified," Mac said. "But I assure you that with the people he's working with, there's no way Clark could get anywhere near Gnarly."

Bernie and Hap exchanged long glances and periodically looked back at Mac, weighing whether they should believe him.

"We have nothing to worry about," Mac said. "As soon as this case is over, Gnarly will be back home safe and sound."

"Hey, Mac," Sheriff Turow said. "You need to hear this. Looks like we've got a situation."

With a grin, Mac looked from Bernie to Hap and back to Bernie again. "Are we good?"

After a pause, they both nodded their heads.

"You've been doing a great job on Gnarly's campaign." Mac took turns shaking their hands. "We all appreciate it. Really, we do. And as soon as Gnarly is back from his secret mission, he'll be calling you."

Mac was halfway across the squad room when he realized what he had said. *Gnarly doesn't have a phone. How is he going to call them?* He shook his head. *I'm losing my mind.*

Bernie paused at the door leading out to the parking lot to study Mac while Sheriff Turow and David briefed him about the situation. "You buying that story about Gnarly being away on a secret mission, Hap?"

Watching Mac, Hap slowly shook his head.

"Neither am I," Bernie said.

With a sense of determination, the two men left the sheriff's department.

On the other side of the squad room, Sheriff Turow directed Nathan Braxton to repeat for Mac what he had told them.

"Well," Nathan said. "It's pretty much common knowledge that Nancy and I led separate lives." He gestured to David. "I told that to the police chief here yesterday. It's a known secret that I sleep with other women and that I have a longtime mistress, Eleanor."

"Eleanor confirmed Braxton's alibi for the time of the murder," Sheriff Turow said to David and Mac.

"But," Nathan said, "since Nancy was here in Deep Creek Lake campaigning and her election team wanted me available for photo ops, I started having a fling with another woman."

"Cassandra Clark," David said to Mac. "I saw the two of them together."

"Bill Clark's wife?"

"They're newlyweds," David said.

"I didn't know she was Bill Clark's wife until after we hooked up," Nathan said. "We were in bed...after...And then she started talking about what a twerp Bill Clark was. One thing after another about how great he thought he was, and then when she started talking about how lousy he was in bed, I thought, 'damn it!' I had just laid the wife of my wife's political opponent. I started looking for hidden cameras. I was absolutely certain that it was going to end up on the news the next day and that Nancy would kill me." Conviction dripped from his voice when he added, "I mean, Nancy literally would have killed me."

"But it didn't make the news," Mac said.

"She hated Clark as much as, if not more than, I couldn't stand Nancy. The fling continued." Waving his hands, Nathan caught their gazes. "We're all men here. You know how it is. It was no love affair. We only got together for sex, and she is—" He chuckled.

Wondering if the fling had turned into a *Fatal Attraction* type of scenario, Mac asked, "Was it only sex on her end, too?"

"Yes," Nathan said. "But then—" He stopped. "The last time we hooked up, Cassie had had a big fight with Clark, and she was mouthing off about how, since I couldn't stand Nancy, we should help each other out."

"In what way?" Mac asked.

Nathan swallowed. "Well, no one knew about our fling. As far as the public was concerned, we barely knew each other. So she said that if I got rid of Clark for her, or at least arranged to make it happen, she would get rid of Nancy for me. Then we would both be free of them."

"Together or—"

With a frown, Nathan shook his head. "We were only having sex together. Nothing serious."

"Serious enough for the two of you to discuss killing each other's spouses," Mac said.

"I didn't take it seriously," Nathan said. "As a matter of fact, I forgot all about it—even when Nancy ended up dead—until this morning, when Cassie tracked me down at the athletic club at the Spencer Inn and reminded me of our conversation. She said that since she'd taken care of Nancy, it was time for me to hold up my end of the bargain by getting rid of Clark."

Mac gasped. "She actually said that."

Nathan nodded his head. "I thought she was joking. But she said she was serious. I don't know if she actually killed Nancy or had her killed. I was too shocked to ask for details. But Cassie said that if I didn't do my part, she would contact you and repeat our conversation about my wanting to get rid of Nancy, and she would testify against me in court and say that I had solicited her to kill my wife."

"What did you tell her?" Mac asked.

Nathan shook his head. "Frankly, I was in shock. I can't believe…This is my fault. If I hadn't slept with Cassie in the first place, Nancy would still be alive. I know she was a pain in the butt and crazy out of her gourd, but still—"

Mac grasped his arm. "How did you leave it with Cassie Clark?"

"I said I'd have to get back in touch with her about it," Nathan said. "She told me not to take too long."

"Good." Mac nodded at Sheriff Turow and David.

"What are you going to do?" Nathan asked.

"What else can we do?" Mac asked with a grin. "Keep Braxton's end of the bargain and arrange to kill Bill Clark."

CHAPTER TWENTY

"Do you see what I see?" Jessica asked Murphy.

From his perch in the backseat, Gnarly stood up and placed his head between theirs. Seeing his face on the billboard overlooking the freeway and the hospital parking lot, where they had parked, he barked and wagged his tail.

Gnarly's head was four stories tall. His mouth was hanging open, and his tongue was hanging to one side and spilling over the edge of the billboard. The sign read, "He's Not Snarly! Vote for Gnarly! Mayor of Spencer."

"Why are they advertising for votes from Washington-area residents?" Jessica grabbed her cell phone from her purse. "I need to text Dad and tell him."

"How much does a billboard cost?" Murphy opened the SUV's driver's side door. "We're going to need to leave Gnarly in the car. Even with his service vest, if he walks in smelling like that, security will evacuate him as a biohazard."

Mac Faraday had not been exaggerating when he'd claimed that Gnarly was lactose intolerant. The odor from his indigestion had filled up the interior of the SUV so badly during the drive to Walter Reed Hospital in Bethesda,

272

Maryland, that they'd been forced to turn off the air conditioning and open the windows and sunroof.

Sensing that he was the source of Murphy's and Jessica's displeasure—or maybe because of the tummy ache caused by the cheese sauce that Tristan had put on his food—Gnarly hung his head, and his ears fell to each side of it.

In spite of the odor, Jessica felt sorry for the dog. He'd been taken away from his home. She wondered if he understood why he was being shuffled from one home to another and then hauled around the city—though Gnarly never complained about a ride in the car.

"You go on in to see Tawkeel, and I'll take Gnarly for a walk around the courtyard." Finished with her text, she threw open the door. Once Gnarly was on his leash, he proudly trotted in the direction of the courtyard to stake his claim on every plant he could.

As a man, Murphy felt weird taking a plant or flowers with him when visiting a friend at the hospital. Unfortunately, in his short career, more than one friend had been injured in the line of duty. But because he was married, he was able to use the excuse that Jessica had sent the flowers, and he was simply delivering them.

Tawkeel Said was Murphy's teammate in the Phantoms. After seeing the agent's condition when they had rescued him in Brussels, Murphy felt that he deserved the largest fruit-and-cheese gift basket available in the gift shop. Filled with apples, oranges, gourmet cheeses, nuts, and spreads, the basket in his arms covered the lower half of his face when he carried it up to the fourth floor to Tawkeel's private room.

Even though Tawkeel had been on an assignment for the CIA, CO had arranged for him to be in a private room for security reasons until the Phantoms figured out what had happened. The door to the patient's room was open, and the privacy screen, pulled back so that Tawkeel could see out into the hallway.

"Hey, Tawkie, are you decent?" Murphy said before entering the room. The greeting served two purposes: it announced who was there and notified Tawkeel that his incoming visitor was a friend rather than a foe.

Their intense military and special-operations training proved to be a double-edged sword. While it had taught them to always be prepared for anything, in some cases, especially right after a mission during which they had spent long periods of time in a constant state of high alert, it caused them to have hair-trigger nerves.

Murphy was relieved to find Tawkeel sitting up in bed and reading. As soon as the team had arrived back in the States, Murphy had called Tawkeel's parish priest, who had immediately visited to check on his parishioner and had even delivered a Bible, which Murphy found his friend reading.

Still, in spite of the fact that Tawkeel was upright in bed, his appearance made Murphy cringe. His face was black and blue and swollen, and he had cigarette burns up and down his arms. Murphy wondered if the scars would ever go away.

Reminding himself to be glad that his good friend was alive, Murphy forced an upbeat note into his tone when he set the basket on the table. "From Jessie."

"Not you?" Tawkeel marked his place in the Bible with a bookmark and closed it.

"I'm not a gift-basket type of guy." After closing the door to give them privacy, Murphy pulled a chair up to one side of the bed. "How are you feeling? You look like hell, but you still look better than you did the last time I saw you."

"Then I feel better than I did when you guys rescued me," Tawkeel said. "I don't even remember that. My first memory is of being on the plane coming home." He grinned. "First thing I remember is opening my eyes and seeing your ugly face. After everything I went through, the least I deserved was something prettier to look at—like Jessie."

"I'm the only man who's allowed to see her face right after waking up." In silence, Murphy reflected on how close his friend had come to being executed—and he would've been if they'd arrived only one day, or even a few hours, later—all because someone had blown his cover.

Tawkeel seemed to have read Murphy's thoughts. "Who blew my cover?"

"That's what I wanted to ask you."

"They told me that my handler was tortured to death," Tawkeel said. "He was a good man. Had a wife and three little kids."

"He didn't out you," Murphy said. "You were grabbed the day before he was."

"I didn't out him," Tawkeel said firmly. "But the agency is saying that I did." His tone was bitter. "They're going to suspend me, and my career as an agent will be over."

"We won't let that happen," Murphy said. "I won't let that happen." He sat forward with his elbows on his knees. "When they grabbed you after finding out that you were CIA, what did they say? What proof did they have that you were agency?"

Tawkeel shook his head. "They ambushed me when I came into the house, and they knocked me to the floor—all of them, six guys—and kicked me in the head. I barely remember anything about those first couple of days. They tortured me, asking me for information, but I kept slipping in and out of consciousness."

"Can you remember anything that they said that could help us identify who gave you up?"

"Word came down from their—" Tawkeel's eyes glazed over. "It didn't make sense."

"What didn't?" Murphy held his breath.

"My mission was to work my way up through their chain of command and to get access to a very senior-level head of ISIS," Tawkeel said. "For a month, this cell in Brussels had been planning and organizing a series of bombings in London."

"That's what all the bombs were for," Murphy said. "Good thing we took them out."

"But the London bombing was supposed to be a rehearsal," Tawkeel said. "According to the information I uncovered right before they nabbed me, their leader in Syria, who I still hadn't met even after nine months of being with those animals, is planning a bigger coordinated attack in America."

"When?"

"Right after they hit London," Tawkeel said. "ISIS has a group leaving for Mexico. They're going to enter America by crossing the Mexican border, and then they'll get set up to make a series of coordinated attacks in the United States. The bombing in London was just supposed to be a test. After that bombing, the leaders were going to critique the slaughter and then fine-tune it in order to launch a bigger attack the next time—with more targets and more casualties."

"How far up the line did you get?" Murphy asked.

"All I know is that the one pulling the strings was located in Syria," Tawkeel said. "And *he* was the one who sent the word down to my group that I was a spy. The guy had never met me, Murphy. How could I have given myself away to him if we'd never even met?"

"You couldn't have," Murphy said. "So that information had to have come from someplace else. Only other place would be Washington."

"Which points back to my handler," Tawkeel said. "The handler is the middleman between the agent and headquarters."

"And we've already eliminated your handler," Murphy said. "That leaves someone at headquarters—Washington." He let out a sigh of relief. "At least now the members of that cell are gone."

"Sorry, mon ami," Tawkeel shook his head. "That does not mean that the attack has been called off. The head coordinator, the one planning the attack, will simply use a different terror cell from someplace else."

"We destroyed all of the bombs," Murphy said. "They're going to have to start over with new phony passports, visas—"

"Training," Tawkeel said. "Point is, all you did was delay the London attack. You didn't cancel it altogether."

"Well," Murphy said, "whoever outed you and your handler is obviously already in communication with the head honcho of this group. If we can identify the traitor, we'll have access to him. We'll nab him and give him a taste of his own medicine and find out what he knows. Any suggestions on where to start looking inside the agency?"

"Tawkeel...Tawkeel Said? Are you in here?"

The unexpected opening of the door and the unexpected voice made both men jump. Murphy reached for the nine-millimeter Smith & Wesson semiautomatic that he had tucked into the pocket of his jacket. Tawkeel reached down under his blankets for what Murphy suspected was a weapon that a fellow Phantom had most likely snuck in for him.

An exceedingly tall, thin man with thin reddish-blond hair entered the room and stepped up to the foot of the bed. "Are you Tawkeel Said?" He looked from the patient to where Murphy was seated next to him.

Tawkeel glanced at Murphy as if to ask if he knew the man. With a shrug of his shoulders, Murphy shook his head. When the visitor went around to the other side of the bed,

Murphy tightened his grip on the gun and watched him closely.

"We never actually met." The visitor stuck out his hand to Tawkeel. "I'm Andrew Collins. I'm one of the chiefs of your division at the State Department." His eyes flickered from Tawkeel's face to Murphy's when he said "State Department."

Tawkeel immediately picked up on Collins' covert message, as did Murphy. As an agent who worked undercover with the CIA, Tawkeel could never publicly acknowledge where he worked. Not knowing who Murphy was, Collins had had to provide a cover story.

"As soon as we got word of your escape from the terrorist cell in Brussels, our director insisted that I come personally to check on you," Collins said while looking Tawkeel up and down. Once again, he glanced over in Murphy's direction. On his face was an unspoken request for Murphy to leave so that he could debrief Tawkeel in private.

Reaching into his pocket for his cell phone, Murphy stood up. "I'm Lieutenant Murphy Thornton. US Navy." After rubbing the screen of his cell phone against the material inside his pocket, he extracted his hand and stuck it out to Collins from across the bed. "I was the CO leading the team that found Tawkeel after he escaped from Brussels." The phone tumbled out of Murphy's pocket, bounced across the bed, and fell to the floor at Collins' feet. "Damn!"

Andrew Collins picked up the phone.

"I hope I didn't break it," Murphy said, which prompted Collins to press his thumb on the screen and to sweep it across the phone. The cell phone unlocked and came to life. With a sigh of relief, Murphy took the phone, careful to touch only its edges.

"Well, Tawkeel, I'll be sure to tell the rest of my team how you're doing. We're all pulling for you." Murphy shook his hand. "We're glad we were able to be there for you."

With a farewell nod to Andrew Collins, Murphy spun on his heels and left the hospital room. While making his way down the hallway, he snatched a plastic trash bag from a cleaning cart and carefully slipped his cell phone inside it before going down the elevator and out to the courtyard to find Jessica and Gnarly.

"Gnarly, you really need to learn to not eat everything that's put in front of you," Jessica said while rubbing the German shepherd's tummy.

She was sitting on a park bench, and Gnarly was sprawled out next to her with his head in her lap. His gas was so intense that even outdoors, Jessica had to turn her head and hold her breath occasionally.

"I'm going to kill Tristan," she said.

A dark-haired man wearing a doctor's jacket strolled down the path and took a seat on the park bench across from them. Nodding a greeting in Jessica's direction, he took a plastic container out of a lunch bag and opened it, revealing a salad.

His nose twitching upon picking up a scent, Gnarly lifted his head and peered over the handrail of their bench to study the doctor eating across from them.

"Gnarly, no," Jessica said in a low voice. But her words meant nothing, and Gnarly scrambled onto his stomach, launched himself off of the bench, and galloped over to the doctor.

"Gnarly, halt! No!" Jessica jumped up to run after the German shepherd, who had stopped directly in front of the doctor and planted his bottom on the ground.

The doctor stopped eating with his fork, filled with lettuce, in midair. He stared at Gnarly, whose tail was wagging.

"I'm so sorry, doctor." Jessica grabbed the dog by the collar. "Bad boy, Gnarly! That's not yours."

"Did you call him Gnarly?" Putting down the fork and the plastic bowl, the doctor stared at the dog, who was wagging his tail with his mouth open. "It is you."

Gnarly yanked free from Jessica's hold and jumped into the doctor's arms. Patting and petting Gnarly, the doctor delivered a kiss to the side of his head. "I can't believe it's you! What a good boy! I'm so glad to see that you're okay."

"You know Gnarly?" Jessica asked.

"Oh, yes." The doctor smiled while Gnarly licked him all over his face. "We served together in Iraq." Breaking free from the enthusiastic dog, he held out his hand to Jessica. "I'm Dr. Drew Samuels. I was a medic on Gnarly's team during my last tour overseas, before going to med school." He sucked in a deep breath and wrapped his arms around the German shepherd's broad chest. "I was there when his handler was killed." He pulled back to look into Gnarly's brown eyes. "That was a bad day for all of us. Huh, boy?"

Gnarly licked his snout.

Jessica slid down onto the bench next to him. "Sergeant Belle Perkins."

Drew nodded his head. "Last I heard, Gnarly had been discharged. I guess you have him now."

"My father does," she said. "Gnarly is visiting." She offered him her hand. "Jessica Faraday, by the way. My husband is Lieutenant Murphy Thornton, navy. He's visiting a friend of his here at the hospital." She smiled when she saw Murphy crossing the courtyard in their direction.

After greeting Murphy with a hug and a kiss, Jessica introduced him to the doctor petting the German shepherd, who had zeroed in on the salad.

"Dr. Samuels served with Gnarly in Iraq." Jessica arched a telling eyebrow in Murphy's direction.

"Then you were there when Gnarly's handler was murdered," Murphy said.

"But Gnarly didn't do it," Drew said. "I heard that that was in the news, but I was there. It's not true. She wasn't attacked by a dog. She was strangled."

"Do you have any idea about who would have done something like that to her, especially when she had a dog like Gnarly in the tent with her?" Jessica asked.

"Gnarly was sedated when it happened," Drew said. "He had gotten injured in an attack earlier in the day. Perkins didn't realize it until much later. A round had grazed his upper leg, near his hip. I know because she came to me for thread so that she could stitch him up."

"So you knew Gnarly would be asleep," Murphy said.

"The whole team knew." Dr. Samuels sat up tall in his seat. "Four members of our team got killed that afternoon. We all would have been wiped out if it hadn't been for Gnarly and Perkins. Why, after they stuck out their necks to save us, would any of us have wanted to kill either one of them? Gnarly should have gotten a medal. I heard that the lieutenant was going to put Perkins in for the Bronze Star, but then she was killed."

"Why didn't she get it posthumously?" Jessica asked.

Dr. Samuels shrugged his shoulders.

"I'm sorry for the questions," Jessica said. "But like you said, you saw on the news that someone said that Gnarly killed his handler, and Perkins' husband asked us to find out the truth and to clear his name."

Dr. Samuels nodded his head. "If there's anything I can do to help."

"Someone told us that there was a female member of the team who Perkins had problems with," Murphy said.

A slow grin crossed Dr. Samuels' face. "Do you mean Private Abigail Moss?"

"We were told that she was the only other woman on the team," Murphy said. "There was some tension between them."

"Yes, there was," Dr. Samuels said. "Some."

"Do you know what that was about?" Jessica asked.

"I know exactly what that was about," Dr. Samuels said. "Private Moss and I started dating shortly before Sergeant Perkins arrived at our camp. Abby is a lovely woman, but she's not one of those soft, feminine girlie girls."

Jessica grinned. "She was jealous."

Samuels nodded his head. "But she never would have killed Perkins. Perkins was very happily married. There was no competition there. Besides, that afternoon, she'd taken out a terrorist who had pinned Abby and me down while we were trying to save one of the four men who got killed. Perkins nailed him solid. And then that night, I spent the whole night in Abby's tent. After what we had gone through…That was the night I proposed to Abby, and she accepted. She had no reason to be jealous of Perkins."

Distracted by the questions, Dr. Samuels lost track of his salad, which Gnarly had pulled down off of the bench to finish. Before Murphy and Jessica could ask another question, he said, "Perkins had a lot of trouble with Lieutenant Watson."

"What kind of trouble?" Murphy asked.

"His commanding style," Dr. Samuels said. "Some of the men called him 'Patton.' He was—is—completely fearless. No zone is too hot for him to go into. Still, he has a reputation for putting himself and his people in situations that other commanding officers would avoid. But then his people do respect him because he doesn't send his people in where he himself won't go first. Many of the people on his team had so much respect for him that they would've followed him to hell and back, which is the mark of an excellent leader. Sergeant Major Scott Scalia, for example, has gone on every tour with Watson that I know of."

He paused. "Perkins was furious after the gunfight that afternoon. And when she saw that Gnarly had gotten hurt—whoa! The medical tent was right next to the lieutenant's—who's a captain now, by the way. You could hear them yelling at each other all the way over in the medic tent."

"What was she saying?" Murphy asked.

"That it was going to stop, and it was going to stop there and then."

"What was going to stop?" Murphy asked.

Dr. Samuels' face went blank. "I…I just assumed…well, his full-speed-ahead type of leading. Actually, you can ask him about it yourself. He's back here in the States. I see him pretty regularly here at the hospital. Maybe he's in PT because of an injury he got on his last tour?"

"Since she was enlisted and he was an officer"—Jessica looked up at Murphy for an answer—"could she have put a stop to how he led his team?"

In deep thought, Dr. Samuels looked down at where Gnarly was lapping up a drop of salad dressing. "Maybe there was something else going on between Watson and Perkins."

CHAPTER TWENTY-ONE

Garrett County Sheriff's Department

"Are we going to tell Bill Clark that his wife is actively looking for a hit man to kill him?" David asked Sheriff Scott Turow.

After sending Nathan Braxton to an interview room with his lawyer, Mac, David, and the sheriff had gone to his office to decide how best to handle the situation. At the top of the list was getting an undercover detective to play the hit man who Cassandra Clark wanted to kill her husband.

Since Bill Clark was a longtime resident of the county, they couldn't take a chance on using a local police officer. Cassandra might have inadvertently met the officer through Bill. Therefore, Sheriff Turow had called the state police who, after a long discussion, had said that they had an agent from the Rockville, Maryland, barracks who had finished up an operation in Fairmont just the night before. They would send the detective to Oakland, Maryland, as soon as possible.

"If we don't give Clark a heads-up and something happens, we'll be liable for it," Mac said to David. "You just don't want to tell him because you have high hopes of messing with his mind."

David nodded his head.

"We can't tell him right now," the sheriff said. "If we do, he could let Cassandra know that we're on to her. We have to keep this between us and Braxton."

"Somehow, this whole scenario doesn't seem right to me." Exhaustion setting in, Mac sat down. "If Cassie Clark killed Nancy Braxton, how did she know she was going to be down at the lake?"

"Maybe she followed her," Sheriff Turow said. "Sat outside of the mansion until Braxton left—"

"In the middle of the night wearing nothing but her jammies? Luckiest murder-of-opportunity killer I ever heard of."

"I still want to know what scared her so badly that she went running out of her home late at night like that," David said. "Nancy Braxton was not one who scared easily."

"What are you two saying?" the sheriff asked.

"We need to find out what meds Nancy Braxton was supposed to be on," David said. "Dallas thinks, and I agree, that she was on some sort of antipsychotic medication, and someone substituted sugar pills for the real meds, wanting her to have a breakdown."

"The outlandish lies, delusions of grandeur, and mood swings," Mac said. "Psychosis would explain all of that. And of course, Braxton's party wouldn't have wanted anyone to know that."

David nodded his head. "The last thing that they would've wanted to get out was that they were pushing a mentally unstable candidate on us."

There was a knock on the door. Before Sheriff Turow could respond, a woman with long legs, each one bearing a tattoo of a long vine with red roses from her ankle up to her upper thigh, opened the door. The red of the roses matched her long, elegant fingernails and the red on her plump lips. Her long red hair was the color of a new copper penny. She wore high-heeled sandals with straps around her ankles and up her calves. She was dressed in a short leather skirt, a mesh top, and what appeared to be a leather bra holding an abundant bosom. Leather and chains were clasped around her wrists and neck.

At first glance, the men thought she was a streetwalker who wanted to beg the sheriff to release her with just a warning for soliciting—until they saw that she was wearing a utility belt baring a side arm, handcuffs, and a state-police badge.

She struck a pose with a hand resting on her shapely hip. "Chris Turow! You owe me sixty bucks, you lyin', cheatin' heartbreaker!"

Behind his desk, Sheriff Turow gazed at her with wide eyes that were even wider than Mac's and David's. His instinctive objection was replaced with a wide grin. "Greyson!" Instantly, he was out of his seat and hugging her. Their hug ended in a quick kiss.

"When did you leave the army?" he asked, taking in her outlandish disguise.

"When the Maryland State Police made me an offer I couldn't refuse," she said. "No more tours in the desert."

Mac was looking her up and down. In particular, he was impressed with the elaborate tattoos on her legs. "You were in the army?"

"Roxie and I met in basic training," the sheriff said. "Roxie held our class record for the obstacle course." With a grin, he shook his head. "No one could scale a wall like Roxanne Greyson."

"Being chased by all those horny recruits in our class helped." She laughed. "They're not real, by the way."

Afraid he'd been caught taking in her bosom, which was quite visible in the leather bra, David said, "We weren't looking."

"I was talking about the tattoos." Pointing to her chest, she said, "These are real. But the tattoos are temporary. I just came off of an undercover assignment with an illegal arms merchant who had a thing for women with tattoos."

"Then they wash off." No longer concerned with discretion, Mac whirled around in his seat and peered closely at her long legs, taking in the detail of the tattoos that snaked up both of them. "They look so real. How long will it take for them to wash off?"

"At least a week." She gazed up at the sheriff. "My department tells me you're looking for a hit man. Who do you need bumped off?"

"Town councilman running for mayor," Sheriff Turow said. "His wife is blackmailing the husband of a murder victim into arranging her husband's murder."

"Did this husband kill his wife?" Roxie asked.

"He has a solid alibi," David said.

"But he could have hired someone to do it for him," Mac said. "He admits that he hated her."

"But then why would he have come running to us saying that Cassandra Clark took credit for killing his wife for him and wanted him to off her husband?" Sheriff Turow said.

"To throw suspicion off of him," Mac said.

"If he'd had his wife killed, then he would've known that Cassandra was lying when she said she'd done it," David said.

"How better to divert suspicion from himself than to throw her under the bus and have her arrested for committing or arranging the murder that he himself had set up?" Mac said.

"I'll let you guys figure out who the real culprit is," Roxie said. "My job is just to role-play. What's the plan?"

287

"Nathan Braxton is going to meet with the suspect and tell her that he has an assassin lined up to kill her husband, Bill Clark," the sheriff said. "He'll be wearing a wire. He's going to try to get her to talk about his wife's murder, the one she claims she committed. Once we get enough information about that crime, you'll join in and get her to talk about the murder that she wants you to commit for her. When we have enough, we'll swoop in."

"When will this happen?" she asked.

"Tonight," David said.

"I'll need to shower and change," she said.

"We can put you up—"

"You can shower and change at my place," Sheriff Turow said, interrupting Mac's offer for her to stay at the Spencer Inn.

"Are you sure your wife won't mind?" she asked.

Sheriff Turow's face fell. An awkward silence filled the office before he cleared his throat. "Belle died four years ago. She was killed during a tour in Iraq."

"I'm sorry." Roxie let out a breath filled with regret.

"Is your husband—"

"We got divorced during my last tour," she said. "It's really hard to be married when just as one partner is coming back, the other one gets shipped out. That's why I joined the state police. I thought that maybe if I had a more stable lifestyle—"

"Going undercover as a hooker," David said, grinning.

"Hey, I'm the best hooker in our department," she said.

Mac noticed that Sheriff Turow was fighting the grin that was working its way to his lips.

Roxanne stood up. "Well, I'd better change into something more suitable for an assassin. I have a go bag in the car."

"I'll get your bag for you." The sheriff hurried to the door. "I'll take you to my place, and we'll get you fixed up in no time."

"Are you sure I won't be any trouble?" she asked on their way out the door.

"No, I want you to make yourself at home."

Once the sheriff and Rosie were gone, Mac and David exchanged glances.

"Did they just leave without saying good-bye to us?" David asked.

"They clearly forgot we were in the room."

At five o'clock, Caleb Montgomery almost tripped over a soaking-wet child running into the Lakeside Inn as he made his way out of the front entrance to go home. He had to grit his teeth to avoid saying what he was really thinking to the urchin's apologetic mother, who was chasing the child with a beach towel. With a forced smile, he glanced up the mountain behind him and saw the clearings for the Spencer Inn's ski slopes.

Now that's a hotel. Where the grown-up guests outnumber the ankle biters. Where most of the food isn't deep fried and served on chipped plates.

"Rough day?"

Caleb had to turn around completely to locate the owner of the familiar throaty voice. Struck by her striking good looks and the way she filled out her faded blue jeans and soft summer-blue off-the-shoulder top, the hotel manager needed a full moment to recall how he knew Dallas Walker.

As though a switch had been flipped, he changed his mind from wanting to invite her to the lounge for a drink and possibly to check out one of the hotel's king-sized beds to wanting to send her on her way.

"What makes you think that?" he said, stepping toward his car in the parking space reserved for the manager.

She lifted one bare shoulder. "Just...You look like a man who's got yellow jackets in his outhouse."

That was enough to make Caleb come to a halt. He was unsure about whether he should engage her in a conversation and find out what that meant. He looked her up and down while she stood before him, clutching an oversized shoulder bag. He liked what he saw until he remembered that the last time he had seen her, she'd been having dinner with Spencer's chief of police.

"Nancy Braxton was murdered the other night," she said.

"So what does that have to do with me? Sure, she was a local celebrity running for office and was married to Nathan Braxton, but she never lowered herself to come in here—"

"Even though her brother owns the place?"

That got his attention.

She could see the wheels turning in his head. "And you"—she pointed a finger at him and moved toward him—"are his silent partner. V & M Enterprises. The *V* stands for 'Vance,' and the *M* stands for 'Montgomery.' I found your business license. V & M Enterprises started operating less than two months after Sandy Burr's murder in this hotel, where you were tending bar while Nancy Braxton was having a long talk with the murder victim. The hotel's owners had been trying to unload it for years, and suddenly it was sold to this brand-new company in which you were a partner. Less than a year later, it was renovated and reopened with you, a former bartender with no hotel-management experience, as its manager. Funny thing," she scratched her ear. "I can't find any record of how much money *you* invested into this venture."

"I didn't do anything wrong."

"Hey," she said with a wave of her arms. "You don't have to convince me as much as you have to convince my readers."

"I told you that I wasn't going to talk to you."

"And you don't have to."

Pleased, he turned away. She followed him.

"I have enough facts and documentation to write the story without an interview with you," she said. "Of course, without your side of the story, readers will have to come to their own conclusions. Do you think your employees are going to respect you when they find out that you aren't the manager but really a one-third owner of the hotel—a position that you didn't earn but rather received as blood money in exchange for your silence?"

Caleb stood with his back to her. After a long silence, he said, "I didn't *ask* for anything. It was *offered* to me."

"And you *took* it, and then you conveniently got amnesia about what you saw that night."

He whirled around. "It wasn't like I saw her kill Burr. I just saw her and Burr together at the table. They ordered two rounds of drinks. Look, that was over twenty years ago. I took care of a lot of customers before that night, and I've taken care of a lot since that night. You expect me to remember two customers having two rounds of drinks one evening decades ago?"

"How many of those customers ended up as buzzard bait less than two hours later?"

"I have nothing to say to you." Caleb Montgomery yanked open his car door.

"She was scared of something," Dallas said.

He paused.

"Nancy Braxton. The night she was killed," she said. "Someone or something scared her. Now, a lot of money has been flowing in and out of Braxton Charities—not all of it clean. Of course, you know that, since Hugh Vance had enough money to pay you off with this hotel. Sandy Burr was asking for information about Braxton Charities, and he ended up dead. Nancy Braxton was the face of Braxton Charities, and she ended up dead. You witnessed the last hour or so of Burr's life, and you must have seen or heard something. Hugh Vance is very slick—his sister was too. They would not have invested what they did if you hadn't seen something—"

"Why would he want me dead now?"

She moved in for the kill. "Because Nancy Braxton was murdered, and the police are asking questions. There's no telling where this investigation is going to lead. Vance can't leave any loose ends lying about." She cocked her head at his back. "Seen any strange-looking characters around the hotel lately? Like maybe the fat man you saw at the bar that night?"

"It's a three-star hotel," Caleb said. "It's a strange night when we don't have strange characters hanging out in the lounge." He slid into the front seat of his car. "You want the truth? I never did think that Burr's murder had anything to do with Nancy Braxton."

"Then why did the killer take Burr's research?"

Caleb looked up at her. His eyes were wide.

"Sandy Burr's sister told the police that he'd brought a boot box with all of his research in it that weekend. However, the morning after his meeting with Nancy Braxton, when he was found dead, the boot box was not in his hotel room. It was filled with articles and notes and his manuscript. A bunch of papers. Why would the killer take a box full of research if the murder had nothing to do with it?"

They stared at each other in silence. Dallas willed him to speak. She could see from his eyes that he was in a quandary.

"I have no idea what you're talking about," he said with conviction.

Dallas grasped his arm. "Was Vance the fat man you saw watching Burr and Braxton that night?"

"No," Caleb said. "I never saw the fat man before or after that night." He put his car in gear. "And I'm sure of that. The guy weighed, like, four hundred pounds. Hard to forget someone like that."

With that, Caleb drove off.

Watching him drive away, Dallas mulled over the one thing he'd offered: Hugh Vance was not the fat man. Also, Caleb Montgomery had seemed extremely certain that Sandy Burr's murder had had nothing to do with Nancy Braxton or Braxton Charities.

If he doesn't know anything about Sandy Burr's murder, then how does he know what it doesn't have to do with?

CHAPTER TWENTY-TWO

"Do you see that?" David asked Mac, who was sitting in the front passenger seat of his police cruiser.

Mac checked the reflection in the side rearview mirror. "They're not very good at tailing, are they?"

David tried to keep his attention on maneuvering the cruiser along the twisting road leading up to the Spencer Inn, but it was difficult to keep from watching Hap's ancient, broken-down pickup truck, which had been following them since they'd left the sheriff's department.

"Why are they tailing us?" David asked Mac.

"They're worried about Gnarly," Mac said. "I don't think they bought my excuse for him being gone for a few days. Ignore them." He took out his cell phone. "I'll give Turow a heads-up."

In the midst of the busy summer season and with an emotionally charged mayoral election going on, the Spencer Inn was hopping. Sheriff Turow and David would have preferred their undercover operation to take place in a less populated place. But it was where Cassandra Clark had insisted they meet when Nathan Braxton had called to inform her that he had run into problems with setting up the hit for her.

A rendezvous with a former football star in a popular resort seemed like a reckless endeavor—especially since that rendezvous was a meeting to arrange a murder. But then Nathan had noted that Cassandra got off on taking such risks.

"When Nancy slugged Clark during the debate and you arrested them," Nathan said to David, "Cassie and I were having a quickie in the men's restroom. We didn't know they were in jail until after you had hauled them both away."

"Bill Clark has a town-hall meeting scheduled for this evening at the Spencer Inn," Mac said. "Cassie will be expected to sit in the front row and to play the role of the devoted wife. So we can expect that she'll want to meet in the rose garden beforehand."

Sheriff Turow uttered an audible groan, which perplexed Roxie Greyson. "Why is that a problem?"

The Spencer Inn was famous for its elaborate floral maze made up of rose bushes and twisting vines. "During the summer months," Mac said, "when the flowers are in full bloom, guests love to lose themselves in the maze. But it's the worst place for the police to keep tabs on suspects. I guarantee that that's where she'll want to meet."

"Then we'll get deputies dressed in plain clothes scattered throughout the garden before they actually meet," Sheriff Turow said.

Nathan Braxton was fitted with an audio wire, and a tiny camera was concealed in the American flag pin that he was wearing on his lapel.

Sheriff Turow and his deputies parked their surveillance van in a contractor's lot next to the landscaper's supply building. From there, they had a view of the gardens, but not a clear view.

Keeping close enough to Nathan to see him but far away enough that it wouldn't be obvious that they were following him, David and Mac entered the Spencer Inn through the main door. One hour before Bill Clark's town-hall meeting, a herd of journalists and cameras operators with television equipment filled the lobby.

The mob was focused on George Ward and on Erin Devereux, who was dressed in a becoming business suit. The sling she had been wearing the day before was gone.

"What's going on with them?" David asked as if Mac would have an answer.

"Ward wasted no time replacing Nancy Braxton on our party's ticket," Salma Rameriz, who happened to have heard the question, said. "With Erin Devereux, Nancy's executive assistant. Interesting, huh? Considering that Erin was the last one to see Nancy alive."

"Can he do that?" Mac asked. "Erin Devereux never ran for mayor. They should replace her with someone who actually *ran* for mayor."

"Erin Devereux isn't even a resident of Spencer," David said.

"Yes, she is," Salma said with a slim smile. "She owns a condo down on the lake. Has for a year. It's listed as her legal residence. That's all she needs to be considered a resident of Spencer, which makes her eligible to run for mayor."

"And she has the right genitalia, which is the most important thing to your party," David said.

"I always suspected you were sexist, Chief," Salma said. "How is it that out of a dozen police officers on your force, not one is a woman?"

"Our desk sergeant is a woman."

"But she doesn't do patrols," Salma said.

"She used to," David said. "Now she's the sergeant and has ten men serving under her. *They* answer to *her*."

Having no comeback, Salma rolled her eyes and scoffed.

"Say a woman comes to me to apply for a police officer's position in my department," David said. "And according to her application, she's had very little actual training and was fired from her last position for botching an arrest. Yet she's a woman. Wouldn't I be just as sexist to overlook her lack of qualifications and hire her because she's a woman? Wouldn't that be unfair to the man I don't hire, who has more training and better experience?"

"I have better things to do with my time than listen to your hate speech." With a shake of her head, Salma Rameriz spun on her heels and walked out into the night.

"It was a question," David said to Mac. "What was hateful about it?"

"She'll come around when she grows up and learns how the world really works," Mac said in a low voice. "In the meantime, when was the last time you read a newspaper?"

David looked in the direction in which Mac was jerking his chin. Sitting in the lounge area in front of the fireplace, Hap and Bernie were hiding behind two newspapers. Despite their effort to blend in, they immediately drew Mac's attention away from the hotel guests who were doing their reading on computer tablets.

"Cassie called Nathan," Sheriff Turow texted to David. "Mtg. in maze."

After tapping David on the arm, Mac led him to the elevator, where he pressed the call button for the private penthouse elevator. Before it arrived, the guest elevator's doors opened, and Bill Clark, along with his entourage, stepped out. Carrying a martini, the councilman was so enthralled in his conversation with a young man whose blond hair was slicked back that he collided with David before the police chief could get out of the way. The drink spilled down the front of Clark's shirt in the collision.

Clark whirled around. "You stupid son of a bitch!" Upon seeing David, he sneered. "O'Callaghan!" Clark waved the martini glass about, spraying David and anyone unfortunate enough to be nearby with the remnants of the drink. "I should have known it'd be you."

David was wiping the drink off of his shoulder and the back of his uniform. "You ran into me."

A member of Clark's entourage took the glass from the councilman's hand, possibly to prevent him from using it as a weapon. His hand then free, Bill Clark poked David in the chest. "Which is unfortunate for you because I've got something to tell you."

David looked down to where Bill Clark was pressing his finger against his breastbone. Seeing David's expression, Mac wondered if he was going to break Bill's finger.

"What's this about you digging into my mother's death?"

"I'm not digging into your mother's death."

"That's not what I heard," Clark said.

"You heard wrong."

"Then why was the sheriff asking my mother's doctor about—"

"Your mother died in Oakland," David said. "Even if I wanted to investigate it, which I don't, I couldn't, because she died out of my jurisdiction. I have no authority."

A smug expression filling his face, Bill Clark moved in closer and peered into David's face. Refusing to be intimidated, David matched the glare in his eyes.

"That's absolutely right," Bill Clark said in a low voice. "You have no authority. I'm warning you—you'd better stop looking for dirt on me, O'Callaghan."

"Afraid of what I'm going to find?" David asked.

"You're the one who should be afraid," Clark said.

"Are you threatening me, Clark?"

Poking David with each word, Bill Clark said, "I'm a member of the town council. That means that you work for me—"

"Wrong." With one hand, David grabbed the offending finger and twisted it. The pain brought Bill Clark down to his knees. "You listen to me, you son of a bitch. I work for the people of Spencer. I do what I have to do to protect and defend them—and you don't." With a shove, he released Clark, who fell backward and was caught by the blond-haired man.

Clutching his finger, Bill Clark sputtered and fought to recoup his demeanor and save face among his underlings. "That's it, O'Callaghan," he said while his assistant helped him to his feet. Once he had his footing, Bill shoved the young man away. "This race is now between Gnarly and me, and you'd better pray that by some miracle, Gnarly wins, because when I win, my first act on my first day will be to fire you." He shot a smug grin in Mac's direction and laughed. "Even your rich bastard brother won't be able to protect you."

His entourage joined in the laughter, and the blond-haired young man laughed the loudest.

"I wouldn't be so certain about winning the election, Clark," Mac said. "Even without his face in front of the camera, Gnarly is still well ahead of you in the polls. He picked up PETA's endorsement after the army confirmed that he wasn't a suspect in the murder of his handler and that he saved that mother cat and her twenty kittens. He's got the vote of every animal lover in Spencer."

Bill Clark's eyes narrowed. He directed his gaze toward David. "Have you met my campaign manager?" Without taking his eyes off of David, he jerked his head in the direction of his companion, who jumped forward at his boss' command. "Simon Spears. He's the best. Last year, he won two senatorial seats for his clients."

"He leaked a picture of one client's opponent shaking hands with a KKK clansman who showed up in the crowd at his college graduation," Mac said, "a man the candidate had never met before and hasn't seen since. And then there was Spears' other client. Spears smeared the opposing candidate by paying Internet trolls to flood social media with accusations of extramarital affairs that never happened. The hired trolls also launched attacks against the opponent's supporters."

"So you've heard of me." Simon grinned with pride.

"I do my homework, Spears, and I know more about you than your own mother does." Mac moved in on the young man, who was several inches shorter than he was. "Don't think we don't know who planted that phony story about Gnarly killing his handler. You sent the story to Rameriz using an e-mail address similar to Devereux's to make everyone think it came from Braxton's camp," he said in a low voice. "You want to take on the big dog? Then you'd better make sure you're man enough to handle yourself in a dog fight." Mac whispered into his ear, "Believe me, you don't want to get Gnarly mad at you. The other night, a mountain lion ticked him off. That lion is now at animal control…in a body bag…in a freezer." He finished by making a cutting motion across his throat.

Swallowing, Simon backed up.

Bill Clark shook his head at his campaign manager's retreat. "You know what the problem is with having a dog run for mayor, O'Callaghan?"

"No, tell me."

"Dogs have a way of just running off and disappearing without a trace," Clark said.

"Don't even think of going near our dog," David said.

With a knowing laugh, Bill Clark sauntered across the lobby and down the hallway toward the banquet room with his entourage surrounding him. Mac and David caught sight of Hap and Bernie trailing behind them.

"Where are they going?" Mac asked as the elevator doors opened again.

"I don't know, but we don't have time to babysit them," David said.

Using his key pass, Mac took David into his private penthouse suite and out onto the balcony, where they had a bird's-eye view of the rose-garden maze.

David called Sheriff Turow. "When you get your eyes on Cassandra, let us know what she's wearing so that we can guide you through the maze."

"They're going to bump into each other at the entrance and then make their way inside and away from everyone to talk," the sheriff said. "Hope Braxton can hold it together."

"He should be able to," Mac said when he heard him on the speakerphone. "He was a winning quarterback. They're trained to keep their cool when things get tough."

They heard the sheriff sigh. "You didn't hear him in the car on the way here."

In the background, Roxie Greyson said, "Don't worry. I'm all wired up and ready to go. If he starts to flake out, I'll take care of things."

"Braxton is at the meeting place," the sheriff said.

After realizing that he was only barely able to pick out Nathan Braxton at the entrance of the maze, Mac went inside the penthouse and returned a moment later with opera glasses.

"Terrible thing, when your eyes get old," David said with a chuckle.

"Don't be a smartass." Mac pointed down to the entrance of the maze. "There's Braxton."

Pointing out a woman in a form-fitting red dress, David said, "There's Cassandra Clark." Then he said, "I wanted so much to tell Clark that his own wife wants him dead."

"If this goes down right, he'll find out soon enough."

"Nathan, why'd we have to meet?" Bill Clark's wife asked in a harsh whisper. "I told you this morning—" She stopped.

Through his opera glasses, Mac saw her looking around at a group of noisy young people leaving the maze.

Starting to set, the sun was casting the garden in a golden glow. In a matter of minutes, the seven-foot-tall rose bushes and thick vines were forming long, eerie-looking shadows throughout the maze.

"I talked to someone, and—"

"Not here." Cassandra entered the maze. Seeing that Nathan wasn't following her, she turned around. "Come on. Follow me."

"They're going in," Mac said.

"You called it right down the line, Mac," the sheriff said. "You predicted she'd want to meet the hour before the town-hall meeting in the garden, and that's the way it's going down. Try to keep your eyes on them, and I'll do my best to have some of my deputies nearby."

"She's spooked," David said. "I can see it from here."

Cassandra led Nathan Braxton to the far end of the maze and then turned down two different corners to take them to a bench. "What is so important that we had to meet?" she asked. "I told you this morning that for this to work, we can't see or speak to each other, or the police will get suspicious."

"Salma Rameriz saw you in the hotel lounge putting moves on the piano player the other night," Nathan said.

David nodded his head. "Actually, it wasn't Salma Rameriz but the bartender. We had to check to see if she had an alibi for the time of the murder."

"Since she has an alibi then she couldn't have committed the murder," Mac said while Nathan rambled on.

"The police said that Nancy was killed between midnight and one o'clock," Nathan said. "The same time you were groping the piano man. That means that you couldn't have killed Nancy. You only told me that you did so that I'd kill your husband for you."

Cassandra stammered when she said, "I-I didn't tell you that *I* killed her. I t-told you that I *had* her killed for you. Do…do you really think that I'd be stupid enough to do it myself? Suppose…suppose someone had seen us together. I would've immediately ended up being suspect number one. So I hired a guy to do it for me."

There was silence.

"Ask her how much she paid, Nathan," Sheriff Turow said from his hideout in the van.

"How much?" Nathan's voice trembled.

"How much what?" Cassandra asked.

"How much did you pay him?"

"Five thousand dollars," Cassandra said. "Half up front, and the rest, I paid him yesterday morning."

"Why didn't you just pay him five thousand dollars to kill Bill for you if that was who you wanted dead?" Nathan asked.

"Good question," Mac said.

After several start and stops, she finally answered him. "Because we agreed to swap murders. That way, the police would never catch us."

Mac was shaking his head. "If Cassandra's ultimate goal was to have her husband killed, why not hire a hit man to kill him while she established an alibi instead of hiring a hit man to kill Nathan's wife and then telling him what she'd done—"

"Which was a huge risk, because how could she have been certain that he wouldn't go to the police?" David finished.

"Which he did." Mac picked up the cell phone. "Turow, tell Nathan to ask her if the hit man told her about how the murder went. Specifically, tell Nathan to ask her if his wife suffered when he drowned her."

"Gotcha," Turow said before relaying the question.

"Cassie," Nathan said in a gentle tone, "This guy you hired, did he tell you how he killed Nancy? Did she suffer? Did your hit man tell you how long it took for her to actually drown to death?"

"He told me it took a few minutes," she said. "She put up quite a fight, but he's a big guy. It wasn't hard for him to overpower her and to hold her under the water until she died. That was about all he told me." Then a note of excitement came to her tone. "When are you going to kill Bill?"

"Like I said, I made a couple of phone calls, and I have someone who can do it," Nathan said.

"When?"

"We have to work out a few details," Nathan said.

"Payment, for one," Roxie said.

The undercover officer had climbed out of the back of the surveillance van to join them in the garden.

Cassandra audibly gasped upon seeing the paid assassin in the flesh. "This isn't very smart—meeting me like this. If you get caught—"

"I don't get caught." Roxie set her foot up on the bench next to the nervous woman. "I'm a highly trained professional."

"And very expensive," Nathan said. "That's what we need to talk about. Madam X here is very expensive, and I need to know how much you're willing to pay."

"Me?" Cassandra said. "I expected you to—"

"Why would I pay to kill *your* husband?"

"I paid to kill your wife," Cassandra said.

"Only five thousand dollars," Roxie said. "I charge twenty thou in advance."

"Bill isn't worth twenty thousand!" Cassandra shouted before catching control of herself.

"Suit yourself." Roxie dropped her foot to the ground. "I'm out of here."

"Wait!" Cassandra turned to Nathan. "If you don't pay her to do it, I'm going to go to the police and tell them that you told me that you were going to have your wife killed."

"Why would they believe you?" Nathan asked.

"Bill has a lot of unsavory friends," Cassandra said. "He'll get them to put pressure on the police and the prosecutor and force them into arresting you."

"All on your word," Nathan said with distaste.

"It shouldn't be hard for me to find someone who'll say that he saw us together and that we were having an affair. That you wanted Nancy out of the way so that you could be with me."

"If I do this," Nathan said, "it will be a onetime thing. Twenty thousand. Your husband will be dead, and we'll never see or speak to each other ever again."

"Deal," Cassandra said.

Nathan reached into his inside breast pocket and took a thick envelope out of it. He handed it to Cassandra, who held it out to Roxie.

Instead of taking the money, Roxie asked, "When and how do you want it done, Ms. Clark?"

"Can you do it tomorrow night? Bill will be giving a speech before a big crowd with a lot of journalists," Cassandra said. "I'll be there. There's a balcony at the back of the auditorium. You can shoot him from up there."

"What if there are spectators in the balcony?" Roxie asked.

"Pu-leeze!" Cassandra said. "Don't let the big phony fool you. Take a look at the pictures on his media page. You'll notice that there aren't any room shots of the crowds. It's because there aren't any crowds. Bill's goons push everyone up close to the stage to make it look like the room is packed."

"Any other special instructions for this hit?" Roxie asked. "Like a specific number of bullet holes?"

"How many bullets have you got?"

"You really don't like him, do you?" Roxie said.

"Have you ever met my husband?" Cassandra asked. "If the sex were halfway decent, I could stand it. He's practically impotent. I only married him for his money. Never expected the tightwad to bitch every time I spend a dime."

"Any other instructions?" Roxie asked.

"After you shoot him, I'm going to run out and throw myself on top of his dead body, and it should make all of the major newscasts."

"Ah, I understand completely." Roxie took the envelope from her. "A dead impotent husband with a big inheritance is worth millions. A dead impotent husband with a big inheritance and fifteen minutes of fame? Priceless."

Cassandra let out a deep breath and smiled broadly. "Thank you so much." She let out a squeal of delight. "I can't wait."

"Neither can I," Roxie said while stuffing the money into the inside breast pocket of her leather vest. "There's just one more thing."

"What's that?"

"You're under arrest." Roxie took her police shield out of her pocket and held it up for Cassandra to see.

CHAPTER TWENTY-THREE

"Nigel, please exclude my prints from the sample, and run the rest through the federal database," Murphy said after lifting the thumbprint left by Andrew Collins off of the screen of his cell phone.

With a "Yes, Murphy," the computer went to work.

Murphy and Gnarly were on the ground floor of the Faraday-Thornton home in the room that was the smart house's brain and heart. When it had originally been constructed in the 1990s, the corner efficiency apartment had been intended to be a servants' quarters. Built into a hillside and with only two small windows, the area consisted of a bedroom, a bathroom, and a kitchenette. The owners prior to Murphy and Jessica had rented the space to a college student.

Murphy had realized that since it had a separate entrance, with the proper reinforcement, it would make a perfect panic room, which could prove to be useful in his line of work. The space was also secure enough to weather a tornado or another natural disaster.

The original glass in the windows had been replaced with specialized bulletproof glass. Those in the room could see outside, and sunlight could shine in, but no one outside could see into the room. The door had been reinforced with secure fingerprint- and retina-scanning locks. Only Murphy, Jessica, Tristan, and other family and friends who had been cleared by Nigel could open the door.

The pantry off of the kitchenette was stocked with enough food to feed four people and two dogs for a week. There was a queen-sized pullout sofa bed and a full bath.

The space was also home to the computerized communications command center in which Nigel's server was based. Nigel had been installed and was monitored by a federal security agency, so Murphy and Jessica's home was able to send and receive data instantly through control panels on computer tablets stationed throughout the house, guesthouse, and garage.

While away from home, Murphy or Jessica could contact Nigel via an application on their cell phones. For example, if a visitor arrived at their house before they did, they could instruct Nigel to open the front gate, turn on the lights, and even pop open the front door and tell their guest to make himself at home. Unlike the application on Jessica's phone, the application on Murphy's secure phone was a classified one through which he could give Nigel instructions to check for information in the Phantom's federal database.

Inside the command center, they could see every room and around the grounds on a bank of security monitors. With the main control panel, they were able to turn on and off lights and to adjust the temperature. They could even turn on water faucets, fireplaces, and various appliances, including televisions and sound systems. While Jessica was able to instruct Nigel to start her bath and to adjust its temperature and jets, she wished she could somehow have the computer take the dog food out of the cupboard and put it in the dogs' bowls—or maybe make the bed in the morning.

Also included in Nigel's command center was a small forensics lab in which Murphy and Jessica, who was pursuing her doctorate at Georgetown University, could do a basic analysis of evidence.

Like the fingerprints of strangers visiting friends at the hospital.

Tawkeel Said had wasted no time and had called Murphy on his secure phone to tell him that he had never seen Andrew Collins before in his life. Tawkeel reported that Collins had confirmed that he was from the CIA and had been sent from security to debrief him—and that he'd wanted to know what had happened in the days leading up to his capture and during his time with the terrorist cell.

"I got the feeling he was digging to see if I knew who had blown my cover," Tawkeel said. "I told him what I told the other security people who debriefed me: I don't know. They're going to make me the scapegoat on this. They're going to say it's my fault that my handler was captured and killed. My career with the agency is over."

"Not if we have anything to say about it," Murphy said.

While Nigel ran the fingerprints through the federal database, Murphy rolled his desk chair over to where Gnarly was curled up in what had been Jessica's chair the few times she'd visited the command center. Gnarly had climbed up into the chair and had tightly curled his hundred pounds of bulk so that he could fit onto the seat. Not quite fitting, one of his hind legs spilled out and hung in the air.

Despite his reclined position, the dog was alert. His head was resting on the arm of the chair; his eyes were moving around the room, taking note of the constantly changing images on the computer monitors; and his ears were twitching to and fro with every noise made by the devices.

"So who do you like in the upcoming presidential election?" Murphy asked Gnarly.

The German shepherd raised his head up from his paws and stretched his neck. Then he shook. Spencer trotted into the room and stopped in front of Gnarly's chair to gaze up at the big dog in complete adoration.

"Murphy," Nigel said over the chaos. "I got a match on the fingerprints you had me run through the federal database. Do you want me to send a report to CO?"

"Yes, Nigel," Murphy said.

Still confused about the disembodied voice, Gnarly cocked his head. Spencer yapped to demand that he direct his attention toward her instead of Nigel.

"CO is on the line for you, Murphy."

Gnarly's sigh reminded Murphy of when he was a child and would have to stop what he was doing to play with a younger sibling. Slowly, the German shepherd unfolded himself to ease out of the chair and left the room. Delighted, Spencer bounced out after him.

Murphy whirled his chair around to face his commanding officer on the web cam, which was transmitting her image from a remote location that could have been anywhere in the world. All he could see on the monitor was her head, and her eyes were hidden behind dark glasses. Her hair was pulled back and hidden under a blue hat.

"Lieutenant, Nigel just sent me a report on a thumbprint that you lifted from someone who visited Tawkeel at the hospital today."

Murphy was reading the report that Nigel had displayed on the computer screen for him. "He said he was State Department—the division chief from where Tawkeel worked. He said that his name was Andrew Collins and that he'd been sent to debrief him." Reading the name and the title on the report, Murphy felt his jaw drop.

"Andrew Collins was one of the aliases used by Newt Wallace when he was out in the field several years ago," CO said.

"Wallace is the executive director of operations in the CIA," Murphy said. "That's pretty high up. This guy made like he was midlevel management. What interest would he have in Tawkeel?"

"Newt Wallace's mentor is Camille Jurvetson, the director of operations at the agency," CO said. "She's been on the fast track through operations since joining the agency a little over twelve years ago. She has a reputation for being able to extract or piece together valid information to make strategic movements that her colleagues can't. Last week, that SEAL strike on the Afghan terrorist compound that took out the third-ranking leader of ISIS? Jurvetson deduced that location by piecing together reports and satellite images. She's so good that she's on the short list for one of the presidential candidates to be appointed director of the CIA." She paused and then said, "Newt became her lapdog about seven years ago. Every step she's taken up the ladder, she's brought him along."

"What's an executive officer who answers to the director of operations doing debriefing a field agent?" Murphy asked.

"Very good question," she said. "We know that the snitch who outed Tawkeel is someone from inside the agency who had contact with the very people Tawkeel was trying to identify."

"Which would mean that whoever outed Tawkeel already knew their identities," Murphy said. "Not only knew them but also was in contact with them."

"I have two questions," she said. "Did Wallace go to question Tawkeel because he knows that there's a double agent inside the agency and is trying to identify him or her, and was he there to cover his tracks because he's the double agent?"

"If he were simply the executive officer for the director of ops," Murphy said, "he wouldn't have gone to a hospital to visit a lowly field agent who might or might not have blown his cover. He'd have sent security, which is what he told Tawkeel he was. He was there because he needed to know firsthand what Tawkeel knows—because he has a personal stake in it."

"In his position, he has access to the information that got leaked in Tawkeel's case."

"Nigel," Murphy said as if the AI were in another room. "Check Newt Wallace's personnel file in the Office of Personnel Management. Was he in any way connected to Bruce Hardy's assignment four years ago in Iraq?"

"We'll also need to check his financials to determine if there's a money trail to whomever he's selling this information to," she said.

"If he's selling information to the terrorist network, there's no telling how many people died because of him," Murphy said.

"Four years ago," Nigel said, "Newt Wallace was the division chief stationed in Langley and was working over Bruce Hardy. At the time, Wallace's supervisor was the director of covert operations, Camille Jurvetson."

"I can tell you right now," CO said, "that without hard proof that Wallace has been selling human sources, Camille Jurvetson will never turn on him. I've heard more than one source say that they are very close."

"Lovers?"

"Most likely. At the very least, he is protected."

"What do you want me to do?" Murphy asked.

"You're a Phantom," she said. "Do what any good Phantom would do."

After Detective Roxie Greyson had arrested and handcuffed her, Cassandra Clark was ushered out of the maze, into the Spencer Inn, and through the lobby, which was filled with guests who were still gathering for her husband's town-hall meeting.

Dozens upon dozens of news journalists got pictures of the mayoral candidate's wife being arrested—though they still didn't know what for. In no time, they speculated that she had possibly murdered Nancy Braxton, her husband's opponent, to better his chances of winning the election.

By the time Cassandra Clark was escorted out of the front door to where the sheriff's police cruiser was waiting, Bill Clark was running into the lobby. When the news journalists saw him, a sea of microphones and recorders was stuck in his face. "Tell us how you feel about your wife being arrested. Has the sheriff been in contact with you about the investigation?"

Bill Clark searched the faces surrounding him until he caught sight of David O'Callaghan coming out of the penthouse elevator with Mac. Enraged, he shoved his way through the throng of people to reach the police chief. "What the hell, O'Callaghan! What kind of trumped-up charges—"

Before Clark could reach David, Mac jumped in between them. "You're talking to the wrong man, Clark! Sheriff Turow is in charge of this case."

"What case?" Bill's eyes grew big. "Not Braxton's murder!"

Aware of the recorders and microphones aimed at them, Mac said, "The county sheriff has had the lead in Nancy Braxton's murder from the get-go, and you know it!" He looked around at the crowd of journalists. "Any questions about what just happened or about the Braxton murder are to be directed to the Garrett County sheriff's department."

Cocking his head to make eye contact with David, Bill Clark narrowed his eyes. "Sheriff Turow may have the official lead in this case, but I know who's pulling the strings behind the scenes." He pointed two fingers first at his own eyes and then at David's. "I'm watching you, O'Callaghan. You're going to slip up in this conspiracy of yours—"

"Your wife just did a perp walk through a hotel lobby, Clark!" Mac said. "Don't you think you should get down to the sheriff's office to find out what she did?"

Clark's campaign manager, Simon Spears, whispered something to Bill Clark that reminded him of the journalists surrounding him and of the many cameras catching the moment. With effort, he contorted his face into a practiced expression of concern for his wife and hurried away.

CHAPTER TWENTY-FOUR

At the sheriff's department, Mac and David slipped in through a rear door to avoid running into Bill Clark or any members of his entourage. They assumed that Simon Spears was already hard at work doing damage control and spinning the event to make it the police department's fault—and to aim most of the blame at Gnarly—even though the candidate wasn't even in the vicinity.

They found Sheriff Turow in his office going over the details of the arrest for his police report. He had already started a case file. Sheriff Turow was comparing the statements that Cassandra Clark had made during her recorded conversation with Nathan Braxton to the evidence that they had collected on Nancy Braxton's murder.

"That was a good suggestion you made, Mac—having Nathan ask her about drowning Nancy Braxton," the sheriff said. "We didn't release the official cause of death—not even to the family. The media reported that she had been found in the lake. It would be natural for someone not involved in the murder to assume she drowned."

"The killer will know that Nancy Braxton had first been struck in the back of the head," David said.

"So," Mac said, "since Cassandra didn't correct Nathan and even went into detail about how she'd drowned, we can assume that the gold digger was lying. She took credit for arranging the murder in order to coerce Braxton into setting up and paying for the murder of her husband."

"Could she have done it?" Sheriff Turow asked. "Maybe she didn't get the details of how the hit man did it and made that part up when Nathan asked for the details."

"If she was going to hire a hit man to kill someone, why not have him kill her intended target?" David asked.

"Because she's a nut," the sheriff said.

"And an opportunist," Mac said. "I'm willing to bet that she and Nathan Braxton did have that conversation. Maybe the shared misery of being married to self-absorbed narcissists brought them together. Then, when Nancy Braxton ended up dead—"

"Cassandra assumed Nathan had done it and decided to take advantage of it," David said.

"And to blackmail him into arranging the murder of her husband," Sheriff Turow said.

"The point is," Mac said, "you can't hang a murder charge on her."

"But if Nathan Braxton ends up being behind his wife's murder, you can use Cassandra as a witness, since she can testify that he did talk about wanting to kill his wife," David said.

"Do you think he did arrange his wife's murder?" Sheriff Turow asked.

"I wouldn't rule anything out right now," Mac said.

"At least we do have Cassandra Clark on extortion and conspiracy to commit murder," Sheriff Turow said. "That's enough to hold her awhile. The fact that his own wife wanted him dead is not going to bode well for Bill Clark in the election."

"Oh, I'm sure he'll be able to spin things around in his favor," David said. "They're both going to be screaming 'entrapment' so loudly that everyone will forget that Clark's wife only married him for his money, thinks he's terrible in bed, and she hates him so much that she wants him dead."

Sitting back in his seat, Mac pressed his fingertips together and concentrated on the many angles of the case. "I can't help but think that the meds Nancy Braxton was supposed to be on figure into the motive for her murder."

"You're still thinking she was on antipsychotic drugs," Sheriff Turow said while reaching for the phone ringing on his desk. "Based completely on her nasty and arrogant behavior during the last few weeks of the election. Has it ever occurred to you two that she behaved that way because she was an ugly human being?" He answered the phone. When a smile crossed his face, they sensed it was good news. After taking down several notes and taking time to ask for the spelling of some words, he hung up and turned back to them.

"It pays to have friends," Sheriff Turow said. "Doc Washington ordered a more comprehensive tox screen on Nancy Braxton's hair and put a rush on it."

"Hair analysis?" David asked.

"Hair analyses are more comprehensive than blood analyses," Mac said. "Blood will only show a recent drug history, whereas your hair can show what chemicals have entered your body and even give a general timeline of when you took them and when you stopped taking them."

"And it looks like Dallas was right." Sheriff Turow was nodding his head. "According to the hair analysis, Nancy Braxton had a long history of taking both a neurotransmitter and antidepressants. But she stopped taking both about six weeks ago."

Squinting, David did a mental calculation. "The primary was six weeks ago. Someone took Nancy Braxton off her meds when she became her party's nominee for mayor"

"Which points toward a motive," Mac said. "Someone wanted her to have a breakdown before the election."

"But why kill her?" Sheriff Turow asked. "She was losing to Gnarly."

"Maybe her breakdown wasn't happening fast enough," David said. "I didn't recognize the symptoms."

"Okay, let's work this one step at a time," Mac said. "We'll start with who had access to Braxton's meds and could've tampered with them. Whoever it was swapped the real meds for sugar pills. Who is that?"

"Let's start with the husband." Sheriff Turow stood up from behind his desk. "He's right down the hall in the interrogation room."

Mac, David, and Sheriff Turow filed into the conference room. Sitting next to his lawyer, Nathan Braxton looked up from where he was reading over the witness statement that they had put together to bring charges against Cassandra Clark.

"We're just about through here." The lawyer placed his finger on the paper to mark their place.

"Good." Feeling weak in the legs after the full day of activity and still suffering from pneumonia, Mac took a seat across the table from them. "We don't think Cassandra had your wife killed."

"You don't believe her story about my doing it," Nathan said. "You recorded her saying it. She said that if I didn't help her—"

Mac waved his hand to silence him. "We think she just took advantage of the situation."

"Who do you think did have something to do with it?" the lawyer asked with a tone of warning in his voice.

318

Ignoring the lawyer, Mac asked, "Was your wife taking any medications?"

Nathan shrugged. "Someone already asked me that. I don't know."

"She was your wife," Mac said. "How could you not know?"

"Because"—Nathan sucked in a deep breath—"our marriage, in the traditional sense, died years ago. I was only with her—and I'm not talking sexually, I'm talking about being in the same room with her—when I had to be. I couldn't stand her, and she didn't really care that I couldn't stand her."

"If you couldn't stand her, why didn't you divorce her?"

"I couldn't divorce her, because she would have stripped me of everything she could've," Nathan said. "She had a whole file of women I'd been with. Then on her end, she couldn't divorce me, because she had Braxton Charities. She couldn't exactly be the face of Braxton Charities, which I started, without being my wife, and it was through Braxton Charities that she made all of the contacts who propped her up in politics." He rolled his eyes. "Now that she's dead, maybe I can get away from those bloodsuckers she called friends, take a shower, and never have anything to do with any of them ever again."

His lawyer shushed him.

After catching his attorney's eye, Nathan said, "Not that I'm glad she's dead." He glanced at the time on his cell phone. "Are we going to be much longer? Eleanor is waiting for me."

"Eleanor?" Mac turned to David, who was leaning against the wall.

"His longtime mistress," David said. "She's got a suite at the Spencer Inn."

"She's his alibi for the time of the murder," the sheriff added.

Resting his head in his hands, Mac let out a deep breath. "That's right. You told me that already." Lifting his head, he said, "Okay. You two were married only in name. We need to find someone who Nancy Braxton was close to—someone who would know what meds she was taking and for what."

"The person Nancy was closest to is Hugh," Nathan said. "I think he was the only person Nancy considered a friend."

"Would he have access to her medication?" David asked.

"You mean like picking up her prescriptions?" Nathan chuckled. "Like lowly servant-type stuff. Nah! That would've been Erin Devereux. Nancy was too important to keep track of her own calendar or to do the shopping and menial tasks like that."

"The same Erin Devereux who George Ward has selected to take your wife's place on the ballot for mayor," Mac said with a sly grin.

"The same Erin Devereux who has been sleeping with the party's state leader for some time now," Nathan said.

"You know that for a fact?" Mac asked.

"Eleanor and I have run into them at the out-of-the-way cheaters' paradises that we go to."

Mac stood up. "Then I think we need to have a word with Erin Devereux."

Her wounds still fresh from the mountain lion's attack, Storm was too skittish to go outside. Rather than risk another attack, she had messed twice in the house. Recalling how Storm had shrieked when the large cat had jumped her and dug her claws into her flesh, Dallas was afraid to take her outside after the sun went down.

Clutching the handgun she had placed in her pocket, Dallas led Storm outside after she had her dinner. While the dog took cautious steps off of the walkway leading to the dock to which David had his boat tethered, Dallas scanned the dark trees and the surrounding area for any sign of a predator.

That time, she was ready to drop him where he stood.

In the stillness of the night, Dallas thought over the Sandy Burr murder. *It really can't be that complicated.*

A journalist went to a hotel to meet with a confidential source for his investigative report. He met with a man who Dallas assumed was his confidential informant during the day—a source who was never identified. Later, the journalist had dinner with a fellow hotel guest who was traveling alone. Then he had drinks with the woman in charge of the charity he was investigating. They argued. The fat man was watching them from the bar. He was never identified either.

The investigative journalist went to his room, and not even two hours later, he was dead.

Who was the source he was seen talking to earlier in the day? Could the fat man have been that source? Why hasn't either of them been identified? Maybe because there was no actual source. Maybe Nancy Braxton set Sandy Burr up—lured him to Deep Creek Lake so that she could have him killed.

Feeling like she was on the brink of something, Dallas stood up tall.

The ring of her phone made Dallas jump and take aim in the direction of the noise.

Equally startled, Storm jumped up onto the walkway and galloped as fast as she could inside. Her attitude told Dallas that she was done for the day.

The caller ID on her cell phone said that the call was from Archie. Dallas grinned. The prospect of becoming friends with Archie made her feel closer to David. She answered the call. "How'd it go?"

There was a smile in Archie's voice. "He's shaken up. I don't know what you told him, but it was enough to get his imagination working overtime. I followed him close enough that he could see that he was being followed. With the tinted windows in the rental, he couldn't see me. Then when he got home, I sat in front of his house until just a bit ago."

"Are you sure he saw you?"

"I've done this before," Archie said, annoyance slipping into her tone. "I know what I'm doing."

"I wasn't saying that you don't." Dallas would have elaborated on how much she respected Archie, but her attention went to Storm, who was curled up on the sofa and had lifted her head. The shepherd's ear stood up tall, and she directed her attention to the door.

The doorbell rang.

Storm barked.

"Wait a minute, Archie. There's someone at the door."

Dallas went over to peer out onto the front deck, which wrapped around the round house. She caught sight of a pair of taillights heading back down the cove.

"Dallas?" Archie said. "Who is it?"

"I don't know." Dallas opened the front door to look out across the front yard and the driveway, where there were two pickup trucks, hers and David's. After searching the area but not seeing anyone, she looked down at her feet and found one addition to the scene: a dusty old boot box resting on the welcome matt.

"Dallas, tell me you're okay."

"I'm fine." Kneeling down in front of it, Dallas checked the lip around its edges to make sure that there weren't any wires or explosive connections. The lid fell aside and revealed that the box was filled with newspaper and magazine clippings, a stenographer's notebook filled with notes, and a typewritten manuscript.

"Dallas." Archie sounded more annoyed by the minute. "What's going on there?"

"It worked," Dallas said with a grin.

"What worked?"

Dallas turned the phone onto speaker and dropped it into the box. Then, carrying it inside, she said, "Montgomery was just here, and he left us everything."

"Everything?"

"It looks like it's Sandy Burr's research." Dallas dipped her hand into the box and shuffled through the thick stack of papers. "There's a whole box of it here."

"I'll be right there!"

Click!

CHAPTER TWENTY-FIVE

Old Towne Alexandria, Virginia

"Pull over here," Murphy said, telling Jessica to park diagonally in the historic district of Old Town Alexandria.

Newt Wallace lived in a colonial brownstone on a cobblestone street only three blocks from the Potomac River. After insisting that Murphy not shut her out of the case, especially since things were really happening, Jessica had appointed herself to be the lookout. For his part, Gnarly moved from window to window in the back of their SUV, peering out into the darkness.

Late in the summer evening, there were some dog owners walking pets who had been cooped up inside all day. The occasional tourist could be spotted roaming out of the historic marketplaces to take in the upscale town homes lining the cobblestone streets lit up by chic streetlamps reminiscent of those of colonial times.

Jessica turned off the engine and waited while Murphy checked the assortment of weapons that he wore strapped and hidden on various parts of his body. He wore a gun on each hip and another in an ankle holster. He also had a knife strapped to his thigh and a backup in a sheath on the other ankle. As if all of that weaponry weren't enough, Murphy was also concealing a small handgun in his jacket pocket.

He stored the rest of the equipment for the mission in a backpack, and he removed two earbuds from its front compartment. He handed one to her. "Do you know how to use this?" He stuck his own in his right ear.

"Yes, I do." She pulled down the visor and lifted the flap so that she could use the mirror when she tucked it into her ear. "Where's the communications control center?"

"I'm right here, Jessica," Nigel said over the speakers.

"Our communications are directly tied into Nigel," Murphy said.

"Everything is tied into Nigel," Jessica said with disgust. "When we decide to have a baby, is Nigel going to deliver it?"

"Now that question is just plain silly, Jessica," Nigel said. "I would need arms in order to deliver a baby. But I would be able to give you instructions on how to breathe, and I could override the department of highways' computer system to give you green lights all the way to the hospital."

"The earbuds also include a GPS." Murphy pressed a series of buttons on the computer monitor built into the SUVs dashboard. A street map appeared on the screen. "This is our car," he said, pointing to an arrow and a red dot. There was a blue dot almost on top of the red one. "I'm the blue dot." He held up his cell phone to show her a nearly identical map that had two dots on it. "You're the red dot. If you have to move the car for some reason, I'll be able to find you on my phone."

He placed his hand under her chin and turned her head, forcing her to look into his eyes. "Repeat for me what I told you before we left the house."

With a roll of her eyes, she said, "No matter what happens, do not go near Wallace's place. If anything happens to you, order Nigel to call CO, then go home and wait for her to contact me."

Murphy was having second thoughts about allowing her to accompany him, even if only to act as a lookout several blocks from Newt Wallace's home. He let out a deep shuddering breath.

"Where's Gnarly on this GPS?" she asked.

"He's in the back." Murphy tucked his cell phone into his jacket.

Jessica looked over her shoulder to where Gnarly was sitting in the back seat. "He's not going with you?"

"No!" he said.

"Then why'd you bring him?"

"I didn't bring him," Murphy said. *"You* brought him."

"No, I didn't. He was already in the car when I got in. I assumed *you* put him in here."

The two of them looked at each other. In unison, they turned to look back at the hundred-pound dog staring at them from over the center console.

"Who put you in the car?" Murphy asked.

"I did," Nigel said.

"How did you *put* Gnarly in the car?" Jessica asked.

"I activated the vehicle's automatic door opener," Nigel said. "You had approved Gnarly for the friends and family list, which includes pets. A scratch at the door communicates the request for me to open the door. Gnarly requested that I open the door for him to access the SUV, so I complied."

"Obviously," Murphy said in a low, "Nigel still has a few glitches."

"Do you think?" Jessica said with sarcasm. "He's *definitely* not delivering our baby. As long as Gnarly is here, you might as well take him with you."

"I'm going to be interrogating a suspect."

"Gnarly is a highly trained canine," she said. "He can be very persuasive."

Looking over his shoulder at Gnarly's intimidating face and size, Murphy said, "I want the guy to tell me why a high-level CIA executive is visiting an agent whose cover got blown—not to pee his pants."

After giving her a kiss on the cheek, Murphy threw open the door and climbed out of the car. He reached back inside for his backpack only to have Gnarly jump into the front of the SUV and leap out of it.

"Gnarly," Murphy said. "You're not going. Come here." He gestured for the dog to go back inside. Instead, Gnarly sat down and gazed up at him. "I'm the alpha. Do what I say. Get in the car." The dog continued to stare up at him. "Now!" To add force to his order, he reached out to grab Gnarly by the collar only for the dog to dodge his reach and gallop off down the street.

"Get back here!" As he took off after the dog, Murphy could hear Jessica laughing behind him.

At the end of the block, Gnarly stopped to look over his shoulder and back to Murphy as if to ask which way to go. Seeing that there was no way to capture the dog without drawing attention to him, Murphy gestured to the left. Looking both ways for traffic, Gnarly trotted across the road and waited for Murphy to catch up.

"Okay, you can come, but remember who's in charge."

Halfway down the next block, Murphy made a right into an alleyway that ran down the middle of the block. A row of eight-foot-tall redbrick privacy fences ran down the length of the block. "Are you reading me, buttercup?" he asked to check that his earbud was working.

"I'm reading both of you," she said.

"Both of us?"

"I tapped into the GPS that the army had installed in Gnarly's microchip," Nigel said.

"He's the dog biscuit on the map," Jessica said with a giggle.

Murphy slipped the phone out of his pocket to check the map. Sure enough, he saw a small dog biscuit next to the blue dot. Tucking it back into his pocket, he stepped up his pace. Gnarly did the same, galloping in tandem with Murphy, who could feel the dog's shoulder against his leg.

Near the end of the block, Murphy came to a halt and pressed his body up against a brick wall, careful to stay in the dark shadows. After looking both ways to ensure that no one was in the alley, Murphy held out his hand in a "stop" signal to Gnarly.

"Okay, I'm going in. You stay here, and act as lookout. If anything goes wrong, run back to the car. You understand?"

Gnarly cocked his head at him.

"Stay." Jogging across the alley, Murphy sucked in a deep breath and then jumped up onto the wall. Grasping the top of it, he pulled himself up and scrambled over it. After hitting the ground on the other side, he peered into the darkness of the small, neatly landscaped courtyard and the brick patio behind the colonial town house.

Searching and listening for any sign that Newt Wallace might have overheard him, Murphy rose to his feet. His sigh of relief over getting into the yard undetected was interrupted by the sound of claws digging into the brick wall behind him. Bits of cinder dust rained down onto him before Gnarly leaped down to the ground beside him, landing gracefully on all fours.

"I told you to stay," he said.

Ignoring Murphy, Gnarly trotted up to the patio door and looked back at him as if to say, "Let's get a move on."

Afraid that Gnarly would give them away, Murphy ran up to the white French door and peered through the window to check for a security monitor. After placing his gloved hand on the doorknob, he twisted it and found that it was unlocked. He pressed on the door. It swung inward.

Before Murphy could reach out to stop him, Gnarly slipped inside.

"We're in luck," he said to Gnarly and Jessica, who was listening in. "The door's unlocked." Careful to stay in the shadows, Murphy slid in through the doorway and pressed up against the wall. He peered into the darkened home to see where Gnarly had run off to.

"Damn dog," he said. "No wonder Mac keeps threatening to sell him on eBay."

"Did you say something, hon?" Jessica asked.

"Nothing." Remembering Gnarly's GPS, Murphy took out his cell phone and zoomed in on their location to search for the dog biscuit that would tell him where Gnarly was.

"She's a traitor to our country!"

Murphy almost dropped the phone when he heard Newt Wallace yelling on the upper floor of the town house. His tone was filled with an equal mixture of panic and anger.

Grabbing one of his guns from his holster, Murphy made his way across the dining room and through the kitchen to the stairs going upward.

The other voice was so quiet that Murphy was unable to make out what it was saying.

There was a glow of light at the top of the stairs. A silhouette resembling that of Batman came into view before Gnarly appeared at the top of the stairs. He peered down at Murphy as if to tell him to hurry up.

Sensing that the coast was clear, Murphy broke into a trot to follow Gnarly up to the second floor, which contained two master suites. The door of the one at the far end of the short hallway was open.

"She's not going to get away with this," Newt Wallace, who was in the bedroom, said.

Flattening himself against the wall, Murphy peered in through the doorway and saw that Newt Wallace was standing on top of a chair in the middle of the room with a noose around his neck. His hands were bound behind his back. His button-down shirt was hanging open, and his clothes were disheveled.

While the intelligence agent was arguing for his life, a man in dark clothing was staging what would appear to be the scene of a suicide. He set an almost-empty bottle of scotch on the nightstand next to a used drinking glass.

"She already has," the man in black said. "If you haven't realized that already, you're a bigger fool than I thought you were." He crossed the bedroom in front of Wallace to place a suicide note on the dresser. "Camille Jurvetson is our DO. She's on the brink of becoming our next DCI. If you had just left well enough alone, you'd be going up to the top with her and those who've been loyal to her. But no, you had to screw things up for yourself."

"By asking questions when critical operations and valuable agents were getting killed in the field! Said and his partner were one of our best teams!"

"Jurvetson got us the location of ISIS's number-three guy!"

"By trading the names, locations, and missions of human resources?"

The man in black stood under Wallace. "There's really no point in arguing about this, Wallace. It's plain to see that we have different viewpoints on this matter. Unfortunately for you, in the end, you lose!"

"No!" Murphy kicked open the door and charged in with a gun in each hand aimed at the intruder. "You lose."

Simultaneously, the intruder kicked the chair out from under Wallace's feet and reached behind his back for his gun. Murphy fired off three rounds from both guns, striking the assassin in the midsection. The force of the shots sent him backward and down to the floor.

Holstering both of his guns, Murphy ran to where Newt Wallace was kicking and fighting for his life. Grabbing the man's flailing legs, he lifted him up so that he could breathe.

"I have you!" Murphy reached up with one hand to try to release the Velcro strap that the assassin had used to bind Wallace's arms.

He hadn't realized that he had forgotten about Gnarly until the room was seemingly filled with the dog's roar. In a black-and-tan flash, the canine raced across the room to slam into the assassin, who screamed out in anguish when Gnarly plunged him down to the floor with his jaws clamped on the killer's arm. The gun he was wielding in an attempt to shoot Murphy tumbled out of his hand.

The ballistic vest under the assassin's shirt had protected him from the gunshots. But he wasn't so well protected from Gnarly's teeth.

Stripped of his gun, the killer struggled to reach for the knife that he had strapped to his ankle. By then, Gnarly's teeth had torn through the flesh of his right arm down to the bone. Wailing in anguish, he extracted the knife and held it up, ready to plunge it into Gnarly's side. But the knife was shot out of his grasp when a bullet from Murphy's gun flew through the inside of his wrist and out the other side before plunging into the floor behind him.

"Gnarly! Release!"

Dropping his grip on the killer, Gnarly scurried around and lay down by Murphy's side. With both of his arms bloody and useless, the assassin dropped back down onto the floor.

"Backup and cleanup are on the way," Nigel said.

"Murphy! Murphy, are you okay?" Jessica asked through the earbud. She was breathless with worry. "I heard gunshots! Is Gnarly okay?"

"We're both fine." Murphy bent over to pet Gnarly on the head. His mouth hanging open, the German shepherd wagged his tail. "Don't get cocky."

CHAPTER TWENTY-SIX

It was late in the evening when Sheriff Turow pulled his cruiser through the front gates of the Braxtons' estate. A black Cadillac was parked near the front porch.

David and Mac waited with the sheriff for a very long time after ringing the doorbell—long enough to suspect that no one was home—and then saw Erin Devereux running down the stairs with her long silk bathrobe flapping behind her. After scurrying across the foyer in her slippers, she pressed her face up against the cut glass of the front door to see who was there. Upon seeing the sheriff and the police chief in their uniforms and Mac Faraday, her mouth dropped open. After quickly checking to make sure that her robe was properly closed, she opened the door.

Her tone oozed with innocence. "Sheriff Turow, what are you doing here? I was just about to go to bed."

"I can see that." Without invitation, the sheriff stepped inside, and David and Mac filed in behind him. "We've had some developments in our investigation of Nancy Braxton's murder—"

"I saw Cassandra Clark being taken out of the Spencer Inn in handcuffs," Erin said. "Did she kill Ms. Braxton to help her husband win the election?"

"We don't think so," the sheriff said.

"She had an alibi for the time of the murder," Mac said. "We have a few more questions, and Nathan thought that you might be able to help us."

Seeing that they were going to be a while, Erin led them across the foyer in the direction of the study, where she had been shot by an intruder only a few days before.

On their way into the study, Mac yelled up the stairs. "You may want to join us, George!"

Erin stopped—frozen with uncertainty about how to proceed.

Mac, David, and the sheriff stared up the stairway, awaiting George Ward's appearance. Finally, he emerged from the upstairs hallway and made his way down the stairs with the demeanor of a guilty child who'd been caught with his hand in the cookie jar. He waited until he reached the last step before asking, "How did you know?"

With a shrug of his shoulders, Mac said, "There are only so many motives for corruption. Sex, money, and power. This evening, after seeing that you'd replaced Nancy Braxton with Erin instead of with a better-qualified candidate who had run for mayor in the primary, I had to ask myself why you'd done that. She has no actual governing experience. She doesn't have money. She can't give you power. All that leaves us with is...sex."

George's face turned bright red. Erin looked down at her feet.

"There's also blackmail," Mac said.

"Blackmail for what?" George said.

"The obvious next question is, when did you two hatch this plot to replace Nancy Braxton on the ballot? Before or after her murder?" Mac said.

"After!" George yelled.

"We had nothing to do with Ms. Braxton's murder," Erin said.

"Are you sure about that?" David asked.

"She was losing it," Erin said. "I saw it happening. Since I was with her all the time, I saw things going on with her. I think she was getting Alzheimer's. I'd been covering for her for months, but it was getting more difficult." She waved at David. "You saw her at the Italian restaurant. She was totally paranoid." She grasped the arm that had been shot days before. "When she shot me, I realized that she was truly unfit to hold an office like that of mayor."

"Which is why you called George from the ambulance on your way to the hospital," David said.

"She was doing the right thing," George said. "Giving me a heads-up about a potentially explosive situation that would've proved very embarrassing to our party."

"Oh, yeah," Mac said, chuckling. "I'm sure that all Erin cared about was doing the right thing for all the right reasons."

"I don't like your tone." George slipped a protective arm around Erin's waist.

"Tell us about the shooting," Sheriff Turow said.

"I was here in the study looking for some files to take upstairs to work on," Erin said.

"What files?" Mac asked.

"What does it matter?" she countered.

"If it doesn't matter, then you should have no problem telling us."

In silence, George Ward was looking at her.

With a shrug of her shoulders, she said, "A list of our campaign donors. I was going to send out invitations to a fund-raising dinner. I was looking through the folders on the desk. Suddenly, the light flipped on—"

"Why were the lights off?" David asked.

"Because I didn't want to wake anyone up."

"Why would the light being on down here wake up anyone?" Sheriff Turow asked. "The bedrooms are upstairs."

Erin's face turned pink. She clenched her jaw. "I was the one who got shot!"

"So the light was turned on," Mac said. "And what happened then?"

"There was Nancy, and she was holding a gun. She started spouting all of this insanity about how I was out to get her and how she hadn't worked all these years courting and sucking up to anyone and everyone so that she could get to where she was and then have a little slut steal it from her." Erin rubbed her injured shoulder. "Then she pulled the trigger and shot me. Hugh and Nathan heard the shot, and they came running in and took the gun from her. They took her upstairs and gave her a strong tranquilizer. Then Hugh got rid of the gun, and they came up with this phony story about a burglar."

"But you called George from the ambulance to tell him the truth," David said.

"At which point you two started maneuvering to remove Nancy from the campaign and replace her with you," Mac said.

"I have a degree in political science," Erin said.

"I'm sure you do." Mac turned to George. "Did Erin tell you that she took Nancy off of her meds without her knowing it?"

"Meds? What meds?" George Ward's mouth dropped open.

"That's right," Mac said. "Your party's chosen candidate was mentally ill."

Guttural noises came out of George's mouth as he looked from Mac to Erin and then back again.

"They're lying!" Erin said.

"That's why Nancy was losing it," Mac said. "The pathological lying. Making herself out to be more important than she really was. Showing signs of having delusions. Paranoia." He grinned. "Though the paranoia might have been because someone close to her really was out to get her."

"You can't prove any of that!"

"Nathan gave her doctor permission to tell us what's in her records," Sheriff Turow said. "He had referred her to a psychiatrist for treatment of her delusions of grandeur and paranoia years ago. She'd been on antidepressants and antipsychotic medication for several years—until Erin here started swapping out her meds for sugar pills."

"The medical examiner found gelatin capsules in Nancy Braxton's stomach," David said, "but no meds in the tox screen. She did a hair analysis and found that up until six weeks ago, she'd been taking regular medication and then had suddenly stopped."

"The primary was six weeks ago," George said.

"When did Erin start putting the moves on you?" Mac asked.

"You can't prove it was me," Erin said. "I didn't even know Nancy was on meds. She obviously didn't want anyone to know. Not even her husband knew."

"Now, why would you say that?" Mac asked. "We just told you that Nathan gave the doctor permission to tell us what's in her records. Why would you think he didn't know—unless Nancy told you that she didn't want him to know?"

"There are no pills in this house," Erin said. "You've already looked."

Mac slipped on evidence gloves. "*I* haven't looked yet."

Sheriff Turow took an envelope out of his pocket and handed it to Erin. "Another search warrant for the house and the entire grounds."

After the sheriff called in one of his deputies who was stationed outside to watch Erin and George, he and David led Mac upstairs to Nancy Braxton's bedroom suite. On their way out of the room, they saw that George was glaring with disdain at Erin Devereux.

Once inside the master suite, Mac stood in the middle of the room and looked around, turning in a complete circle.

"My people tore this room apart," Sheriff Turow said. "Went through all the garbage, too."

"No, she has them in the house," Mac said. "She's smart. As soon as she found out that Nancy Braxton was dead, they all went into cover-up mode. Nancy didn't tell her husband about the psychiatrist and the meds. I doubt that she told her brother. She was not a woman who got close to anyone."

"Erin was the first assistant she had who lasted more than a year," David said.

"Only because she was as ambitious as Nancy Braxton." Mac went into Nancy's bathroom and looked around. He peered up at the shower-curtain rod. "Knowing that no one knew about Nancy's condition, Erin bided her time until the right moment and then took her off the meds." He reached up and tapped the rod with his fingertips. "Then she went about seducing George Ward and priming him for blackmail so that when Nancy Braxton had her breakdown, she could swoop in like Wonder Woman to save the party."

Without touching anything, Mac hurried out of the room to the hallway. "Where's Erin's room?"

Sheriff Turow pointed to the room across the hallway. Mac threw open the door and went inside.

"You mentioned blackmail," Sheriff Turow said. "George Ward was adamant that he wasn't being blackmailed."

Mac went into Erin's bathroom. "That's how I know he's lying. Erin said she was in the study looking for a list of donors to Nancy's campaign." He peered up at the curtain rod and grinned. "That information would have been digital—on her laptop." Climbing into the tub, he studied the brace holding the rod in place.

"Which wasn't in the study," David said before turning to Mac. "Be careful. You were in the emergency room just a couple of days ago."

"Yes, Dad," Mac said with sarcasm. "I'm willing to bet that she was really looking for the charities that Braxton Charities pays out to." He tapped on the curtain rod. His taps made a noise that indicated that the rod was not hollow. Mac held out his hand to David, who slapped a multitool pocketknife in his palm.

"More than one person has told us that Nancy Braxton was not qualified to be the mayor of Spencer," Mac said while unscrewing the brace that held the rod in place. "She didn't have the experience or personality to win the election. George was literally taking a big chance by backing Nancy Braxton. Erin had been working with Nancy. She must've seen what was going on and realized that George Ward was taking bribes. But in order to blackmail him into replacing Nancy with her, she needed proof."

"Nathan Braxton told us on the night of the shooting that both Erin and Hugh used the study," David said.

Mac yanked the curtain rod down. "Erin was in the study looking for records showing a money trail from Braxton Charities to George Ward. She needed to prove that Nancy Braxton was paying him off so that he would get her elected into some leadership position that would fulfill her fantasy of being queen."

Mac turned the curtain rod vertically and shook it. With a rattle, four prescription bottles, each of which contained several pills, fell out of the tube and onto the floor. Realizing that there was something else still in the rod, he took a toothbrush from the bathroom counter and pushed its handle down the rod until he managed to pry out a clear plastic bag containing powdered sugar.

"Looks like we have our killer." Sheriff Turow stuffed the pill bottles into evidence bags.

"Nah," David said.

"Nah?" the sheriff said. "We have the pills and the sugar that she replaced them with—"

"According to the security recording from the night of the murder, Erin Devereux never left the grounds," David said. "Hugh went looking for Nancy. Erin stayed here."

"Why would Hugh Vance have killed his sister?" Sheriff Turow asked.

Mac took the pills and the powdered sugar. "Let's go find out."

"This confirms everything that Mac and I uncovered about Braxton Charities." Archie picked up one of the stacks of paper work and thumbed through it.

Archie had raced over to David's house as soon as Dallas had told her about the box that had been left on the doorstep. While sorting through the paper work, which included government reports collected from the Freedom of Information Act and witness statements, and scanning Sandy Burr's unpublished manuscript, they drank a whole bottle of white wine.

After sorting through each piece of paper, Dallas went into the kitchen to open a second bottle and to freshen their drinks so that they could sit back and digest what they had learned.

"How did Caleb Montgomery end up with this box?" Archie asked while accepting the glass of wine being offered to her.

"I assume he found it in Sandy Burr's room." Dallas sat on the arm of the sofa and stroked her sleeping dog.

"What was he doing in Sandy Burr's room?" When Dallas had no answer, Archie grinned. "You know what they say: when you assume, you make an ass out of you and me."

"Are you thinking he killed Sandy Burr?" Dallas asked. "Like, Hugh Vance paid him to do it? That's why Caleb was so insistent that Hugh Vance wasn't the fat man at the bar."

"If Hugh hired Caleb to kill Sandy Burr, he wouldn't have let this business-slash-extortion-business continue for all of these years," Archie said. "Vance would've made damn sure that he got this box as part of the arrangement. Caleb came upon the box in another way. Like, he happened upon it."

"He witnessed the murder," Dallas said, "or the killer running away. Went into the room to check it out and found the box with the manuscript. Before that he had witnessed Sandy Burr's meeting with Nancy Braxton—had seen them arguing. All he had to do was read the first few pages of the manuscript to realize how valuable it would be, so he took it."

Archie's brow furrowed while she leafed through the paper work.

"What do you see?"

"It's what I don't see." Archie paused to take a sip of her wine. "While we've been going through all of this and talking about it, one name keeps coming up in regard to Braxton Charities."

"Hugh Vance," Dallas said.

"Not Nancy Braxton, who was the person Sandy Burr interviewed and argued with that night." She shook a copy of a contract at Dallas. "Yes, Nancy signed some stuff, but the guy who is really running things is—"

"Hugh Vance." Dallas stood up. "What was it I heard someone say? Nancy Braxton is the face of Braxton Charities. She goes around hobnobbing with all the big wheels and getting them to donate to it, but it's her brother who runs things behind the scenes."

"Which means that when Sandy Burr met with her to discuss the money laundering, she most likely honestly had no idea what he was talking about."

"Which would have given Hugh a big motive to want Burr dead." Dallas sat down across from her.

"We need to confirm all of this." Archie picked up a dusty weekly organizer that they'd found in the box and thumbed through the contacts listed in it. "We know he met his contact in Deep Creek Lake the afternoon of the day he died."

Dallas was looking through the appointment section. "Maybe he made a note—" She jumped in her seat. "Someone with the initials 'NB.' Can't be Nancy Braxton, can it?"

"Of course he would've used initials," Archie said.

"Who does he have listed in the *B*s?" Dallas asked. "We want a last name starting with *B* that has a Deep Creek Lake phone number listed with it."

"But not Nancy Braxton." Archie ran her finger down the list of contacts. Her eyes widened with surprise.

"There is someone, isn't there?" Dallas held her breath.

"You're never going to believe who it is."

As Mac, David, and Sheriff Turow had expected, when they returned to the study with the pill bottles and the powdered sugar they'd found in her bathroom, Erin Devereux immediately claimed that someone else had planted them there.

"I can see you learned from the best," Mac said. "You're going to claim that your political enemies are perpetrating a vast conspiracy."

"I am being framed."

"So when we dust these pill bottles for fingerprints, your prints won't be on them?" Sheriff Turow asked.

"They will be. I ordered the pills for Nancy, and I opened the package and gave them to her—"

"And after Nancy Braxton had a breakdown and ran out of the house and into the night—ending up dead—you didn't hide the pills to keep her condition from being made public?" When Erin shook her head, Mac grinned. "Not even to protect the image of your party?"

With a sigh, she relented. "Not because I'd done anything wrong. You have to understand. Ms. Braxton was a brilliant woman. If it got out that she had a psychiatric condition, her legacy would have been ruined." Pleased with how well she had thought on her feet, Erin grinned.

Impressed, Mac chuckled. "There's only one problem with that explanation. Why would you have been so concerned about preserving Nancy Braxton's legacy before you even knew she was dead?"

"Allegedly," David said, "you didn't know she was dead until I came here to tell you she was at nine thirty the next morning."

"Until then," Mac said, "supposedly, you only thought she was missing."

"I hid them after Chief O'Callaghan told us she was dead," Erin said, "but before they searched her room."

David and Sheriff Turow both shook their heads. "My officers and I kept everyone down here on the main floor," David said. "You had no access to Nancy's bedroom, and an officer was with you at all times."

"Which means that you hid Nancy Braxton's medications the night before," Mac said. "Which means that you knew she was dead before Chief O'Callaghan arrived here the next morning. You had to get rid of the pills so that we wouldn't discover that you had tampered with them."

Erin turned to George Ward, hoping he would defend her. Instead, he turned away. "I'm the party's mayoral nominee! If I go down, you're going down with me."

"I had no idea that Nancy was on antipsychotic medication and that Erin was tampering with her meds," George said. "I had seen Nancy losing it, but she was always demanding, and I swear that she wouldn't have known the truth if it'd bit her on the butt. But I didn't think—" He paused and pointed at Erin. "She called me from the ambulance on the way to the hospital and told me that Nancy had lost her mind and shot her. She told me that Nancy was having a breakdown from the stress of the campaign. That's all I thought it was."

"And the night of the murder?" Mac asked.

"Erin called and told me that Nancy had had a complete breakdown and run out," George said. "She asked me what to do. I told her to wake up Hugh and send him out to find her before she did something crazy and ruined everything we had done for her."

"What set Nancy off?" David asked them.

Erin looked from George to her feet and then cast her eyes around the room.

Mac folded his arms across his chest. "You're looking at being charged with negligent homicide and accessory to murder, Ms. Devereux."

"I didn't kill her!"

"You tampered with her medication, causing her to have a breakdown and to run out into the night," Sheriff Turow said. "While she was out there, someone killed her."

"If a prosecutor wanted to, he could argue that if you hadn't tampered with Nancy Braxton's medication, she never would have had the breakdown that sent her out into the night to be murdered," Mac said. "If you help us, we'll put in a good word for you."

Erin folded her arms across her chest. "I saw that Nancy was at the breaking point—especially when she told that outlandish lie at the debate about landing in sniper fire in Somalia. Then, when those nuts called threatening her life after someone planted that story about Gnarly, she completely lost it. She fired me, saying that I was out to get her."

"But you said you got fired a couple of times a week," David said.

"Not like that time," Erin said. "That time was for real. I did dismiss it, and just like always, I went to my room to go to bed. But then Nancy came banging on my door, screaming for me to get out and saying that she wasn't going to have me in her house for even one more night. We got into a huge fight, and then my cell phone rang. She looked over and saw George's picture and name on the caller ID. Then she totally lost her grip and said that we were conspiring against her to oust her from the campaign."

"Which was true," Mac said.

Erin frowned when she saw George step away from her. "That was when she became completely unwrapped and ran out of my room, down the staircase, and out of the house. I ran outside to try to find her, but I couldn't."

"But not right away," David said. "According to the time stamp on the security tape, you were seven minutes behind her. Instead of going after her to make sure she was okay, you called George to snitch on her."

"I didn't know she was going to die!" Erin said.

"You wanted to give him a step-by-step play of how unbalanced Nancy was," Mac said. "You knew that if you didn't call him, she would just come back, and everything would be fine—no harm done. But if you did call in the midst of the crisis, he would see for himself that his candidate needed to be replaced—and needed to be replaced quickly."

"Are we right, George?" David asked.

George Ward nodded his head.

"Hugh went to go find her and then came back and said that he had found her down by the lake," Erin said. "He said that one of the fanatics who'd threatened her must have found her and bashed her brains in."

"That's what he said?" Mac looked from Erin to David and the sheriff.

"That's what Hugh told you?" David asked.

"Hugh told us he never found her," the sheriff said.

"That was a lie," Erin said with a casual shrug of her shoulders. "He told me that he found her down at the lake and her head had been bashed in with a rock."

David turned and whispered to Mac and Sheriff Turow. "The way Nancy's body was found, she was lying with her head facedown in the water. If Hugh had really found her like that in the dark, he would've assumed that she'd drowned."

"The only way Hugh could've known that she'd been hit in the head with a rock would've been by hitting her with it," Mac said.

"Where is Hugh?" Sheriff Turow asked.

"He left this afternoon," Erin said.

"This afternoon?" David asked.

"After you guys had finished questioning him. He said that you guys had told him that he was cleared and could go. So he came home and packed a suitcase and left."

Chapter Twenty-Seven

Spencer Police Department

David was on one phone putting out a BOLO—a "be on the lookout"—for Hugh Vance, who was a suspect in the murder of his sister, while Mac was sitting behind Bogie at a computer doing a search for airline reservations. Everyone was talking at once when Archie called Mac on his cell.

"We just found the mastermind for the money laundering at Braxton Charities," Archie said. "It was Hugh Vance. Nancy was just a front man—or, rather, a front woman. Hugh Vance did all of the moving around of the funds—"

"And he killed his sister," Mac said. "We've got a BOLO out for him right now. He chartered a plane from McHenry to Chicago. Now we're trying to find out where he's going from there. He has to be running."

"He's got an alias," Archie said.

"How'd you find that?"

"Once I found out that he was in charge—"

"We need to know his alias," Mac said.

"Van Kruger," Archie said. "And he's got a big bank account in the Cook Islands, so that's where he'll be heading, because that's where the bulk of his money is."

"That's in the South Pacific," Bogie said while Archie continued to tell them about her and Dallas' discoveries. "There won't be any direct flights there from Chicago, so he'll have to take a connecting flight."

"Try looking at flights to Australia," Mac said.

"He's got, like, thirty-one and a half million dollars stashed away there," Archie said. "He also bought an estate on one of the islands about four years ago—"

"Here!" Bogie practically jumped out of his chair while pointing at the screen. "Chicago to Sydney."

David relayed the message to airport security. "Bogie, what's the flight and gate?"

Thanking Archie for her help, Mac disconnected the call without realizing that she was still excitedly telling him about Caleb Montgomery turning over Sandy Burr's research. They could tell by Bogie's expression that what he was reading on the computer screen was not good news.

"He's gone," Mac said.

Bogie nodded his head. "Plane took off two hours ago."

Everyone visibly slumped.

Mac read the flight itinerary over Bogie's shoulder. "Well, that makes it more difficult, but it's not impossible." He picked up his cell phone and hit a speed-dial button. When the call was picked up, Mac said, "Remember when you told me that if I ever needed anything, I could just call? Well, I need something, and I'm calling."

"Sure, that won't be any problem," Murphy said into his cell phone. "But don't forget to gas it up when you're done."

The back door of the limousine opened.

"Gotta go." Murphy disconnected the call and slipped the phone into the case on his utility belt, which held his double holster, as the woman in the red pantsuit climbed into the back of her limousine.

Startled to see the young man dressed in black waiting for her in the seat facing away from the driver, Camille Jurvetson stopped. Her plump frame made her incapable of turning around fast enough to curse her security detail before he closed the door on her.

"Who the hell are you, and how did you get into my limo?"

"I have friends," Murphy said.

"So do I." She plopped down across from him. Her eyes, which were small to begin with, disappeared in her bloated face, which was weathered after years of manipulating and maneuvering her way to the top of what had once been a man's game. Every setback she had suffered while working to achieve her goal was etched into her face.

"We have some mutual friends," Murphy said. "I just left one of them. Newt Wallace."

For a second, Murphy was able to see her eyes widen in surprise. She regained her demeanor quickly. "He wasn't in the morning briefing," she said. "Is he sick?"

"He's in protective custody."

Adopting an expression of concern, she folded her hands in her lap. "What did Newt get himself into?"

"He trusted the wrong person."

She offered what was supposed to be a demure, even motherly smile. "Well, we are in the spy game. Even the most experienced intelligence agents can fall victim to a particularly cunning adversary who pretends to be their ally."

"Like their mentor?" Murphy asked.

She gasped. Her hand flew to her chest. "You don't think I—"

"Newt Wallace is not as naïve as you think he is," Murphy said. "All of the years that you were fast-tracking your rise to the top at the agency, you conned everyone into thinking that you had brilliant deductive reasoning—that you were able to piece together the information that came in from the agents in the field to figure out who the key figures were and where the most important targets were located." He shook his head. "Your mentors and bosses all thought you were a hotshot agent who they were lucky to have on their side. When in reality"—he leaned toward her—"you're nothing more than a lowly muck-eating traitor to your country and fellow agents."

She held her expression, which was one of shock, long enough for Murphy to see that she was launching into a well-rehearsed performance. In all of the years that she had been trading secrets, she'd known that his accusation could surface eventually. "I don't know what Wallace told you—"

"He recorded your phone conversation yesterday."

The demure smile fell.

"You know the one," he said. "The one where you told him that he didn't have the stomach to make it to the big time after he called you out for trading information about *our* undercover agents—for putting *our* people in danger and getting *our* people killed—to advance your own career."

"Those were hard choices that had to be made, and I made them!" With each word, she jabbed her finger at him.

"You don't deny giving classified information to foreign agents," Murphy said.

"Everyone does it!"

"Four agents!" Murphy held up his hand and showed her four fingers. "Four agents! That's how many agents Wallace was able to track down who had been killed due to your making deals with our enemies! Four brave Americans—all of whom had families—were serving their country, and they died because you blew their covers, abandoned them, and let them die out in the field!"

Her voice sounded like the hiss of a demon. "You can't prove anything."

"After Tawkeel Said and his handler were captured, Newt Wallace recalled your asking him about what agency operation was going down in Brussels and which agents were involved. He gave you the file with everything in it. Seventy-two hours later, Said's cover had been blown, his handler had been tortured to death, and you had learned the current location of ISIS's number-three man and his compound."

"They offered it to me," she said.

"Who offered it to you? ISIS's number-four man? The one who moved up to fill the number-three slot after you had his competition taken out?"

Her silence brought a slow grin to Murphy's face. "That's what happened, isn't it? Terrorists can be ambitious, too. The number-four guy, who Tawkeel had gone undercover to identify and locate, came to you. You'd been in contact with him all along—helping each other move up the ladder. He'd give you information, and you'd use it to make yourself look good to the folks on the seventh floor." He cocked his head at her. "You look like a smart woman. I think you knew that your source was using you. High up in ISIS, he would give you information that he knew would make you look good while helping him move up in his organization. Because you would use his information to eliminate his competition. And you'd do the same. Of course, if your source got captured, then you'd be up a creek and you couldn't have that. So you'd pass on information that would help him evade capture—like information about our agents who were moving in on him—even if it meant our people ending up tortured to death."

Through gritted teeth, she said, "You have no idea who you're dealing with."

"I know exactly who I'm dealing with," Murphy said. "A traitor to our country."

"A traitor with the whole CIA behind her." She held up her hand with her first two fingers crossed. "I am like this with the front-runner for president of the United States. She's going to make me Director of Central Intelligence. Do you honestly think anyone is going to believe a disgruntled CIA employee over me? If anyone does, do you think they're going to stand in the way of the appointment of the first woman DCI?"

"No."

"You're not as naïve as I thought." Arrogance filled her face. "Why are you wasting your and my time telling me this? Nothing is going to happen."

"I'm giving you a chance to come out of this alive," Murphy said.

She scoffed. "Seriously?"

"We have all we need—undeniable proof that you are a traitor who traded American lives to advance your own career."

"You're repeating yourself," she said. "I don't know who you work for. NSA? FBI? Doesn't matter. The fact is that I am protected, and no one can touch me."

"You're wrong," Murphy said. "That's why I'm giving you a choice. Resign now. Quietly. You can forget about your benefits, because we will strip you of those—"

She laughed.

"Your benefits will be split between the families of the four men you sentenced to death."

Her amusement dropped. "You have no idea how the world works."

"I know how it works," he said. "It's been a big mess for a very long time because good people have allowed themselves to get beaten down into silence by people like you. But here's some breaking news for you, Ms. Jurvetson. There's a revolution going on. Politics and personal ambition have destroyed our country, and good Americans have died. It's going to stop—here and now." Murphy leaned toward her. "You have twenty-four hours to resign."

"Go to hell."

"Your choice." Reaching for the door handle, he said in a whisper, "I wouldn't waste my time packing to move to the DCI's office quite yet."

"You can't protect Newt Wallace from the CIA," she said.

Without a word, Murphy slammed the door on her.

Fuming, Camille Jurvetson picked up her cell phone and hit a button. "There was a young man who was just in the back of my limo. I want you to get his name, the names of his family members, his home address—everything about him! I don't care how you get it. Make an example of him."

Spencer Inn

Archie Monday ordered a tomato juice, a glass of water, and two aspirins to go with her breakfast of a vegetable omelet. Across the table in the resort's restaurant, Dallas Walker had an unbelievable amount of food spread out in front of her. The Texan had a large steak, eggs over easy, home fries slathered in sausage gravy, and Texas toast, of course.

"Wait until you hit thirty, and your metabolism changes," Archie said to the woman who was more than ten years younger than she was.

"Huh?" Dallas stopped with a forkful of steak halfway to her mouth.

The two women had spent the whole night scouring Sandy Burr's research and drinking wine. Around three o'clock in the morning, Archie realized that Dallas had drunk her under the table. A wine aficionado who couldn't remember the last time she had imbibed too much alcohol, Archie was thoroughly annoyed with David's new girlfriend,

His computer tablet tucked under his arm, Nathan Braxton followed the host into the restaurant and took a seat several tables away from them.

"That's him," Dallas said. "That's Nathan Braxton." Tossing her napkin onto the table, she stood up.

"We can't just go running up to him like a couple of football players and tackle him," Archie said in a hushed voice.

"Why not?"

"We need to play it cool." Taking a deep breath, Archie gracefully rose from the table and strolled across the dining room to where Nathan Braxton was reading the news on his tablet while the server filled his coffee cup. She waited for the server to leave before introducing herself.

"You're Mac Faraday's wife," he said while shaking her hand.

"Actually, he's my husband." Archie slipped into the seat across from him.

"If this is about Nancy's murder, I've already—"

"That's not the murder I wanted to talk to you—"

"It's about Sandy Burr." Dallas plopped down in the empty seat between them.

Nathan Braxton's jaw dropped open slightly.

"You know all about Sandy Burr," Dallas said, grinning. "You were the confidential source he came out here to Deep Creek Lake to meet with."

Nathan Braxton's cheeks grew pink.

"We found your initials in his calendar under the day he was killed and found the phone number of your private line in his list of contacts," Archie said. "What I don't understand is why you had to be a confidential source. Braxton Charities was your foundation. You set it up. If something illegal had been going on, you would've had the power to stop it."

"Not really," Nathan said while glancing around to make sure that no one was listening to their conversation. "You see, I set up Braxton Charities for Nancy. Her ego refused to allow her to work for anybody. She had this need to be in charge—to snap orders and to have everyone ask 'how high?' when she said 'jump.' I thought that by setting up Braxton Charities and making it big enough, I could kill two birds with one stone. If I created a foundation that would disburse money to a wide variety of charities, money and help would go to those who needed it. And if I allowed Nancy to be in charge of it, it would help her fulfill her need to be a bigwig and to rub elbows with movers and shakers with big wallets around the world."

"But while she was hobnobbing around the world, her brother, Hugh, set up a money-laundering branch for the more unsavory movers and shakers," Dallas said.

Nathan Braxton nodded his head. "By the time I realized it, it was too late. Nancy didn't want to hear anything about my suspicions—that's all they were at that point. Then Sandy Burr came to me because my name was on the foundation. He was investigating how Braxton Charities had awarded some medical grant. I thought—" He shrugged. "I told him all about my suspicions and pointed him in the right direction." He sighed. "It's my fault that he's dead."

"Did Hugh Vance kill him?" Dallas asked.

"He couldn't have," Nathan said. "I purposely scheduled Sandy's and my meeting for when Hugh would be out of town. He had no idea that I was having the foundation investigated. Hugh was in Canada meeting with some foreign companies that wanted to donate to us."

"But Hugh did buy the bartender's silence by buying the hotel and making him a partner," Dallas said. "He saw Sandy meeting with your wife—"

"The meeting was my idea," Nathan said. "Nancy refused to believe any of my suspicions about Hugh. I thought that if a third party, an investigative journalist who had dug deep into the charity, confronted her with solid evidence, she'd see that Hugh was a crook. But it didn't work."

"Why do you say it didn't work?" Archie asked.

"She refused to believe it," Nathan said. "Instead, she accused me of trying to frame her brother and trying to shut down Braxton Charities because I was out to get her. She then turned around and told Hugh." He waved his hand. "From what I was able to pick up, that bartender found Sandy's research when he found the body after the killer had taken off. Maybe he left the door of his hotel room open. Instead of calling the police, he kept it and blackmailed Hugh with it." With a shake of his head, he added, "Nancy could be very paranoid. But no matter how paranoid she got, she never would have thought that her brother was in any way capable of doing anything wrong or illegal—even after all those years."

Dallas and Archie exchanged glances.

"Who was bribing Nancy's political party to support her for her elections?" Dallas asked.

"That was more like blackmail," Nathan said. "Think about it. Since Hugh runs the laundromat, he knows all about everyone's dirty laundry."

"But it sounds like you're saying that Nancy wasn't really involved at all," Archie said.

"She wasn't," Nathan said. "But not everyone knows that."

"So," Archie said, "George Ward and everyone who was laundering their money through Braxton Charities probably assumed that Nancy, the face of Braxton Charities, knew things about them that they didn't want to be made public. So they backed her for whatever she wanted."

"Making her think that their support was based on a sincere belief in her abilities," Dallas said, "which fed her delusions of grandeur."

"When really, they were just plain scared to death of her." Nathan looked up and saw a lovely blonde making her way across the dining room to him. "Well, I'm glad everything is now coming out into the open. Now I can close up Braxton Charities and start a new chapter of my life."

Thanking him, Archie stood up.

"Wait!" Dallas said. "If Hugh was out of town during Sandy Burr's murder, then he really wasn't the fat man watching from the bar. Do you know who the fat man the bartender saw was?"

"I have no idea," Nathan said while holding out a chair for his date. "I've always assumed it was just a coincidence, and the guy had a beef with Sandy about something else that had nothing to do with Braxton Charities."

Life is good indeed.

Flashing what he hoped was a charming grin at the server, Hugh Vance accepted the glass of champagne from her and took a sip of it as he took in the view from the Virgin America Loft at Los Angeles International Airport. Sitting back in his padded seat, Hugh sighed and took a moment to admire the long legs of a woman sitting in a padded chair at the next table. He wondered if she was one of those women who would be impressed by a man with money—and whether she'd be impressed enough to tumble into bed with him.

While Hugh couldn't see her eyes behind her dark glasses or see the color of her hair under her wide-brimmed white hat, he could see enough of her legs to know that he wanted her.

After catching the steely eye of the mountain of a man sitting across from her, Hugh decided that it would be safer to simply let her be a fantasy.

You may be bigger and stronger than I am, but I have enough money to buy and sell you like that! In his mind, Hugh snapped his fingers. *And with all of the dirt I have on some of the most powerful people in our nation, I could have you killed just by asking.* Sticking out his chin in a show of bravado, Hugh took a sip of his champagne and directed his attention back out the window. He picked up his briefcase. In it was his computer tablet, which held all of his banking information and the information for the paper work he'd need to start a new life.

Movements around him drew Hugh's attention from the window to where passengers were leaving the lounge. At first, he thought they were leaving for a flight, but then he noticed four men in suits making their way from one table to the next, quietly speaking to the other guests in the lounge. During their hushed conversations, the men would show the guests what appeared to be badges, and then the guests would gather up their belongings, casting quick glances in Hugh's direction, and rush out of the lounge.

No, no, no, no, no! Maybe this has nothing to do with me. A thick layer of sweat formed on his brow. He clutched his leather briefcase to his chest. *I was so careful while creating Van Kruger. Spent a lot of money making a new identity and years storing up nest eggs all over the world. I even have my own estate on a private island.*

The lounge was empty except for the men in suits, each of whom had weapons on his hip, stationed at the exit. Even the bartender had left.

Hugh's heart pounded against the smooth leather. He considered making a run for it, but he doubted that the men guarding the exit would let him get very far.

Three men were being escorted by two uniformed Maryland State Police officers and two California State Police officers into the lounge. After flashing their badges to the plainclothes officers, they crossed the lounge to where Hugh was trembling in his seat.

Sheriff Turow stepped up to the side of his chair. Police Chief O'Callaghan took a position behind it. The other police officers boxed Hugh in. There was no escape.

Mac Faraday slipped into the seat across from him. "Hello, Hugh. Do you know why we're here?"

"How'd you get here so fast?"

"You forgot that a lot of very wealthy people live in Spencer," Mac said. "One of them is Randolph York, the owner of SuperMart. He always has a private jet on standby. As soon as we found out where you were, we just had to go to McHenry and get on board the jet. We were on our way here within an hour."

David reached out to extract the briefcase from Hugh's grip. Like a child refusing to give up a favorite toy, Hugh clung to his new life for all it was worth until David pried it from his fingers.

"Why did you kill her?" Mac asked while David handcuffed him. "She was your sister. She considered you her only friend. She believed in you—even when others confronted her with evidence of what you were doing."

"Because she couldn't stop," Hugh said.

"Stop?"

"Nancy had this insane need—not desire but *need*—to be in charge. When we were kids, it was to be president. Then a governor or a senator. What she really wanted was to be queen, but since we live in a democracy—"

"But why kill her?"

Hugh Vance looked down at Mac. "Because with every race she ran, there was always a danger that her opponents would look too closely at Braxton Charities. I saw from day one that Bill Clark would dig far and wide to uncover something on her. Then when Chief O'Callaghan here brought up Sandy Burr—" He shook his head with remorse.

"It was only a matter of time before someone found out that you had turned Braxton Charities into a money laundromat," David said.

"When those death threats came in and Nancy lost her mind, I couldn't have asked for a better time to get rid of her and to finally be free to live my new life." Hugh Vance pursed his lips together. "It was her fault, you know. I had worked too long and too hard to let her ruin everything I had built just because she wanted to be the mayor to a bunch of hicks who can't stop clinging to their clotheslines!"

Chapter Twenty-Eight

The Next Morning

Her head resting on Murphy's bare chest, Jessica listened to the thrum of his heartbeat. Lightly, he brushed his fingers through her hair. His chest rose as he took in a deep breath.

"Don't tell me that you're going back to sleep," she said with a smile. "Not after all the trouble I went to waking you up."

"Not a chance." Chuckling, he pulled the comforter up from where they had kicked it while making love and covered their naked bodies. After wrapping his arms around her, he buried his face in her tousled hair and enjoyed the scent of her. "Gnarly snores."

"I know." Reminded of the German shepherd, she raised her head to look around their bedroom. "Where is Gnarly?"

"I kicked him out at about three thirty this morning."

As if to announce that he could not be kept out, he quickly opened the bedroom door. Standing in the doorway, Gnarly regarded them. Seeing the opening, Spencer scurried into the room, scampered across the floor, took a running jump from the middle of the room, and landed on the bed.

"Did he just open that door?" Murphy asked her.

Jessica nodded her head. "He just presses down on the door lever and pushes it open. He can open doors with round doorknobs too. I thought it was cute until now."

"Does he pick locks, too?"

"I wouldn't be surprised." She lay back down. "I'm sorry you didn't sleep well."

"It's wasn't Gnarly's fault." He gazed into her violet eyes. "I kept thinking about those four agents working under Camille Jurvetson—the ones she got killed."

With a heavy sigh signaling his resignation of the fact that his breakfast was not going to be immediately served to him, Gnarly plopped down in the middle of the floor.

Murphy took Jessica's hand and fingered the wedding band on her ring finger. "Every time I go out on a mission for the Phantoms, I leave my wedding band in the night-stand because I can't risk one of our enemies getting ahold of it and tracing it back to you. Our missions are that dangerous. Every time I kiss you good-bye and walk out that door, I know that there is a very good chance that I won't be coming home to you." He met her eyes. "I knew that when I signed up for it."

She swallowed. "So did I when I married you."

"And so did those agents," Murphy said. "They didn't become intelligence agents for glory. They signed up for the same reason I did: because our country needs people who are willing to put their lives on the line every day to protect their families, their neighbors, and their freedom—to protect everything we stand for. We know that we're on the front line, and we're there willingly and because someone has to be." He gritted his teeth. "Those four agents didn't sign up to be sold out because of their own leader's personal ambitions."

Jessica stroked his face. "She will be held accountable for it, Murphy. CO said Jurvetson will never be able to put another agent in danger ever again."

"I know, but—"

"Did CO say what she's going to do?"

Murphy shook his head. "Nigel said she's out of country, but she is working on the case."

"Basically," Jessica said, "the case is closed. We identified the traitor. We know who blew Bruce Hardy's cover when he was working with Gnarly's handler's team. I guess we can take Gnarly back home in a couple of days so that he can resume his campaign for mayor."

"Your dad wanted us to clear his name," Murphy said.

"The army put out a press release saying that the journalist who broke the story was wrong," Jessica said. "Between that, the release of Gnarly's birth certificate proving that he's an American citizen, and him saving that mother cat and her twenty-four kittens, there's no way he can lose the election."

"But we promised Sheriff Turow that we'd find out who killed his wife," Murphy said. "We have to finish that case."

Impatient for his breakfast, Gnarly leaped up onto the bed. The addition of a hundred pounds at the foot of the bed forced Spencer to move farther up toward the head of the bed, which pried Murphy and Jessica apart.

"I admit that we don't know who actually killed Belle Perkins," Jessica said. "But I kind of thought that she was killed by someone who came into the camp to find Bruce Hardy and happened upon her."

"An Islamic terrorist wouldn't have stopped with Perkins," Murphy said. "He would have continued through the camp. Plus he would have brought a group of soldiers with him to take out the whole camp. That's how they work. No," he shook his head. "this was personal."

"Strangling someone is up close and personal," Jessica said. "You're looking someone in the eye while you're killing him." She stroked Spencer.

Lying sphinxlike and with his ears up straight, Gnarly eyed both of them.

"Does that mean that we have to start back at the drawing board?" Jessica asked.

"No, we have made headway." Murphy moved down toward the foot of the bed to stroke the German shepherd. "Belle Perkins and Gnarly were sent to Iraq to that unit to investigate something."

"But CO hasn't told you what yet," Jessica said.

"Not exactly, but look at what we do know." He looked into Gnarly's eyes. "Both Dr. Samuels and Bruce Hardy said they heard Perkins arguing with the lieutenant."

"Dr. Samuels said she told the lieutenant that she was going to put a stop to something."

"He also said that Lieutenant Watson had a reputation for being a real go-getter. Respected by his people but always taking on high-risk missions." He lowered his voice. "He also said Watson was always on the front lines with his men."

Jessica sat up. "What are you thinking?"

Murphy sprang out of bed and grabbed his sweat pants. "I think I want you to do some psychological profiling for me," he said while stepping into his pants and pulling them up.

Hoping for breakfast, Gnarly and Spencer followed Murphy out of the bedroom.

"But if Hugh Vance wasn't the fat man, who was?" Dallas said in the kitchen, piercing the sleep and dreams of David, who was all the way upstairs in the bedroom.

Who's she talking to? Curious, he opened one eye and squinted against the late-morning sun streaming in through the window.

Seeing a sign of wakefulness, Storm slithered up from where she had been sleeping down by the foot of the bed to lick his face.

"I don't know." Archie sounded annoyed. "Maybe he had nothing to do with the murder?"

"Caleb Montgomery said in his statement back at the time of Burr's murder that the guy was watching Nancy Braxton and Sandy Burr very closely. So closely that he ordered a fresh drink and pretty much left it there so that he could follow Sandy Burr out of the lounge."

"Montgomery is a blackmailer," Archie said. "He probably made up the fat man in order to turn attention away from Hugh Vance."

"Who Nathan Braxton says was out of the country and had no idea about Sandy Burr's investigation," Dallas said.

"That we know of," David said while making his way down the stairs in his bathrobe. He paused to hug and kiss Dallas on his way to the coffeemaker. He lifted the mug in a toast to Archie, who was sitting at the kitchen table and looking at copies of case files and Sandy Burr's research. There was no room for him to set his mug down. "Where's Mac?"

"Home in bed," Archie said. "Remember, he has pneumonia. I can't believe you guys let him fly to California."

"He insisted on going," David said. "I would have had to shoot him to stop him."

"Well, after bringing Vance back last night," Archie said, "he crashed, and he's still out like a light."

Dallas was petting Storm, who had followed David down the stairs. "Could Caleb have killed Sandy Burr?"

"He was there in the lounge when Burr was interviewing Nancy Braxton," Archie said. "He would have heard what Burr had against Braxton Charities, and he could've realized that that information would make good blackmail."

"So he killed Sandy Burr to steal his research," Dallas said with a wave of her hands.

Both Dallas' and Archie's smiles fell when they saw David shaking his head over his coffee mug.

"Where are we wrong?" Archie asked. "Montgomery had to have been in the room to steal Burr's research."

"Not at the time of the murder," David said. "Caleb Montgomery was cleared as a suspect back then because he was working in the lounge. He didn't get off until one o'clock, and Sandy Burr was murdered at around ten o'clock." Before Dallas could voice her opposition, he added, "Montgomery was the only employee working in the lounge, so there was no one to cover for him. Plus Burr's room was all the way over on the other side of the hotel, which was off of the employee parking lot. Montgomery must have seen something in Burr's room and gone in to check it out after the murder and found the research."

"After overhearing Braxton and Burr arguing, he realized Burr's research was valuable," Archie said. "So he grabbed it."

"But didn't bother calling the police about Burr's murder." Dallas turned to David. "You don't think he would've been capable of killing Burr?"

"He didn't have the chance," David said. "This murder was not a crime of opportunity. It had been planned. The killer took the time to control his victim, to kill him in a manner that would look like a suicide, and to stage the scene. Montgomery couldn't have been gone from his post for that long."

"Maybe Nathan Braxton only thought that Hugh Vance didn't know about the investigation," Dallas said. "Hugh did know, and he hired someone to kill Burr while he was out of the country."

"Then why not kill Montgomery when he started blackmailing him?" Archie asked.

"Hugh is not a cold-blooded killer," David said. "He is remorseful about his sister. It took years of stress and worry about her continued campaigning to push him over the edge. If he'd had it in him to hire someone to get rid of Burr, he would have eliminated Montgomery as soon as he started blackmailing him."

Uttering a growl, Dallas grabbed her head with both hands.

"Remember what Nathan Braxton said?" Archie asked.

"What did Braxton say?" David asked.

"He said he always believed that someone else with a motive that had nothing to do with Braxton Charities killed Sandy Burr." Archie shuffled through the papers on the table until she pulled out a case file. "Has anybody ever taken a look at that?"

"I doubt it," David said.

Archie opened the folder she had pulled from the batch. "Fiona Davis."

Dallas sat up at attention. "I actually forgot all about her."

"Who's Fiona Davis?" David asked.

"The woman who Sandy Burr had dinner with the night he died," Archie said.

Excited, Dallas bounced in her seat. "They didn't know each other. She was just a guest at the hotel, and the two of them met in the lounge and had drinks and ended up having dinner together."

"Six weeks later she committed suicide," Archie said.

"Only it wasn't suicide," Dallas said to David. "Archie showed me that it couldn't have been suicide because you can't drown to death in a toilet. Want me to show you?"

The doorbell rang.

"Maybe another time, dear." On his way to answer the door, David called back to the two women. "Two strangers have dinner together in a hotel, and both of them end up dead—they're murdered, but the deaths look like suicides. What do you think are the odds of that?"

Dallas and Archie smiled at each other. "We have work to do," Archie said.

David peered through the cut glass in the front door. Seeing Bernie and Hap, he dreaded the interrogation that would surely be coming his way about Gnarly's whereabouts. Forcing a grin onto his face, David opened the door. "Hello, gentlemen. What brings you here?"

Bernie cast a glance at Hap, who shoved his hands into his pockets and looked down at his feet. "Uh, Chief, we're sorry to bother you on your day off"—Bernie had clearly taken note of David's bathrobe—"but Hap and I have a confession to make."

David looked the two men up and down. Hap shuffled his feet. Curious about what they could have possibly done that was so serious that they had to go to the police chief's home to make a confession, David opened the door and gestured for them to enter.

Once they were inside, Storm galloped over to check them out. After sniffing their legs, she decided that they were okay and returned to lie down under the kitchen table, where Dallas and Archie were working. Recognizing Bernie and Hap, they greeted the two men before returning back to their work on the Fiona Davis case.

Looking like a couple of guilty children about to confess to breaking a window, Bernie and Hap hung their heads.

Unsure of whether he should be worried or amused, David folded his arms across his chest. "Do I need to go get my handcuffs?"

With a shake of his head, Bernie glanced over at his friend. "Tell 'im, Hap."

"Tell me what?" David asked.

Hap raised his eyes from the floor. Slowly, he pulled his right hand out of his pocket and held the gnarled, weathered appendage out for David to see. Uncertain of what the old man was showing him, David touched his hand. Hap's fingernails were short. His knuckles were swollen, and his fingers were crooked with arthritis.

A scratched-up gold signet ring with a blue stone adorned his pinkie finger. Upon examining it, David noticed that the stone had an odd shape resembling a family crest cut onto its face.

"He can't get it off," Bernie said.

"I'm a police chief, not an EMT." David went over to the kitchen and opened the refrigerator. "Have you tried butter?"

The two elderly men followed him into the kitchen. "Yeah, but that's not the problem, Chief. You see—"

David plunged his hand into a tub of butter and removed it when he had a thick blob on his finger. He then grasped Hap's hand and worked the butter up and down his pinkie and under and around the ring. "What's the problem?"

"It doesn't belong to us," Bernie said. "The ring."

David stopped with his hand grasping the ring in question.

At the kitchen table, Archie and Dallas stopped talking about their case to observe what had become a curious situation.

"What do you mean, it doesn't belong to you?" David asked. "Where did you get it? Who does it belong to?"

Bernie cleared his throat and then said, "Bill Clark."

Silence filled the kitchen.

"Bill Clark?" David asked in a soft voice. "This ring belongs to Bill Clark. Am I correct in assuming that he didn't give it to you?"

"Well," Bernie said.

Hap had slipped his hand out of David's grasp and was tugging on and pulling at the ring, which was then covered in a thick layer of butter.

"You see," Bernie said, "when we heard Bill Clark and you talking the other night, when he said that dogs sometimes just take off, and you never see them again, we thought that maybe he had kidnapped Gnarly to keep him from being around for the election. So Hap and I went to Bill Clark's house while he was in the town-hall meeting to look around."

Seeing that Hap was becoming desperate to get the ring off, David grabbed it and put more butter around it.

"While we were searching his house, we went into the study, and Hap here went through the desk drawers—"

"Gnarly is kind of big to fit in a desk drawer," David said while studying the knuckle that was preventing the ring from slipping off his finger.

"We were looking for clues," Bernie said. "Well, Hap saw this ring sitting right there in the top drawer of Clark's desk, and he thought it was pretty, and the next thing you know— we couldn't get it off."

At the same time that Bernie said the words, David slipped the ring off of Hap's finger. Both old men uttered sighs of relief. In the next breath, Bernie said, "I guess we're in trouble now, huh? I'm surprised Clark hasn't been screaming bloody murder about someone breaking into his house."

"Did you break anything when you broke in?" David held the ring under hot running water.

"No, we were real careful," Bernie said. "We just wanted to know where Clark was keeping Gnarly."

"Clark does not have Gnarly." David held the ring up to the light to study the design cut into the blue stone. "Gnarly will be back home by next week, and I assure you that he'll be right back out on the campaign trail with you guys."

"We certainly hope so," Bernie said. "Ever since it hit the news about Gnarly risking his life to run into that inferno to save that momma cat and her thirty kittens, folks all over have been asking to interview him." He pounded his fist into his palm. "We need to strike while the iron is hot if we want to ride this wave into a win this November!"

"You can count on Gnarly." David patted Bernie on the shoulder. "As for Clark, he hasn't reported any break-ins or missing items. Maybe you're lucky, and he didn't notice the ring was missing."

"What are you going to do?" Bernie asked. "Are we under arrest?"

David shook his head. "No, I'll take care of this. Leave it to me."

With enthusiastic thanks, Bernie and Hap left. Studying the signet ring, David strolled back into the kitchen and found Dallas and Archie staring at him.

"You look like you've seen a ghost," Dallas said.

"More like a revelation." Spinning around, he ran up the stairs to his bedroom to put on his uniform.

CHAPTER TWENTY-NINE

Impatient for his breakfast, Gnarly barked at Jessica and stomped his feet while she prepared three bowls of food. It was as if he were saying, "Hurry up! I'm hungry! You're not doing that fast enough!" By the time she set the bowls down on the floor so that he, Spencer, and Newman could chow down, Jessica was ready to take her adopted brother home to Daddy. The German shepherd was equally loud while chowing down.

In less time than it took Jessica to brew a fresh pot of coffee, Gnarly inhaled his breakfast and went about his day. Enjoying the silence that came with the canines' full tummies, she poured a cup for herself and a mug of green tea for Murphy and went downstairs to what she had started referring to as "Nigel's office."

Whatever it was that had struck Murphy hadn't let up long enough for him to get dressed. Wearing nothing more than his sweat pants, not even slippers on his feet, Murphy was jotting down one note after another on a notepad while referring to reports on the computer monitor.

Since Gnarly was squeezed into her chair, Jessica took a seat on the sofa. "Okay, you said you wanted me to do a psychological profile. Who do you want me to do one on?"

"Lieutenant Frank Watson." Taking his notes with him, Murphy got up from his chair and went over to sit down next to her. "Remember what Dr. Samuels said? Many of the men called him 'Patton.' You do know who Patton is, don't you?"

"I may be new to military life, but I do know my history," she said. "General Patton was a great general during the Second World War."

"Fearless," Murphy said with a nod of his head. "His men used to call him 'Old Blood and Guts.' He was known for leading his troops into the worst places, like Nazi Germany."

"Dr. Samuels said that there's no zone too hot for Lieutenant Watson," Jessica said.

"But"—Murphy held up his finger—"Samuels also said that Watson doesn't just send his men into those situations. He goes himself, which is why the men respect him."

"What are you thinking?"

"I don't want to lead you in your profile. Just listen." He referred to his notes. "Watson's team suffered four casualities on the day Perkins was killed. A couple of weeks before that, there were two others."

"They were being tracked by a terrorist cell that was after Agent Hardy," Jessica said.

"The tour before that, Watson's team suffered three casualties in battle," Murphy said. "In the last six years, the two years before Perkins was killed and the four years after, teams serving under Lieutenant, now Captain, Watson suffered a mortality rate twenty percent higher than that of most other teams."

"Did the army suspect that his leadership was reckless?"

"*I* suspect that Perkins and Gnarly were sent to serve with Watson's team because after seeing the high number of casualties, the army wanted to know why his teams kept ending up in situations where his people were getting killed."

"During the fight between Perkins and Lieutenant Watson that Dr. Samuels overheard, Perkins said it was going to stop—it being his reckless leadership."

"But she was killed before she could report it to CID," Murphy said.

She shook her head. "Watson is now a captain."

"With more soldiers under his command," Murphy said. "More lives are at risk."

"Would Watson have been promoted to captain if the army had suspected him of getting his team killed?"

"Hard to say," Murphy said. "He was brought back stateside. Nigel says he's due to fly out to Syria in the next couple of weeks. Now, if I'm right about what I think Perkins uncovered—"

"What?"

"Dr. Samuels told us that he regularly sees Watson at the hospital."

"He thinks that maybe he was wounded and is doing physical therapy," Jessica said.

"I had Nigel do a search for Watson's medical records," Murphy said.

"Did he find anything?"

"No," Murphy said. "So I asked Nigel to see if he could find a record of any regular prescriptions under Frank Watson's name that he hadn't submitted to his health insurance. Nigel found Tetrabenazine."

"That's a dopamine-depleting agent," Nigel said. "I also found a prescription for a neuroleptic, which is a dopamine-receptor antagonist. Together, the two are used to treat the symptoms of Huntington's disease."

"Huntington's disease?" Jessica said. "That's a neuro-degenerative disease. There's no cure for it. If Lieutenant Watson has Huntington's disease, then—"

"He should've been given a medical discharge," Murphy said with a nod of his head. "He would not be serving overseas—no way would he be able to lead a unit in Syria."

"Huntington's is hereditary," Jessica said. "There are tests to determine whether you've got the disease long before the symptoms show up."

"Exactly. Now, suppose someone in Lieutenant Frank Watson's family had Huntington's disease. Knowing that it's hereditary, Watson got tested. But he wouldn't have had it done by an army doctor, because then it would've gone on his record. The test came back positive, so Watson knows that eventually, this degenerative disease is going to eat away at his body, and he's going to end up in a wheelchair."

"For a strong, gung ho alpha male," Jessica said, "that would be a bitter pill to swallow."

Murphy held out both of his hands to symbolize a scale. "On the one hand, he'd be forced to take a medical discharge from the army and to watch his body fall apart one iota at a time. On the other hand, he'd be able to go out in a blaze of glory on the field of battle serving his country."

Jessica sucked in a deep breath. "You think that he's suicidal. That he's purposely putting his people in danger to get himself killed in action."

Murphy's eyes met hers. "That would explain why as soon as he gets back from a tour, he signs up to go out again. Perkins must have figured out that he was suicidal. Maybe based on the decisions and calls he made during the gunfight that got four of his men killed. I don't know. Whatever she'd observed, she called him on it."

"And said she was going to put a stop to him risking his soldiers' lives in order to get himself killed."

"But Watson couldn't let her do that," he said, "because he wanted to die in action."

"Why would he do that?" Jessica asked, "There are a lot of ways to kill yourself without putting men and women whose lives have been entrusted to you in danger. Doesn't he realize that the rest of his team wants to go home?"

"Why do some suicidal men kill their whole family and then put a gun to their head and blow out their brains?" Murphy asked with a shrug of his shoulders. "There's no telling what's going through his mind."

"The symptoms of Huntington's disease include dementia and behavioral changes," Nigel said.

"Lieutenant Watson has a wife and two children," Murphy said. "His wife is a schoolteacher. Most likely, he's doing this because he doesn't want to saddle his family with an invalid. Also, if he is medically discharged, his family won't get the same death benefits that they'll be entitled to if he's killed in action."

Agreeing, Jessica said, "Lieutenant Watson could be rationalizing that this is all for the greater good—he'd rather die serving his country than being a burden to his family. If you're right, we need to stop him before he goes back overseas. Is there any way Nigel could find out for certain if Watson is receiving those meds for Huntington's?"

"We'll start by confirming Perkins' mission," Murphy said. "Proving that she was sent to evaluate his leadership would make him an actual suspect in her murder. That may be enough to keep him stateside. Once we tell CO about our discovery of the meds he's been taking, she'll report it to the army chief of staff who will order a test to see if Watson does have Huntington's."

"Right now," she said, "all we have are a bunch of theories based on one witness' statement and Nigel's finding records of Watson getting a couple of drugs. How do we move Watson all the way up to murder suspect?"

He grinned. "You forgot. We have a witness." He pointed behind her to where Gnarly was resting his head on the arm of her chair. His eyes closed, he was sound asleep.

"I thought you were taking the day off." Tonya was so shocked to see David burst through the front door that she almost fell out of her seat.

"I have a killer to catch." Without slowing down, he hurried through the squad room to Bogie's corner office, where he slammed the door behind him.

"Just like his father," Tonya said while returning to what she'd been working on.

"What's got your shorts in a knot?" Bogie asked David, who was standing before his desk with a wild look in his eyes.

David yanked the blue ring out of his pants pocket and thrust it out for Bogie to see. "Recognize this?"

Bogie put on his reading glasses and then took the ring. Squinting, he adjusted his glasses on his nose to bring the shape cut into the blue stone into view. "I'm not sure." He lifted his eyes to look at David over the top of his glasses. "Should I?"

"You knew Bill Clark's dad."

"Yeah." Bogie examined the ring again. "I knew Harvey Clark. This could very well be his ring—the one he always wore on his pinkie."

The deputy chief took a magnifying glass out of his desk's side drawer and used it to examine the inside of the band. David moved around Bogie's desk to see what he was looking at. The inscription inside the ring read, "With Pride and Honor to the Patriarch. Clan of Clark."

Bogie set the ring down in the center of his desk. "That's Harvey's ring all right. Where'd you get it?"

"Someone turned it in to me," David said.

Bogie's bushy silver eyebrows rose up on his forehead.

"Bernie and Hap broke into Bill Clark's house to look for Gnarly and found that ring in his desk drawer."

"Why were they looking for Gnarly in Clark's desk? One, Clark's so scared of Gnarly that he won't go near him. Two, Gnarly's too big to fit in any desk drawer."

David waved his hands, indicating that Bogie should be quiet. "Fact is, Lisa, Bill's sister, told me that her mother gave their father's ring"—he held up the ring for Bogie to see—"to *Leroy*, their younger brother."

"The one who got drunk and drove his truck into the lake," Bogie said.

"Bill was furious because this ring was supposed to go to the firstborn," David said. "Lisa told me that Bill was so upset that he got into a fight with Leroy at their father's funeral."

Bogie was nodding his head. "I remember the two of them getting into a scuffle over something, but I didn't think anything of it. Those two were always fighting."

"Because their mother had given the ring to Leroy, who was her favorite," David said. "One could say that symbolically, she was passing Bill's rightful birthright as the firstborn to his younger brother." He pointed to the inscription. "This ring is supposed to go to the patriarch, the head of the family. Then, after their mother died, Leroy sued Bill, the executor of their mother's will, because Bill was cheating him out of his half of the estate." He tossed the ring to Bogie. "But that suit was conveniently dropped after Leroy drove his truck into the lake."

"Leroy was a drunk," Bogie said. "And I remember that accident. The medical examiner said his blood-alcohol level was twice the legal limit."

"And so no one looked any closer at the accident, did they?" David asked. "Dad didn't look into it, because he was sick."

"I handled it," Bogie said. "I didn't see anything suspicious. I knew about the suit, but—" He peered at the ring in his hand. "Why would this ring make you think that Leroy was murdered?"

"How did Bill end up with it?"

"After Leroy died, Bill inherited it," Bogie said with a shrug of his broad shoulders.

"He wanted it so badly that he got into a fight over it with Leroy at their dad's funeral. If he inherited it after Leroy died, why isn't he wearing it?"

Bogie responded with silence. His eyebrows furrowed.

David leaned over Bogie's desk. "You read the inscription. It goes to the leader of the family—the patriarch. It signifies Bill's birthright, which is being the leader. If he got that ring legally, he'd be wearing it proudly—with honor. The fact that he's *hiding* it in his desk tells me that he didn't get it lawfully."

"I know that you don't like Bill Clark and that you have no respect for him," Bogie said in a low voice. "I've heard rumors for years saying that he killed his mother—"

"I already looked into that," David said. "Turow confirmed that there's nothing there."

"Do you realize what you're suggesting?" Bogie asked. "Bill Clark is a liar and a cheat, but do you really think he would've been capable of killing his brother for a *ring?*"

"And to end a lawsuit that threatened to cost him a lot of money," David said. "Bill was living in Oakland. He'd always wanted the status of living here on the lake, but he hadn't been able to afford it—at least not until after his mother died, and he inherited the family fortune. If Leroy had won his suit, Bill would have lost half of everything. Now, I don't know the specifics of his financials, but even if he hadn't been in financial trouble—"

"Bill hates to lose anything to anyone," Bogie said. "I'll get that case file for you."

CHAPTER THIRTY

Fort Belvoir, Fairfax, Virginia

"I don't know if I can get used to this." While keeping one eye on the road, Jessica glanced down at the white button-down shirt and the blue slacks of an enlisted army soldier. "Why can't I be an officer, like you?"

She glanced across the front compartment of their SUV to where Murphy was dressed in the blue uniform of an army lieutenant. Gnarly was strapped into the dark-gray vest of an army canine and sitting in a crate in the back, which the dog did not like at all. He would've much preferred to ride in the backseat. Ideally, he would've been riding in the front passenger seat.

"Because I am an officer," Murphy said. "Your ticket into this case is that you're Gnarly's handler. Only enlisted personnel are dog handlers in the army. Be happy. This is your first undercover job."

"Why are you undercover as army?" she asked. "I mean, you're investigating—"

"Because the existence of the Phantoms is a highly classified secret," Murphy said, "that has been neither confirmed nor denied by the Joint Chiefs of Staff. If I go in as a navy officer, these soldiers will spit in my face. But if I go in in an army uniform and tell them that General Johnston sent me, they'll kiss my feet." He checked his reflection in the mirror. "You should see me in my marine uniform."

"Maybe later on tonight we can play show-and-tell," she said with a naughty grin.

"I love show-and-tell."

They were on their way to Fort Belvoir to meet with the army's CID agent tasked with solving First Sergeant Belle Perkins' murder. Over the years, the case had officially grown cold. After Murphy had contacted his CO with his suspicions about the motive for Perkins' murder, she'd requested that the Joint Chiefs of Staff enlist the investigator to go along with Murphy's plan to reveal the killer.

It was a simple but ambitious plan. Murphy and Jessica would meet with the army's investigator at Fort Belvoir. Then Murphy and the agent would simply walk into wherever Captain Frank Watson was training his team, many of whom had been members of the same team that Sergeant Belle Perkins had been stationed with in Iraq. Murphy would be introduced as a special investigator who was working for the army's chiefs of staff and had been sent to gather information about Sergeant Belle Perkins' murder. After a few standard questions, without warning their suspect, Jessica would walk in with Gnarly, who they hoped would in some way identify Captain Frank Watson as the killer.

Basically, Gnarly was going to a suspect lineup.

At the gate, Jessica flashed the phony military ID that Murphy had picked up from the Joint Chiefs of Staff's office that morning. The CID agent, an older man in a summer suit, met them in the visitors' parking lot. He introduced himself as Special Agent Logan Silverman.

Greeting Murphy with a firm handshake, he said, "Lieutenant Thornton, I heard about Sergeant Major Gnarly running for the office of something or other and about the army releasing a statement saying that he wasn't a suspect in First Sergeant Perkins' murder, but I had no idea that General Johnston was going to be personally overseeing this investigation."

"It's been cold for a long time," Murphy said, "and the family wants answers."

Jessica had unloaded Gnarly from the crate in the back of the SUV and put him on his leash.

The CID agent, a civilian tasked with investigating crimes involving military personnel, eyed Gnarly. "I broke out the case file a few days ago, after the news of Perkins' murder thawed out the case. I had inherited it from an agent who retired three years ago. He'd considered it one of those cases where everyone knew who did it but couldn't prove it."

"Who was that?" Murphy asked.

"Benjamin Frost," Agent Silverman said. "A contractor the team was escorting. He went missing the night Perkins was killed. Was never found. It was assumed that he'd either been captured by the terrorist cell shadowing the team or had died in the desert after killing Perkins."

"Well," Murphy said, "General Johnston figures that as long as we have a witness"—he gestured at Gnarly—"we should let him tell us if your assumption is right or wrong and if the person who killed his partner was one of her teammates."

Agent Silverman shook his head. "I don't know why they never thought of this before." With a jerk of his thumb, he gestured toward a classroom building a short walk away and led them toward the front entrance. "We're in luck. Most of the team is still intact. Only four who were on Perkins tour have been discharged or requested reassignment. The members of Captain Watson's team are very close knit and extremely loyal. As a matter of fact, First Sergeant Scalia was recently offered a promotion to another unit in Florida. He turned it down because he wanted to stay with this team. He's been with Watson since boot camp. It'll be near impossible to get any of them to turn in a fellow teammate."

"But Sergeant Perkins and Gnarly saved their lives when they all got pinned down by those snipers." Jessica was relieved that Gnarly was heeling nicely between her and Murphy. Usually when she walked him, the German shepherd would drag her down the street.

"Captain Watson charged Sergeant Gnarly with negligence since he didn't defend Sergeant Perkins when she was attacked and murdered," Agent Silverman said.

"We talked to witnesses who told us that Sergeant Perkins had sedated him so that she could stitch up a wound he'd received in the gunfight that afternoon," Jessica said.

"I read witness statements in her case file saying that as well." Agent Silverman held the door open so that Jessica, Gnarly, and Murphy could enter the building used for training. He then led them down the hallway. "How do you want to do this, Lieutenant?"

"Our witness will remain out in the hallway until after you introduce me, and I'll ask a few preliminary questions to get us started."

Gnarly uttered a low growl from deep in his throat.

Jessica jerked his leash. "Gnarly, shush."

Ignoring her, the German shepherd pulled on the leash. Behind them, Murphy stepped up his pace so that he could grab the leash and help Jessica, but he wasn't fast enough. His hackles up, Gnarly practically pulled Jessica's arm out of her shoulder socket when he bolted down the hallway. Afraid she was going to lose her footing and land face first on the floor, Jessica dropped the leash.

Upon reaching the classroom at the end of the corridor, Gnarly jumped up, grabbed the round doorknob in his jaws, turned his head to open the door, and flew inside.

In the classroom, a dozen army combat soldiers jumped up onto their desks when a hundred pounds of fur, claws, and teeth charged through the door. Not certain of what the attack was about, they all reached for their weapons. But upon recognizing the army vest the dog was wearing, they realized that he must have been a friend—possibly a dog that a new handler had lost control of.

"Gnarly! Down!" Murphy tried to grab Gnarly, who dodged his attempts to capture him.

"Gnarly?" some of the soldiers said. "Is that Gnarly?"

Seeing that their former teammate had only one man in his sights, most of them holstered their guns and climbed down from their desks.

"What's this about?" the army captain at the front of the classroom asked

Agent Silverman showed Captain Frank Watson his badge and identified himself. "Who is that man?" The agent pointed to the young man standing like a statue on top of his desk with his weapon clutched to his chest.

"Sergeant Major Scott Scalia," Captain Watson said. "What's going on here?"

"Thank you, Gnarly!" Murphy yelled. "You did good! Sit!"

Breathing hard, Gnarly sat down with his eyes trained on Sergeant Major Scott Scalia. He dared the sergeant to make a false move.

Knowing that he was a hairbreadth away from being torn to shreds, the sergeant held his gun and was ready to aim and fire it.

Feeling foolish for allowing Gnarly to escape, Jessica rushed over to gather up his leash.

"Sergeant Major Scott Scalia," Murphy said, "as in your protégé who has done every tour with you since boot camp, Captain?"

"Yes," Captain Watson said. "I thought Sergeant Major Gnarly was dishonorably discharged after he let his handler get murdered."

"But they never caught Perkins' killer," Agent Silverman said. "General Johnston has personally sent Lieutenant Thornton to get to the bottom of this case."

"It was that contractor," Captain Watson said. "Frost was his name. That's why he took off. Disappeared the same night Perkins was murdered."

"No," Murphy said. "It was your sergeant. Our witness just identified him. Out of everyone in this classroom who was on the team and in the camp when his partner was killed, Sergeant Major Gnarly picked you, Sergeant Scalia. You're the only one he wants to kill. Why is that?"

"Because when he came out of the anesthesia after Sergeant Perkins stitched him up," Jessica said, "he could still smell your scent on her from when you strangled her."

Captain Watson stepped up to the desk. "Is that true, Scalia? You killed Sergeant Perkins? Why?"

"Because she was going to ruin your career," Sergeant Scalia said. "We all heard her. She was going to report you to command for getting your people killed. She was ignoring all of those missions that we did together. All of the good you did. All of the men and women who gave their lives for you—for *you*. She was going to have you drummed out of the army in disgrace. Don't you see? I did it for you."

Jessica saw the captain's hands shaking. His chin quivered. The disease that had been dogging him was creeping up on him.

There was silence in the classroom.

Murphy reached up to where the sergeant was still standing the desktop. "Give me your gun, soldier."

Instead of obeying the order, Sergeant Scalia clutched the gun tighter. His eyes seemed to glaze over.

Moving slowly, Murphy turned slightly to the side so that his side arm would be out of sight and laid his hand on his weapon.

"Perkins and Gnarly saved our lives," a young soldier in the back of the room said. "I was there that day. Most of us were. They were both heroes, and you killed her and disgraced Gnarly. How could you have done that, Scalia?"

Tears came to the sergeant's eyes. "Captain, tell them. Make them understand. We're all a team, and you're our leader. Someone messes with you, and they mess with all of us."

"Sergeant," Murphy said, "yes, your captain is your team's leader, and your team is your family. You're not out there to serve your commanding officer. You're first loyalties are to your country and your team, and when you have a leader who makes bad decisions—putting your team in danger—he's putting your mission and your country in danger." He moved in closer in hopes of getting within grabbing distance of the weapon in the soldier's hand. "Give me the gun. Please."

"No!" Tears spilled from Sergeant Scalia's eyes.

"Get him out of my sight," the captain said to Agent Silverman.

Captain Frank Watson turned his back on the sergeant who had been so devoted to him during his whole career.

"Don't leave me, Captain!" Before Murphy could react, Sergeant Major Scott Scalia's arm shot out and he pulled the trigger on his gun.

Murphy yanked his gun out of its holster.

The soldiers flew in every direction, taking cover.

Jessica was tackled by half a dozen soldiers, and they plunged her to the floor. In the pileup, she lost Gnarly's leash—again.

Agent Silverman fumbled for his weapon.

When Murphy threw up his arm to take aim, his target was already gone.

Sergeant Scalia's abrupt move was all the excuse Gnarly needed to leap up and capture his arm in his jaws. Gnarly, Scalia, and the desk all fell to the floor.

Murphy scrambled over to where Sergeant Scalia had been forced to release his grip on the gun. With the sergeant's arm locked in the grip of his jaws, Gnarly was dragging the soldier kicking and screaming across the floor to the front of the classroom as if he wanted to show off his prize for show and tell.

Murphy picked up Scalia's gun. "Gnarly, release him." He took out his handcuffs and knelt down to secure the killer.

That was when Murphy noticed that Jessica, Agent Silverman, and many of the soldiers had crowded around the one fallen man in the room—Captain Frank Watson.

Tears in her eyes, Jessica broke away from the crowd.

"Captain Watson?" Murphy asked.

Jessica shook her head. "Bullet to the back—through the heart."

CHAPTER THIRTY-ONE

It was one of those moments when Bogie heard himself say, "How did I miss that?" As soon as David opened the file on Leroy Clark that the deputy chief had brought to his office, he tossed the first crime-scene picture of Clark down in front of him and pointed to his hand. Not only was the Clark family ring absent from Leroy's right hand, but there was also a visible tan line around his pinkie finger.

The picture had been taken at the crime scene by a forensics officer as soon as Leroy Clark's body had been pulled up from the bottom of the lake. His truck had been found empty with the driver's side door open, prompting them to send divers in to search for Leroy.

After a routine accident investigation, Bogie had concluded that Leroy had missed the turn onto the Glendale Road Bridge and driven his truck into the lake. He'd figured that as the truck had begun to sink, Leroy had opened the door to escape, but he'd been too drunk to swim to shore—causing him to drown.

Even though the deputy chief hadn't been aware that Ida Clark had cheated her elder son by giving the ring to his brother, Bogie should have noticed that a piece of jewelry was missing from his finger.

"The only reason I knew about the ring was because Lisa told me." David picked up the autopsy report. "If it had been anyone else, I probably would've given him the benefit of the doubt when Bernie and Hap brought it to me, but knowing Bill—"

"What's your problem with Clark?" Bogie asked.

"He's a bully," David said. "I grew up with his sister, Lisa. He used to beat her up. When she'd complain, he'd lie, and his father would take Bill's side—calling him a real man."

"So you hate the guy because when he was a kid, he beat up his sister? David, we've dealt with a lot of jerks in our time—"

"Did I ever tell you how Lisa died?" David asked.

"We were told that she was killed in action—"

"Well, I know the truth," David said. "She was stomped to death by an abusive boyfriend—beaten, kicked, and stomped with a pair of combat boots. Bill Clark and his father had sent a message to her that it's okay to beat up women, and I was trying to convince her otherwise." He gazed down at the words in the report. "But it was too little, too late."

"You're too much like your pappy." Bogie's voice was soft. "You can't save the world, David. You can try, but there are times when you just have to accept that there are bad people in this world, and while they may escape justice here on earth, they'll have their due handed to them by the big guy upstairs."

Without looking up from the autopsy report, David asked, "On which side of the bridge did Leroy's truck end up in the lake?"

"South side," Bogie said. "We decided that he missed the bridge and the bridge embankment, drove through the weeds and tall grass, and went right into the lake. He had to have been driving at least forty miles an hour to miss that turn."

David stood up from behind his desk.

"You know that turn," Bogie said. "People go too fast, can't make the turn, and end up off the road. Since Leroy had such a high blood-alcohol level and—"

"We're going to the scene." With the case file in his hand, David left the office.

Wondering what David had seen to make him jump up and leave, Bogie stood in the middle of the vacant office until David stepped back inside. "You're driving."

It was a fast drive. They drove along the twisting country road to the bridge, which was less than ten minutes from the police station.

During the drive, David's cell phone rang, and the call was from Dallas. "Hey, lover boy, I'm on my way out of town!"

"Was it something I said?" David said with a grin.

"Archie and I are goin' to Gettysburg to meet with the police chief who investigated Fiona Davis' murder. We're gonna stay at a charmin' hotel."

David heard Archie say something in the background that he didn't catch. Luckily, Dallas repeated it for him. "It's haunted!" she said before squealing with laughter. "Can you be a love and stay with Mac tonight? Archie is worried about him. Be sure to take Storm over with you." After some giggles mixed with information about her and Archie following up on a lead they thought they had uncovered, Dallas hung up.

Bogie pulled the police cruiser off of the road next to a marshy area of the lake. From there, the road sharply curved up onto the bridge that crossed into McHenry.

Depending on the water level, the grassy-field area that sloped forty feet down to the lakeshore was usually dry, but it didn't take many rainy days to turn the area into a marsh.

391

When the lake's water level was particularly high, the marshy area would rise to within a few feet of the road.

Because it was early in the summer season and there hadn't been any rain for over a week, the grassy field was somewhat dry.

David climbed out of the passenger side of the cruiser and waded through the tall grass until he was down by the water's edge. "How far up was the water?"

"About where it is now." Bogie joined David down by the shore. "The truck was submerged right about there." He pointed to approximately twenty feet out from shore. "It was submerged when I got here."

David squatted down. "And Leroy wasn't in the truck?" He ran his fingers through the mud.

Bogie watched him pick up one handful of mud after another and let the cool lake water wash the mud from his hand. "He was at the bottom of the lake. They think he was too drunk to swim to shore."

"And so he drowned? Here?" David looked up and down the lakeshore.

"That's what Doc and the forensics people said."

David picked up a handful of the mud. Rising to his feet, he held it out to his deputy chief. "What's this?"

"Mud."

"Mud. All around here is mud. Along the shore. At the bottom of the lake." He turned his hand over and allowed the mud to land at his feet with a *plop*. "Doc found sand in Leroy's lungs."

"Sand?"

"Sand. Beach sand. Who do we know who has a private beach in the backyard of his lakefront home?" David shook his head. "Leroy Clark didn't drown here." With a sweep of his hand, he said, "This was all staged."

"I can't believe I slept all day." Mac Faraday pulled himself up and fluffed the pillows behind him before accepting the hot tea with honey that David was holding out to him.

Mac had wakened up to Storm licking his face. Once she had completed her task of waking him up, she rested her head on his chest as if to commune with a fellow creature who needed mending. She had healed enough that David had removed the cone of shame that she'd been wearing around her neck to prevent her from chewing her stitches. Taking in her wounds, Mac shuddered to imagine the horror Storm had experienced when the mountain lion had jumped her.

"You overdid it the last couple of days. Now your body needs to catch up." David picked up the pill bottles on the nightstand. "Did you take your meds?"

To answer him, Mac opened one of the bottles and shook out a pill. David took the water glass into the bathroom and filled it with fresh water. While washing down his medication, Mac watched David sit on the edge of the bed and proceed to stare off into space. Mac set the glass on the end table and picked up the cup of tea.

"Sand in Leroy's lungs despite the fact that his body was found in a part of the lake where there is no sand proves that he drowned someplace else," Mac said. "At the very least, his body was moved."

"He was murdered by his own brother," David said with certainty.

"Maybe."

"Bill Clark had his ring."

"Clark's lawyers will say Leroy gave it to him, and we can't prove otherwise," Mac said. "A jury will find it hard to believe that a man killed his brother over a ring."

"Plus Leroy was suing him because Bill cheated him out of his half of the estate," David said. "Bill was furious that his mother gave the ring to Leroy. If he'd acquired it legally and rightfully, he would have been wearing it all these years instead of hiding it in his desk drawer."

With a sigh, Mac set the cup down and clasped his hands behind his head. He stared up at the ceiling.

"You do believe me that Clark is capable—"

"I believe that everybody is capable of murder when the circumstances are right," Mac said. "The problem is proving it. Leroy's case was closed as an accident. It will be impossible now to match the sand found in Leroy's lungs to the sand on Bill's beach because so much time has passed. Every lake house around here has private beaches with sand. You can't prove he drowned on Clark's beach and not on some beach someplace else on the lake—like on the state park's public beach."

"I know," David said.

"The ring can't be used as evidence, because Bernie and Hap stole it," Mac said. "Where was Leroy drinking before the so-called accident?"

"There's nothing about that in the file. Leroy really didn't have much in the way of friends." David shrugged his shoulders. "He was a drunk, which was why Bogie and everyone else pretty much went through the motions when his truck ended up in the lake. His blood-alcohol level was twice the legal limit. Bogie feels terrible about this. Maybe if he had—"

"Give me the case file."

David grabbed the case file he had left on the dresser when he'd arrived at Spencer Manor. While he was crossing the room, Storm resumed licking Mac's face.

"Any word from Jessica about their case?" David held out the case file to him.

"They got the guy and a confession," Mac said while turning his head from one side to the other in an effort to escape Storm's flapping tongue. "They'll bring Gnarly back on their way up to West Virginia to visit Murphy's twin brother. Murphy missed his law-school graduation." He allowed Storm to nuzzle his ear while he reached around her for the folder.

"You really miss Gnarly," David said.

"No, I don't." Mac attempted to gently push Storm away. "Gnarly has been getting me up at six o'clock every morning since the day I met him. Now that Archie and I are married, he still gets *me* up. And he snores. I never knew dogs snored. Frankly, I enjoy the break."

David sat on the edge of the bed. "Well, take your mind off of how much you don't miss Gnarly by figuring out how we can catch Bill Clark."

"We're going to need a confession." Mac opened the folder.

"Even if we get one, he'll get it suppressed and go free," David said. "His supporters will never believe he killed his own brother over a ring."

"But he *did* kill his brother over a ring." Mac turned a page in the folder. "Do you have it with you?"

David took the ring out of his breast pocket and handed it to Mac, who took his time studying the gold jewel with the blue stone. He then read the inscription inside the band.

"Dollarwise," Mac said, "this is worth a little over a thousand dollars. But the real value is attached to what it signifies. Back in the old days, a ring with the family seal would be passed from the father to the firstborn son. The carving in the stone is the Clark family crest. When the family patriarch would write a letter, he would press the ring into hot candle wax to seal the letter with the mark of the family crest."

"Now we use e-mails," David said.

"This ring"—Mac held it up—"signifies Bill Clark's birthright. The firstborn is the patriarch, the leader, and the head of the family. When his mother gave it to Leroy, she gave Bill's birthright to the family's black sheep. That's why he went nuts and killed him to get it back." A slow grin worked its way across Mac's face while he studied the ring.

"What are you thinking?" David finally asked.

Mac held out his hand with his palm up. "Give me your hand."

David hesitated. "Which one?"

"Doesn't matter. Either one." When David placed his right hand in his palm, Mac corrected him. "Give me your left."

With a roll of his eyes, David placed his left hand in Mac's palm. Mac slipped the signet ring onto his little finger. It fit perfectly.

Holding up David's hand to admire the gold jewel with the blue stone, Mac chuckled. "That'll work."

CHAPTER THIRTY-TWO

Archie Monday could not believe that they'd managed—in a most spur-of-the-moment way—to travel two and a half hours to Gettysburg, Pennsylvania, and to reach the borough's police department one hour before it closed for the day.

Considering the way Dallas Walker had raced her big pickup truck up and down the mountains and across the rolling farmlands of Maryland and Pennsylvania, Archie was grateful that they'd arrived at their destination in one piece.

As if Dallas' adventurous driving style hadn't been enough for Archie to deal with, when they'd crossed the state line into Pennsylvania, they'd been greeted by Gnarly's smiling face—four stories tall—and the words "Don't Give a Paws! Vote for Gnarly!" The unexpected sight had caused both women to shriek. Luckily, there hadn't been any other vehicles on the freeway, so both lanes had been clear for Dallas to zigzag in while regaining her composure.

Upon reaching Gettysburg, Archie said a silent prayer of thanks, pried her fingers from the edge of her seat, and made an ironclad decision that she'd drive for the rest of the trip or take a bus home.

If nothing else, Dallas Walker was entertaining. She'd filled their roller-coaster drive with one story after another about growing up on her pappy's ranch, her first real cattle drive when she was six years old, her mother's teaching her the Walker family's secret chili recipe, and the day she squealed on her brother for breaking their mother's vase after he had paid twenty bucks for her silence. Dallas insisted it hadn't been her fault. When Phil had said, "Don't tell anyone," he hadn't told her that "anyone" included their momma and pappy.

As Dallas' loud enthusiasm filled the interior of the truck, Archie quickly forgot that her pappy's ranch was spread over three counties in Texas, that the Walker chili her momma had taught her to make was the world-famous specialty served at the ranch house of the Walker dude ranch, and that the vase her brother, Phil, had broken had most likely been worth no less than several thousand dollars.

If only she'd learn how to drive.

They were so anxious to get started on their case that Dallas went straight to the borough's police department instead of going to the hotel to check in.

In addition to being home to one of the most famous battles in the Civil War, Gettysburg was the meeting place of several major roads going north and south and east and west, as it had been founded over three hundred years earlier. Despite the tourist traffic and the fact that it had three times the number of residents of Spencer, it still held on to its rural historic atmosphere.

Located in a red-brick building, the police department was only slightly bigger than Spencer's.

Dallas shoved their unofficial case file, which was made up of news articles and their copy of the bootlegged police report about Fiona Davis' death, into her oversized bag, and they marched into the police department. At the business counter, the desk sergeant, an attractive woman in her fifties wearing a name tag that read "Gladstone," welcomed them with a pleasant smile.

Taking the lead, Archie introduced herself and Dallas and explained that they were investigative journalists working on a death that had taken place in Gettysburg close to twenty years ago.

"Twenty years ago?" The desk sergeant looked from Archie to Dallas. "You two must have been just little girls when it happened. Was the person a relative?"

"Her death came to our attention while we were investigating another case," Archie said. "She was a witness. She died only a few weeks later under what appears to have been questionable circumstances, so we think the two deaths could be related."

That seemed to catch the attention of the chief of police, who strolled out of his office in the corner of the spacious squad room. Big boned and with a barrel chest, the balding middle-aged man eyed the two visitors while he made his way up to the counter.

"Sounds exciting," the desk sergeant said in a pleasant manner. "What's the name?"

"Fiona Davis," Dallas said.

The desk sergeant's eyes looked like they were about to pop out of her head. The police chief stopped in midstride. Both of their faces went white.

The first to recover, the police chief stepped up to the counter and introduced himself as Jarrett Hill. After shaking both of their hands, he asked, "What was that name again?"

"Fiona Davis," Archie said while the desk sergeant stepped aside to allow the police chief to take over the conversation.

Chief Hill placed his hands on a computer keyboard and went into the police database. Archie noticed that the desk sergeant, who had returned to her desk, was watching him.

"Davis," the police chief said over and over again. "What was that first name again?"

"Fiona," Dallas said.

"Spell it for me."

Casting quick glances at the desk sergeant, who was visibly upset, Dallas slowly spelled out the name while the police chief pecked each key on the keyboard. When the case file came up, the chief uttered an "aha" before saying, "Fiona Davis. Twenty-seven years old. She committed suicide. Sad."

"By drowning herself in a toilet," Dallas said with a chuckle.

"I admit it's not something you see every day," Chief Hill said. "But she did leave a note."

"But you can't drown in a toilet," Dallas said with certainty.

"Yes, you can," the police chief said. "Fiona Davis did drown, and her body was found in a toilet. So, yes, you can drown in a toilet."

"Not without help," Dallas said. "If you want, we can take you into the bathroom and prove it."

"She left a note saying that she wanted to die, and she took a whole bottle of migraine pills," the chief said. "When they didn't kill her, she stuck her head in the toilet and passed out and drowned—or maybe she held her head under the water. In either case, there was no one else involved. It was a suicide."

"You said she was a witness to another murder?" the desk sergeant asked from her seat behind her desk.

"Six weeks earlier, a man who Fiona Davis had had dinner with in Deep Creek Lake was murdered," Archie said. "That was made to look like a suicide, too. That's why we think it could be the same killer."

"She wasn't murdered," Chief Hill said with a laugh. "You two ladies have very active imaginations."

"How can you be so certain that your department didn't make a mistake?" Dallas asked. "A few minutes ago, you didn't know who Fiona Davis was. All you did was look at the statement on your computer screen."

In an effort to keep their conversation with the police chief congenial, Archie patted Dallas on the arm. "Do your records show any family members who still live in the area?"

"Yes, but I don't think any of them would like my giving out their names." The police chief turned off the monitor so that they couldn't read what was on it. "Enjoy your stay in Gettysburg, ladies." He spun on his heels and went back to his office.

The desk sergeant was staring up at them with wide eyes.

Furious at the roadblock, Dallas slammed her hand down on the counter and went over to the door to leave.

"Can you give us directions to the Gettysburg Hotel?" Archie asked in a surprisingly friendly tone.

The desk sergeant jumped out of her chair and hurried up to the counter. While giving Archie detailed directions to the hotel, she scribbled on a notepad that was resting on the counter. Then she ripped the sheet of paper off of the pad, folded it in half, and handed it to Archie.

"I hope you have a pleasant stay in Gettysburg." She flashed them a wide grin.

"Thank you," Archie said before sauntering past Dallas to go out into the parking lot.

"Why did you have to be so nice?" Dallas said as soon as they were outside. "This whole trip has ended up bein' a waste of time. No way is that police chief gonna help us."

Archie unfolded the note that the desk sergeant had handed to her and held it out for Dallas to read. "Ms. Gladstone in there will help us."

The desk sergeant had not written out driving instructions but rather a note that read, "I found Fiona's body. Was murdered. Will meet you @ Gettysburg Hotel @ 5:30. Sally Gladstone."

A wide grin filling Dallas' face, she snatched the note out of Archie's hand to read it a second time.

Pleased with herself, Archie stuck out her hand. "Keys, please. I'm driving."

The grand old hotel was elegant with its hardwood floors, off-white walls, and sitting areas in the lobby and the lounge that were furnished with wing-backed chairs.

"You did make sure we got a ghost with this room, right?" Dallas said after they had arrived in their room, which was decorated in tan with blue accents. "I am so looking forward to seeing a ghost."

"No," Archie said with a laugh while going into the bathroom to unpack her cosmetic bag.

To Archie's surprise, Dallas was serious. "But I requested a room with a ghost when I made the reservations," she said with a whine in her tone.

That was enough to prompt Archie to fly out of the bathroom. "You better not have!"

Sitting on the edge of her bed, Dallas nodded her head. "I paid an extra hundred bucks ghost fee for it."

Sucking in a deep breath, Archie reminded herself that Dallas was David's girlfriend. For family harmony she needed to get along with her. With a forced grin, she turned around and went back into the bathroom to continue unpacking.

"Don't worry, Archie," Dallas called into her. "If we don't get haunted tonight, I'm gonna demand a refund."

After checking in with Mac and David, they hurried down to the lounge, where they snagged a table with three wingbacked chairs in front of the fireplace. While waiting for their first round of martinis, they both eyed the doorway leading into the lobby, looking for any sign of their informant, who arrived at the same time as their drinks—a good ten minutes before the appointed time.

Sally Gladstone had hurried to the hotel straight from the police station as soon as she'd gotten off duty. Immediately, Dallas ordered a martini for their guest and a second round for her and Archie, even though they had only tasted their first round.

Hoping to ease Sally's nervousness, Archie patted her hand. "We really want to thank you for meeting with us. We both know that you're taking a big chance by talking to us."

"Yeah," Dallas said. "If your boss catches you, you'll probably be fired in half time less than no time."

Sally jumped when Dallas put the reality of her situation into words, and Archie shushed her. "Let me do the talking. Okay?"

Sally took a generous sip of her drink when it arrived and cleared her throat before she began. "Fiona and I went all through school together. We were friends. She was a bridesmaid at my wedding."

"So you were close," Archie said in a gentle tone. "You wrote in your note that you found her body."

Sally nodded her head. "She and I were supposed to go out to lunch that day, and she didn't show up. I waited for close to an hour. I knew immediately that something was wrong. I had a key to her place because I had collected her mail and fed her cat when she'd taken a trip the month before. So I let myself in when she didn't answer the door." Reminded of the horror of her discovery, she took another sip of her drink. After setting the glass down, she covered her face with a trembling hand. "I found her in the bathroom. She was lying in front of the toilet. There was vomit everywhere."

"The autopsy said she had taken a whole bottle of migraine medicine," Dallas said.

"Fiona got horrible migraines," Sally said with a nod. "She had a hard time because of them. She'd get them so often that it was hard for her to hold a job." She sucked in a deep breath. "But she didn't kill herself. That note was forged. It had to have been."

"According to the police investigation," Dallas said, "Fiona was depressed about her mother's death."

"Yes," Sally said with a wave of her hand. "That was a murder, too. I didn't think so at the time, but I think it was."

"She fell down a flight of stairs," Archie said.

"I think he did it to get back at her," Sally said.

"He who?" Dallas asked.

"I don't know." Sally frowned.

Dallas and Archie exchanged glances.

"Fiona was twenty-seven years old. She was at the point— all of her friends were married," Sally said. "She couldn't hold a job. She was afraid of being alone. So…She started seeing someone. He was married. At first, he treated her really good."

"Except for being married," Archie said.

Sally agreed. "Fiona got all wrapped up in it. He paid for her apartment. Bought her clothes and gifts. Bought her a car. She had money for the first time in her life. She was happy."

"Until?" Archie asked.

"He became very possessive. I mean, like, insanely possessive. He'd call her at all times of the day and night wanting to know where she was, who she was seeing, and what she was doing. It was okay that he was going home and sleeping with his wife, but Fiona couldn't go out to lunch with a friend without his knowing who, what, when, and where."

"Sounds like a stalker to me," Dallas said. "Only she was sleeping with this stalker."

"It got insane," Sally said. "Fiona knew that she'd have to start over with nothing if she cut it off, but I think she also realized that it was not a healthy relationship at all. I mean, the guy was obsessed with her. He was nuts. She was really torn about the whole situation. That was why she went away for that long weekend. She didn't tell anyone where she was going, because she was afraid he'd follow her. You said she witnessed a murder?"

"Fiona had dinner with the victim a few hours before he was killed," Archie said.

Sally covered her mouth with her hand. "She never told me."

"What did Fiona decide during her trip?" Dallas asked. "Did she end it with the married man?"

Sally nodded her head. "And a week later, her mother fell down the stairs and broke her neck. Fiona was devastated."

"Don't tell me," Archie said. "She ended up going back to him."

"Yeah," Sally said. "But that only lasted a couple of weeks, because the last time I talked to her, she said she was going to apply for some clerical jobs in Washington, DC. I asked her how her boyfriend felt about that, and she said that she didn't care how he felt. It was time to move on and to stand on her own two feet." She looked from Archie to Dallas and back again. "Now does that sound like a woman who was about to kill herself?"

"No, it doesn't," Dallas said.

"You have no idea who this guy was?" Archie asked.

Sally shook her head.

"The night of the murder in Deep Creek Lake," Dallas said, "a fat man was seen in the lounge watching the man who Fiona had had dinner with—"

Dallas stopped when Sally's eyes grew wide with recognition. Seeing it too, Archie leaned over in her seat.

"Fat—fat man?"

"Like, three to four hundred pounds," Dallas said.

"Son of a bitch," Sally said.

"Do you know who that could've been?" Archie asked.

Sally was still cursing. "Of course. It all makes sense now. Why Jarrett didn't want you two looking into this case—why he insisted that it was a suicide."

"You mean the chief of police?" Dallas said. "He's not three to four hundred pounds."

"But he used to be!" Sally said. "Back then, Jarrett was obese. His father was a big-shot engineer and had designed some big—" She waved her hands. "Forget it. Point is that they had a lot of money. Jarrett got married, and they had a couple of kids, but he'd always wanted to be a police officer. He'd gotten a degree in law enforcement and stuff, but he couldn't get into the academy because of his weight. One day, he buckled down and started really working out and dieting. He lost two hundred pounds and got into the academy—that was over fifteen years ago. They even did a big spread about it in the local papers because he came back home to join our local police department. He made chief about five years ago. That was when I started working there as a desk sergeant."

She wagged her finger at both of them. "Jarrett always had a thing for Fiona. He asked her out when he was engaged to his wife. Why didn't I see it?"

"Because you were too close," Archie said.

"Okay, so the chief of the police is our killer," Dallas said. "How do we prove it—especially after all this time?"

"You said he bought her a car and rented an apartment for her." After Sally confirmed that he had, Archie said, "Apartments usually have leases that need to be signed. Cars need insurance and titles. If Jarrett Hill was her sugar daddy, he had to have left some sort of a trail somewhere."

"We'll start by following the money," Dallas said.

Chapter Thirty-Three

The Next Morning

"Mr. Clark, I want to thank you for coming in to help us clear this up," David said with as much congeniality in his tone as he could muster. He and Mac had just walked into the police station's interview room to meet with the town councilman and his lawyer.

"I just want to get this over with." Despite years of practice, Bill Clark couldn't completely erase the disgrace from his face. His own wife of less than a year had admitted to hating him so much that she wanted him dead—in front of Police Chief O'Callaghan, no less.

David and Mac sat across the conference table from them, positioning themselves so that David was directly across from Bill Clark.

"Sheriff Turow asked us to go over the facts as we have them in the case against your wife." David opened the folder containing the police report that stated that Cassandra Clark had conspired with an undercover police officer to have her husband killed. "The whole purpose of this meeting is to answer the questions that I'm sure you may have." He laid his hand bearing the gold ring on his little finger flat on the police report. "If there's anything you want to offer that you think may be helpful, we'll be very glad to hear it."

Mac saw that Bill's eyes were drawn to the ring on David's finger like metal to a magnet.

David's gaze met that of the town councilman. "Is there anything you'd like to tell me, Bill?"

"No."

"In light of the situation," the lawyer said, "my client feels that it would not be beneficial for us to cooperate in prosecuting his wife."

"What dirt does Ms. Clark have on your client?" Mac asked.

"My client stands for devotion to family."

"He's been divorced twice," Mac said, "after his wives caught him cheating on them."

"Oh, yeah," David said. "We know all about how devoted your client is to family." Holding a pen in his hand, David gently rapped the ring on the tabletop.

His gaze never leaving the gold ring with his family crest on it, Bill smoldered.

"Was your client aware of his wife's affair with Mr. Braxton?" Mac asked.

"No," the lawyer said without needing to check with the councilman. "Unfortunately, political candidates can become so wrapped up in campaigning and meeting voters and listening to their concerns and trying desperately to help them that their spouses, especially young, insecure women like Cassandra, can become vulnerable to players like Mr. Braxton. He took advantage of her."

"She tried to blackmail him into hiring a paid assassin to kill your client," Mac said. "We recorded the whole thing."

"We're going to have that recording tossed out of court," the lawyer said.

"You're representing her?" Mac asked.

"Mr. Clark hired me to defend her. We're going to have the charges dropped on the grounds of entrapment."

"She wants your client dead," Mac said. "If the police hadn't stepped in and arrested her, he'd be dead now."

"The problems between the Clarks would be best worked out between the two of them, without the help of the police. As soon as the election is over, they're going to go away for a long holiday together."

"I'd suggest she stay away from water," David said in a low voice that only Bill Clark could hear.

"Excuse me," the lawyer said. "Did you say something?"

"Just that Bill is very good at working out family problems," David said. "I used to be friends with his late sister. When it comes to putting an end to family differences"—he rubbed his fingers across the blue jewel on the ring—"he's an expert."

Bill lifted his gaze to glare into David's blue eyes. The tension in the room was palpable.

"Do you need anything else from us?" the lawyer asked Mac.

"No, I think we're done here for now."

"Thank you for finding time to meet with us." Archie's tone oozed with gratitude that Police Chief Jarrett Hill had agreed to meet with Dallas Walker and her to go over their findings in the Fiona Davis case.

Concealing her nervousness, Sally Gladstone busied herself at her desk outside of the police chief's office.

Jarrett Hill closed his door and went around behind his desk. "Well, like I told you two yesterday, I believe you're wasting your time. After you left, I went to the trouble of bringing up Fiona Davis' case file and going over the evidence and the autopsy report. There's no evidence of any foul play."

"Even the fact that it's impossible to accidentally drown in a toilet?" Dallas set a typewritten report on the center of his desk. "Forensics experts have proven that in more than one case."

"I don't care what your science says." Chief Hill refused to look at the report. "Fiona left a suicide note. She was extremely close to her mother, who had died the month before. She wanted to be with her. She took a bottle of migraine medicine—"

"Funny thing about that," Archie said. "When you look at the autopsy report, it shows enough gelatin capsules for two pills, but the actual level of medication in her system was much, much higher. Like, maybe someone got the medication and ground it up into a powder and then mixed it into a drink—like the wine he had brought over as a peace offering."

"Only instead of dying of an overdose like her killer had planned," Dallas said, "she threw it up."

"That wasn't good," Archie said. "The stuff that was supposed to kill her had gone down the toilet. So he shoved her head down into the bowl and held it there until he killed her."

Police Chief Jarrett Hill looked from one of them to the other and back again. They could see his mind working to come up with an argument. "Most likely, when she was throwing up on the pills she'd taken to kill herself, she passed out from the overdose, fell into the toilet, and died."

"If Fiona had passed out," Dallas said, "her body would have acted as a counterweight, and she would have slipped out of the toilet before she had time to drown and landed on the floor. No"—she shook her head—"someone would have had to hold her head under the water in order for her to drown."

"Does this mysterious someone have a name?" the police chief asked.

"Jarrett Hill," Archie said.

Police Chief Jarrett Hill laughed. "I barely even remember Fiona Davis. When you came in here yesterday—"

"Cut the crap," Dallas said. "It's a small town. The landlord of the apartment you rented for Fiona remembers you setting up the whole thing. You found the apartment. You paid the rent in cash every month. He even remembers you going to visit her on a regular basis."

"We also found the friend who sold you the little sports car that you gave to her," Archie said.

"And all of that was while you were married to your wife," Dallas said. "You remember your wife, don't you? The one who tragically died in a fire less than a year after Fiona died. Did she try to leave you, too?"

They all stared at one another in silence.

Jarrett Hill broke the standoff. "You yourself said that Fiona's death was connected to a murder she witnessed in—where is it that you said you were from?"

"Deep Creek Lake," Dallas said.

"The murder of Sandy Burr at the Lakeside Inn," Archie said. "Yes, it was six weeks before Fiona's murder. Have you ever been there?"

"No," he said. "And I never met this Sandy whatever. Since I never met him, I had no reason to kill him. No motive. No opportunity. Based on your theory that the two murders are connected, I guess I didn't kill Fiona." He flashed them a grin. "Well, it was nice meeting you."

"Are you sure you've never been to the Lakeside Inn in Deep Creek Lake?" Archie asked.

"Positive."

"Because Caleb Montgomery, the bartender who was tending bar the night Sandy Burr was killed, remembers you." Archie took a copy of a newspaper article out of her purse, unfolded it, and laid it flat on his desk. The article included two pictures, one of Jarrett Hill in his present slender shape and a "before" picture of him from when he was obese.

"Mr. Montgomery told the police that the night Sandy Burr was killed, there was a customer at the bar—he called him the 'fat man'—who was clearly watching Mr. Burr," Dallas said. "He was so intent that he left a fresh drink behind to follow Mr. Burr when he left. We texted this picture to him, and he identified you at your former weight as that man."

"He's wrong," the police chief said. "That was so long ago that his memory has to be foggy. I've never been to Deep Creek Lake. I wouldn't have had any reason to kill Sandy Burr, so I wouldn't have had any reason to follow him."

"You didn't start out following him," Archie said. "You started out following Fiona. You were obsessed with Fiona. Her friends confirm that. You tried to hide it, especially after you got married. But then Fiona started having health and money issues, which made her vulnerable. You saw your chance to have her, so you took advantage of it. But you couldn't just have her as a mistress—you had to have her completely. When your love became suffocating, Fiona wanted out. She went to Deep Creek Lake to think about your relationship—but you couldn't let her go. You followed her and saw her having dinner with another man."

"You assumed then that Fiona had gone to Deep Creek Lake to cheat on you," Dallas said. "But that wasn't the case at all. They were simply two people traveling alone who decided to keep each other company over dinner."

413

"But in your jealous rage," Archie said, "you watched Sandy Burr after Fiona had left, and then you followed him to his room and killed him."

"Very good story," Jarrett said with a smug grin. "But you can't prove any of it. Your witness who said I was at the bar is wrong. No jury will ever believe him. Fiona was distraught about her mother's death."

"The mother I'm willing to bet you shoved down the stairs to punish Fiona for breaking up with you," Dallas said. "She went back to you but only temporarily. She left you again. So you decided to kill her so that no one else could have her."

"I've never been to Deep Creek Lake," Jarrett Hill said with a laugh. "So I didn't kill this Sandy guy. Fiona's mother was a klutz, and Fiona left a suicide note behind. And as for my late wife, that was faulty electrical wiring."

"Are you sure you've never been to Deep Creek Lake?" Archie asked.

"How many times do I have to tell you? No!"

"That's weird, because your fingerprints were there," Dallas said.

Jarrett Hill fell silent.

"Forensics picked up a beautiful set of prints on the door to Sandy Burr's room," Dallas said. "I know what you're thinking. You planned everything so well while you were sitting there in the bar watching Burr have drinks with that woman. You wore evidence gloves and were very careful to not leave prints. But after he was dead and you'd staged the room to make it look like he'd committed suicide, you went to leave, and that was when you let your guard down. I can see you taking off your evidence gloves, opening the door, propping it open with your foot, and then—being careful to wipe your prints off the door handle—closing the door behind you. Thing is, you were so focused on not touching the handle that you didn't notice it when you touched the door itself with your bare fingers, which were moist with sweat and the talc that's inside those gloves." She grinned. "You left a perfect set of prints on the door."

"After Caleb Montgomery identified you as the man at the bar watching Sandy Burr," Archie said, "we had Maryland State Police compare those prints to your prints in the Pennsylvania police database, and they're a match. Burr's murder happened before you got accepted to the police force, before your prints were put into the system. So when they ran the prints back then, nothing came up." She flashed him a grin. "This time they did."

"A witness puts you in Deep Creek Lake at the same hotel on the same night that Sandy Burr was murdered," Dallas said. "And your fingerprints put you at the murder scene."

"And your affair with Fiona Davis gave you a motive to kill him." Archie stood up and went to open the police chief's door.

Bogie was standing in the doorway. "Jarrett Hill, we have a warrant for your arrest in the death of Sandy Burr in Spencer, Maryland."

"Any sign of Bill Clark?" David asked his officers on the radio while driving home from the police department.

"He hasn't left his house since getting home before noon, Chief," Officer Fletcher said.

During that report, David petted Storm, who had her nose pressed up against the passenger's side window, and headed toward the grocery store on the other side of Deep Creek Lake. Hopefully, the timing would work out, and he could prepare another Chateaubriand for two to have waiting for Dallas when she got home that evening. While driving

415

across the lake, he saw dark, heavy clouds signaling the end of the bright, sunny weather they'd had for the last couple of weeks.

After Bogie had arrested Jarrett Hill for Sandy Burr's murder, Dallas and Archie had gone to meet with homicide detective Cameron Gates of the Pennsylvania State Police to go over the evidence they had dug up on Fiona Davis' death. Murphy Thornton's stepmother, Cameron Gates, would certainly latch onto the case like a dog with a bone and refuse to let up until she uncovered the evidence necessary to put Jarrett Hill in jail for the murder of Fiona Davis, her mother, and possibly his own wife.

Not long after he had left the police station with his lawyer, Bill Clark had canceled his appearances for the rest of the day, saying that he was not feeling well. David had called in his off-duty officers to keep Bill under surveillance and to keep close in case David needed back-up when Bill made his move.

Mac's hunch had been proven right. David had been able to see the fury in Bill Clark's eyes by the end of the meeting. Bill had killed his own brother to steal the ring that signified his birthright. Bill had hated David even before he'd seen that ring on his finger. If he had to kill David to retrieve it, he would do so with glee.

"You're not eating this dinner," David said to Storm when he put the bags of groceries into the back compartment of his police cruiser. Hearing a low rumble from the dark clouds overhead, he hurried to cross back to Spencer's side of the lake and to get home and unload the groceries before the clouds opened up and dumped all of the precipitation they'd been storing up.

"Hey, Brewster, are you awake?" David said into the radio after turning onto the narrow road that led to the cove where he lived.

"Yeah, Chief, wide awake, but nothing is happening."

David waved to the officer staking out the police chief's home from inside his truck, which he had tucked back off the road behind some trees.

After kicking the door closed behind him, David stopped, his arms filled with grocery bags, to take in the silence of his home. He wished he hadn't insisted that Mac return to Spencer Manor to go back to bed. The pneumonia had been sapping all of his strength, which made him of little use in this stage of their investigation.

Something about being aware that someone hated him—and very definitely wanted him dead—made the solitude of his home seem…scary.

Shaking off the feeling of dread, David carried the grocery bags to the kitchen, where he dumped them on the counter.

Storm had plopped down on the sofa. With her head propped up on the arm, she tracked his movements with her eyeballs.

David took off his utility belt, which held his service weapon, police baton, radio, and cell phone, and hung it up on the coat hook next to the door before going to work putting away the food. After popping the package of tenderloin filets into the fridge, he yanked a bottle of beer out, twisted off its cap, and took a big gulp from the bottle. Then, he put the rest of his groceries away and took the bag of dog food out of the lower cupboard to prepare Storm's dinner.

Upon smelling the scent of her food, Storm's ears perked up. She focused in on the bowl David had set on the kitchen counter.

"I guess you're hungry," he said in response to her lifting her head from the arm of the sofa.

As soon as he set the bowl on the kitchen floor, she jumped off of the sofa. Storm was not the least bit ladylike when it came to eating. She'd plunge her snout into the bowl and send dog-food pellets flying in her effort to inhale every bite.

Smiling, David recalled that Dallas had said that it was like Storm was determined to eat her food before it ate her first. Gently, he brushed his fingertips across the dog's wounds from the mountain lion's attack. They were healing nicely, and the patches of sable fur that had been shaved were already starting to grow back.

Leaning against the counter, David drank his beer and watched Storm gulp down her food and then lick the inside and outside of the bowl to get every morsel. She even pushed the bowl aside to check underneath it and around its edges. Once she was satisfied that she had indeed eaten every bite, she looked up at David and licked her chops.

"Ready to go outside?"

She answered by trotting across the living area of the great room to the French doors that opened to the back deck and the lake at the rear of the house. Sipping his beer, David followed her. As soon as he opened the door for her, she shot out of it and galloped down the walkway to the dock, where a small flock of ducks was gathering. She was so intent on chasing away the intruders that she didn't notice or care that heavy drops of rain had started to fall.

Assuming she would be right back as soon as she realized that she was getting wet, David closed the door. He then took out his cell phone to check the locater application for Dallas' location to see what time he could expect her to get home. He didn't want the filets to dry out from overcooking.

"Nice place."

David froze. *How?* Slowly, he turned around to face Bill Clark, who was aiming a .357 Magnum, not unlike the one Clint Eastwood used in *Dirty Harry*, directly at him.

"I considered shooting you in the back," Bill said, "but I decided I wanted to see your face when I killed you."

David tried not to look at the front door, beyond which Officer Brewster was supposed to have been watching for him.

Seeming to see the flicker of his eyes, Bill chuckled. "Really, O'Callaghan, I expected more of you. I've known Fletcher and Brewster and all of your officers for as long as you have. I know their vehicles. As soon as I saw Fletcher following me from the police station, I realized what you were doing." His face hardened. "You stole my ring because you knew I'd try to kill you to get it back. Then you would have your men arrest me and ruin my chances of becoming mayor."

David heard Storm scratching at the door behind him. The rain was falling in sheets then, and she wanted in.

"You think this is about politics?" David asked. "That's what you think this is about? No. I don't give a damn about politics. This is about murder." He held up the hand holding the cell phone so that Bill could see the ring. "Your mother gave this ring to your brother, Leroy—not to you. He wasn't wearing it when he died, and I know—Lisa told me—that he would have never given up this ring *willingly!*"

"It's mine!" His face filled with rage, Bill stepped toward him. "Give it to me!"

"How did you get it?"

"Like you don't know!" Aiming the muzzle of the gun at David's face, Bill laughed. "You said it. Leroy refused to give it to me. It was mine! Dad told me ever since I was a kid that he would give it to me because I was to take his place as the patriarch—the leader of our family! It was my birthright!" he said, spitting out his words.

"But your mother gave it to Leroy."

"Because he was a loser, and she felt sorry for him!" Bill Clark was close enough that David could see the insane quest for greatness in his bloodshot eyes. "She totally didn't get it! Leroy was not worthy of that ring and what it represented!"

"Is that why you killed him?"

"If he had just given me the ring like I'd asked him to," Bill said. "I made him a very good offer. If he gave me the ring that rightfully belonged to me, I'd give him his half of the family's estate. But you know what he did?"

David set his half-empty beer bottle and the cell phone on the table next to the doors. "What did he do, Bill?"

"He said no! He said Mom gave it to him because she wanted him to have it! She felt he deserved it! Deserved it!" Bill bounced with rage. "I am the firstborn! I am the oldest! I deserved it! Not him! But he couldn't get it! He just didn't get it, and he would not give it to me, and it belonged to me!" He clenched his teeth. "If he had just given it to me like I'd asked, then—"

"Then what, Bill?" David asked.

His voice was dreadfully calm. "Then I wouldn't have had to kill him." He held out his hand. "Give it to me, or you're going to end up like Leroy."

David could hear Storm scratching and whining at the door behind them. The rain was pouring down on her. Unable to look, he could only imagine that she was soaked to the skin and shivering.

"Now!" Bill said.

"You'll have to take it off my dead body," David said.

A slow grin came to Bill's face. "Gladly." He lowered his gun and aimed it to David's right. "But first I'm going to shoot your dog."

Bill Clark pulled the trigger as David's leg shot out and hit him in the chest, sending him flying backward and onto the glass coffee table, which gave way under his weight. Broken glass flew everywhere as the table collapsed.

The gun fell from his hand and slid under the sofa.

The stray bullet shattered the glass door.

David heard Storm yelp.

The anger that had built up over the years from the abuse the councilman had heaped on the police chief, his friends, his neighbors, and his town bubbled up to the surface. His taking a shot at Dallas' beloved Storm was the straw that broke the camel's back.

David descended on Bill Clark like an enraged bear. Grabbing him by the front of his shirt, he pulled him to his feet. "This is for Lisa." He heard Bill's nose break under the force of his punch to his face.

Falling back onto the floor, Bill covered his face with his hands. When he saw the blood, he charged at him. "You bastard!" Grabbing David by the middle, he shoved him back against the wall, shattering a series of candid pictures that the former owner had taken around the lake.

David had known Bill his whole life. During those years, he'd never known him to be athletic, though he regularly golfed and took occasional trips to the athletic club— usually only to network with fellow politicians and business associates. For that reason, David had expected him to go down easy and to stay down. But insane rage does things to a person. It gives him strength and endurance that he would not have under normal circumstances.

Years of resentment of the respect that David had from those in the community, not to mention of the charisma that won him affection from women without the use of money and power as bait, exploded into blind rage.

Holding David against the wall, Bill delivered one punch after another to his midsection until David kneed him in the face and shoved him back. Before Bill could recover his footing and stop stumbling backward, David advanced on him, delivering one blow after another. Occasionally, Bill would deliver wild punches, but seldom did they hit home.

Finally, in desperation, Bill grabbed a lamp from an end table and took a swing, trying to hit David in the side of the head.

The blow was hard enough to make David see stars. He staggered. Shaking his head in an effort to chase away the stars, he staggered back, turned, and dropped down onto one knee.

Approaching David from behind, Bill lifted the lamp up over his head. "You have no idea who you're messing with." He prepared to bring it down on David's head with every ounce of strength he had to finish him off.

"Hey, Brewster, any sign of Clark?" After parking his sports car next to the officer's truck in the turnoff, Mac banged in the truck's passenger side window. He had to yell in order for Officer Brewster to hear him over the downpour.

Caught in the midst of sending a text to his girlfriend, the officer dropped his phone onto the passenger seat. "None." He took note of the dark circles under Mac's eyes. "Aren't you supposed to be in bed?"

"I'll rest after we get Bill Clark locked up." Mac tugged on the collar of his yellow slicker to block the chill in the air.

"Hey, Brewster!" Officer Fletcher's voice came out of the radio. "We've got trouble!"

Officer Brewster pressed the button on his radio. "What do you mean we have trouble?"

"I've been watching Clark's house all day," Officer Fletcher said, "and then this storm came in and it got dark. But I noticed no lights came on in Clark's place. So I decided to go check—"

Mac wasn't waiting around to listen to the rest. Ripping open his rain coat to grab his gun out of its holster, he sprinted up the driveway and across the front lawn toward the round

422

house on the lake. Officer Brewster was directly behind him. They were galloping up the steps to the front deck when they heard the unmistakable sound of two gunshots.

Mac felt his heart up in his throat when Officer Brewster threw open the door and stood off to the side. The officer covered Mac who charged into the foyer with his gun ready to fire.

They heard Bill Clark wailing before they saw him.

Sweeping the great room with his gun, Mac located the councilman sprawled out spread-eagle in the dining area with two gunshot wounds—one to his thigh and the other to his lower abdomen. He was in tremendous pain and furious.

"He shot me!" Bill Clark said, playing every bit the victim. "All I asked was that he give me the ring he stole and he shot me!"

Officer Brewster proceeded to radio for an ambulance.

Mac looked over to see David carry Storm in from the deck. Cold, wet, and scared, she was trembling and whining almost as loud as Bill was cursing.

"When I'm elected mayor, O'Callaghan, you're fired if you're not in jail first!"

Ignoring the councilman's threats, David sat down on the steps of the drop down living room to comfort Storm, who rested her head on his shoulder.

"Are you okay?" Mac grabbed an afghan from the sofa to help dry the dog off.

"He took a shot at Storm." Finding no injuries, David reached around behind his back to take out his gun, which he handed to Mac. "I shot him with the back-up weapon from my ankle holster when he tried to smash in my skull with a lamp. You'll find his gun under the sofa where it slid when I disarmed him."

"I didn't bring any gun!" Clark said. "I was unarmed and he shot me."

Officer Brewster looked up from where he was offering the councilman some first aid until the emergency crew arrived. "You better hope he doesn't by some miracle win the election, Chief."

Busy calming the dog in his lap, David nodded his head in the direction of the end table on which he had placed his beer bottle and cell phone. "He's not going to be mayor."

Mac crossed over to the end table and bent over to observe the cell phone. With a swipe of his finger, he activated the screen to show that it had been recording. "How much did you get, David?"

"Everything."

For the first time, Mac saw an expression of genuine fear in the councilman's face. "Clark, I'm willing to bet money that you're going to be in jail before election day."

CHAPTER THIRTY-FOUR

Even after a year of married life, Murphy felt like every day with his bride was one of discovery. After their first official case working together, they were able to take a deep breath, gaze into each other's eyes, and marvel at what a perfect fit they were for each other.

For Jessica, it was an excellent excuse for a date night. She'd made reservations at Marcel's, one of Washington's most popular five-star restaurants on Pennsylvania Avenue, for one of his fabulous seven-course meals for two.

The sun had begun to set behind the trees on the other side of the Potomac River when Jessica stepped out onto the front porch in time to see Tristan and Sarah trotting down the path from his guest cottage. Seeing Sarah dressed in shorts and an oversized T-shirt from the naval academy, Jessica was reminded that Murphy's sister had been visiting Jessica's brother.

Strange. My brother is dating my husband's sister. Or is it really dating? She searched her mind but couldn't recall their ever going out on a real bona fide date.

Gnarly and Spencer clawed and barked at the front door until it popped open—the lock and latch had been released by

Nigel—and then they galloped across the yard with their tails wagging to greet the visitors.

Seeing Jessica dressed up in a silver-sequined cocktail minidress with a crisscross halter top and a daring plunging back, Sarah stopped and let out a low whistle. Jessica's long legs were accentuated by four-inch sequined heels. "If Murphy hadn't already married you, he would probably pop the question after seeing you in that."

Jessica did a model-like turn. "Do you think?" Cocking her head at Tristan, she asked, "Would you two like to join us? I can call in to change the reser—"

"We're going to watch a movie in the home theater," Tristan said. "Since you two are going out, we—"

"How did you know we were going out?"

"I asked Nigel if you had anything on your calendars."

"The always helpful Nigel." Somehow, Jessica felt like her brother had walked in on her and Murphy while they'd been otherwise engaged.

Murphy drove Jessica's purple Ferrari up to the front porch. "Hey, sis!" He waved to Sarah. "You didn't put gas in my motorcycle after taking it out. You promised when you called the other day that you'd gas it up."

"I will tomorrow before I leave." Sarah leaned over the driver's side door of the convertible to hug Murphy and give him a quick kiss. "I promise."

On the other side of the car, Tristan opened the door so that Jessica could climb in. "We'll all go out for breakfast together tomorrow."

"We're taking Gnarly back to Spencer." Jessica strapped on her seatbelt. "Then we'll be going to West Virginia for a few days to see J.J. since Murphy missed his graduation."

"Guess I'll see you when you get back," Tristan said.

Wrapping her arms around Tristan, Sarah told Murphy, "Tell J.J. I said hi."

"Be sure to let Gnarly and Spencer in before you two watch the movie," Jessica said. "And please clean up after yourselves."

With that, Murphy put the sports car into gear, and they sped around the circular drive to head down the driveway and through the gate, which closed after them.

"What do you wanna do first?" Sarah asked while lifting her shirt up over her head and waving it about. "Make out naked in the spa or go see the movie?"

With a husky laugh, Tristan swept her up into his arms and carried her inside and then to the spa in the back—forgetting about Gnarly and Spencer, who had taken off to chase a rabbit through the woods.

At Marcel's, after they had toasted each other, Jessica with her first glass of wine and Murphy with his glass of water, Jessica saw that Murphy's smile didn't fully reach his eyes as he glanced around at the various patrons of the high-priced restaurant. Many of the diners were the upper echelon of the nation's capital—those who held the reins of power.

Jessica laid her hand on Murphy's. "Don't tell me that you'd rather be home drinking a beer and watching a game."

"No." He kissed her fingertips before shooting a glance over his shoulder to a group decked out in tuxedos and gowns for a show taking place in one of the many theaters nearby. "That's the DCI over there. The members of his security detail are eating at the other tables around him and over by the door."

Jessica spotted the earbuds of the security officers protecting the head of the Central Intelligence Agency. Silently, she kicked herself for her lack of observational skills.

Murphy nodded his head toward a table behind her. "That's an undersecretary of state and his wife."

"Do you feel intimidated, like you aren't worthy of dining in the same restaurant as them?"

Shaking his head, Murphy let out a breath. "No, that's not it." He leaned toward her. "Jurvetson is a hairsbreadth from becoming the DCI, Jessica."

"That's not going to happen," she said. "CO said she'll take care of it. She hasn't let you—us—down yet."

"And what about the next time?" Murphy asked. "The next Camille Jurvetson who puts her own ambitions ahead of our country's security?"

"There have been power-driven narcissists since the beginning of time," Jessica said, "especially in this town. But the way I see it, good and good people like you and the Phantoms always win out in the end."

The server arrived with their first course, which was caviar.

"What if we hadn't reached Tawkeel in time?" Murphy asked her in a whisper. "What if I hadn't walked in on her assassin killing Wallace?"

"But you did," Jessica said. "And I believe that the Phantoms saved Tawkeel and you tracked down Jurvetson for a reason." She shook her cracker, which was covered with caviar, at him. "God hates slimy power-hungry fiends like Jurvetson, and you may not think so right now, but they always get their just desserts in the end." She popped the cracker into her mouth. After taking time to chew and swallow, she added, "If we're lucky, we'll get to see it happen ourselves."

Delighting in the thrill of the chase, Spencer zigged and zagged around the trees on the outer perimeter of the estate. Yapping merrily away, she suddenly realized that Gnarly was no longer behind her. After spinning around, the blue-furred shelty raced back through the trees until she found the German shepherd, who was standing tall and still and staring out beyond the trees and through the security fence at a black-paneled van. Gnarly crouched down on the ground and peered at the vehicle that had for some reason captured his attention.

Spencer picked up on the change in Gnarly's demeanor.

Inside the van, six men were lined up against either side of the rear compartment, checking the frequency of the communications devices they were wearing in their ears. They were dressed in black from head to toe, and each one was wearing a ballistic vest. They were heavily armed with assault rifles, handguns, and fighting knives.

"We'll be using secure network number seven," their leader, a short, stocky man with a black goatee, said. "Our target is Murphy Thornton, a navy lieutenant."

"You sure we have the right place, Elmo?" the largest of the men asked. "This place seems pretty rich for a simple navy lieutenant."

"That's because Thornton married money, Tucker," Elmo said. "Jessica Faraday, daughter of multimillionaire Mac Faraday, a retired homicide detective who has put a lot of bad people in jail. Our job is to take them and everyone in the house out. Make it look like she's the prime target. That way, the police will assume that this was revenge for one of Faraday's past cases and never suspect that it was the agency."

"What'd Thornton do to get on our hit list?" Tucker asked.

"I don't know, and I don't ask," Elmo said. "Jurvetson ordered that he be taken out, so that's what we're gonna do."

"Does that mean we get to have a bit of fun with the rich wife before we off her?" Cody, the youngest member of the death squad, wiped a drop of drool from his mouth.

"Cody, how many times do I have to tell you to focus on the job?" Tucker gave his head a slap.

"Mom told you to stop pounding on me!" Cody said.

"Everybody, focus on the job," Elmo said. "We need to make this look like a hit by a mob or a drug cartel. If you want to torture them, fine—but don't leave any physical evidence that could be traced back to us. You all know what happens to you if a cop comes knocking on your door. There's no room in our business for loose ends." To mess up was the equivalent of a death sentence—executed by a member of their own team.

The solemn reminder made each man nod his head.

The leader turned to the laptop he had attached to a series of computer monitors and set up toward the front of the van. "Everybody ready?"

They all acknowledged that they were ready.

"Go!"

The team of six men each carrying gear in a backpack jumped out of the back of the van. With a sense of determination, Tucker led them up to the control panel attached to the gate. He used a knife to pry open the access panel in the back and plugged one end of a USB cord into an outlet. The other end was then attached to a specially configured smart phone that was already open to an application. After he pressed a series of buttons, the phone beeped, and the gate swung open.

Their weapons drawn, all six men sprinted through the open gate and spread out across the estate.

On the other side of the trees, Gnarly jumped to his feet. Not quite sure about what had happened to excite the German shepherd, Spencer circled him and yapped for his attention until he nipped her on the butt and herded her into the woods toward the river.

"I wish you didn't have to go back tomorrow," Tristan whispered into Sarah's ear. "I like having you here."

"You only say that because it's true." Pulling him close to her, she hooked one of her legs behind his knee and rolled him over onto his back, landing on top of him.

A wide theater screen filled the wall on the other side of the room. Tristan and Sarah were so immersed in their last night together before she returned to Annapolis and he went back to his college studies that they had managed to tune out the first installment of the *Scream* series.

Not bothering to dress after their time in the spa, they had carried their clothes into the home theater and started the movie. Before the villain had killed his first victim, they were making love on the wet towels they had spread out on the floor.

But no amount of passion would've been able to drown out the high-pitched sirens and the red-and-white flashing lights that had abruptly gone off in every room of the house. The urgent nature of the alarm made Sarah and Tristan feel as if they had been transported onto a spaceship that was under attack.

"Code sixty-six!" Nigel said. "Intrusion! Intrusion! This is not a drill. Code sixty-six has been activated. Intruders are approaching the house from the north, south, east, west, and northeast—"

"Who the hell is that?" Sarah screamed.

"Nigel!" Tristan said.

"Who's Nigel!"

"Our butler," Tristan said while searching the floor for his eyeglasses. "Get dressed!" After putting on his glasses, he grabbed his pants. He didn't think there was time to find his underwear. "We've gotta go!"

"Where? Murphy has a butler? Why haven't I met him?" Sarah managed to find her panties and to yank on her shirt. "Where are my shorts?"

"Intruders are one hundred feet from the main house," Nigel said.

"We don't have time to look." Leaving his shirt, her shorts, and their shoes behind, Tristan grabbed her hand and yanked her out of the home theater.

"We need to call the police!" Sarah pulled him toward the stairs leading to the main level. "Where are our phones? Murphy's gun is in the bedroom upstairs."

"Nigel has already contacted security." Tristan dragged her behind him toward the panic room.

"Intruders are fifty feet from the main house," Nigel said.

Tristan was almost to the door when he remembered Newman, Spencer, and Gnarly. He stopped. "The dogs!"

"Gnarly has taken Spencer to the guest cottage," Nigel said. "Newman is in the game room watching the presidential debate."

Tristan shoved Sarah into the panic room. "Where are you going?" Seeing the panel of keyboards and monitors, she asked, "What is this?"

Without answering, Tristan ran to the end of the hallway. "Nigel, if I'm not in the panic room before the intruders enter, close and lock the door. Keep Sarah safe."

Nigel said, "I am programmed to keep all allies safe, even if they're not secure in the panic room. Intruders are now within striking distance of all entrances to the main building."

Tristan scooped the overweight Bassett hound up into his arms. Without stopping, he ran down the hall toward the panic room. In the doorway, Sarah beckoned for him to hurry.

"Intruders are now here."

Saying a prayer, Tristan hit the brass plate inside the room. The steel-paneled door slid across the doorframe and latched into place. They could hear the door lock. The lights inside the room turned on. The monitors flashed on to reveal views of every room in the house.

"Panic room is now secure," Nigel said.

In the hallway on the other side of the door, a pocket door disguised as a bookcase slid out and concealed the entrance of the panic room.

"Where is this Nigel?" Sarah asked Tristan, who'd set the Bassett hound on the sofa and turned on the television.

"He's a virtual butler," Tristan said.

"All buildings on the estate are now in lockdown," Nigel said. "Code sixty-six has been activated and launched."

The youngest member of the hit squad, Cody, made his way across the swimming-pool area in the back of the main house and jumped when he heard a motor kick on. Aiming his assault rifle in the direction of the noise, he paused when he saw covers unrolling and covering both the swimming pool and the spa.

The lights inside the house turned off, leaving the house in total darkness.

At the side door, Tucker used the same cord and cell phone application to bypass the home's security system. After the phone beeped, he said, "Security is terminated." He then picked the lock and opened the door.

Unaware of the pair of canine eyes watching from under the hedges on the outer perimeter of the backyard, the hit team entered the house.

"You need to taste this soup." Jessica held out the spoon so that Murphy could taste the delectable dish. He found her violet eyes so much more mesmerizing than the soup.

"What do you think?" she asked.

He licked his lips. "I think I want to take you home and get you out of that dress." His phone vibrated on his hip.

When she saw him take it out of his pocket, her bottom lip stuck out in a pout. "Please don't tell me you have to go on a mission now. CO promised you a week off."

"It's not CO," Murphy said while reading the screen. "It's Nigel. Code sixty-six. Someone is breaking into our house. We have to go."

"I should have known," Sarah said. "If anyone would have a bat cave, it'd be Murphy." She stomped one of her bare feet. "I am so jealous."

"I helped design it." Tristan pressed buttons and studied readings on the applications throughout the room. "If our lives weren't in danger, you would be turned on right now."

Taking in the array of monitors showing them the intruders moving from room to room throughout the house, Sarah said, "Well, even though the timing is inappropriate, I have to admit that I am very turned on."

With a naughty grin, Tristan leaned back in his chair and patted his leg. "I won't tell if you won't." She jumped into his lap and kissed him.

"What have you two done?" Jessica's sharp voice interrupted their embrace. Her face filled one of the monitors. They could see that she was in the car and racing home.

Tristan pushed Sarah out of his lap, causing her to plop down onto the floor. "*We* did nothing. It looks like a bunch of military dudes have broken into the house."

"How many are there?" Murphy asked offscreen.

"We count six." Sarah scanned each of the monitors. "They're armed with heavy military weapons and dressed in special-ops uniforms. They're all throughout the house. We're locked up in your bat cave." With a shriek, she pointed at one of the monitors. "There's Gnarly!"

While Tristan and Sarah watched, Nigel opened the side door to allow Gnarly inside. The door then closed and latched behind him.

"Send a text to CO. Tell her that Camille Jurvetson has just upped the ante," Murphy said to Jessica.

On the main level of the house, Tucker used hand signals to send two of his men down the stairs to the lower level of the house. He and another man took the main level, and his brother, Cody, and the sixth man went upstairs.

On the upper level, Cody and his partner moved with the utmost stealth down the hallway toward the master suite, where they expected to find the young couple in a loving embrace in the safety of their bed.

They were unaware that at the opposite end of the hall, a highly trained creature was creeping equally stealthily up the back staircase.

Upon bursting into the bedroom, the two assassins were disappointed to find the bed not only empty but also still made. "Maybe they're not home," Cody's partner said into his com device.

"Keep searching," Tucker said.

After sending Cody to check the other rooms on the floor, the older gunman went into the master bath. He opened the door to the steam bath and peered into the darkness. Abruptly, he felt a pair of jaws with the force of a bear trap clamp down on the back of his knee. The sharp pain brought him to his knees. His head banged on the wall and then on the glass enclosure as Gnarly dragged him out of the steam bath and across the floor.

The ambush caused the gunman's rifle to discharge. The shot bounced off of the steam bath's bulletproof enclosure before striking the gunman in the neck.

Abruptly, the lights throughout the house flashed on and reached a bright intensity before the house returned to black.

When the television on which Newman, the Bassett hound, was watching the presidential debate turned off, Newman growled at the interruption. Glaring at Sarah, the dog barked.

Sarah grabbed the remote and pressed the "power" button. "What's the big deal?" she said to Newman. "It isn't like you're planning to vote."

"Shots fired," Nigel said. "Code ninety-nine activated and launched. Lethal force activated."

"Is that a good thing?" Sarah's voice trembled.

"Not if you're a bad guy," Tristan said.

"Damn it!" Murphy pounded the Ferrari's steering wheel as if that would make the traffic in the clogged streets of downtown Washington move. It was a weekend, and everyone was out to take in the shows or visit the clubs.

After reading the screen of her cell phone, in a strained voice, Jessica said, "Murphy?"

"What?"

"Nigel just authorized lethal force." She held up the phone so that he could read the message himself.

Throughout the house, the remaining gunmen bellowed in pain when every earbud began to emit a high-frequency squealing noise of such intensity that it hurt their ears. Unable to stand the pain, they tore the devices out of their ears.

At the same time, in the van outside of the security fence, all of the computers and communications shut down.

"No," Elmo said while hitting one button after another. "This can't be happening. We're the CIA. No one can shut us down." He took his secure cell phone out of the case and checked the screen. He had no bars. "Are you kidding me? That's never happened before."

Cody ran into the master bedroom in search of his partner. Upon seeing the gunman lying in a pool of blood in the middle of the bathroom floor, Cody backed out of the room.

"You bastard, Thornton!" Peering through the sights on his gun, Cody searched each corner of the bedroom. "Come out like a man, and show yourself."

As Cody swept the room with his weapon, Gnarly darted out of a dark corner to collide with the back of his knees. Cody hit the floor so hard that the wind was knocked out of him. Before Cody could recover, Gnarly lunged for the rifle.

In a life-and-death tug-of-war, Cody struggled to keep at least one hand on his weapon as he reached for the knife in his belt.

On the ground floor, a gunman was searching the game room when he heard what sounded like a woman sobbing.

Maybe it's that rich man's daughter.

Licking his lips in anticipation of some fun with the wife of their target before they killed her, he made his way toward the sound of the crying, which seemed to be coming from a room at the end of a small, dark corridor.

"Stop crying, or they'll find us." The male voice that shushed her confirmed that the gunman was on the verge of striking gold.

"But I'm so scared!"

They continued to whisper until the gunman entered the wine cellar. Shadows and movement behind a shelving unit in the corner gave away the couple's location.

"I see you there," he said. "Come out now, and I won't hurt you."

He waited.

There was no response.

"We have you trapped, Thornton. There's no escape. Come out now, and you won't get hurt."

Still not receiving any response or seeing any action, the gunman charged around the corner only to find a lava lamp. He was still cursing when the heavy metal door slid across the doorway, sealing him in the wine cellar.

Enraged, he pounded on the door. "Thornton, open up this door!" Checking his cell phone to see if he could call for help, he found that there was no signal. It was useless. In frustration, he hurled it to the floor.

"When I find you, Thornton, you're a dead man."

After yanking his handgun out of its holster, he aimed it at the door and unloaded the clip. The shots bounced off of the bulletproof door and around the room. He realized his mistake when a shot hit him in the back of the leg—a split second before a second bullet struck him in the back and the fatal shot struck him in the back of the head.

Tucker was searching the sun-room when he heard a scream on the floor above him. Recognizing his brother's voice, he ran to the bay window in time to see Cody's body fall from the balcony above and crash down on top of the outdoor kitchen's grill.

"Co-Cody!" Tucker tore through the French doors to run over to his brother's broken body.

Screaming with rage, he ran back inside and up to the top of the stairs in time to see a shadow of a figure run down the back stairs.

"Thornton! When I catch you, I'm going to tear you limb from limb!"

Up on the roof, a sliding door opened. In silence, a drone rose up out of its rooftop housing and made its way up toward the treetops. Gracefully, it circled around the house and made its way out toward the road.

On the ground floor, one of the gunmen entered the home theater. Seeing the articles of clothing thrown around the room, he sensed that they had interrupted the young couple at an inopportune time.

"There you are. I know you and your wife are in here, Thornton. You might as well come out. There's no way you can escape us."

Lights all around the room, including on the ceiling and the floor, turned on. Each light was directed toward the center of the home theater to create a life-size image—a hologram—of Murphy Thornton.

The gunman chuckled.

"I'm Murphy Thornton, this is my home, and you are not welcome here. I'm only going to tell you this once: leave now, or we will use lethal force to end this invasion."

"Seriously? I'm not afraid of a movie," the gunman said.

"Is that your final answer?" Murphy asked.

"No, this is my final answer." The gunman fired three shots through the hologram, which disappeared in the gunfire.

Across from the gunman, Murphy's face filled the movie screen. "You chose poorly."

The gunman's face filled the wall-sized monitor. The red cross hairs aimed between his eyes zeroed in on him.

Confused by and curious about the image on the screen, the assailant stepped closer to it, noticing that every move he made was projected up onto the wall. Too late, he noticed a small hole in the wall and saw the muzzle of the gun. Before he could react, a shot was fired and struck him in the very center of the cross hairs.

Inside the van, Elmo was punching his phone and waving it out the window in an effort to get a cell-phone signal.

Lieutenant Thornton couldn't have blocked the signal. He's a pencil pusher at the Pentagon. Doesn't he know we're the CIA?

The remaining gunman went into the kitchen. Smelling something strange, he made a face. "Is that—" He saw the gas stove in the middle of the shiny granite counter top.

Without being touched by human hands, the burner turned on.

As he was hanging out of a window, Elmo heard the whir of an engine. Looking up into the sky, he saw a drone gracefully flying his way. The drone moved closer to the van and circled it.

As the drone closed in on him, Elmo spotted the camera hanging from the bottom of it and realized where the drone must have come from. "Lieutenant Thornton, I don't know who you think you are, but you're playing way out of your league. Don't you know who we are? We're the CIA, and no matter how cute you think you are with your Wi-Fi-blocking devices and drone, you're no match for us. So you might as well bend over and kiss your ass good-bye now—because before morning, you're going to be a dead man."

As if to say farewell, the drone swung around and moved to the back of the van. A small door on the front of the drone opened and fired what looked like a dart with a rubber tip. The projectile attached itself to the side of the van.

The *ping* noise that the dart made prompted Elmo to laugh even harder.

The drone then flew up and sailed back toward the house.

Elmo was admiring the peaceful night sky beyond the drone when an explosion from the main house rocked the night. He was in the middle of a curse when the van exploded.

At the edge of the woods, Tucker stopped when he heard the two explosions and realized what had happened. Furious, he returned to the woods into which he had seen the dark figure disappear. Bringing his rifle up to his shoulder, he said, "Okay, Thornton! That's it. I'm going to kill you—all of you! First, I'm going to start with skinning your dog alive."

CHAPTER THIRTY-FIVE

"Who did that?" Jessica asked when their Ferrari came upon the van engulfed in flames. "Nigel or Gnarly?"

Murphy pressed his foot down onto the gas pedal to speed through the open gate.

After determining that the house was clear of intruders, Nigel unlocked the panic room. Arming themselves with the guns that were stored inside the room, Sarah and Tristan made their way upstairs. They reached the main level just in time to hear Jessica scream upon seeing that the kitchen was engulfed in flames.

During the renovations, the kitchen walls had been reinforced to prevent such a blast from spreading throughout the house. While the blocks had been unable to prevent smoke damage, they had been able to contain the flames.

"My kitchen! Nigel blew up my beautiful kitchen!" Jessica said.

"I apologize, Jessica, but the use of lethal force was necessary to terminate the invasion," Nigel said.

Trying to comprehend the extend of the damage, Jessica held her hands to her head while turning around. "But did you have to blow up my kitchen? Couldn't you have just hit them over the head with a frying pan and locked them in the pantry?"

Spotting Tristan, she charged across the room. Before she could tackle her brother, Murphy intercepted her and lifted her off her feet. "You did this! You booby trapped our home!" Twisting in her husband's arms in an effort to escape, she yelled, "I'm telling Dad!"

"Contrary to what your emotions are communicating to you, Jessica," Nigel said, "lethal force was required to terminate the intruders' mission, which was to kill you and all occupants on site. I have downloaded the assailants' communication with their leader from the command center in the van and stored them on my hard drive. They have already been backed up off site and copies have been sent to CO."

Sensing that Jessica had moved beyond the shock and no longer wanted to do bodily harm to Tristan, Murphy set her down. "Who gave the orders?" he asked Nigel. "Do you have that name from the recordings?"

"Camille Jurvetson."

"Who's that?" Sarah asked.

"A traitor." Noticing that Tristan and Sarah were undressed, Murphy asked, "Are you two okay? Maybe you'd like to put some clothes on before the emergency and fire fighters get here?"

Getting over her shock, Jessica interrupted their response. "Where are the dogs? Don't tell me they got caught in a cross fire."

"Newman is downstairs watching the presidential debate, which is rather ugly," Nigel said. "Based on the guidelines set up by the FCC for family viewing, the content presented in the presidential debate is not appropriate for a lifeform of Newman's age. I have tried to change the station, but he objects when I do so."

"Where are Spencer and Gnarly?" Jessica asked.

"Gnarly is leading the surviving assassin down to the river," Nigel said. "Spencer was safe in the guest cottage, but Gnarly moved him. Based on Gnarly's recent movements, I have concluded that he is setting a trap."

"Gnarly's gone rogue!" Murphy dropped down to one knee and extracted his backup weapon from an ankle holster. "Nigel, why didn't you tell us that?"

"I just did," Nigel said, "Did you not hear me, Murphy?"

Murphy ran out the door. Jessica pulled her small handgun out of her purse and, clattering in her high heels, followed him.

"We're coming with you." Tristan, with Sarah directly behind him, ran downstairs to the home theater to find their shoes.

Receiving no answer to his question, Nigel asked, "Murphy, would you like me to adjust my volume so that you may hear me better?"

After midnight, the woods were enveloped in complete darkness. It was only with the assistance of night goggles that Tucker was able to make out the German shepherd's form darting behind a tree or scurrying out from behind a bush or a shrub before they finally reached the riverbank.

The footpath ran along a steep, rocky ledge high up above a rapid portion of the Potomac River.

"Where are you, you mutt?" Peering through the sights of his semiautomatic with his finger on the trigger, Tucker scoured the trees and rocks for the dog that he had come to realize had killed his brother.

A high-pitched yap gave away the dog's location.

Anticipating the sweet taste of revenge, Tucker sprang around a boulder and saw a young Shetland sheepdog squirming with excitement. With her tail wagging, she seemed genuinely happy to see him.

Lowering the gun, he asked, "What are you so happy about?"

He didn't care who she was or to whom she belonged. At that moment, all he wanted to do was kill someone or something.

A blue dog would do.

He raised the gun and took aim. His finger was on the trigger when he heard a roar from high up above him. He was in the midst of turning to look up when Gnarly's body collided with his, sending them both plunging over the ledge and down into the rapids.

Murphy broke out through the woods just in time to see Gnarly and the gunman hit the churning water.

"Gnarly's in the rapids!" Tearing off his suit jacket and kicking off his shoes, Murphy yelled back to Jessica, who was running as fast as she could in her high heels. She reached the riverbank as he dove into the river.

Seeing her master, Spencer galloped up the path to join her. Squinting down into the dark river, Jessica tried to pick out Murphy and Gnarly in the fast-moving water. She was still looking when Tristan and Sarah reached her side.

"Where's Murphy?" Sarah asked.

"He jumped in after Gnarly," Jessica said.

"What about the gunman?" Tristan asked.

"There!" Sarah pointed to where a man with a knife in his hand was fighting the current to make his way to Murphy. Seemingly unaware of the danger, Murphy was trying to swim toward Gnarly, who was paddling as hard as he could to get to the shore. The dog's progress was hampered by the current smashing him against the rocks.

"I'll get Gnarly!" Tristan said while running down the shore to get closer to where Gnarly was about to be washed over the falls. "Try to tell Murphy to watch out for that guy!" He dove into the water.

Screaming and waving their arms to warn Murphy of the danger making its way to him, Sarah and Jessica ran along the riverbank.

Through the roar of the rapids swirling around him, Murphy finally heard Sarah's voice calling out the word "killer." He saw her and Jessica pointing to an area behind him. Taking his attention off of Gnarly, he turned in time to see that the man was riding a wave that was about to come down on him. Murphy saw the flash of a knife slicing through the water. After diving underwater, Murphy grasped a rock and held on to it, hoping that Tucker would sail past him. As his attacker flowed by him, Murphy kicked him in the ribs, sending the middle of his back into a rock. Murphy hoped that if he hit the rock hard enough, he would drop the knife.

Not caring who was the good guy or the bad guy, the river washed both Murphy and his assailant downstream.

Exhausted from paddling against the current, Gnarly had lost all fight, and the swift current plunged him into a rock. After bouncing off of the rock and back into the swift current, he was carried toward the falls. Determined not to let his canine brother down, Tristan grasped Gnarly with both arms, rolled him over, and held him to his chest as the two of them rode the current together—and plunged down into the water below.

At the other end of the falls, Sarah and Jessica joined hands. Jessica anchored herself to the shore by digging her high heels into the mud, and Sarah waded out into the river to catch Tristan and Gnarly when they floated by.

Tristan tucked Gnarly under his arm and reached out to grab Sarah's hand. With what little strength he had left and Sarah's and Jessica's help, he dragged Gnarly to shore.

"Is he okay?" Seeing Gnarly's limp body, Jessica feared the worst.

Tristan and Sarah laid Gnarly on the shore. All three of them stared at the German shepherd. Spencer sniffed him.

Then they saw Gnarly's chest expand. He let out a deep breath. A deep gurgling sound came out of his throat.

Tristan and Sarah smiled at each other.

Frantically, Jessica turned back to the river to search for her husband.

The waterfall had plunged Murphy down to the bottom of the river. Fighting to get to the surface so that he could get some air into his lunges, Murphy was aware of someone else nearby when he hit the surface. As luck would have it, that someone was Tucker, who had hit the surface before him.

With his knife poised to strike, he was waiting for Murphy to come up for air.

After taking in one quick gulp of air, Murphy dove back down and plunged his shoulder into Tucker's chest. His hope was that he would knock the air out of the gunman, who would then be at a disadvantage if Murphy managed to get him back underwater.

When the knife came down, Murphy dodged the blade and grabbed Tucker's arm.

The river's current continued to sweep the two men downstream. Kicking and punching, they were battling not only each other but also Mother Nature. At one point, after they had been pushed against a rock, Murphy was able to pound Tucker's hand and to make him release the knife, which washed downstream. Grabbing Murphy around the neck with both hands, Tucker shoved him down into the water.

Holding his breath, Murphy fought to keep his wits about him and to think his way out of the situation.

Grabbing his assailant, Murphy recognized the feel of the items he was wearing on his utility belt. Finally, he recognized the shape of a Taser.

Feeling Murphy's body go limp, Tucker grinned.

Mission accomplished.

Never had it occurred to him that a simple navy lieutenant who pushed paper at the Pentagon would be so hard to kill.

Give him another minute underwater to make sure he's dead.

Before Tucker could start counting, an electric shock shot through his body and sent him flying backward. Jerking and flailing, he hit the water like a human lightning bolt.

Murphy jumped up out of the water and gulped in as much air as he could before shooting Tucker once again with his own Taser until his body went limp.

In silence, he floated facedown in the river's current.

"Murphy!" Jessica's cry was like a song to Murphy's ears.

Exhausted, he searched the shoreline to get his bearings until he felt a pair of arms wrap around his chest. "I've got you, bro," Tristan said into his ear before helping him swim to where Jessica and Sarah were waiting on the shore with Spencer and Gnarly.

Upon reaching the shore, Murphy dropped to his knees and let Jessica take him into her arms. Tristan and Sarah went back out into the river to retrieve Tucker's dead body. Offering her own comfort, Spencer gave Gnarly a tongue bath.

Tightening her arms around Murphy, Jessica uttered a sigh. The reality of how events could have played out that evening hit her. *What if Nigel hadn't worked? The death squad would have killed Tristan and Sarah.*

She watched Tristan and Sarah drag the last assassin— drowned in the river after Murphy had knocked him unconscious with his own Taser. *That could be Murphy that they're dragging out of the river.*

Suddenly, a blown-up kitchen didn't seem so bad. She tightened her arms around Murphy, who, in his wet clothes, was shivering in the cool night air. He reached up to kiss her on the neck.

"Call me conservative, but I think three dogs are one too many," Murphy said, "especially when one is Gnarly."

EPILOGUE

Potomac, Maryland

Camille Jurvetson sensed that her luxurious million-dollar home was too quiet when she woke up. Upon checking the time on her clock, she found that she had slept in.

"Ingrid!" Camille threw back the covers and marched to the door of her master suite. "You didn't wake me up!" Snapping orders, she snatched her bathrobe from the bed and rushed down the stairs. "Where's my breakfast? Call the DCI, and tell him that I'm going to be late for the morning briefing."

When she arrived in the dining room and found no breakfast waiting for her, Camille realized that something had to be wrong. She charged into the kitchen. No cook.

"Brett!" she said, calling for her assistant, who always went over her day with her during breakfast.

"Breaking news," a voice coming from the television said. "The Department of Defense just confirmed that one of ISIS's top leaders, the third in command, was killed two hours ago in a drone attack—"

No! Not him! How did they find him!

She rushed to the front door and hurled it open. No car or driver. Worse yet, no security.

Camille Jurvetson was alone.

"What the hell!" She ran for the phone. Her fingers shook when she dialed the emergency phone number.

"Yes, Ms. Jurvetson?" a sultry, feminine voice said.

"My security detail is gone!" Camille fought to keep the panic out of her tone.

"Yes, it is. You terminated your security detail as of midnight last night."

"I did not."

"I'm afraid you did," the voice on the other end of the line said. "We recorded it."

"I need it back—immediately! I'm the director of operations at the CIA! If our enemies find out that I don't have any security—"

"Ms. Jurvetson, you sound frightened," the voice said in a cool tone.

"I did not cancel my security," Camille said with a hiss. "Someone else did it to leave me vulnerable to our country's enemies."

"Oh," the voice said. "How does it feel to have been abandoned?"

The click behind her brought home the price she would have to pay for her betrayal.

Camille placed the phone back on the table. Slowly, she turned around and found Tawkeel Said aiming a gun at her.

"Good morning, Ms. Jurvetson. We have not formally met. I am one of the agents who you sold out. Now it is time for you to pay up."

Election Night

Dallas Walker's blog announced the news to the world:

"American Politics Goes to the Dogs! Gnarly Wins by a Landslide!"

One week before the election, Gnarly had been awarded the Canine Congressional Medal of Honor for saving the lives of his unit during a firefight in Iraq. He had made the national news. The picture of his girl Storm "kissing" him on the face while he proudly wore his medal was shared across the social media worldwide.

The Belgian shepherd's sable coat had grown back and Storm was once again her conniving self—especially when Gnarly was around.

During the same ceremony, First Sergeant Belle Perkins had been posthumously awarded the Soldier's Medal. Her daughter, Kelly, had tearfully accepted the award for her.

After Murphy briefed Sheriff Turow about the details of his wife's murder, the sheriff and his daughter went public about their family's special relationship with Gnarly, even offering darling pictures of the national hero as a puppy. Once they had closure, Sheriff Turow and his daughter were able to move on. Even Mac and David didn't miss the fact that Roxie Greyson was becoming a regular visitor to Spencer.

Once his name had been cleared, how could anyone have not voted for Gnarly—the only candidate who had risked his life by running into a fiery inferno to save a mother cat and her one-hundred-and-one baby kittens?

Gnarly was not only the best choice but also the only choice.

One of his opponents had been murdered, and the other had been arrested for murdering his brother. David's cell phone recording proved invaluable to the prosecution's case against Bill Clark. Not only did it prove the councilman's intention to kill the police chief, but the recording also captured Clark admitting that he'd killed his brother. The town councilman had gone directly from the emergency room to jail.

Both political parties ended up in hot water. Hugh Vance's laptop contained a wealth of evidence about Braxton Charities. It turned out that Hugh had been a bipartisan money launderer who'd kept very good records. His unsavory clients had included politicians, party leaders, presidential appointees, lobbyists, and even a few judges—enough to launch a major federal investigation with a special prosecutor.

However, the list of Braxton Charities donors also included celebrated members of the mass media who either accepted hush money or buried stories of corruption involving politicians of their favorite political party. As a result, the mainstream media attempted to ignore the federal investigation of what appeared to be widespread political corruption—until Dallas Walker published the details, complete with a list of names and dollar amounts, on her blog. Immediately, the story was picked up by a few brave news services and shared on social media. Gradually, people learned about the hard-to-ignore proof of what many had suspected for a very long time—politics and morals did not necessarily go hand-in-hand.

Dallas' news breaking exclusive captured the attention of her late mother's publisher, who offered her a huge advance to write a book detailing her investigation of the Sandy Burr murder and Braxton Charities, which she turned down in favor of co-authoring the book with Archie Monday. Both agreed to credit Sandy Burr and give royalties from all book sales to his family.

Upon hearing about Dallas and Archie's partnership, Mac chuckled. "Admit it. Dallas is growing on you."

"No, she is not," Archie said. "It's just...she made me an offer I couldn't refuse."

"What kind of offer?"

"Let's just say the next cruise we're going on will be on the Walker yacht, which is Texas huge."

Mac folded his arms across his chest. "Oh, so Dallas is buying your friendship?"

He swore he saw sparks shoot out of Archie's eyes. "Now you know full well that my friendship can't be bought!"

"Yes, I do," Mac said. "I also know you refuse to work with anyone who you don't like. So, Dallas must be growing on you."

Growling about the lack of a come-back to his accusation, she trotted downstairs to the study to go over the outline Dallas had sent for *their* book.

With a shake of his head, Mac returned to writing Gnarly's acceptance speech.

With only one mayoral candidate left standing, election day ended up simply being a formality and a celebration.

Gnarly's campaign headquarters was the Spencer Inn, which was packed with seemingly every resident of Spencer, all of whom wanted to meet and congratulate the new mayor. Every section of the media was on hand to interview Mac, who was Gnarly's representative, and Gnarly's campaign managers, Bernie and Hap. Everyone wanted a picture with Gnarly, Spencer's first canine mayor. Not wanting to be left out, Storm, wearing a diamond encrusted collar for the event, often barged in and had her picture taken as well.

In the evening, the polls closed, and the votes were tallied—even though it was only a formality.

In a small conference room off the stage area, Mac went through the speech that he had so carefully prepared.

Exhausted after a day of pictures, hugs, and stealing goodies out of every handbag that he could stick his snout into, Gnarly was sprawled out at Mac's feet. Some of his stolen goodies were cheese cubes, which had given him a tummy ache. Upon spotting Archie and Dallas looking for Mac, he rolled over onto his back and groaned. As he had hoped, Archie knelt to give him a belly rub. Storm joined in by licking his snout.

"He brought this on himself," Mac said. "You should let him suffer."

"You don't mean that," Archie said.

"I'd be nice to him if I were you," Dallas said, "he's your new mayor."

"Only because both humans running against him are either dead or in jail," Mac said.

"I wonder what that says about us humans?" Dallas asked. "I mean what are the odds of both human candidates being slicker than a couple of slop jars?"

"I don't think it's as much a comment about humans as it is about what our country has turned politics into," Archie said, "and the type of people our political system attracts."

Mac set down his notes. "Have you ever heard of the butterfly effect?"

While Dallas shook her head, Archie said, "It's the chaos theory, which I think very much applies to what happened when Gnarly entered the race for mayor."

"According to the butterfly effect," Mac said, "a butterfly flapping its wings in New Mexico can cause a hurricane in China."

"Not all the time," Archie said. "If the butterfly flaps its wings at just the right time and place, then the hurricane will happen. If not, then the hurricane won't. It illustrates how small changes in the initial condition can cause drastic results."

Finished with the tummy rub, Archie stood up and took Mac's notes for his speech to look over. Storm moved in to lick the top of Gnarly's head. Content with the the pampering, the German shepherd appeared to have fallen asleep.

"Small changes," Dallas said. "Yes. Like Gnarly and Storm eating our dinner, which made us go to the Spencer Inn where Bill and Nancy got into a brawl, causing David to arrest them. They made David mad, so he threw Gnarly into the race for mayor."

"Which threw the whole race into chaos," Mac said. "If Tonya hadn't told you about the Sandy Burr case, you and Archie would have never looked into the case to find his and Fiona Davis' killer."

"Gnarly entering the race brought national attention to the campaign," Archie said. "Between the scrutiny of the media, Bill Clark being a dirty politician, and David suggesting another look at the Sandy Burr case, Hugh was pushed over the edge and killed Nancy.

"And if Erin hadn't taken Nancy off her meds," Dallas said, "then she wouldn't have become a loose cannon, which presented the opportunity for Hugh to kill her."

"If Gnarly's opponents hadn't dug up Belle Perkins' murder," Archie said, "then Murphy and Jessica would have never uncovered the truth. The army would have just gone on assuming that it was a runaway contractor."

"Which led to uncovering a traitor who was in line for a presidential cabinet position," Mac said.

"Not only that," Archie said, "but if Gnarly hadn't run for mayor, then Bernie and Hap would never have broken into Bill Clark's house and found the evidence to prove he killed his brother. He would have gotten away with murder for the rest of his life."

"All that happened because Gnarly broke in off the deck to steal our dinner," Dallas said. "Whoever would have thought?"

The three of them looked down at where Gnarly was sprawled out at their feet. With Storm licking the side of his head, he was in a state of complete contentment. Without moving a muscle, he flicked his eyes from one of them to the other.

Spotting Mac, Bernie and Hap trotted into the room. "We're so glad we caught you," Bernie said. "We didn't want to forget to give this to you." At Bernie's direction, Hap shoved an envelope into Mac's hand. "It's our bill."

"Bill?" Mac's eyes grew wide.

"For managing Gnarly's campaign."

"I thought you were volunteers." Mac's voice went up an octave. With trepidation, he opened the envelope. Equally concern, Archie peered at the bill while he opened it.

Bernie and Hap laughed and jabbed each other in the ribs. "See, Hap, I told you. Even with all of his millions, Mac Faraday is just like a regular guy—with a sense of humor and all."

Upon reading the final figure at the bottom of the bill, Mac clutched his chest. "Seriously? Are you guys serious?"

"You can't say we didn't do a good job," Bernie said. "Gnarly got two thousand five hundred four percent of the vote. And only eight percent of the votes were from dead people."

With tears in his eyes, Mac scanned the itemized list. "Website. Nationally televised commercials?" He shook the bill in his hand. "This is a small town! Fewer than a thousand registered voters. Gnarly didn't need a nationally televised commercial during *Saturday Night Live*."

"He needed the millennial vote to win," Bernie said. "And it worked. Twenty-two percent of Gnarly's votes were from millennials."

"But only two percent of them actually *reside* in Spencer."

"Well, if you're gonna be legalistic about it."

Mac held out the bill so that Archie and Dallas could see it. "This is insane!"

"Does that mean you won't allow Gnarly to go to New York to be the guest host on *Saturday Night Live* next month?" Both men stuck their bottom lips out in a pout. "Hap and I were really looking forward to meeting Tina Fey. She's gonna do a skit with Gnarly."

Onstage, David said, "Ladies and gentleman, our best friend and mayor, Gnarly!"

"We'll take a credit card." Bernie held out his cell phone, which had a credit-card swiper attached to it.

Without answering, Mac grabbed Gnarly's leash, and the two of them trotted out onto the stage to where David was waiting at the podium.

Exhausted and sick with a tummy-ache, Gnarly plopped down next to the podium. Oblivious to the standing ovation in his honor, Spencer's new mayor closed his eyes and went to sleep.

When David reached out to shake Mac's hand, Mac shoved Bernie and Hap's bill into it. Giving his brother a hug, Mac whispered, "You nominated him. It's your bill."

David's brow furrowed with confusion. Taking the sheet of paper, he made his way off of the stage as Mac turned to the mic. "Good evening, ladies and gentlemen! The people have spoken, and they said—"

"Are you kidding me!"

The End

ABOUT THE AUTHOR

Lauren Carr

Lauren Carr is the best-selling author of the Mac Faraday Mysteries, which takes place in Deep Creek Lake, Maryland. *Candidate for Murder* is the twelfth installment in the Mac Faraday Mystery series.

Candidate for Murder features characters from Lauren Carr's latest series, Murphy Thornton and Jessica Faraday in the Thorny Rose Mysteries. Look for the second installment in this series, *A Fine Year for Murder*, in Fall 2016.

In addition to her series set on Deep Creek Lake, Lauren Carr has also written the Lovers in Crime Mysteries, which features prosecutor Joshua Thornton with homicide detective Cameron Gates, who were introduced in *Shades of Murder*, the third book in the Mac Faraday Mysteries. The third installment in this series, *Killer in the Band*, will be released Summer 2016.

Lauren is a popular speaker who has made appearances at schools, youth groups, and on author panels at conventions. She also passes on what she has learned in her years of writing and publishing by conducting workshops and teaching in community education classes.

She lives with her husband, son, and three dogs on a mountain in Harpers Ferry, WV.

Visit Lauren Carr's website at www.mysterylady.net to learn more about Lauren and her upcoming mysteries.

CHECK OUT
LAUREN CARR'S MYSTERIES!
Order! Order!

All of Lauren Carr's books are stand alone. However for those readers wanting to start at the beginning, here is the list of Lauren Carr's mysteries. The number next to the book title is the actual order in which the book was released.

Joshua Thornton Mysteries:

Fans of the *Lovers in Crime Mysteries* may wish to read these two books which feature Joshua Thornton years before meeting Detective Cameron Gates. Also in these mysteries, readers will meet Joshua Thornton's five children before they had flown the nest.

1) A Small Case of Murder
2) A Reunion to Die For

Mac Faraday Mysteries

3) It's Murder, My Son
4) Old Loves Die Hard
5) Shades of Murder
    (introduces the Lovers in Crime: Joshua Thornton
    & Cameron Gates)
7) Blast from the Past
8) The Murders at Astaire Castle
9) The Lady Who Cried Murder
    (The Lovers in Crime make a guest appearance
    in this Mac Faraday Mystery)
10) Twelve to Murder
12) A Wedding and a Killing

13) Three Days to Forever
15) Open Season for Murder
!6) Cancelled Vows
17) Candidate for Murder
   (featuring Thorny Rose Mystery detectives
   Murphy Thornton & Jessica Faraday)

Lovers in Crime Mysteries

6) Dead on Ice
11) Real Murder
18) Killer in the Band *(Summer 2016)*

Thorny Rose Mysteries

14) Kill and Run
   (featuring the Lovers in Crime in
   Lauren Carr's latest series)
19) A Fine Year for Murder

Killer in the Band

A Lovers in Crime Mystery

Summer has arrived! The Thorntons expected it to be a summer of change and change it does, but not in the way Joshua had expected.

Joshua's eldest son, Joshua Thornton Jr. (J.J.) has graduated at the top of his class from law school and is returning home to spend the summer studying for the bar exam. However, to the Thornton's shock and dismay, J.J. decides to move in with Suellen Russell, a lovely widow twice his age.

The May/December romance, bonded by a love for music, between the symphony conductor and young musical prodigy had bloomed many years earlier.

The move brings long buried tensions between the father and son to the surface. When a brutal killer strikes, the father and son must set all differences aside to solve the crime before J.J. ends up in the crosshairs of a murderer.

Coming Summer 2016!

A Fine Year for Murder

A Thorny Rose Mystery

After months of marital bliss, Jessica Faraday and Murphy Thornton are still discovering and adjusting to their life together. Settled in their new home, everything appears to be perfect...except in the middle of the night when, in darkest shadows of her subconscious, a deep secret from Jessica's past creeps to the surface to make her strike out at Murphy.

When investigative journalist Dallas Walker tells the couple about her latest case, known as the Pine Bridge Massacre, they realize Jessica may have witnessed the murder of a family living near a winery owned by distant relatives she was visiting and suppressed the memory.

Determined to uncover the truth and find justice for the murder victims, Jessica and Murphy return to the scene of the crime with Dallas Walker, a spunky bull-headed Texan. Can this family reunion bring closure for a community touched by tragedy or will this prickly get-together bring an end to the Thorny Rose couple?

Coming Fall 2016!